TOKYO YEAR ZERO

Tokyo Year Zero

DAVID PEACE

faber and faber

First published in 2007
by Faber and Faber Limited
3 Queen Square London WC1N 3AU

Typeset by RefineCatch Limited, Bungay, Suffolk
Printed in England by Mackays of Chatham Ltd

A CIP record for this book
is available from the British Library

ISBN 978-0-571-23645-9

ISBN 978-0-571-23782-1 (Limited edition)

2 4 6 8 10 9 7 5 3 1

For my children

Tokyo, 1945–6

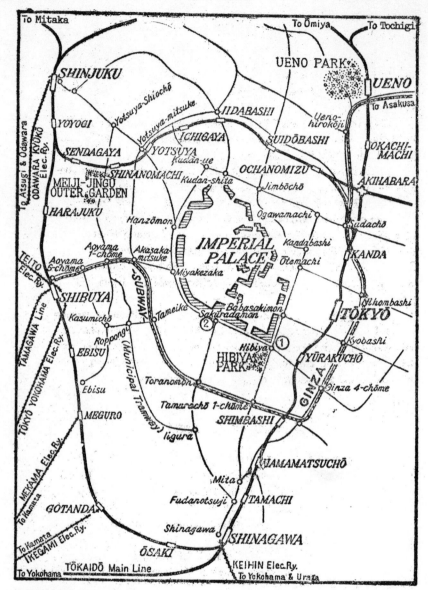

Legend:
1 GHQ/Dai-Ichi Bldg.
2 Metropolitan Police Board

For an explanation of Japanese words and phrases used in the text, please refer to the Glossary on pp. 347–50.

51. Defeat

The hand taking up the pen had started to tremble.
He drooled.
Only after a 0.8 dose of Veronal did his head have any clarity.
But even then, only for half an hour or an hour.
Day by day he lived in this half-light.
The blade nicked, a slim sword for a stick.

A Fool's Life, Akutagawa Ryūnosuke, 1927

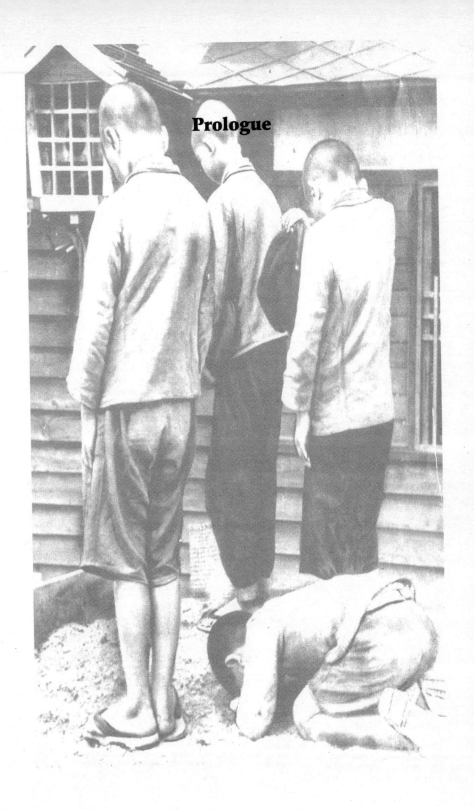

Prologue

I lie among the corpses. **One Calmotin, two**. Hundreds of them, thousands of them. Dead leaves, floating in the autumn breeze. I try to raise my head but I cannot. Flies and mosquitoes swarm over me. I want to brush them away but I cannot. Low dark clouds shift across the sky. *It is time to reveal the true essence of the nation*. Last night, sometime between midnight and dawn, between retreat and defeat, rain drenched this place and, though the storm has now passed, fresh torrents of rain still fall upon the corpses and onto my face. My head is numb, my thoughts the fleeting shadows of delirium. Images of my wife and my children float before my eyes, among the corpses. **Ten Calmotin, eleven**. Beneath the eaves of the Black Gate of Zōjōji Temple. *Oh so bravely, off to Victory*. My son has a little flag in his hand. My daughter has a little flag in hers. *Insofar as we have vowed and left our land behind*. My parents are here. Friends from school, teammates from my high school baseball club, colleagues with whom I graduated. *Who can die without first having shown his true mettle?* Each holds aloft a big banner, each banner bearing my name, each before the Black Gate. *Each time I hear the bugles of our advancing army, I close my eyes and see wave upon wave of flags cheering us into battle*. There are sight-seeing buses full of girls on school excursions. *The earth and its flora burn in flames, as we endlessly part the plains*. The clock strikes noon as my truck approaches the Black Gate. *Helmets emblazoned with the Rising Sun*. The truck stops in front of the gate and I jump down from the Nissan. *And, stroking the mane of our horses, who knows what tomorrow will bring – life?* I stare into the crowd, up at the banners and the flags, and I salute. Now the departure signal sounds. *Or death in battle?* **Twenty Calmotin, twenty-one**. The print of dear faces floating in a sea of flags as the mountains fade, the rivers retreat, waving our flags until our hands are numb, floating and waving. *We are bound for Siberia*. Down the Shimonoseki Channel, the waters choked with transports and cargo boats. *We are bound for Dairen*. I lie among the corpses, the damp bodies and the fetid air. *We are bound for Shanghai*. The two tiers of cheap bunks on the decks below. *We are bound for Canton*. The men shout, the men applaud, as Yamazaki begins to recite 'The Bloody Handkerchief of Kioi Hill'. More shouts, more applause, as Shimizu tells of 'Konya, the Harlot'. I love you, I love you, I love you, says Konya to her customer. The bell rings for the evening meal. The war horses stabled in the hatch below scream, their ribs exposed. The steam winch hoists their corpses into waiting boats. In their bunks, men hold their *sennin-bari* tighter, their belts of one thousand stitches, touching the charms and talismans sewn into the silk. The Eight Myriads of Deities and a Buddha from Three Thousand Worlds. I lie among the corpses, a three-inch image of the Buddha in my hands. No bullet ever touched the man who carried it, said my father. Through the Shino War, the Boxer Rebellion and the Russo War, without a scratch. Bags of five-sen or ten-sen pieces, vests of dried cuttlefish, every man has his charm. *How far we have come from the homeland*. The transport ploughs on through the black ocean. *'Tis the land of Manchuria, far, far from home*. I lie among the corpses and I listen

The fifteenth day of the eighth month of the twentieth year of Shōwa

Tokyo, 90°, fine

'Detective Minami! Detective Minami! Detective Minami!'

I open my eyes. *From dreams that are not my own.* I sit up in my chair at my desk. *Dreams I do not want.* My collar is wet and my whole suit damp. My hair itches. My skin itches –

'Detective Minami! Detective Minami!'

Detective Nishi is taking down the blackout curtains, bright warm shafts of dawn and dust filling the office as the sun rises up beyond the tape-crossed windows –

'Detective Minami!'

'Did you just say something?' I ask Nishi –

Nishi shakes his head. Nishi says, 'No.'

I stare up at the ceiling. Nothing moves in the bright light. The fans have stopped. No electricity. The telephones silent. No lines. The toilets blocked. No water. Nothing –

'Kumagaya was hit during the night,' says Nishi. 'There are reports of gunfire from the Palace . . .'

'I didn't dream it, then?'

I take out my handkerchief. It is old and it is dirty. I wipe my neck again. Then I wipe my face. Now I check my pockets –

They are handing out potassium cyanide to the women, the children and the aged, saying this latest cabinet reshuffle foretells the end of the war, the end of Japan, the end of the world . . .

Nishi holds up a small box and asks, 'You looking for these?'

I snatch the box of Muronal out of his hands. I check the contents. *Enough.* I stuff the box back into my jacket pocket –

The sirens and the warnings all through the night; Tokyo hot and dark, hidden and cowed; night and day, rumours of new weapons, fears of new bombs; first Hiroshima, then Nagasaki, next is Tokyo . . .

Bombs that mean the end of Japan, the end of the world . . .

No sleep. Only dreams. No sleep. Only dreams . . .

Night and day, this is why I take these pills . . .
This is what I tell myself, night and day . . .
'They were on the floor,' says Nishi –

I nod. I ask, 'You got a cigarette?'

Nishi shakes his head. *I curse him.* There are five more days until the next special ration. *Five more days . . .*

The office door swings open –

Detective Fujita storms into the room. Detective Fujita has a *Police Bulletin* in his hand. Fujita says, 'Sorry, more bad news . . .'

He tosses the bulletin onto my desk. Nishi picks it up –

Nishi is young. Nishi is keen. Too young . . .

'It's from the Shinagawa police station,' he says, and reads: 'Body discovered in suspicious circumstances at the Women's Dormitory Building of the Dai-Ichi Naval Clothing Department –'

'Just a moment,' I tell him. 'Surely anything to do with the Naval Clothing Department falls under the jurisdiction of the Kempeitai? This is a case for the military police, not civilian . . .'

'I know,' says Fujita. 'But Shinagawa are requesting Murder Squad detectives. Like I say, I'm really sorry I pulled it . . .'

No one wants a case. Not today. Not now . . .

I get up from my desk. I grab my hat –

'Come on,' I tell Fujita and Nishi. 'We'll find someone else. We'll dump the case. Just watch me . . .'

I go out of our room and down the main hallway of the First Investigative Division of the Tokyo Metropolitan Police Department; down Police Arcade, room to room, office to office, door to door –

Door to door. *No one.* Office to office. *No one.* Room to room. *No one.* Everyone evacuated or absent –

No one wants a case. Not today . . .

Just Fujita, Nishi and me now –

I curse. I curse. I curse . . .

I stand in the corridor. I ask Nishi, 'Where's Chief Kita?'

'All chiefs were summoned to a meeting at 7 a.m. . . .'

I take out my pocket watch. It's already past eight –

'7 a.m.?' I repeat. 'Maybe today is the day then?'

'Didn't you hear the nine o'clock news last night?' he asks. 'There's to be an Imperial broadcast at noon today . . .'

I eat acorns. I eat leaves. I eat weeds . . .

'A broadcast about what?' I ask –

4

'I don't know, but the entire nation has been instructed to find a radio so that they can listen to it . . .'

'Today *is* the day then,' I say. 'People return to your homes! Kill your children! Kill your wives! Then kill yourself!'

'No, no, no,' says Nishi –

Too young. Too keen . . .

'If we're going to go,' interrupts Fujita, 'let's at least go via Shimbashi and get some cigarettes . . .'

'That's a very good idea,' I say. 'No cars for us, anyway . . .'

'Let's take the Yamate Line round to Shinagawa,' he says. 'Take our time, walk slowly, and hope we're too late . . .'

'If the Yamate Line is even running,' I remind him –

'Like I say,' says Fujita again. 'Take our time.'

Detective Fujita, Nishi and I walk down the stairs, through the doors, and leave Headquarters by the back way, on the side of the building that faces away from the grounds of the Imperial Palace –

That looks out on the ruins of the Ministry of Justice.

The shortest route to Shimbashi from Sakuradamon is through the Hibiya Park, through this park that is now no park –

Black winter trees in the white summer heat . . .

'Even if we are routed in battle,' Nishi is saying, 'the mountains and the rivers remain. The people remain . . .'

Plinths without statues, posts with no gates . . .

'The hero Kusunoki pledged to live and die seven times in order to save Japan,' he states. 'We can do no less . . .'

No foliage. No bushes. No grass now . . .

'We must fight on,' he urges. 'Even if we have to chew the grass, eat the earth and live in the fields . . .'

Just stark black winter trees . . .

'With our broken swords and our exhausted arrows,' I say. 'Our hearts burnt by fire, eaten by tears . . .'

In the white summer heat . . .

Nishi smiling, 'Exactly . . .'

The white heat . . .

Nishi in one ear and now the harsh noise of martial music from a sound-truck in the other as we leave the park that is no park, down streets that are no streets, past buildings that are no buildings –

'Oh so bravely, off to Victory / Insofar as we have vowed and left our land behind . . .'

5

Buildings of which nothing remains but their front walls; now only sky where their windows and their ceilings should be –

'Who can die without first having shown his true mettle / Each time I hear the bugles of our advancing army . . .'

The dates on which these buildings ceased to be buildings witnessed in the height of the weeds that sprout here and there among the black mountains of shattered brick –

'I close my eyes and see wave upon wave of flags cheering us into battle . . .'

The shattered brick, the lone chimneys and the metal safes that crashed down through the floors as these buildings went up in flames, night after night –

'The earth and its flora burn in flames / As we endlessly part the plains . . .'

Night after night, from the eleventh month of last year, siren after siren, bomb after bomb –

'Helmets emblazoned with the Rising Sun / And, stroking the mane of our horses . . .'

Bomb after bomb, fire after fire, building after building, neighbourhood after neighbourhood until there are no buildings, there are no neighbourhoods and there is no city, no Tokyo –

'Who knows what tomorrow will bring – life?'

Only the survivors now –

'Or death in battle?'

Hiding under the rubble, living among the ruins, three or four families to a shack of rusted iron and salvaged wood, or in the railway or the subway stations –

The lucky ones . . .

'We must fight on,' repeats Detective Nishi. 'For if we do not fight on, the Emperor himself will be executed and the women of Japan will be subjected to methodical rape so that the next Japanese will not be Japanese . . .'

I curse him . . .

Beneath telegraph poles that stand as grave markers, down these streets that are no streets, we walk as Nishi rants on –

'In the mountains of Nagano, we shall make our final stand; on Maizuruyama, on Minakamiyama, on Zōzan!'

There are people on these streets that are no streets now, people that are no people; exhausted ghosts in early morning queues, bitter-enders waiting for lunches outside hodge-podge dining halls in old movie theatres, their posters replaced by slogans –

'We Are All Soldiers on the Home Front . . .'

The sound-truck has gone and with it that song we have heard every day for the last seven years, 'Roei no Uta' –

Just the noise of Nishi's voice now –

'Every man under sixty-five, every woman under forty-five will take up a bamboo spear and march off . . .

'To defend our beloved Japan . . .'

I stop in the middle of this street that is no street and I grab Nishi by the collar of his civil defence uniform and I push him up against a scorched wall, a scorched wall on which is written –

'Let us All Help One Another with Smiling Faces . . .'

'Go back to Headquarters, detective,' I tell him –

He blinks, open mouthed, and now he nods –

I pull him back from the black wall –

'I want to make sure one of us, at least, is able to hear this Imperial broadcast,' I tell him. 'You can then report what was said, if Fujita and I are unable to hear it . . .'

I let go of his collar –

Nishi nods again.

'Dismissed,' I shout now and Nishi stands to attention, salutes and then he bows –

And he leaves.

'Thank you very much,' laughs Detective Fujita.

'Nishi is very young,' I tell him.

'Young and very keen . . .'

'Yes,' I say. 'But I don't think he'd be too keen on our old friend Matsuda Giichi . . .'

'Very true,' laughs Fujita again as we walk on, on down these streets that are no streets, past buildings that are no buildings –

In this city that is no city –

To Shimbashi, Tokyo.

There are lines of soldiers unloading wooden crates from two Imperial Army trucks outside the temporary offices of Matsuda Giichi and his affiliates in an open lot near the back of the Shimbashi railway station; Matsuda Giichi himself giving the orders –

'Sellers and Buyers Are All Comrades in Arms . . .'

Matsuda Giichi in a new silk suit, stood on a crate with a

Panama hat in one hand and a foreign cigar in the other –

The brand new Emperor of Tokyo . . .

Matsuda smiles when he sees Fujita and me –

The only man smiling in Tokyo . . .

'I thought you lot had all run off to the mountains,' he laughs. 'The last stand of the Japanese race and all that . . .'

'What's in the crates?' I ask him –

'Ever the detective, aren't you?' says Matsuda. 'But you two might want to start thinking of changing your line of work . . .'

'What's in the crates?' I ask again –

'Army helmets,' he says –

'Not thinking of joining the war effort, are you?'

'Little late for that,' he says. 'Anyway, I did my bit on the continent – not that anyone ever thanked me for my trouble. But, past is past; now I'm going to help this country get back on its feet . . .'

'Very patriotic of you,' I say. 'But we've not lost yet.'

Matsuda looks at his watch, his new foreign watch, and nods. 'Not yet, you're quite right, detective. But have you seen all those columns of smoke rising from all those government buildings . . .?'

Both Detective Fujita and I shake our heads –

'Well, that means they're burning all their documents and their records. That's the smoke of surrender . . .

'The smoke of defeat.'

Two more army trucks pull up. Horns sound. Matsuda says, 'Now I am very sorry to be rude but, as you gentlemen can see, today is a very busy day. So was there anything you specifically wanted? Like a new job? A new name? A new life? A new past . . .?'

'Just cigarettes,' Fujita and I say simultaneously.

'Go see Senju,' says Matsuda Giichi.

Both Fujita and I thank him –

'Senju's round the back.'

Fujita and I bow to him –

And curse him.

Detective Fujita and I walk round the back of Matsuda's temporary office to his makeshift warehouse and his lieutenant –

Senju Akira stripped to his waist, a sheathed short sword in his right hand, as he supervises the unloading of another truck –

Its boxes of Imperial Chrysanthemum cigarettes –

I ask, 'Where did you get hold of all these?'

'Never ask a policeman,' laughs Senju. 'Look, those in the know, know, and those who don't, don't . . .'

'So what's with your boss and all those helmets?' I ask him.

'What goes around, comes around,' smiles Senju again. 'We sold the army saucepans to make helmets, now they're selling us helmets to make saucepans . . .'

'Well then, you can sell us on some of those Chrysanthemum cigarettes,' says Fujita.

'Don't tell me you've actually got hard cash,' says Senju.

Detective Fujita and I both shake our heads again –

'Fucking cops,' sighs Senju Akira as he hands us each five packs of Imperial cigarettes. 'Worse than thieves . . .'

We thank him and then we bow to him –

And we curse him and curse him . . .

We share a match in the shade –

In the shade that is no shade . . .

We smoke and walk on –

There are uniformed police officers on duty at Shimbashi railway station, checking packages and bundles for contraband –

Knapsacks and pockets for black-market cigarettes –

Detective Fujita and I take out our *keisatsu techō*, our police notebooks, to identify ourselves at the gate –

The station and the platform are almost deserted, the Yamate Line train almost empty –

The sun is climbing, the temperature rising. I wipe my neck and I wipe my face –

I itch –

I itch as I stare out of the windows; the elevated tracks of the Yamate Line now the highest points left in most of Tokyo, a sea of rubble in all directions except to the east –

The docks and the other, real sea.

The uniforms behind the desk at Shinagawa police station are expecting us, two waiting to lead us down to the docks –

One called Uchida, the other Murota –

To the scene of the crime . . .

'They think it might be a woman called Miyazaki Mitsuko,' they tell us as we walk, panting and sweating like dogs in the sun. 'This Miyazaki girl was originally from Nagasaki and had been brought up to Tokyo just to work in the Naval Clothing Department and so she was living in the workers' dormitory . . .'

The sun beating down on our hats . . .

'Back in May, she was given leave to go back home to visit her family in Nagasaki. However, she never arrived there and she never returned to work or the dormitory . . .'

The neighbourhood stinks . . .

'Most of the workers have actually moved out of the dormitory now as the factory of the Naval Clothing Department is no longer in operation. However, there have been a number of thefts from the buildings and so the caretaker and his assistant were searching and then securing premises . . .'

It stinks of oil and shit . . .

'They went down into one of the air-raid shelters, one that has not been used in a while, and that was when they . . .'

It stinks of retreat . . .

'Found the naked body of a woman . . .'

Surrender . . .

This neighbourhood of factories and their dormitories, factories geared to the war effort, dormitories occupied by volunteer workers; the factories bombed and the dormitories evacuated, any buildings still standing now stained black and stripped empty –

This is the scene of the crime . . .

The Women's Dormitory Building of the Dai-Ichi Naval Clothing Department still standing, next to a factory where only the broken columns and the gateposts remain –

No equipment and no parts –

The workers have fled –

This is the scene . . .

Two men sit motionless before the abandoned dormitory, sheltering from the sun in the shadow of a cabin-cum-office –

'I really can't understand it,' the older man is saying. 'I really can't understand it. I really can't understand it at all . . .'

The older man is the caretaker of the dormitory. The other, younger man is the boiler-man. It was the boiler-man who found the body and it is the boiler-man who now points at the two corrugated metal doors to an air-raid shelter and says, 'She's down there . . .

'In a cupboard at the back of the shelter . . .'

The sun beating down on our hats . . .

I pull back the two corrugated tin doors and then immediately

I step back again. The smell of human waste is overwhelming –

Human piss. Human shit. Human piss. Human shit . . .

Three steps down, the floor of the shelter is water –

Not rain or sea water, the shelter has flooded with sewage from broken pipes; a black sunken pool of piss and shit –

'We could do with Nishi now,' says Fujita.

I turn back to the caretaker in his shade –

'When did this happen?' I ask him –

'In the May air raids,' he says.

'How did you find the body, then?' I ask the boiler-man –

'With this,' he replies, and holds up an electric torch.

'Pass it over here,' I tell the boiler-man –

The boiler-man gets to his feet, mumbling about batteries, and brings the torch over to Fujita and me –

I snatch it from him.

I take out my handkerchief. I put it over my nose and my mouth. I peer back down the steps –

I switch on the torch –

I shine the light across the black pool of sewage water, the water about a metre deep, furniture sticking up here and there out of the pool. Against the furthest wall a wardrobe door hangs open –

She is down here. She is down here. Down here . . .

I switch off the torch. I turn back from the hole. I take off my boots. I take off my socks. I start to unbutton my shirt –

'You're never going in there, are you?' asks the caretaker.

'That was my question too,' laughs Fujita –

I unbutton my trousers. I take them off –

'There are rats down there,' says the caretaker. 'And that water's poisonous. A bite or a cut and you'll be . . .'

I say, 'But she's not going to walk out of there, is she?'

Fujita starts to unbutton his shirt now, cursing –

'Just another corpse,' he says –

'You two as well,' I say to the two uniforms from Shinagawa. 'One of you inside, one of you holding these doors open . . .'

I tie my dirty handkerchief tight around my face –

I put my boots back on. I pick up the torch –

Now one, two, three steps down I go –

Fujita behind me, still cursing –

'Nishi back in the office . . .'

I can feel the floor of the shelter beneath the water, the water up to my knees. I can hear the mosquitoes and I can sense the rats –

The water up to my waist, I wade towards the wardrobe –

My boots slip beneath the water, my legs stumble –

My knee bangs into the corner of a table –

I pray for a bruise, a bruise not a cut –

I reach the far side of the shelter –

I reach the wardrobe doors –

She is in here. In here . . .

I glimpse her as I pull at the doors, but the doors are stuck, submerged furniture trapping her within, closing the doors –

Detective Fujita holds the torch as the uniformed officer and I clear the chairs and the tables away, piece by piece –

Piece by piece until the doors swing open –

The doors swing open and, *she is here . . .*

The body bloated in places, punctured in others –

Pieces of flesh here, but only bones there –

Her hair hangs down across her skull –

Teeth parted as though to speak –

To whisper, *I am here . . .*

Now the uniform holds the torch as Fujita and I take the body between us, *cold here,* as we carry and then hoist it out of the black water, *warm there,* up the dank steps, *hard here,* out –

Out into the air, *soft there,* out into the sun –

Panting and sweating like dogs . . .

Fujita, the uniform and I flat on our backs in the dirt, the badly decomposed and naked body of a young woman between us –

Bloated, punctured, flesh and bones, hair and teeth . . .

I use my jacket to wipe myself, to dry myself –

I smoke a Chrysanthemum cigarette –

Now I turn to the two men sat in the shade, the caretaker and the boiler-man, and I say, 'You told these officers that you think this might be the body of a Miyazaki Mitsuko . . .'

Flesh and bones, hair and teeth . . .

The caretaker nods his head.

'Why did you say that?' I ask him. 'Why do you think that?'

'Well, it was always a bit strange,' he says. 'The way she left and never came back. Never went home and never back here . . .'

'But thousands of people have gone missing,' says Fujita.

'Who knows how many people have been killed in the raids?'

'Yes,' says the caretaker. 'But she left after the first raids on this place and she never arrived back in Nagasaki . . .'

'Who says so?' I ask him. 'Her parents?'

'They might have been lying,' says Fujita. 'To keep their daughter from coming back to Tokyo . . .'

The caretaker shrugs. The caretaker says, 'Well, if she did get back to Nagasaki, she's as good as dead anyway . . .'

I finish my cigarette. I nod at the body in the dirt and I ask, 'Is there any way you could identify this as her?'

The caretaker looks at the remains of the corpse on the ground. He looks away again. He shakes his head –

'Not like that,' he says. 'All I remember is that she had a watch with her name engraved on its back. It was a present from her father when she moved to Tokyo. Very proud of it, she was . . .'

Fujita puts his handkerchief back over his mouth –

He crouches down again. He shakes his head –

There's no watch on the wrist of this corpse –

I nod back towards the air-raid shelter and say to Detective Fujita, 'It might still be down there somewhere . . .'

'Yes,' he says. 'And it might not be.'

'How about you?' I ask the boiler-man. 'Did you know her?'

The boiler-man shakes his head. He says, 'Before my time.'

'He only started here this June,' says the caretaker. 'And Miyazaki was last seen around here at the end of May.'

I ask, 'Can you remember the exact dates?'

He tilts his head to one side. He closes his eyes. He screws them up tight. Then he opens his eyes again and shakes his head –

'I'm sorry,' he says. 'But I lose track of the time . . .'

I can hear an engine now. I can hear a jeep . . .

I turn round as the vehicle approaches –

It is a military police vehicle –

It is the Kempeitai.

The jeep stops and two Kempei officers get out of the front, both wearing side-arms and swords. They are accompanied by two older men sporting the armbands of the Neighbourhood Association –

I want to applaud them. The Kempeitai. I want to cheer –

No one wants a case. Not today. Not now . . .

This body was found on military property; this is their

dominion, this is their body, this is their case.

Detective Fujita and I step forward. Fujita and I bow deeply –

These two Kempei officers look very much like Fujita and I;
the older man is in his late forties, the other in his late thirties . . .

Detective Fujita and I introduce ourselves to the men –

I am looking in a mirror. I am looking at myself . . .

We apologize for being on military property –

But they are soldiers, we're just police . . .

There are briefer reciprocal bows –

This is their city, their year . . .

The younger officer introduces the older man as Captain Muto and himself as Corporal Katayama –

I am looking in a mirror . . .

I bow again and now I make my report to the two Kempei officers, the two men from the Neighbourhood Association still standing close enough to hear what I am telling them –

The times and dates. Places and names . . .

I finish my report and I bow again –

They glance at their watches.

Now Captain Muto, the older of the two Kempei officers, walks over to the corpse stretched out in the dust. He stands and he stares at the body for a while before turning back to Fujita and me –

'We will need an ambulance from the Keiō University Hospital to transport this body to the hospital. We will need Dr. Nakadate of Keiō to perform the autopsy on the body . . .'

Detective Fujita and I both nod –

This is their body, their case . . .

But Captain Muto turns to the two uniforms now and says, 'You two men return to Shinagawa and request that the Keiō University Hospital send an ambulance immediately and that Dr. Nakadate is made available to perform the autopsy.'

Uchida and Murota, the two uniforms, both nod, salute and then bow deeply to the Kempei man –

Fujita and I both curse –

No escape now . . .

Now Captain Muto gestures at the caretaker and then the boiler-man and asks us, 'Which of these men work here?'

'They both do,' I reply.

Captain Muto points to the boiler-man and shouts, 'Boiler-

14

man, you go get a blanket or something similar and as many old newspapers as you can find. And do it quickly as well!'

The boiler-man runs off inside the building.

The older Kempei officer glances at his watch again and now he asks the caretaker, 'Do you have a radio here?'

'Yes,' he nods. 'In our cabin.'

'There is to be an Imperial broadcast shortly and every citizen of Japan has been ordered to listen to this broadcast. Go now and check that your radio is tuned correctly and in full working order.'

The caretaker nods. The caretaker bows. The caretaker goes off to his cabin, passing the boiler-man as he returns with a coarse grey blanket and a bundle of old newspapers –

The younger Kempei man now turns to Fujita and me and tells us, 'Lay that body out on these newspapers and then cover it with this blanket ready for the ambulance . . .'

Fujita and I tie our handkerchiefs back over our mouths and our noses and set to work, laying the newspapers and then the body out, partially covering it with the blanket –

This is not our case any more . . .

But now the boiler-man nervously approaches the younger of the Kempei officers. The boiler-man's head is bent low in apology, first mumbling and then nodding, pointing here and there in answer to the questions the officer is asking –

The conversation ends.

Now Corporal Katayama strides over to his senior colleague and says, 'This man says there have been a number of thefts from our property and that he suspects these robberies to have been committed by the Korean labourers billeted in that building over there . . .'

The younger Kempei man is pointing to a scorched three-storey building on the opposite side of the dormitory –

'Are these workers under any kind of supervision?' asks the older man. 'Or are they just free to come and go?'

'I heard that they were under guard until the end of May,' says the boiler-man. 'Then the younger and stronger ones were taken to work in the north but the older, weaker ones were left here.'

'And do they do any kind of work?'

'They are meant to help us with the repairs to the buildings but they are either too sick or there are not enough materials available, so usually they just stay in there . . .'

Captain Muto, the older Kempei officer, who still keeps looking at his watch, now abruptly waves at all of the surrounding buildings and shouts, 'I want all these buildings searched!'

Fujita and I have finished laying out the body on the newspapers. Now I glance at Fujita. I am not sure if Captain Muto means for us to search or not. Fujita doesn't move –

But now the Kempei captain barks –

'You two take this dormitory!'

Not our case any more . . .

Fujita and I both salute him. Fujita and I both bow to him. Then we march off towards the building –

I am cursing. Fujita cursing . . .

'Nishi back in the office . . .'

Detective Fujita takes the top floor. I take the second floor. The knotted wooden floorboards of the corridor squeak. Knock-knock. Door to door. Room to room. Every room exactly the same –

The tatami mats, frayed and well worn. The single window and the blackout curtain. The thin green walls and the chrysanthemum wallpaper, limp and peeling –

Every room empty, abandoned.

The very end of the corridor. The very last room. The very last door. *Knock-knock.* I turn the handle. I open the door –

The same old mats. The single window. The same blackout curtain. The thin walls. The same peeling paper –

In another empty room.

I walk across the mats. I pull back the curtain. The sunlight illuminates a partially burnt mosquito coil on a low table –

The stench of piss. The stench of shit –

Human piss and human shit . . .

I open the closet built into the wall and there, among a heap of bedding, crouches an old man, his face buried in a futon –

I crouch down. I say, 'Don't be afraid . . .'

Now he turns his head from the bedding and looks up at me; the old man's face is flat and his lips are chapped and parted, showing broken yellow dirt-flecked teeth –

He stinks of piss and of shit –

The old man is a Korean –

I curse and I curse . . .

He is a *Yobo* –

'Congratulations!'

I look round; Corporal Katayama, the younger Kempei officer, is stood in the doorway, Fujita behind him, shaking his head –

'Bring him downstairs!' orders the Kempei man –

I stare at this Corporal Katayama –

I am looking into a mirror . . .

'Quickly!' he barks.

The old man buries his head back in the bedding, his shoulders shaking, mumbling and moaning –

'I didn't do anything! Please . . .'

His breath foul and rotten –

I take him by his shoulders and start to pull him from the bedding, from the closet, the old man wriggling and struggling –

'I didn't do anything! Please, I want to live!'

'Help him!' the corporal orders Fujita –

Fujita and I drag the old man from the closet, from the room, by his shoulders, by his arms, then out into the corridor, back along the floorboards; we have an arm each now –

The man's trunk and legs aslant –

His feet are trailing –

The Kempei officer marching behind with his sword in one hand, kicking at the soles of the old man's feet, striking him with his sword to hurry him along –

Down the stairs –

Into the light . . .

'That's *him*!' cries the boiler-man now. 'That's *him*!'

'Get me two spades now!' shouts the older Kempei officer and the caretaker runs back inside his cabin-cum-office –

'You two, bring the suspect over here.'

Fujita and I march the old Korean man over to Captain Muto in the shade of the other dormitory –

Into the shadows . . .

The caretaker comes back with the two spades. Captain Muto takes one of the spades from the caretaker and hands it to the boiler-man. He nods at a patch of ground that might once have been a flowerbed, then perhaps a vegetable patch, but now is nothing but hard, packed soil stained black –

'Dig a hole,' he says.

The caretaker and the boiler-man begin to dig up the ground, the caretaker already sweating and saying, 'He made a peephole to spy on the women workers as they bathed . . .'

The boiler-man wiping his skull, then his neck and agreeing, 'We caught him and we beat him but . . .'

'But he kept coming back . . .'

'He couldn't keep away . . .'

Captain Muto points at a spot just in front of where the two men are digging. The captain orders Fujita and me to stand the old Korean man in front of the deepening hole –

The old man just blinking –

His mouth hanging open.

Fujita and I push the Korean towards the spot, his body weaving back and forth like rice-jelly. I tell him, 'There's nothing to worry about. Just stand over here while we sort this out . . .'

But the old Korean man looks at each of us now –

The two Kempei officers, the Neighbourhood Association officials, the caretaker, the boiler-man –

Detective Fujita and me –

The dead body lain on the newspapers, the dead body partially covered by the blanket –

I am here . . .

Then the Korean glances back at the freshly dug ground, at the hole that the caretaker and the boiler-man are digging, and now he tries to run but Fujita and I grab him and hold him, his body shaking, his face contorted as he cries out, 'I don't want to be killed!

'I didn't do anything! Please, I want to live!'

'Shut up, *Yobo*!' says someone –

'But I didn't do anything . . .'

'So why did you just try to escape, *Yobo*?' asks Captain Muto. 'In Japan, innocent men don't run away.'

'Please don't kill me! Please!'

'You lying *Yobo* bastard!'

'Shut up!' shouts the younger Kempei officer now and he points over to the body beneath the blanket, the body lain out in the dirt and the sun by the corrugated metal doors to the air-raid shelter, and he asks the old Korean man, 'Did you rape that woman?'

And the old Korean man glances again at the body on the newspapers, the body beneath the blanket –

Bloated and punctured . . .

'Did you kill that woman?'

He shakes his head –

Flesh and bone . . .

Captain Muto steps forward. The older Kempei officer slaps the Korean's face. 'Answer him, *Yobo*!'

The Korean says nothing.

'This *Yobo* is obviously a criminal,' says Captain Muto. 'This *Yobo* is obviously guilty. There's nothing more to say . . .'

The old man looks up at us all again; the two Kempei officers, the Neighbourhood Association officials, the caretaker, the boiler-man, Detective Fujita and me; the old man shakes his head again –

But now all our eyes are fixed on Captain Muto's sword, the Kempei man's bright and shining military sword –

The sword unsheathed and drawn –

The blade raised high –

All our gazes slowly falling to one single spot above the old Korean man's back –

One spot . . .

'It's time!' shouts the younger Kempei officer suddenly –

The caretaker rushing back into his cabin-cum-office, shouting, 'The Imperial broadcast! The Imperial broadcast!'

Everyone turns to stare at the office, then back again to Captain Muto. The Kempei man lowers his sword –

'Bring the *Yobo* over to the radio,' he shouts and marches off towards the caretaker's cabin himself –

And everyone follows him –

To stand in a semi-circle before the open window of the caretaker's cabin-cum-office –

To listen to a radio –

Listen to a voice –

His voice . . .

A voice hollow, sorrowful and trembling –

'*To Our good and loyal subjects . . .*'

The voice of a god on the radio –

'*Oh so bravely, off to Victory / Insofar as we have vowed and left our land behind . . .*'

I can hear the strains of that song from a sound-truck again, the strains of 'Roei no Uta' and the voice of a god on the radio –

'*After pondering deeply the general trends of the world and*

19

the actual conditions in Our Empire today, We have decided to effect a settlement of the present situation by resorting to an extraordinary measure . . .'

'Who can die without first having shown his true mettle / Each time I hear the bugles of our advancing army . . .'

The strains of the song, the voice of a god, and the heat of the sun beating down on all our hats and all our heads –

'We have ordered Our government to communicate to the governments of the United States, Great Britain, China, and the Soviet Union that Our Empire accepts the provisions of their Joint Declaration . . .'

'I close my eyes and see wave upon wave of flags cheering us into battle . . .'

The strains of the song, the voice of a god, the heat of the sun, and the men from the Neighbourhood Association on their knees, heads in their hands, already sobbing –

'To strive for the common prosperity and happiness of all nations as well as the security and well-being of Our subjects is the solemn obligation handed down by Our Imperial Ancestors, and which We hold close to heart. Indeed, We declared war on America and Britain out of Our sincere desire to ensure Japan's self-preservation and the stabilization of East Asia, it being far from Our thought either to infringe upon the sovereignty of other nations or to embark on territorial aggrandizement. But now the war has lasted for nearly four years. Despite the best that has been done by everyone – the gallant fighting of military and naval forces, the diligence and assiduity of Our servants of the State, and the devoted service of Our one hundred million people, the war situation has developed not necessarily to Japan's advantage, while the general trends of the world have all turned against her interests. Moreover, the enemy has begun to employ a new and most cruel bomb, the power of which to do damage is indeed incalculable, taking the toll of many innocent lives. Should We continue to fight, it would not only result in the ultimate collapse and obliteration of the Japanese nation, but also it would lead to the total extinction of human civilization. Such being the case, how are We to save the millions of Our subjects, or to atone Ourselves before the hallowed spirits of Our Imperial Ancestors? This is the reason We have ordered the acceptance of the provisions of the Joint Declaration of the Powers . . .'

'The earth and its flora burn in flames / As we endlessly part the plains . . .'

The song, the voice, and the heat; men on their knees, heads in hands, sobbing and now howling –

'We cannot but express the deepest sense of regret to Our allied nations of East Asia, who have consistently cooperated with the Empire towards the emancipation of East Asia. The thought of those officers and men as well as others who have fallen in the fields of battle, those who died at their post of duty, or those who met an untimely death and all their bereaved families, pains Our heart night and day. The welfare of the wounded and the war sufferers, and of those who have lost their home and livelihood, are the objects of Our profound solicitude. The hardships and sufferings to which Our nation is to be subjected hereafter will be certainly great. We are keenly aware of the inmost feelings of all ye, Our subjects. However, it is according to the dictates of time and fate that We have resolved to pave the way for a grand peace for all generations to come by enduring the unendurable and suffering what is insufferable . . .'

'Helmets emblazoned with the Rising Sun / And, stroking the mane of our horses . . .'

The endless song, the endless voice, and the endless heat; men on their knees, howling, now prostrate upon the floor in lamentation, weeping in the dust –

'Having been able to safeguard and maintain the structure of the Imperial State, We are always with ye, Our good and loyal subjects, relying upon your sincerity and integrity. Beware most strictly of any outburst of emotion which may engender needless complications, or any fraternal contention and strife which may create confusion, lead ye astray, and cause ye to lose the confidence of the world . . .'

'Who knows what tomorrow will bring – life?'

The song is ending, the voice ending, the sky darkening now; the sound of one hundred million weeping, howling, wounded people borne on a wind across a nation ending –

'Let the entire nation continue as one family from generation to generation, ever firm in its faith of the imperishableness of its divine land, and mindful of its heavy burden of responsibilities, and the long road before it. Unite your total strength to be devoted to the construction for the future. Cultivate the ways of rectitude; foster

21

nobility of spirit; and work with resolution so as ye may enhance the innate glory of the Imperial State and keep pace with the progress of the world.'

'Or death in battle?'

It is over and now there is silence, only silence, silence until the boiler-man asks, 'Who was that on the radio?'

'The Emperor himself,' says Fujita.

'Really? What was he saying?'

'He was reading an Imperial Rescript,' says Fujita.

'But what was he talking about?' asks the boiler-man and this time no one answers him, no one until I say –

'It was to end the war . . .'

'So we won . . .?'

Only silence . . .

'We won . . .'

'Shut up!' shouts Captain Muto, the older Kempei officer –

I turn to look at him, to bow and to apologize –

His lips still moving but no words are forming, tears rolling down his cheeks as he brings the blade of his sword up close to his face, the thick blade catching the last sunlight –

His eyes, red spots on white . . .

He stares into the blade –

Bewitched.

Now he turns from the blade and looks into each of our faces, then down at the old Korean man still in our midst –

'Move!' he shouts at the Korean –

'Back over there, Yobo!'

But the old Korean man stands shaking his head –

'Move! Move!' shouts the Kempei man again and begins to shove the old Korean back over towards the hole –

Kicking, prodding him with the sword –

'Face the hole, Yobo! Face the hole!'

The Korean with his back to us –

The sword raised high again –

Eyes, red spots on white . . .

The man begging now –

The last sunlight . . .

Begging then falling, falling forward with a shudder as a cold chill courses through my own arms and legs –

The sword has come down –
Blood on the blade . . .
Now a desperate, piercing lament whines up from out of the mouth of the old Korean –
My blood cold . . .
'What are you doing?' the man cries. 'Why? Why?'
The Kempei officer curses the Korean. He kicks the back of his legs and the Korean stumbles forward into the hole –
There is a foot-long gash on the man's right shoulder where he has been cut by the Kempei's sword, the blood from the wound soaking through his brown civilian work clothes –
'Help me! Please help me! Help me!'
Now he claws wildly at the earth, screaming over and over, again and again, 'I don't want to die!'
'Help me! Help me!'
But Captain Muto has lowered his bloody military sword now. He is staring down at the old Korean in the hole –
Each time the Korean comes crawling back up from the hole, the officer kicks him back down into the dirt –
The blood draining from his body –
Into the dirt and into the hole . . .
'Help me!' gasps the man –
The Kempei captain now turns to the caretaker and the boiler-man and commands, 'Bury him!'
The caretaker and the boiler-man pick up their spades again and begin to heap the dirt back into the hole, over the man, faster and faster, as they bury his cries –
Down in the hole . . .
Until it is over –
Silence now . . .
My right hand trembles, my right arm, now both of my legs –
'*Detective Minami! Detective Minami! Detective Minami!*'
I close my eyes. *Eyes that are not my own.* There are scalding tears streaming from these eyes. *Eyes I do not want . . .*
I wipe the tears away, again and again –
'*Detective Minami! Detective Minami!*'
Finally I open these eyes –
'*Detective Minami!*'
There are flags falling to the ground, but these flags are no

flags, these buildings no buildings, these streets no streets –

For this city is no city, this country no country –

I eat acorns. I eat leaves. I eat weeds . . .

The voice of a god on the radio –

Hollow and sorrowful . . .

Everything distorted –

Heaven an abyss . . .

Time disjointed –

Hell our home . . .

Here, now –

Ten minutes past noon on the fifteenth day of the eighth month of the twentieth year of the reign of the Emperor Shōwa –

But this hour has no father, this year has no son –

No mother, no daughter, no wife nor lover –

For the hour is zero; the Year Zero –

Tokyo Year Zero.

I

The Gate of Flesh

to them weep. **Thirty Calmotin, thirty-one**. To my father: I hope you have been well. We land tomorrow. I shall do my best, as you would wish. To my wife: the great moment has come. To me, there is no tomorrow. I know well what you are thinking about, my dear wife. But be calm and serene. Take care of our children. To my son: Masaki, dear, your daddy is going to fight with the Chinese soldiers soon. Do you remember the big sword that your grandfather gave me? With it, I shall cut and stab and knock down enemy soldiers, like your hero, Iwami Jutaro. Daddy is going to bring home a sword and a steel Chinese helmet as a souvenir for you. But Masaki, dear, I want you to be a good boy always. Be nice to your mummy and Grandmother and all your teachers. Love your sister, and study so that you may become a great man. I see your little figure, waving a little flag in your little fist. Daddy cherishes that picture forever in his mind. *Masaki, Banzai! Daddy, Banzai!* **Forty Calmotin, forty-one**. Heavy fog hides everything but the railway station. Hints of Chinese houses, echoes of Chinese voices. *Everything is yellow.* Now we can smell acacia flowers, now we see Rising Sun flags. *Everything khaki.* Lookout patrols are dispatched, sentries posted. This unit to the noodle factory, that unit to the match factory. *The Chinks rob the Japanese.* The soldiers cook and clean. *The Chinks rape the Japanese.* The soldiers guard and patrol. *The Chinks murder the Japanese.* The soldiers build defence zones. *The Chinks rob the Japanese.* Barbed wire and barricades throughout the city. *The Chinks rape the Japanese.* Every Chinese is challenged at every intersection. *The Chinks murder the Japanese.* There are sandbags and there are roadblocks. More units arrive. There is always sand, there is never water. More units arrive. Always dust and always dirt. More units arrive. I itch and I scratch. *Gari-gari.* Daytime duty is followed by nighttime duty. I itch and I scratch. *Gari-gari.* Nighttime duty followed by daytime duty. I itch and I scratch. *Gari-gari.* The mattresses are torn, the bedbugs hungry. I itch and I scratch. *Gari-gari.* There among the corpses, I cannot sleep. *Bayonets fixed.* I can hear their screams. *Rifles loaded.* I can hear their pleas. *The Chinks rob the Japanese.* The Japanese bosses don't pay their Chinese workers. *The Chinks rape the Japanese.* The Chinese workers complain to their Japanese bosses. *The Chinks murder the Japanese.* The bosses insert cotton-thread needles into the gaps between the flesh and the nails of their workers' fingers. *I can hear their screams.* The bosses thrust the needles into their ring fingers, their middle fingers and their index fingers. *I can hear their pleas.* The Japanese bosses do what they want now. *I was impertinent, lazy and bad.* Workers are lashed with wet leather whips. *This is a warning.* Workers are hung from the branches of trees. *I was impertinent.* **Fifty Calmotin, fifty-one**. A child shits behind a sorghum straw fence. Single-wheeled carts rush down the street. *In this city of robbery.* A woman with bound feet hurries past. The solitary wheels groan beneath the weight of huge gunnysacks. *In this city of rape.* Coolies the colour of dust sift through peanut shells and watermelon rinds. The rhombus-shaped sails of the carts inflate and disappear. *In this city of murder.* Long-eared donkeys lead a lengthy funeral

1

August 15, 1946

Tokyo, 91°, overcast

Ton-ton. Ton-ton. Ton-ton. Ton-ton. Ton-ton. Ton-ton . . .
The sound of hammering and hammering –
Ton-ton. Ton-ton. Ton-ton. Ton-ton . . .
I open my eyes and I remember –
Ton-ton. Ton-ton. Ton-ton . . .
I am one of the survivors –
One of the lucky ones . . .
I take out my handkerchief. I wipe my face. I wipe my neck. I
push my hair back out of my eyes. I look at my watch –
Chiku-taku. Chiku-taku. Chiku-taku . . .
It is 10 a.m.; it is only 10 a.m. –
*Just four hours gone, eight still to go, then down to
Shinagawa, down to Yuki. Three, four hours there and then out to
Mitaka, to my wife and my children. Try to take them some food,
bring them something to eat, anything. Eat and then sleep, try to
sleep. Then back here again for 6 a.m. tomorrow . . .*
Chiku-taku. Chiku-taku. Chiku-taku . . .
Another twelve hours in this oven . . .
I wipe the sweat from my shirt collar. I wipe the sweat from
my eyelids. I look down the length of the table. Three men on my left,
two men on my right and the three empty chairs –
No Fujita. No Ishida. No Kimura . . .
Five men wiping their necks and wiping their faces,
scratching after lice and swiping away mosquitoes, ignoring their
work and turning their newspapers; newspapers full of the First
Anniversary of the Surrender, the progress of reform and the gains of
democracy; newspapers full of the International Military Tribunal,
the judgment of the Victors and the punishment of the Losers –
Day in, day out. Day in, day out. Day in, day out . . .
Turning our newspapers, thinking about food –

Day in, day out. Day in, day out . . .
And waiting and waiting –
Day in, day out . . .

The telephones that can't ring, the electric fans that can't turn. The heat and the sweat. The flies and the mosquitoes. The dirt, the dust and the noise; the constant sound of hammering and hammering, hammering and hammering, hammering and hammering –

Ton-ton. Ton-ton. Ton-ton. Ton-ton. Ton-ton . . .

I get up from my chair. I go to the window. I raise the blind –

Ton-ton. Ton-ton. Ton-ton. Ton-ton . . .

Three floors above Sakuradamon, I look out over Tokyo –

Ton-ton. Ton-ton. Ton-ton . . .

The Palace to my left, GHQ to my right –

Ton-ton. Ton-ton . . .

Under a low typhoid sky –

Ton-ton . . .

The Capital City of the Shōwa Dead, the Losers on their hands and knees, the Victors in their trucks and jeeps –

No resistance here.

I hear the door open. I turn round; Kimura is stood there –

Early twenties. Repatriated from the south. Only three months here and no longer the most junior member of our room, Room #2 . . .

Kimura is staring down the length of table at me; half in contempt, half in deference, a piece of paper in his hands –

Idiot. Idiot. Idiot. Idiot. Idiot. Idiot. Idiot . . .

My stomach knots, my head pounds –

Idiot. Idiot. Idiot. Idiot. Idiot. Idiot . . .

Kimura holds out the paper marked *Police Bulletin* and says, 'Maybe this one's a murder, Detective Inspector Minami, sir.'

*

There is only one working car for the whole division. It is not available. So we walk again, like we walk everywhere. They promise us cars, like they promise us telephones and guns and pens and paper and better pay and health care and holidays but every day we tear apart old bicycle tires to cut out new soles to hammer onto the bottom of our boots so we can walk and walk and walk and walk and walk –

Hattori, Takeda, Sanada, Shimoda, Nishi, Kimura and me –

Ton-ton. Ton-ton. Ton-ton. Ton-ton. Ton-ton . . .
Through the heat, through the flies and the mosquitoes –
Ton-ton. Ton-ton. Ton-ton. Ton-ton . . .
From Metropolitan Police Headquarters to Shiba Park –
Ton-ton. Ton-ton. Ton-ton . . .
Jackets off, hats on. Handkerchiefs out, fans out –
Ton-ton. Ton-ton . . .
Down Sakurada-dōri and up the hill to Atago –
Ton-ton . . .

Detective Nishi has the *Police Bulletin* in his hand. Nishi reads it aloud as we walk: 'Naked body of unidentified female found at 9:30 a.m. this morning, August 15, 1946, at Nishi-Mukai Kannon Zan, 2 Shiba Park, Shiba Ward. Body reported to Shiba Park police box at 9:45 a.m. Body reported to Atago police station at 10:15 a.m. Body reported to Metropolitan Police Headquarters at 11:00 a.m. . . .

'They took their time,' he says now. 'It'll be two hours by the time we see the body. What were they doing at Atago . . .?'

'She ain't going nowhere,' laughs Detective Hattori.

'Tell that to the maggots and the flies,' says Nishi.

'No cars. No bicycles. No telephones. No telegraphs,' replies Hattori. 'What do you expect the Atago boys to do about it?'

Nishi shakes his head. Nishi doesn't answer him.

I wipe my neck. I glance at my watch again –
Chiku-taku. Chiku-taku. Chiku-taku . . .
It is almost 11:30 a.m.; only 11:30 a.m. –
Five and a half hours gone, six and a half to go. Then down to Shinagawa, down to Yuki. Three, four hours there and then out to Mitaka. The wife and the children. Eat and then sleep, try to sleep. Back here again for 6 a.m. and another twelve hours –
Chiku-taku. Chiku-taku. Chiku-taku . . .
If this body isn't a murder . . .

'This way is quicker,' says Nishi and we pick our way over the hills of rubble and through the craters of dust until we come out on to Hibiya-dōri near Onarimon –
Ton-ton. Ton-ton.

*

Two very young men from the Atago police station are waiting for us in their ill-fitting, dirt-stained uniforms. They bow and they salute, they greet us and they apologize but I can't hear a word they say –

Ton-ton. Ton-ton. Ton-ton. Ton-ton. Ton-ton . . .

The uniformed policemen lead us off the road, away from the sound of the hammering, and into the temple grounds –

Huge scorched trees, their roots to the sky . . .

There is nothing much left of Zōjōji Temple since it was burnt to the ground in the May air raids of last year –

Branches charred and leaves lost . . .

The two uniforms lead us through the ashes and up the hill, out of the sunlight and into the shadow; the graves forgotten here, this place is overgrown and its paths lost, the bamboo grass taller than a man and as thick as the insects that cloud the air; this place of foxes and badgers, of rats and crows, of abandoned dogs that run in packs with a new-found taste for human flesh –

In this place of assignation –

Of prostitutes, of suicides –

This place of silence –

This place of death –

She is here . . .

In this sudden clearing where the tall grass has been flattened and the sun has found her, *she is here*; lying naked on her back, her head slightly to the left, her right arm outstretched, her left at her side, *she is here*; her legs parted, raised and bent at the knee, *she is here . . .*

Possibly twenty-one years old and probably ten days dead –

Namu-amida-butsu. Namu-amida-butsu. Namu-amida . . .

There is a piece of red material round her neck –

Namu-amida-butsu. Namu-amida-butsu . . .

This is not a suicide. This is murder –

Namu-amida-butsu . . .

This case ours –

I curse her . . .

I look at my watch. *Chiku-taku.* It is almost noon –

Chiku-taku. It is August 15, 1946 –

The defeat and the capitulation. The surrender and the occupation. The ghosts all here today –

I curse her. I curse myself . . .

It has been one year.

*

In among the tall weeds, an old man is on his knees, bowing and mumbling his prayers with an axe on the ground before him –

'*Namu-amida-butsu*,' the old man chants. '*Namu-amida . . .*'

'This man discovered the body,' says one of the uniforms.

I squat down beside the old man. I swat at a mosquito with my hat. I miss. I wipe my neck. I say, 'It's hot today, isn't it?'

The old man stops his chanting. The old man nods.

'This man is a lumberjack,' says the uniform.

'And you found the body?' I ask the man.

The old man nods his head again.

'Found her just like this?'

He nods his head again.

'Are you sure you didn't find any of her clothes, a bag or a purse or anything else near her?'

He shakes his head.

'You haven't stashed away her things to sell later, have you? Not put away some of her things to come back for?'

Again, he shakes his head.

'Not her ration card?'

The old man looks up at me now. The old man says, 'No.'

I nod and I pat him on his back. I apologize to him and I thank him. I put my hat back on and I stand up again –

I see her out of the corner of my eye . . .

Detectives Hattori, Takeda, Sanada and Shimoda are sat down in the shade of the trees with their Panama hats in their hands, fanning and wiping themselves, swatting at flies and mosquitoes –

In the shade with the Shōwa Dead . . .

The two uniformed policemen from Atago shifting from foot to foot, foot to foot; Detectives Nishi and Kimura still stood over the body, still staring at her, waiting for me –

In this City of the Dead . . .

I walk over to the body –

She is here . . .

'I knew it,' Kimura is saying. 'Knew it'd be murder.'

'And she'll have been a whore,' agrees Nishi.

'I doubt that,' I tell him, tell them both.

'But this place is notorious for prostitutes,' says Nishi. 'We know the ones from Shimbashi bring their men up here . . .'

I stare down at the body, the pale grey and decaying body, the legs parted, raised and bent at the knee –

'This woman was raped,' I tell them both. 'Why would you rape and then murder a prostitute?'

'If you had no money,' says Kimura. 'There are a lot of destitute and desperate men . . .'

'So just rape her and leave her, beat her if you must, but she's not going to tell anyone.'

'Unless she knew him,' says Nishi. 'Knew his name . . .'

'We need to find *her* name,' I tell them now, tell them all, my men and the two men from Atago. 'And we need to find her clothes and any other belongings she might have had with her.'

'Just a moment!' barks out a voice from behind me, and everyone jumps to attention, to bow and to salute –

I turn round. *I know this voice.* I bow and I salute. *I know this face well.* I greet Chief Inspector Adachi –

Adachi or Anjo or Ando or whatever he calls himself this week; he has changed his name and he has changed his job, his uniform and his rank, his life and his past; he is not the only one . . .

Now no one is who they say they are . . .

No one is who they seem to be . . .

Behind him stand Suzuki, the First Investigative Division photographer, and two men in white coats from the Keiō University Hospital with a light, wooden coffin –

They are all sweating.

Adachi points at Suzuki and tells everyone, 'Move out of the way and let this man get on with his work, then these other two can get this body out of here.'

Everybody steps back into the taller grasses, among the taller trees, to watch Suzuki load his film and start his work –

Click-click-click. Click-click-click . . .

I look at my watch –

Chiku-taku . . .

12:30 p.m. –

Everything is lost; there will be a meeting of all the section heads of the First Investigative Division; there will be verbal and written reports; there will be the assignment of command, the delegation of responsibility, the division of labour, of investigation and of evaluation; more lost hours in more hot rooms . . .

'Bad luck, your room pulling this one,' laughs Adachi.

32

'Twenty-one days straight. No time off. You all stuck down here in Atago, knowing you'll never solve the case, never close it, knowing no one cares but knowing it's yet another failure on your record . . .'

'It'll be just like the Matsuda Giichi case then,' I say.

Inspector Adachi leans closer into my face now –

No one is who they say they are . . .

'That case is closed, corporal,' he spits.

No one who they seem to be . . .

I take a step back. I bow my head. I apologize.

'You're two men short,' says Adachi –

I bow again. I apologize again.

'Where's Detective Fujita?'

Another bow, another apology.

'That's not an answer,' says Adachi. 'Just an admission . . .'

*

The photographer has finished his work. *The ground beneath her is crushed and darker.* The two men from Keiō Hospital have lifted up the body. *The ground is infested with insects.* The men from Keiō have lifted the body into the wooden coffin. *She is stiff and refuses to bend.* The two uniforms from Atago were called to help and the arms were folded, the lid fitted and secured with ropes and knots, bound. *She is resisting the box.* The two men from Keiō Hospital have taken her back down the hill. *She is no longer here . . .*

Now I take out my watch again –

Chiku-taku. Chiku-taku . . .

It is almost 3 p.m. –

I am stood on the top of a wall behind the ruined Tokugawa tombs, looking up the hill and out over a sea of bamboo grass and zelkova trees, islands of fallen stone lanterns and broken down graves; I am searching for her clothes or her bag, when suddenly I see it –

I jump down from the top of the wall into the long, long grasses and I wade through the dead leaves and weeds towards it –

Namu-amida-butsu. Namu-amida-butsu. Namu-amida . . .

The white cloth grinning through the long, long grasses –

Namu-amida-butsu. Namu-amida-butsu . . .

White cloth around white bones –

Namu-amida-butsu . . .

33

I curse myself again!

Another body . . .

A second body wearing a white half-sleeved chemise, a yellow and dark-blue striped pinafore dress, pink socks and white canvas shoes with red rubber soles; a second body ten metres from the first; a second body now nothing but bones –

Tangled up in the weeds and leaves . . .

I curse her and I curse this place –

I curse and I curse again . . .

This place of shadow, of forgotten graves and lost paths, of foxes and badgers, of rats and crows, of abandoned dogs and human flesh, of prostitutes and suicides in this place of assignation –

This place of silence. This place of death –

In this place of defeat and capitulation. This place of surrender and occupation. This place of ghosts –

The body now nothing but bones . . .

In this place of no resistance.

*

It takes three hours for us to report the finding of the second body to Metropolitan Police Headquarters. *I stare at her white half-sleeved chemise.* Three hours for them to send Suzuki back here to photograph the second body. *I stare at her yellow and dark-blue striped pinafore dress.* Three hours for the Keiō University Hospital to send out another ambulance to take away the second body. *I stare at her pink socks.* Three hours for my men to seal off the crime scene and the immediate area around the second body. *I stare at her white canvas shoes.* Three hours for us to requisition the necessary uniformed men from the Atago, Meguro and Mita police stations in order to secure the area where the bodies were found. *Their red, red rubber soles.* Three hours sweating and swatting, itching and scratching, *gari-gari*, while I stand and I stare at this second body –

Her flesh far from here, carried in the mouths of others . . .

I stare at the bleached white bones of her fingers –

I stare at the bleached white bones of her hands –

Her wrists and her forearms and her elbows –

The bleached white bones of her face –

The permed hair. The yellow teeth –

34

Her last, contorted smile . . .

The shadows have lengthened now, the tall grasses and zelkova trees closer here.

*

The good detective visits the crime scene one hundred times. I have walked away from that place. *The good detective knows nothing is random.* I have walked out of the shadow and into the sunlight. *The good detective knows in chaos lies order.* I have walked back down the hill and into the temple grounds. *In chaos lie answers . . .*

But there is nothing left of the Zōjōji Temple –

Huge scorched trees, their roots to the sky . . .

Nothing but the ruin of the old Black Gate –

Branches charred and leaves lost . . .

In this lonely place, I stand beneath the dark eaves of the gate and I watch the ambulance drive away –

We have seen hell, we have known heaven, we have heard the last judgment and we have witnessed the fall of the gods . . .

Under the Black Gate, a stray dog pants –

But I am one of the survivors . . .

His house lost, his master gone –

One of the lucky ones . . .

In the Year of the Dog.

*

It is another long, hot walk back to Metropolitan Police Headquarters, a walk made worse by the dirt and the dust from the trucks and the jeeps with their big white stars and their big white teeth –

The constant, constant sound of hammering –

Ton-ton. Ton-ton. Ton-ton. Ton-ton . . .

I knock on the door to Chief Kita's office. I open it. I apologize. I bow. I enter. I take my seat at the table –

Chief Kita sits at the head of the table with his back to the window, its frame still buckled from the bombs; Chief Kita, the *kachō* of the whole of the First Investigative Division, an old but lean man with a deeply tanned face, a close-shaven head and hard, unblinking eyes; Chief Kita, the best friend my father ever had –

I don't want to remember. I don't want to remember . . .

To his right, Chief Inspector Kanehara with Adachi –

But in the half-light, I can't forget . . .

To his left Inspector Kai, leader of the First Team, and me; Inspector Minami now, leader of the Second Team –

No one is who they seem to be . . .

The report for the Public Safety Division is on the table. It has been translated into English, probably by Kanehara, and then typed up. It is passed round the table for all our signatures and seals –

I take out my pen. I stare at the report –

It could be Das Kapital . . .

The typed Roman characters –

Mein Kampf . . .

I sign it.

The report is returned to Chief Inspector Kanehara. Now Chief Kita nods at me and I begin my report; I repeat the timetable of the discovery and reporting of the first body; I detail the state and environment of the first body on our arrival; I recount my initial interview with the lumberjack; I defer then to Adachi who reports the timetable involving the photographer and the ambulance –

'My initial deduction upon seeing the body was that a murder had been committed. Therefore, I ordered Inspector Minami and his men to conduct a thorough search of the immediate area surrounding the body. It was during the course of this search that Inspector Minami himself discovered the second body, which was approximately ten metres from the site of the first body.'

'Detective Inspector Minami, please . . .'

'As Chief Inspector Adachi has said, the second body was approximately ten metres from the site of the first body. The second body was badly decomposed and largely skeletal, but it appears to be the body of a young woman. However, unlike the first body, it was not naked but wearing a white half-sleeved chemise, a yellow and dark-blue striped pinafore dress, pink socks and white canvas shoes with red rubber soles. Initial inspection and experience would suggest that death occurred between three and four weeks ago but of course that will be precisely determined by the autopsy. It is clear though that the two women did not die at the same time.'

'Do you believe these deaths are connected?' asks Chief Kita.

'Until the results of the autopsy are known, the location and sexes of the two bodies remain the only connecting factors,' I reply. 'Despite their proximity, the nature of the vegetation meant that the site of one body was not visible from the other. As you are all aware, there was what would seem to be a piece of material tied round the neck of the first body, leading us to assume that death was a result of murder. On preliminary examination of the second body, no such material was found, nor were there any other obvious signs of a murder having occurred. As we know, in the last year a number of bodies have been found in the environs of Shiba Park. However, before today's discovery, only one of these has proved to be murder. The other deaths were as a result of either suicide or disease.'

Chief Kita nods. Chief Kita says, 'Chief Inspector?'

Adachi nods, reluctantly. 'I agree with Inspector Minami.'

'Then we'll handle the two cases separately,' says the chief. 'Until we have the results from the autopsies which will be . . .?'

'The day after tomorrow,' says Adachi.

'From Keiō or Tokyo?'

'From Keiō . . .'

'By?'

'Dr. Nakadate.'

Kanehara and Kai pretend not to look up from their notes. Kanehara and Kai pretend not to look from me to Adachi to Chief Kita. Kanehara and Kai pretend not to see our exchange of glances –

I don't want to remember. I don't want to remember . . .

'It can't be helped,' says the chief. 'Let's proceed . . .'

Now comes the structure of the investigation. The delegation of responsibility. The division of labour . . .

'Inspector Kai and Room #1 will open the investigation into the first body. Inspector Kai and Room #1 will set up their Investigation Headquarters at the Atago police station. Inspector Kai will report to Chief Inspector Kanehara.'

Inspector Kai bows. Inspector Kai shouts, 'I understand! Thank you! I will not let you down!'

Chief Inspector Kanehara bows. Kanehara shouts, 'Thank you! I will not let you down!'

'Inspector Minami and Room #2 will investigate the second body found at Shiba Park . . .'

I bow too hastily; there must be a hint of relief, a glimpse of respite in my action, because Chief Kita's tone is harsh now –

'Inspector Minami and Room #2 will conduct the investigation as a murder inquiry. Inspector Minami and Room #2 will also set up their investigation headquarters at Atago police station until further instructions are received. Inspector Minami and his team will report to Chief Inspector Adachi.'

I curse him. I curse him. I curse him . . .

I bow again to the chief. I tell him I understand. I thank him. I promise I will not let him down –

So tomorrow morning Room #2 will take their trunk to Atago. Tomorrow morning our banner will be unfurled and raised on its poles. Tomorrow the investigation will begin. Day and night, night and day. From tomorrow morning there will be no rest, no time off for twenty days or until the case is closed . . .

'Has anyone anything else they wish to say?' asks Chief Inspector Kanehara. 'Anything they wish to clarify?'

There is nothing to say. Nothing to clarify –

There is silence now, almost –

Ton-ton. Ton-ton. Ton-ton . . .

'Then tidy up all your affairs tonight,' Chief Kita tells us. 'Leave nothing unfinished. No loose ends, please.'

The chief looks away now –

I glance at my watch –

Chiku-taku . . .

It is 8:30 p.m.

*

I run down the corridor of Police Arcade to the back stairs. I leave through a back door. I cut through Hibiya Park. The temperature not falling with the night, the flies and mosquitoes hungrier than ever –

Pan-pan girls calling through the shadows and the trees –

'*Asobu . . .? Asobu . . .? Asobu . . .? Asobu . . .?*'

I run across Hibiya-dōri. I reach the elevated tracks –

Pan-pan girls in the shadows and the arches –

'*Asobu . . .? Asobu . . .? Asobu . . .?*'

I follow the Yamate train tracks –

To the Shimbashi Market –

'*Asobu . . .? Asobu . . .?*'

To Senju Akira.

Kettles and pans. Crockery and utensils. Clothes and shoes. Cooking oil and soy sauce. Rice and tea. Fruit and vegetables. The *kakigōri* stalls and over and over, again and again, the 'Apple Song' –

'Red apple to my lips, blue sky silently watching . . .'

All laid out on the ground, on stall after stall –

Half of it Japanese. Half of it foreign. All of it illegal. But there are no police here. No Victors. No Occupiers –

'Apple doesn't say a thing, but Apple's feeling is clear . . .'

Here there is only one law; buy or be bought. Sell or be sold. Eat or be eaten; this is where the cannibals come –

'Apple's loveable, loveable is apple . . .'

To the Shimbashi New Life Market –

'Shall we all sing the Apple Song?'

The old Outside Free Market is gone. The old Black Market is finished. This is the new market for the new Japanese yen –

'If two people sing along, it's a merry song . . .'

This is the two-storey Shimbashi New Life Market with its modern arcades for over five hundred stalls –

'If everyone sings the Apple Song . . .'

The dream of Matsuda Giichi –

'It's an even merrier song . . .'

But Matsuda Giichi never lived to see his New Life Market open because two months ago, on the night of the tenth of June, Matsuda Giichi was attacked and shot in his office by Nodera Tomiji, one of his own former gang members, one who had been expelled during Matsuda's reorganization of his own gang, the Kantō Matsuda-gumi, in their amalgamation with the Matsuzakaya gang –

But nobody really knows if Nodera killed Matsuda –

Nobody saw Nodera pull the trigger and fire –

Nobody really knows because Nodera Tomiji was drunk when *persons unknown* found him in a bar on the Ginza –

And he was dead when they left him –

'So let's all sing the Apple Song and . . .'

Now Senju Akira is the new boss –

'And pass the feeling along . . .'

This is the man I've come to see. This is the man whose men are waiting for me. The man whose men are watching for me –

They know I'm here. They know I'm back . . .

In their pale suits and patterned shirts, with their American sunglasses and Lucky Strikes, they are whispering about me –

They know why I'm here, why I'm back . . .

Among the kettles and the pans, they come up behind me now, one on either side, and they take an arm each –

'You're more brave than you look,' whispers one of them –

'And more stupid,' says the other as they whisk me past the mats and the stalls, the crockery and the utensils, out into the alleys and the lanes, through the shadows and the arches, until we come to the wooden stairs and the open door at the top with its sign –

Tokyo Stall Vendors Processing Union.

Now they let me go. Now they let me wipe my face and wipe my neck, straighten up my shirt and put on my jacket –

The calls of odd, even and play . . .

There is a foreigner coming down the stairs, an American in sunglasses. At the foot of the stairs, the American turns his face to look at me and then looks away again. He nods to Senju's men as he disappears into the alleys and the shadows –

No one is who they say they are . . .

There is no 'Apple Song' playing here as I walk up the stairs towards the open door, just the dice and his voice –

'You got good news for me, have you, detective?' calls out Senju before I even reach the top of the stairs –

I stop on the stairs. I look down at his two goons. They are laughing now. I turn back to the door –

The sound of dice being thrown. The calls of odd, even and play, odd, even and play . . .

'Don't be a coward now,' he shouts. 'Answer me, detective.'

I start walking again. I reach the top. *I am a policeman.* I turn into the doorway. Into the light –

'Well?' asks Senju –

I kneel down on the tatami mat. I bow. I say, 'I'm sorry.'

Senju spits his toothpick onto the long low polished table. He turns his new electric fan my way and shakes his head –

'Just look at you, officer,' he laughs. 'Dressed like a tramp and stinking of corpses. Investigating murders when you could be getting rich, arresting Koreans and Formosans and bringing home two salaries for the pleasure. Taking care of your family and your mistress, fucking the living and not the dead . . .'

'I'm sorry,' I say again. 'I'm sorry.'

'How old are you now, detective?'

'I am forty-one years old.'

'So tell me,' he asks. 'What do they pay a forty-one-year-old detective these days, officer?'

'One hundred yen a month.'

'I pity you,' he laughs. 'And your wife, and your children, and your mistress, I really do.'

I lean forward so my face touches the tatami mat and I say, 'Then please help me . . .'

And I curse him; I curse him because he has what I need. And I curse Fujita; I curse him because he introduced us. But most of all I curse myself; I curse myself because of my dependence; my dependence on him . . .

'You chase corpses and ghosts,' he says. 'What help are you to me? And if you can't help me, I can't help you.'

'Please,' I say again. 'Please help me.'

Senju Akira throws down five hundred yen onto the mat in front of my face. Senju says, 'Then get a transfer to a different room; a room where you can find things out, things that help me . . .

'Like who paid Nodera Tomiji to kill my boss Matsuda; like who then killed Nodera; like why this case is now closed . . .'

'I will,' I say, then over and over. 'Thank you.'

'And don't come back here until you have.'

'Thank you. Thank you. Thank you.'

'Now get out!' he shouts –

I shuffle backwards across the mats then down the stairs, past the goons and through the alleys, back into the market –

'Shall we all sing the Apple Song?'

The Shimbashi New Life Market –

This is the New Japan . . .

This is how we live –

'Let's all sing the Apple Song and pass the feeling along.'

*

I haggle. *To eat.* I barter. *To work.* I threaten. *To eat.* I bully. *To work.* I buy three eggs and some vegetables. There was no fish and there was no meat. Now there is another problem on the Yamate Line and the trains have stopped running in the direction of Shinagawa, so I take the streetcar. It is crowded and I am crushed and the eggs were a mistake. I get off at Tamachi and then I walk or run the rest of the way. The vegetables in my pockets. The eggs in my hands –

To eat. To work. To eat. To work . . .

There is only this now.

*

I have waited hours to lie again here upon the old tatami mats of her dim and lamp-lit room. *I think about her all the time.* I have waited hours to stare again at her peeling screens with their ivy-leaf designs. *I think about her all the time.* I have waited hours to watch her draw her figures with their fox-faces upon these screens –

I think about her all the time . . .

Yuki is the one splash of colour among the dust, her hair held up by a comb. Now Yuki puts down her pencils and stares into the three-panelled vanity mirror and says, 'Oh, I wish it would rain . . .

'Rain but not thunder,' she says. 'I hate the thunder . . .

'The thunder and the bombs . . .'

She haunts me . . .

'Rain like it used to rain,' she whispers. 'Rain like before. Rain hard like the rain when it fell on the oiled hood of the rickshaw, drumming louder and faster on the hood, the total darkness within the hood heavy with the smell of the oil and of my mother's hair, of my mother's make-up and of her clothes, the faces and the voices of the actors we had seen on the stage that day, in those forbidden plays of loyalty and of duty, those plays of chastity and of fidelity, of murder and of suicide, those faces and those voices that would swim up through the darkness of the hood towards me . . .'

She has haunted me from the day I first met her, in the thunder and the rain, from that day to this day, through the bombs and the fires, from that day to this . . .

Yuki is lying naked on the futon. *Air raid! Air raid! Here comes an air raid!* Her head slightly to the right. *Red! Red! Incendiary bomb!* Her right arm outstretched. *Run! Run! Get a mattress and sand!* Her left arm at her side. *Air raid! Air raid! Here comes an air raid!* Her legs parted, raised and bent at the knee. *Black!*

Black! Here come the bombs! My come drying on her stomach and on her ribs. *Cover your ears! Close your eyes!*

'Make it rain again,' she says –

And then she brings her left hand up to her stomach. *I think about her all the time.* She dips her fingers in my come. *I think about her all the time.* She puts her fingers to her lips. *I think about her all the time.* She licks my come from her fingers and says again, 'Please make it rain, rain like it rained on the night we first met . . .'

She haunts me here. She haunts me now . . .

I place an egg and two hundred yen on her vanity box and I say, 'I might not be able to visit you tomorrow.'

Here and now, she haunts me . . .

'I am a woman,' she whispers. 'I am made of tears.'

*

The Shinagawa station is in chaos. *Every station.* There are queues but no tickets. *Every train.* I push my way to the front and I show my police notebook at the gate. *Every station.* I shove my way onto a train. *Every train.* I stand, crushed among people and their goods –

Every station. Every train. Every station. Every train . . .

This train doesn't move. It stands and it sweats –

Finally, after thirty minutes, the train starts to move slowly down the track towards Shinjuku station –

Every station. Every train . . .

I force my way off the train at Shinjuku. I fight my way along the platform and down one set of stairs and then up another. I have the two eggs in one hand, my notebook out in my other –

'Police. Police,' I shout. 'Police. Police.'

People hide their eyes and people clutch their backpacks. People stand aside as I heave my way onto the Mitaka train. I stand crushed again among more people and more goods –

This is how we live, with our houses lost . . .

I jostle my way off the train. I go through the ticket gate at Mitaka. I put the eggs in my jacket pocket. I take off my hat. I wipe my face. I wipe my neck. I am parched –

Itching and scratching again –

Gari-gari. Gari-gari . . .

I follow crooked, impotent telegraph poles down the road

to my usual restaurant, half-way between the station and my home –

The one lantern amidst the darkness where once there had been ten, twenty or thirty others, illuminating the street, advertising their pleasures and their wares. But there is no illumination –

No wares or pleasures to be had here now.

I step inside. I sit down at the counter.

'A man was here looking for you last night,' says the master. 'Asking questions about you. After your new address . . .'

No one who they say they are. In the half-light . . .

I shrug my shoulders. I order some sake –

'No sake left,' says the master. 'Whisky?'

I shrug my shoulders again. 'Please.'

The master puts the glass of whisky on the counter before me; it is cloudy. I hold it up to the light bulb –

I swirl the mixture around –

'If you don't want to drink it,' says the master. 'Then go.'

I shake my head. I put the glass to my lips. I knock it back –

It burns my throat. I cough. I tell him, 'And another!'

I drain glass after glass as the old men at the counter joke with the master, horrible jokes, terrible jokes, but everyone smiles, everyone laughs. *Ha, ha, ha, ha! He, he, he, he!*

Then one old man begins to sing, softly at first, then louder and louder, over and over –

'Red apple to my lips, blue sky silently watching . . .'

*

In the half-light, my wife sits sewing at the low table, my children asleep under the mosquito net, and suddenly I feel too drunk, too drunk to stand, to stand and face her with tears in my eyes –

The two eggs broken in my pocket –

But she says, 'Welcome home.'

Home to where the mats are rotting. Home to where the doors are in shreds. Home to where the walls are falling in –

Home. Home. Home. Home. Home. Home . . .

I sit down in the *genkan* with my back to her. I struggle with my boots and then ask, 'How are the children?'

'Masaki's eyes are much better.'

'How about Sonoko?'

44

'They are still inflamed and swollen.'

'Haven't you taken her back to the doctor?'

'They washed them out at the school yesterday but the nurse told her to stay at home until they have cleared up. They are worried it will spread to the rest of the class . . .'

Now I turn to face her and ask, 'So what did you do today?'

'We queued at the post office most of the morning . . .'

'And did you get the money? Did they give it to you?'

'They told us to come back tomorrow. So then we went to the park in Inokashira but their eyes hurt and they were hungry and it was so hot that we came back here before lunchtime . . .'

'Have you eaten anything today?'

'Yes.'

'What?'

'Some bean-paste buns.'

'Fresh?'

'Yes.'

'How many?'

'One each.'

'One each for the children and one for you?'

'I wasn't hungry.'

'Liar!' I shout. 'Why do you lie?'

My wife stops darning the children's clothes. She puts away her needle and thread. She closes her sewing box. She bows slightly and says quietly, 'I am very sorry. I will try harder.'

Now I stand up. I walk across the mats –

These rotting mats . . .

'There was a murder today, maybe two murders,' I tell her. 'My room has pulled the case and so you know this means I'll be away for the next twenty days or . . .'

My wife bows again. My wife says, 'I know. I understand.'

I take the three hundred yen from my pocket. I put it on the table and I say, 'Take this.'

My wife bows a third time. My wife says, 'Thank you.'

'It's not much, not with the way prices rise,' I say. 'But if I can get away, I'll try to come back and bring what I can.'

'Please don't think about us,' she says. 'We will be fine. Please just think about solving the case.'

I want to upend the table. I want to tear apart the children's clothes. I want to slap her face. I want to beat her body –

I want to make her really, really hate me –

I want to make her really leave me –

This time. This time. This time . . .

To take the children and go –

'Don't try and make me feel sorry for you,' I tell her and close the doors to the other room. 'Martyrdom is out of fashion!'

*

Behind the shredded doors, I close my eyes but I cannot sleep –

I think about Yuki all the time, all the time . . .

I could never sleep because I thought about her –

Because she haunted me even then . . .

From the day I first met her, even here –

She is lying naked on the futon, her head slightly to the right, her right arm outstretched and her left arm at her side. Her legs are parted, raised and bent at the knee . . .

I get up from the tatami. *She brings her left hand up to her stomach.* I go into the other room. *She dips her fingers in my come.* I search through the kitchen cupboards and drawers. *She puts her fingers to her lips.* Through all the cupboards and the drawers. *She licks my come from her fingers.* But there is no Calmotin and no alcohol to be found, not one pill, not one drop –

She haunted me even here . . .

I gently slide open the doors. I step inside the room in which we sleep. My two children still lain together beneath their net. I lie down beside my wife. Her eyes are closed now. I close mine but I cannot sleep. I cannot sleep. I cannot sleep –

In the half-light, I can't forget . . .

I remember when the bombs began to fall on Mitaka. I remember their evacuation, out to my wife's sister's house in Kōfu. I remember the platform on which we parted. I remember the train on which they left. I remember their tears; that they would live and I would die. Then, when the bombs began to fall on Kōfu, when her own sister called her cursed, I remember their return to Mitaka. I remember the platform and I remember my tears –

That they would die and I would live –

In the half-light, the walls falling in . . .

'But we're already dead,' they'd said. 'We're already dead.'

46

2

August 16, 1946

Tokyo, 89°, fine

I itch from black-headed lice. I scratch. *Gari-gari.* I get up from the low table. I itch. I scratch. *Gari-gari.* I go over to the kitchen sink. I itch. I scratch. *Gari-gari.* I comb my hair. I itch. I scratch. *Gari-gari.* The lice fall out in clumps. I itch. I scratch. *Gari-gari.* I crush them against the sink. I itch. I scratch. *Gari-gari.* The skin lice are harder. I itch. I scratch. *Gari-gari.* They are white and so more difficult to hunt. I itch. I scratch. *Gari-gari.* I turn on the tap. I itch. I scratch. *Gari-gari.* The water starts. The water stops. The water starts again –

I itch. I scratch. *Gari-gari.* I itch. I scratch. *Gari-gari . . .*

Brown and then clear, clear and then brown again –

I rinse my face. I search for soap to shave –

But there is none to find, again –

I rinse out my mouth and spit –

I am one of the survivors . . .

I put on my shirt and my trousers, the same shirt and the same trousers I have worn every day for the last four or five years, the same shirt and the same trousers that my wife has tended and mended, stitched and re-stitched, like the socks and the shoes on my feet, the winter jacket on my back and the summer hat on my head –

I itch. I scratch. *Gari-gari.* I itch and I scratch –

I am one of the lucky ones . . .

There is one small dish of *zōsui* on the low table, a porridge of rice and vegetables. I leave it for my wife and my children –

I take out my watch. *Chiku-taku.* And I wind it up –

It is 4 a.m. My wife and children still asleep –

I still itch and I still scratch. *Gari-gari . . .*

I put on and lace up my old army boots in the *genkan*. I gently open the front door and then close and lock it behind me. I walk down the garden path of our house. I close the gate behind me –

Ton-ton. Ton-ton. Ton-ton. Ton-ton. Ton-ton . . .

I walk away from my house, away from my family –
Ton-ton. Ton-ton. Ton-ton. Ton-ton . . .
I walk down our street towards the station –
Ton-ton. Ton-ton. Ton-ton . . .
Through the sound of the hammers –
Ton-ton. Ton-ton . . .
The dawn of a New Japan –
Ton-ton . . .

The reconstruction work starts early; the surviving buildings being repaired or demolished, new ones built in their place; the roads being cleared of the rubble and ash, the rubble and ash tipped into the canals, the canals filled up and hidden. But the rivers and roads of Tokyo still stink of piss and shit, of cholera and typhus, of disease and death, death and loss –

Ton-ton.

This is the New Japan; Mitaka station swarming with hundreds, thousands of people waiting for trains in both directions; to travel out into the countryside to sell their possessions off cheap to buy food; to travel into Tokyo to sell food to buy other people's possessions cheap: endlessly back and forth, forth and back, endlessly buying and selling, selling and buying; the New Japan –

Every station. Every train. Every station . . .

People in two solid lines along both platforms, swaying as newcomers try to push their way to the front, treading and trampling on the bodies of those who have slept out all night upon the platform, a last huge surge as the first Tokyo-bound train approaches –

Every train. Every station. Every train . . .

Two empty carriages exclusively reserved for the Victors, one second-class hard-seat carriage for the privileged Losers, and a long string of run-down third-class carriages for the rest of us –

The ones who've lost everything . . .

The third-class windows already broken, the carriages filled to the last inch at 5 a.m., the people on the platform pushing more bundles through the windows to take into Tokyo as others silently fight for a foothold on the steps or on the couplings –

Every station. Every train . . .

I take out my notebook –
I itch and I itch . . .
I shout, 'Police!'

I manage to climb on board the train. *I itch but I cannot scratch.* I force my way inside one of the carriages. *I itch but I cannot scratch.* People continue to push from behind me. *I itch but I cannot scratch.* The train begins to move slowly down the track. *I itch but I cannot scratch.* My arms are pinned to my sides in the crush. *I itch but I cannot scratch.* There are people and there is baggage in every possible place. *I itch but I cannot scratch.* They squat on seat backs and they squat in the luggage racks. *I itch but I cannot scratch.* I can only move my eyes. *I itch but I cannot scratch.* The young boy's head in front of me covered in ringworm. *I itch but I cannot scratch.* Lice crawl in and out of the hair of the young woman to my left. *I itch but I cannot scratch.* The scalp of the man to my right smells of sour milk. *I itch but I cannot scratch.* The train lurches over another set of points. *I itch but I cannot scratch.* I close my eyes –

I think about her all the time . . .

It takes over an hour to reach Yūraku-chō station and then it takes a fight to get off the train and onto the platform –

I scratch. *Gari-gari.* I scratch. *Gari-gari . . .*

I walk from Yūraku-chō station down to Police HQ. I itch and now I sweat and it is not yet 6 a.m. and Tokyo stinks of shit; shit and dirt and dust, the shit and the dirt and the dust that coats my clothes and coats my skin, that scars my nostrils and burns my throat with every passing jeep, every passing truck –

I stop. I take out my handkerchief. I take off my hat. I wipe my face. I wipe my neck. I stare up at the bleached-white sky, searching for the invisible sun hiding somewhere up above the clouds of typhus, the clouds of dust, of dirt –

Of shit, of human shit . . .

The side of the road is littered with people on mats, men and women, young and old, soldiers and civilian, their eyes blank or closed, exhausted –

My fists ball, my chest constricts, my lungs scream, *What are you waiting for?*

It has been one year since people knelt upon the ground across the moat and wept. It has been one whole year, but still the people are on their knees, on their knees, on their knees, on their knees –

Get off your knees! Get off your knees!

*

49

Ishida is back. Ishida is cleaning Room #2, wiping down the chairs and the tables, sweeping up the floor and the doorway, straightening the telephones that can't ring and dusting the fans that can't turn –

Ishida is too young for this room, for this work, this place, but his family have connections, connections that have kept him alive and given him this job in this place and he is grateful and eager to prove himself, his face permanently to the floor, his back slightly bent, he is here to clean and make the tea, to make the tea and take our shit –

'This is disgusting! The worst tea I've ever tasted!' Fujita is shouting at Ishida; Fujita spitting his tea across the desk –

Fujita is back too. Fujita always comes back –

Late forties. Passed over and bitter . . .

Detective Fujita knows he should be the head of this room, knows I am too young for this position, for this work, this place. But Detective Fujita knows my family had connections, connections that have kept me alive and given me this job in this place –

In his place. But Detective Fujita knows –

No one is who they say they are . . .

Ishida apologizes. Ishida mops up the tea Fujita has spit out on the desk. Ishida apologizes again –

'Don't apologize like that,' shouts Fujita. 'Your apologies are always insincere. Your apologies make me feel worse than your silence. Apologize sincerely!'

Ishida has his face to the floor, his back bent. Fujita smacks the top of Ishida's head. Fujita pushes him through the door, out of the room into the hallway –

'You stay out there until you learn how to make decent tea!'

Ishida is on his knees in the hallway. Ishida is apologizing –

Fujita turns his back on him. 'And learn how to apologize with some sincerity!'

I follow Fujita back into the room. I say, 'Good morning.'

'Good morning,' he mumbles. 'You got a cigarette?'

I shake my head. I ask him, 'How was yesterday?'

'I hate the countryside,' he says. 'And country people.'

I nod. I ask, 'They fleece you?'

'They tried,' he laughs. 'Until they found out I was a policeman and then I quickly managed to get some bargains.'

I point at the doorway. I ask, 'Did Ishida turn up?'

'Unfortunately,' says Fujita. 'No use, as usual.'

'But you got some rice? Some supplies?'

'Yes,' he says, and then, 'Thank you.'

I shrug. I say, 'For what?'

'For covering for us.'

'It's nothing.'

'No, but I heard about Shiba Park, about your two bodies. That was bad luck. And I heard they were asking where I was.'

I shrug. I say, 'Forget it. You'd do the same for me.'

Fujita bows slightly and says, 'Of course.'

I look at my watch. *Chiku-taku*. I am late, again.

*

I knock on the door to the chief's office. I open it. I apologize. I bow. I take my seat at the table; Chief Kita at the head, Adachi and Kanehara to his right, Kai and I on the left; the same people, the same place, the same time and the same two conversations every day –

The rumours of purges and SCAP's so-called reforms –

In October last year, following the issuance of SCAPIN 93, forty-seven out of fifty-one prefectural police chiefs were purged along with fifty-four superintendents, one hundred and sixty-eight inspectors, one thousand assistant inspectors, one thousand, five hundred and eighty-seven sergeants and two thousand, one hundred and twenty-seven patrolmen, each of these assistant inspectors, sergeants and patrolmen being members of the disbanded Tokkō –

In January this year, following a new Purge Directive known as SCAPIN 550, two further police chiefs lost their jobs along with sixty superintendents and twenty-eight inspectors –

This Purge Directive not only removes men from public office, it also disqualifies them from all other positions –

And the Victors have not finished –

'I was talking with this old friend from Nerima last night,' says Chief Inspector Kanehara. 'And he was telling me that SCAP sent the Public Safety Division into the Nerima police station to check the career histories of every single police officer in the building, the dates of all their transfers and appointments . . .'

'Why Nerima?' asks Adachi –

Or Anjo or Ando or . . .

'Because some uniformed patrolman complained directly to

SCAP that last August, just after the surrender, some former high-ranking Tokkō and Kempei officers at Nerima had changed their names to those of dead or retired men and then transferred to other, better positions and ranks under their adopted new names . . .'

No one is who they say they are . . .

'While men who had served in the Tokkō and Kempei sections for only a few months were now being purged . . .'

No one who they seem to be . . .

'Snitch!' spits Adachi –

And everybody nods –

Except me . . .

Now the talk around the table turns to an overnight spate of muggings in the Setagaya area, of a three-man gang with handguns, of possible connections to last month's armed burglaries in the same area of Tokyo, of the continuing rise in violent crime, the use of guns when we have none and back then to SCAP's so-called reforms –

'We've asked them for guns,' says Kanehara. 'More guns. Better guns. Guns that work. Guns with ammunition to match . . .'

'And they've promised us guns,' says Adachi –

'But that's all they've done,' says Kanehara –

The same people, the same place, the same time and the same two conversations every day, meeting after meeting, until there is a knock on the door, until there is an interruption –

'Excuse me,' mumbles the uniform –

'What is it ?' barks Chief Kita –

'The mothers are here, sir.'

*

It is 8:30 a.m. on the day after the bodies were discovered and there are already twenty mothers here. Twenty mothers who have read the morning paper or heard the news from neighbours. Twenty mothers who have taken out their last good kimonos. Twenty mothers who have called upon their other daughters or their sisters. Twenty mothers who begged the streetcar or train fare to Sakuradamon –

Twenty mothers looking for their lost daughters –

'They're quick enough to read the papers,' Kai is telling me. 'Quick enough to come down here, but where were they when their daughters went missing? They're too late now . . .'

Inspector Kai and I are walking down the stairs of Metropolitan Police Headquarters to one of the reception rooms –

'There used to be just twenty missing persons a month, before the war. Now we've got between two and three hundred . . .'

To the reception rooms to face the twenty mothers –

'And forty per cent of them are young women aged fifteen to twenty-five, and they're just the ones who get reported . . .'

The twenty mothers looking for their daughters –

'You watch,' says Kai. 'Not one of these mothers will have reported their daughters missing before today.'

A uniformed officer opens the door to the reception room for Inspector Kai and me. Kai and I enter the room. Kai and I introduce ourselves to these twenty mothers before us, these twenty mothers in their last good kimonos with their other daughters or their sisters –

These twenty mothers looking for their lost daughters –

Praying they do not find them here, in this place.

But because the bodies are at Keiō, because the autopsies have yet to be performed, because the search of the area has yet to be completed, because we have yet to formally open the investigation, Inspector Kai and I have nothing to show these twenty mothers, nothing to tell them, so Inspector Kai and I will ask our men to interview these twenty mothers, to take down the descriptions of their daughters, their heights, their weights and their ages, the places they were going, the people they were meeting, the clothes they were wearing, the bags and belongings they were carrying –

On the days they were last seen . . .

The meals they had eaten –

'But why?' they'll ask –

The scars they carry or the teeth they have lost or any other unique features that might help to eliminate or identify their daughters from among the rotting flesh and bleached bones we found in Shiba Park, but not today –

'But if not today?' these mothers ask. 'Then when?'

Today there is no consolation for these mothers –

'When?' they ask, again and again . . .

The day after the autopsies these twenty mothers must return, these twenty mothers and the one father –

The one father in his last good suit with his hat in his hand who steps from the mothers to ask – 'May I speak with you?'

'My name is Nakamura Yoshizo and I am a grocer in Kamata. My daughter's name is Nakamura Mitsuko. She is my only daughter. She graduated from the Aoyama Domestic Science College and she had a number of wartime jobs with the Yasuda and Taito Yokosan companies as well as some volunteer work. But she is my only daughter and so, as the situation worsened in Tokyo last year, my wife and I decided to send Mitsuko to live with her elder brother and his wife in Ibaraki Prefecture. And so, on the twelfth of July last year, she left our home in Kamata to travel to Ibaraki. Mitsuko never arrived at her brother's house. She was twenty-two years old, but she will be twenty-three now. She is my only daughter, detective.'

'Did you report Mitsuko missing?' I ask him –

The father nods. The father says, 'Of course.'

'And what did the local police tell you?'

'That they could find no clue . . .'

I open my notebook. I lick the tip of my pencil and I ask him, 'Can you remember what clothes your daughter was wearing on the day she went missing last year?'

'A pair of brown *monpe* trousers and a pale yellow blouse.'

'Can you remember her footwear that day?' I ask him.

'A pair of traditional wooden *geta* sandals . . .'

'And can you describe Mitsuko for me?'

Mitsuko's father takes a deep breath and says, 'She is one hundred and fifty-five centimetres tall and she weighs about fifty kilograms. She has long hair which she usually wears in two plaits. Mitsuko also wears round silver spectacles.'

In the half-light, no one forgets . . .

'Anything else?' I ask him.

'On the day she went missing,' he nods. 'She was carrying a beige-coloured cotton rucksack . . .'

'And what was inside?'

'A *bentō* lunch box.'

'Anything else?'

Nakamura Mitsuko's father nods again, wipes the sweat from his face and says, 'For her twentieth birthday, I gave her an elliptical-shaped ammonite brooch . . .'

No one forgets . . .

I stop writing now. I close my notebook. I put away my pencil. I tell him, 'As you know, the autopsies on the two bodies have yet to be performed. However, one of the victims died very recently and the clothing found on the other does not match that of your daughter, at least on the day she went missing. So it's doubtful your daughter is one of these bodies . . .'

The father holds a handkerchief to his face. His shoulders begin to tremble –

'It was in the newspaper,' he whispers. 'About the two unidentified bodies in Shiba Park and so my wife and I thought that we should . . .'

'I understand,' I tell him. 'And I will contact you if I do find anything . . .'

He bows his head –

'Thank you.'

*

The first trunk is packed and ready. Nishi and Shimoda will each take a handle. The second trunk is packed and ready. Kimura and Ishida will each take a handle. The others have got their things together. They have tidied up their loose ends. They have cleared their desks. They are ready to go to Atago. They know there will be no days off now. They know there will be no rest now. They are waiting to go, passing round the newspaper, talking of the latest suicide –

A Rear Admiral Satō Shiro, a fifty-four-year-old former commander of the Japanese Naval Forces in the New Guinea area, committed suicide at his home in Yokosuka at about 5 a.m. yesterday morning after having first murdered his forty-two-year-old wife, his eleven-year-old son and nine-year-old daughter as they were sleeping. The former officer who returned home from New Guinea in January this year had been suffering from a nervous condition and is believed to have been contemplating killing himself and his entire family since the latter part of July . . .

'Too many good men,' say my own men. 'How many more good men are needlessly going to give their lives in apology . . .?'

'While bad men are still lining their pockets . . .'

'Too many ceremonies for the dead . . .'

Turning the page of the paper, talking of the latest fugitive –

Yet another Kempei man on the run –

'They'll catch him, you see . . .'

'You can't run forever . . .'

'Too many snitches . . .'

The next two pages of the newspaper, talking of the latest convictions and sentences –

Five men found guilty of mistreating Allied prisoners of war. Evidence showed that as guards at Hakodate Prisoner of War Camp Number One, they had mistreated prisoners and stolen food and clothing from them. The Commission found all five men guilty of crimes against war prisoners and meted out prison sentences ranging from thirty to five years. In the closing hours of the trial, one of the accused, Takeshita Toshio, told the court that former Prime Minister Tōjō was responsible for everything and that he and his co-accused were merely conscripted soldiers given orders that they had to obey on pain of death . . .

'It's never-ending; it just goes on and on and on . . .'

'They're not criminals, just soldiers . . .'

'Too many trials . . .'

The bottom corner of the last page of the last newspaper and there is our story; *the bodies of two women found in Shiba . . .*

I look at my watch again. *Chiku-taku . . .*

I stand up now. They all stand up –

I bow. They all bow –

I say, 'Let's go.'

*

Through the doors of Atago police station, Nishi and Shimoda carry the first trunk, Kimura and Ishida carry the second trunk; up the stairs of Atago Police Station, Nishi and Shimoda carry the first trunk, Kimura and Ishida carry the second trunk; Sanada, Hattori, Takeda, Fujita and I marching behind, through the doors and up the stairs –

Nishi and Shimoda put the first trunk down. Kimura and Ishida put the second trunk down in a corner, to stay locked until tonight. Now Nishi and Shimoda open the first trunk. Nishi and Shimoda take out the white banner and the bamboo poles. Nishi and Shimoda raise the banner on the poles beside the door –

Two metres tall and fifty centimetres wide –

In beautiful, bold, bright-red stitching:

Special Investigation Headquarters.

The men of the Second Team assemble before the banner. The men stand to attention as I tell them –

'This banner remains here until this case is closed with honour or until we are forced to retreat back to HQ in disgrace –

'Which is it to be, honour or disgrace?'

'Honour!' they shout. 'Honour!'

'Then every single one of us must give his very utmost, must give his very best,' I tell them. 'Only then can this case be solved and our team return with honour to HQ –

'So give your utmost!'

'We will give our very utmost,' they reply. 'Our very best!'

Across the hallway, Inspector Kai and his First Team have already raised their banner, already made their pledges and their exhortations; now they are waiting for us –

'Meeting time!'

The First Team, the Second Team and all the uniforms from the Atago, Meguro and Mita police stations are gathered in the hot, dark second-floor room which the First Team is using at Atago –

I stand up at the front of the room beside Chief Inspectors Adachi and Kanehara and Inspector Kai, the four of us facing the First Team, the Second Team and the uniformed men –

'Attention!' shouts one of the uniformed sergeants and everyone in the room jumps to attention –

'Bow!' shouts the sergeant –

Everyone bows –

'At ease!'

Everyone stands at ease now or sits back down except Chief Inspector Adachi; Adachi has a piece of paper in his hand; Adachi reads out lists of names and lists of teams; Adachi assigns names to teams and teams to leaders; Adachi points to a map on the board behind him; Adachi reads out lists of grid coordinates; Adachi assigns coordinates to teams, teams to search and teams to find –

Finally Adachi exhorts every one of us to do our best –

And every one of us promises we will do our best –

'Attention!' shouts the uniformed sergeant again and every one of us stands back to attention –

'Bow!' he shouts –

And we bow –
'Dismissed!'

*

There are journalists waiting for us downstairs again. There are always journalists waiting for us these days. There are hundreds of new newspapers and magazines now, thousands of new journalists –

Freedom of Press. Freedom of Press. Freedom of Press –

Things are better since the defeat of the *Yomiuri* strike last month, but there are still far too many newspapers and magazines, still far too many journalists, too many press freedoms –

Too many questions. Too many questions . . .

Far too many press scumbags –

Scumbags like Hayashi Jo –

My personal scumbag . . .

Hayashi writes for *Minpo* under one name and *Minshū Shimbun* under another. Hayashi would write anything for anyone as long as they paid him and they usually do so he usually does –

Hayashi is waiting for me downstairs –

I take his arm. I take him outside –

Out of sight and out of earshot, across the road and among the trees, a crippled soldier burning weeds in an old black metal drum –

Fire upon fire, heat upon heat, a furnace within a furnace . . .

Hayashi inhales and says, 'I hate the smell of burning . . .'

I tell him, 'You better have something this time.'

'It's not that it reminds me of the air raids . . .'

'Have you got something? Something new?'

'That smelt more like pork fat,' he says. 'This smoke reminds me of the day of the surrender . . .'

'Quickly,' I tell him. 'What have you got?'

'They turned the sky black with the papers they burnt . . .'

'Enough memories!' I shout now. 'Talk or walk.'

'Up in smoke,' he says. 'All the evidence . . .'

I curse him. I curse him . . .

'And all the names . . .'

'That's it,' I tell him and I turn to go –

He grabs my arm. He holds out a piece of folded paper. He says, 'Read this before it goes up in smoke.'

I take it. I open it. I read it –

'Fujita Tsuneo,' he says like I cannot read the characters of the name. 'He was seen drinking with Nodera Tomiji at the New Oasis in Ginza on the night of the Matsuda Giichi hit . . .'

'The Detective Fujita of my room?'

Hayashi nods. 'The very same.'

I curse and I curse . . .

I shake my head. I tell him, 'It's a mistake.'

Hayashi shakes his head. 'No mistake.'

I ask him, 'Who told you? Who?'

Hayashi shakes his head again.

'Who else knows about this, then?' I ask him. 'Your snitch knows, you know, and so how many others know?'

'No one else,' says Hayashi. 'No one still breathing.'

'Except for you,' I tell him –

'And now you,' he smiles.

I stare into Hayashi's eyes. I say, 'Who says you're not lying? Who says you haven't just made this up . . .?'

'Bastard,' snaps Hayashi now. 'It was you who came to me. You who wanted to know who ordered the hit on Matsuda. You who wanted to know who paid Nodera. And then who killed Nodera . . .'

I turn to go, to walk away –

Out of the shadows . . .

He grabs my arm a second time. He says, 'So what now?'

I pull my arm free of him. I say, 'Nothing.'

'What do you mean, *nothing*?' he asks. 'I did what you asked me to do. I got you your information. Now I want my money!'

'But I can't use this information,' I tell him.

'That's not my problem,' he laughs.

'But I can't pay you.'

Hayashi has stopped laughing. Now Hayashi says, 'Well then, I'll just have to take it to someone who can pay me.'

'Like who?' I ask him.

'Like Boss Senju.'

Now I laugh. 'Boss Senju?'

'He'll pay me,'

I step towards him. I lean into him. I say, 'You think Boss Senju will pay you? A lowlife scumbag journalist who couldn't tell someone the right time if they asked him because he wouldn't know what that right time was because he lies and he lies and he lies? You think Senju will pay a lowlife scumbag piece of shit like you just because he says he heard that one of my detectives was seen in a Ginza bar with the very lowlife scumbag who later that same night shot his boss, his mentor, his surrogate father ... is that the information you think Boss Senju is going to pay you for? Is it? Is it really? Because the first thing Senju will do before killing Fujita and then killing me is to torture you to find out how you came upon this piece of information, when you came upon it, and why you never said anything to anyone about it before and believe me, Hayashi, whatever you tell Senju will be the wrong answer and it will also be your final answer before he then kills you! So if I was you, I would forget you ever heard Fujita's name in connection to Matsuda Giichi.'

Hayashi shrugs. Hayashi says, 'You're no better than me, inspector. You think you are, but you're not ...'

I smile. I turn. I leave. I walk away –

Fire upon fire, heat upon heat, a furnace within a furnace ...

'I know you,' he shouts after me. 'I know your secrets ...'

I turn back. I say, 'We lost a war. We've all got secrets.'

Hayashi smiles. Hayashi shakes his head –

'Not like yours, inspector.'

*

There are thirty men on the slopes of Shiba Park. Thirty men with their towels and their sticks. *To search in the long grass.* Thirty men in three teams of ten. Three teams of ten sweating in their plainclothes and sweating in their uniforms, swatting at mosquitoes and swatting at flies. *For the secrets of the dead.* They stare up at the sun. They look back down at the ground. *In the long grass.* They take out their handkerchiefs. They take off their hats. *Their skulls to the sun.* They wipe their heads. They wipe their necks. *In the long grass.* They put their hats back on. Their handkerchiefs away. *That strangles and binds.* They reach for their sticks. They start to search. *In the long grass.* To search again. To try to find. *The long grass ...*

Chiku-taku. Chiku-taku. Chiku-taku. Chiku-taku ...

From eleven in the morning till six in the evening –

But there are no clocks in the land of the dead ...

In these forgotten graves. By these fallen trees –

Just the sound of the crows, the many crows . . .
There is only resignation, no enthusiasm –
In this place of assignation . . .
I am searching too –
For Fujita . . .
'Looking for someone?' asks Chief Inspector Adachi –
'Aren't we all?' I say and I turn away, again.

*

I find Ishida alone in our borrowed upstairs room at Atago. Ishida is smeared in the dirt and the sweat from the search. He is wiping down the chairs and the tables, sweeping up the floor and the doorway, straightening our banner. Ishida senses my shadow. He looks up –

Ishida stands to attention. He bows. He apologizes –

I smile at him and I tell him, 'Stand at ease.'

Ishida bows again. He apologizes again –

'Your apologies are always insincere.'

'You've worked hard today,' I tell him. 'Thank you.'

Again, he bows. Again, he apologizes –

'How was yesterday?' I ask him. 'With Detective Fujita?'

Ishida turns his face to the floor now, his back slightly bent. He is unwilling to look up, to look me in the eye –

'Yesterday?' I ask him again. 'Were you and Detective Fujita able to get some rice and some supplies?'

Ishida turns his head slightly to his left, his back still bent –

'You went out into the country, didn't you?' I ask him –

Ishida nods his head once, back still bent –

'And so where did you go?'

Ishida turns his head again and now he says, 'I went with Detective Fujita at his request, sir.'

'I know that,' I tell him. 'Now I am asking you where it was you went with Detective Fujita.'

Ishida sucks the air in between his teeth but does not answer –

I smack the top of his head. I shout, 'Answer me!'

Ishida starts to bow again, to apologize again –

I smack him again. I shout again, 'Quickly! Answer me!'

But Ishida does not answer, he only apologizes –

'Your apologies are always insincere.'

61

'Idiot!' I shout and I turn to leave –

Nishi and Kimura stood there –

'Chief Kita is here, sir,' says Nishi. 'In the reception room with Chief Inspector Adachi.'

*

The head of the entire First Investigative Division has come to Atago police station. Chief Kita is here for the results of the initial search. I stand outside the reception room. I wait until Chief Kita and Adachi have finished their meeting, until Adachi comes out of the room and walks past me without a word, without even a glance in my direction, and then I knock on the door of the reception room and enter –

I bow to Chief Kita. I apologize to Chief Kita. I take the seat the chief offers me. I tell him what we have done today, what we have found and what we will do next, tomorrow –

Chief Kita listens and then Chief Kita says, 'But I hear you want to leave Room #2. To transfer . . .?'

I have told no one this. But I ask nothing and I say nothing. I bow deeply to the chief. I apologize for asking for a transfer –

'It's interesting you don't deny it,' smiles Chief Kita. 'And apparently it's a transfer to Room #6 you want?'

I ask nothing and I say nothing . . .

I bow. I apologize again.

The chief asks, 'Why?'

'I have been in Room #2 for almost a year now,' I tell him. 'Maybe they need a new leader.'

'But why do you want Room #6?' the chief asks me again. 'It's the gangs and the markets. You'd know nothing . . .'

'I knew nothing when you put me in Room #2.'

Chief Kita smiles and asks, 'And now?'

'One can never know enough . . .'

Chief Kita inhales deeply, closes his eyes and then he says, 'You identify that girl's body. You find out how she died. If she was murdered, you find out who killed her and why –

'Then you can have your transfer.'

I bow. I apologize. I repeat –

'Thank you. Thank you.'

Up the stairs again, back to the same hot, dark second-floor room and the last meeting of the first full day of the two investigations –

'Attention!' shouts the same uniformed sergeant –

'Bow!' shouts the sergeant –

'At ease!' he shouts.

Chief Inspector Adachi and I stay standing at the front of the room, in front of the table on which are lain out the things that have been found today on the slopes of Shiba Park, the many things –

The wicker basket containing a set of carpenter's tools, found fifteen metres from the first body; the child's undershirt and material found near the basket; the soiled women's underwear; the soldier's shoulder bag in the bushes on the Northern Path; the long Chinese-style pipe and the empty lunchbox; the *Asahi Shimbun* from the eleventh of August this year; the old man's glasses, broken in two; the rusted Western-style razor and the red *haramaki* with five darned holes found on the Eastern Path, five darned holes for identification –

'It would seem that the material from the *haramaki*,' reports Adachi, 'matches the material found around the neck of the first body. However, we will have to wait until the results of the autopsy tomorrow before we can be certain. Inspector Minami . . .'

'The military shoulder bag,' I continue, 'was found to contain a statement of employment for a Takahashi of Zōshigaya, Toshima Ward. Detectives have already left for the Toshima ward office to follow up on this information . . .'

'Scientific tests will also be conducted', states Adachi, 'on the various items of clothing found during the search. The underwear may aid in identification.'

Chief Inspector Adachi and I sit down. Chief Inspector Kanehara stands up now –

'Tomorrow morning', he says, 'we resume the search.'

*

The chief has reserved a room in a recently reopened restaurant near Daimon, near one of the kitchens of the Victors. The chief is treating the whole of the First Investigative Division to a meal. The whole of the First Investigative Division sitting sleeve against sleeve, knee against knee on new tatami mats. There is no menu. No choice. But there is beer and there is food; we are eating leftovers, *zanpan*, from the Victors' dustbins, just grateful not to have to eat *zōsui* again –

Dogs starved at their masters' feet, beneath their tables . . .

Everyone still talking about this former naval commander who murdered his wife, his eleven-year-old son, his nine-year-old daughter and who then shot himself and the message he left:

'Dispose of our bodies as you would a dog's . . .'

Everyone talking now about the one million unclaimed ashes of the war dead, the four million repatriated soldiers and civilians, many bearing the bones and ashes of their comrades and kin in small white boxes around their necks, the million more yet to come –

'To live lives as broken jewels, not common clay . . .'

Everyone talking then about the piss and the shit in the rivers, the cholera and the typhus, the train disasters and the union demonstrations, the strike slogans on the sides of the trains –

'I don't feel free. I don't feel I have rights . . .'

Talking about the GI who raped and sodomized a thirteen-year-old girl, the two other Victors who kidnapped and raped a girl on her way home from a flower-arranging class, talking about the Japanese man who attacked and beat up two GIs in Kamata –

'There was spirit in the war, stimulation . . .'

Everyone talking about the minutes that feel like hours. The hours that feel like days. The days that feel like weeks. The weeks that feel like months. The months that feel like years –

This year that has felt like a decade –

'For now there is only monotony . . .'

Talking about purges. Talking about trials. Talking about all our trials; to work, to eat. Talking about food. Talking about food. Talking about food, food, food, food, food, food, food, food –

In whispers. In screams. In whispers. In screams –

If you've never been defeated, never lost –

If you've never been beaten before –

Then you don't know the pain –

The pain of surrender –

Of occupation . . .

In whispers, in screams, this is how the Losers talk –

Their chests constricted and their fists balled –

Their knees bleeding and backs broken –

By the fall . . .

This is how the Losers talk –
To whisper, to scream –
'*We are the survivors. We are the lucky ones.*'

*

Back at Atago on the second floor, the second trunk has been opened, the blankets distributed, but this borrowed room is an oven, another furnace, and the stench of sweat and the whine of mosquitoes is unbearable. From across the hallway, from the other room, drift the low voices of the First Team singing their drunken lullabies –

'*Red apple to my lips, blue sky silently watching . . .*'

But they are soon asleep in here, in their chairs or under their desks, snoring and farting, all except Detective Fujita –

The one empty chair. The empty desk . . .

I get up from my own chair and tiptoe as quietly as I can over the bodies. I open the door. I go down the corridor. Down the back stairs. Out of the back door –

She haunts me . . .

I start to run, to run through the night, the black and starless night, the hot and humid, damp and dark cloth hanging down –

Down to Yuki.

*

In the half-light of her dim lamps, in the three glass panels of her vanity mirror, she puts her hand to her hair and says, 'You had just bought a packet of cigarettes at the corner shop when a man ran past shouting, *It's going to rain! It's going to rain!* Old women in their aprons and young children with their toys scurried indoors as a gust of wind blew a reed blind to the ground and newspapers skated like ghosts down the street. Then came the flash of lightning. The clap of thunder. The great drops of rain. But you did not run. You finished your cigarette and you opened your umbrella. And that was when I first saw you, standing beneath your umbrella, when I first called out to you, as I was leaving the hairdresser's shop, do you remember?'

I don't want to remember. I don't want to remember . . .

'May I walk with you?' she'd said. 'Just over there?'

Her white neck beneath my dark umbrella, her high chignon

just freshly dressed, tied up in long silver threads, I remember –

Shipped home from China, discharged from hospital . . .

'Don't worry about me,' I said. 'Take the umbrella. . .'

'You don't mind?' she smiled. 'Just over to there . . .'

My umbrella in her right hand, she hitches up the skirt of her kimono with her left and then turns back to ask –

'Does this umbrella become me?'

In the half-light, I can't forget . . .

I itch and I scratch. *Gari-gari . . .*

In the half-light. Thinking about my wife. In the half-light –

I am sorry. I am sorry. I am sorry. I am sorry. I am sorry . . .

Thinking of my children. In the half-light. Her back to me –

I am sorry. I am sorry. I am sorry. I am sorry . . .

In the half-light. Her face to the wall. In the half-light –

I am sorry. I am sorry. I am sorry . . .

To the paper. In the half-light. To the stains –

I am sorry. I am sorry . . .

In the half-light, the half-things –

I am sorry . . .

Half-lives, all gone.

3

August 17, 1946

Tokyo, 90°, fine

I itch and I scratch. *Gari-gari*. I have not slept again. I have not closed my eyes. My eyes tired and sore. The early morning sun coming through the window now, illuminating the dust and the stains of her room, the sound of the hammering trailing in with the light –

Ton-ton. Ton-ton. Ton-ton. Ton-ton. Ton-ton . . .

I sit up on the futon. I look at my watch –

Chiku-taku. Chiku-taku. I am late –

Idiot! Idiot! Idiot! Idiot! Idiot!

I get up from the futon. I itch and I scratch. *Gari-gari*. I put on my shirt and my trousers. *Gari-gari*. I go over to the *genkan*. *Gari-gari*. I lace up my boots. *Gari-gari . . .*

I curse. I curse. I curse . . .

I turn to say goodbye –

But she does not move, her back to the door, her face to the wall, to the paper, the stains –

I curse myself . . .

I close her door and I run down the corridor. Down the stairs and out the building. Out of the shadows, into the light. The light so bright this morning, the shadows so dark, bleaching and staining the city in whites and blacks. The white concrete hulks, the black empty windows. The white sidewalks and roads, the black telegraph poles and trees. The white sheets of metal, the black mountains of rubble. The white leaves, the black weeds. The white eyes and the black skin of the Losers, the white stars and the black uniforms of the Victors –

Ton-ton. Ton-ton. Ton-ton. Ton-ton. Ton-ton . . .

No colours today. No colours on this moon.

*

Detective Fujita is at his borrowed desk in our borrowed room. *Fujita does not look up*. Ishida is pouring the tea. *Fujita is going through his jacket pockets*. Nishi and Kimura are repairing their notebooks, rolling up thin pieces of waste paper into tight threads to bind together the coarse rough paper on which they take their notes. *Fujita takes an envelope out of his inside jacket pocket*. The others waking up, yawning and stretching, coughing and scratching. *Fujita has not slept*. The windows are open but the room is still hot and stinks of stale breath and sweat. *Fujita glances at his watch*. They drink their tea and start to grumble. *Fujita writes a name on the front of the envelope*. They want cigarettes but the next ration is not until Monday and today is Saturday. *Fujita puts the envelope back in his inside jacket pocket*. They want breakfast but the next meal will be cold *zōsui* again. *Now he looks up*. Detective Fujita looks up at me –

I wait for him to speak but he says nothing. Now I stand up at my desk. I bow to everyone and I say, 'Good morning, Room #2.'

They all stand. They bow. They say, 'Good morning.'

I tell them, 'This morning I will accompany Inspector Kai of Room #1 to the Keiō University Hospital for the autopsies. In my absence, Detective Fujita will be in charge of the continuing search of the crime scene. The identification of the second body will not be easy and so the smallest scrap of evidence may prove crucial, so I would ask you all to be as diligent as possible in your search.'

'We will be as diligent as possible,' they reply.

I bow to them again. They bow to me –

Everyone but Detective Fujita.

*

Back out into the light, back out to the shadows. Into the white and into the black. Into the dirt and into the dust. The hot walk up to Tokyo Metropolitan Police Headquarters. The morning meeting –

I knock on the door to the chief's office. I open it. I apologize. I bow. I take my seat at the table; Chief Kita at the head; Adachi and Kanehara to his right; Kai and me on the left; the same people, the same place, the same time and the same two conversations –

Purges and reforms. Reforms and purges . . .

Last year seven thousand, eight hundred and ninety-one policemen voluntarily gave up their jobs, three thousand, seven hundred and sixty-nine left due to illness or injury, one thousand, six hundred and forty-nine died and two thousand, eight hundred and fifty-six police officers were purged and fired –

'Now they want to issue a further Purge Directive,' Kanehara is saying. 'We have few enough men as it is and, if they carry out this purge, there'll be no one left at all . . .'

'That's why they are promising better working conditions,' says Adachi. 'To recruit new men . . .'

Reforms and purges. Purges and reforms . . .

From this coming Monday new regulations are to be put into practice; uniforms are presently working an average of thirteen hours a day over three shifts. The Victors have decreed they will now work an average of eight hours a day over three shifts; on the first shift they will work from 8 a.m. to 6 p.m., on the second shift from 5 p.m. to 9 a.m., then the third shift on the third day will be a day off –

'But there aren't the numbers for these shifts,' says Kanehara. 'There aren't the men yet to cover these kinds of hours . . .'

'And we all know their answer to that,' says Adachi. 'Transfer seven hundred of our Metropolitan Police Board officers back onto local patrol duties to cover the shortfall . . .'

'It's our own fault,' says Kanehara. 'We asked them for better conditions; better hours, better holidays, better benefits, better pensions and better salaries. We asked them so we could recruit better men and keep the good men we had. We asked them and this is their answer, this is what they do . . .'

'They just keep purging the leadership,' says Adachi. 'And transferring the men we have . . .'

'We ask and we ask,' says Kanehara. 'And they promise us this and they promise us that . . .'

'That's all they do . . .'

The same people, the same place, the same time and the same two conversations every day, meeting after meeting until there is a knock on the door, until there is an interruption –

'Excuse me,' mumbles the uniform –

'What is it?' barks Chief Kita –

'Keiō Hospital are ready, sir.'

*

There has been another accident on one of the streetcars, a mother

69

and her child killed. The system is suspended and so Inspector Kai and I get off our bus and walk the rest of the way. The route takes us through the old parks and the gardens of Moto-Akasaka –

The sound of crows, the sound of crows . . .

Here too the light is so bright that the green leaves shine white against the black trunks of the trees, though much of this area was untouched by the bombs, just like the Imperial Palace and its grounds, and now these grand houses and former palaces of Moto-Akasaka are homes and offices to the Victors and their families –

'They still hunt round here,' Kai tells me.

'Hunt?' I ask. 'Who still hunts here?'

'The nobility and the Americans.'

'They go hunting together?'

'Yes,' says Kai. 'I heard that members of our nobility entertain the American top brass with falcons. Even MacArthur . . .'

'The Americans don't trust the nobility with guns, then?'

'They take the Americans cormorant fishing too.'

'I'd like to eat *ayu* now,' I tell him. 'Even *ayu* caught by Americans. I can taste it now, washed down with sake.'

Kai laughs. 'I'd even eat the cormorant.'

Two hills to the north of us stand the former War Ministry buildings at Ichigaya, the large three-storey pillbox that was once the headquarters of the Imperial Army but which since May has been the site of the International Military Tribunal for the Far East –

A different kind of hunt. A different kind of sport.

*

The Keiō University Hospital is at Shinanomachi, in the Yotsuya district of Tokyo. The main building is scarred but standing, the approaches and grounds scorched or overgrown. The sick or lost wander in and out, back and forth. There are queues out of the gates. Policemen on the doors. Inside the plaster is peeling from the walls and the linoleum torn from the floorboards. The corridors are crowded with the dying and the dead, the waiting and the grieving –

I don't want to remember. I don't want to remember . . .

I step over or around them and try not to breathe in –

I hate hospitals. I hate hospitals. I hate hospitals . . .

The air thick with screams and sobs, death and disease, DDT

and disinfectant. The only drugs are aspirin and Mercurochrome, the only bandages grey and bloody. The gurneys lined up against the walls, limbs fallen loose from their sides. Remains of meals and scraps of food standing, stinking in cardboard boxes and battered tins under beds of coarse blankets and soiled sheets –

But in the half-light I can't forget . . .

I try not to stare, to just walk on –

I have spent too long here . . .

Through the waiting rooms and down the long corridors, past the consulting rooms and the operating theatres, the surgeries and the wards, to the Chief Medical Officer –

The Chief Medical Officer is either eighty or ninety years old, his face grey and sunken, his eyes black and empty. He is wearing an unpressed morning coat and a pair of striped trousers, both two sizes too big for him, smelling of mothballs –

'You're late,' he says.

Inspector Kai and I bow deeply to him. Inspector Kai and I apologize repeatedly to him –

The Chief Medical Officer shakes his head and says, 'I have to make an important report to the Public Health and Welfare Section. I don't want to be late . . .'

'We are really very sorry,' I tell him again. 'But there was an accident on one of the streetcars . . .'

'More work,' he groans –

'They're dead,' I say –

'Who are dead?'

'The mother and her child,' I tell him. 'The mother and her child who fell from the running board of the streetcar . . .'

He hands us two files from the pile on his desk. He says, 'You know the way.'

Each with our file, reading as we walk down another long corridor towards the elevator. There are the mothers sat here. Five of the mothers here, looking for their missing daughters –

Five mothers whose descriptions of their missing daughters most closely resemble the two bodies found in Shiba Park. Five mothers praying they do not find them here . . .

'What do they want now?' spits Kai. 'We told them to wait until tomorrow. They shouldn't be here . . .'

I have skimmed the evidence and statements in the files. I

have seen the hopes and fears in their eyes. I say, 'Let them look.'

'They can wait,' says Kai. 'Until after the autopsies . . .'

'Why not just let these five look? It might help us . . .'

'Why?' he says. 'They'll either be lucky or late.'

'Let them look before the autopsy,' I say again.

'No.'

'What if it was your daughter that was missing?' I ask him. 'Would you want to see her after an autopsy?'

Inspector Kai stops in the corridor now. Inspector Kai says, 'My daughter is dead. My daughter burned to death in an air-raid shelter. My daughter had no autopsy . . .'

Now I shut up. Now I remember. Now it's too late. Now I say, 'I am sorry. I'm really sorry . . .'

But Kai is away from me now and away from the five mothers, already half-way down the corridor. Down the narrow corridor to the service elevator. To push the elevator button. To wait. To watch the elevator doors open. To step inside. For me to follow him. To push another button. To watch the elevator doors close –

There are no electric light bulbs in here, for the sake of economy one of the orderlies tells us, and so we ride down in an elevator so dark that I cannot see my hand before my face –

I think about her all the time . . .

I cannot see the body on the gurney beside me. The body on the gurney parked up against my leg. The body that smells –

That smells of fruit, that smells of rotten apricots . . .

The elevator stops. The elevator doors open –

The light returns. *The half-light.* The basement not much brighter than the elevator. *Half-things move in the half-light.* People and insects drawn like magnets towards the few naked bulbs there are. *Half-things.* The people working in their shirtsleeves or their undershirts; the insects feasting on their sweat and their skin, their flesh and their bone. *In the half-light.* This labyrinth of corridors and rooms. *Here where the dead come.* The tiled walls of sinks, of drains. *Where the dead live.* The written warnings of cuts, of punctures. *Here in the half-light.* The orderlies washing and rinsing their hands and their forearms, again and again. *Here. Down here . . .*

The autopsy room is along the corridor to the right, beyond the mortuary. There are slippers waiting for our feet, the room itself back beyond a set of glass doors, bomb tape still upon the glass –

She is coming now. She is coming . . .

Dr. Nakadate is waiting for us outside the autopsy room, before the glass doors, before the tape. Nakadate is finishing his cigarette, smoking it right down to the stub –

A familiar face, a familiar place . . .

Dr. Nakadate glances up at us. He greets us with a smile. 'Good morning, detectives.'

'Good morning,' we reply. 'We are very sorry we are late.'

'There are no clocks down here,' says Dr. Nakadate –

He puts out his cigarette and opens the glass doors to the autopsy room where five junior medical examiners in grubby grey laboratory coats are already gathered round the three autopsy tables and two smaller dissecting tables; the three autopsy tables which stand on the concrete floor in the centre of the room, three elongated octagonal tables made of white marble and of German design, slanted for drainage with raised edges to prevent leakage –

I itch and I scratch. *Gari-gari . . .*

She is coming . . .

The glass doors open again. The first body is brought in from the mortuary under a grey sheet on old wheels. The grey sheet is removed. The body lifted from the gurney –

In the half-light, she is here . . .

The naked body of the first woman lain out on the table –

Here where half-things move in the half-light . . .

Her body seems longer, paler. Eyes open, mouth ajar –

'And I am here because of you,' she says . . .

Her sex is noted. Her age estimated at eighteen –

'Here where there is pain . . .'

Her weight is taken. Her height measured –

Here in the half-light . . .

Dr. Nakadate puts on a stained surgical gown and a pair of rubber gloves. The orderlies raise the body. The orderlies place a rubber body block beneath it. Her breasts and chest rise upwards, her arms and neck fall backwards –

I turn away now.

'There is still no name?' asks the doctor. 'No identification?'

I glance over at Inspector Kai and I say, 'No names yet.'

'Then this is Number One. The next is Number Two.'

I nod. I take out my pencil. I lick its tip.

Nakadate begins his gross observations on the exterior condition of the first body, one of his assistants noting down everything he says on the chalkboard on the wall, another writing in a large hospital notebook, the observations in German and Latin –

Mumbled evocations. Muttered incantations . . .

'Irises are black, corneas clouded,' intones the doctor. 'Haemorrhaging in the surfaces . . .'

I look up again –

She is watching the doctor, watching him work . . .

'Removal of a piece of material from the neck reveals a ligature mark – to be known as Ligature A – below the mandible . . .'

She is staring up at the fabric he holds . . .

'Minor abrasions present in the area of Ligature A but the lack of haemorrhage suggests Ligature A is post-mortem . . .'

She opens and closes her eyes . . .

'Heavy bruising on the neck is of a pattern that suggests an attempt was made to throttle the victim . . .'

She swallows now as . . .

'In the same area as the bruising on the neck, a second ligature mark is present – to be known as Ligature B – which encircles the neck, crossing the anterior midline of the neck just below the laryngeal prominence . . .'

As she remembers . . .

'The skin of the anterior neck above and below Ligature B shows petechial haemorrhaging . . .'

Her own death . . .

'The absence of abrasions here is consistent with the use of a softer ligature . . .'

'Like a *haramaki*?' asks Kai.

Dr. Nakadate looks up from her neck. He nods. 'Yes, like a *haramaki*, Inspector Kai.'

Kai looks across at me. I open my mouth to start to speak. To ask him again. Inspector Kai shakes his head. I stop –

Dr. Nakadate has moved down her body to her genital area. 'There is evidence of forced sexual activity here . . .'

Here there is pain. Pain is here . . .

'Pre- or post-mortem?' I ask him –

'I am here because of you . . .'

Dr. Nakadate looks across her body at me. He holds up a

finger. 'One moment please, inspector.'

Her cheeks blush, her eyes close . . .

'Possibly both,' he says –

Here is pain. Pain is here . . .

Dr. Nakadate and his assistants now minutely examine every part of her skin, every nail and every hair, every tooth and every orifice, every spot and every blemish –

'Are there any distinguishing features for identification, doctor?' I ask him. 'Anything . . .'

'Yes,' he says. 'There is evidence of a small whitlow scar on her left thumb . . .'

I look over again at Inspector Kai. Kai making his own notes. I cough. I clear my throat. I start to speak again, to say, 'Then maybe we should let the mothers see the body now, Inspector Kai?'

Dr. Nakadate stops his observations. He looks up –

'No,' says Inspector Kai again.

'But with this scar,' I say. 'And the *haramaki*, the five darned holes in the *haramaki* . . .'

'No,' says Kai.

'I believe positive identification is now possible . . .'

'No.'

'But we're wasting time . . .'

'Room #1 has been assigned to this body . . .'

'Yes,' I say. 'But . . .'

'And Room #2 the next body.'

'But obviously, until this body has been identified, I can't . . .'

'Then I believe I am in charge of this case, detective.'

'Yes, but . . .'

'But what, detective?' asks Inspector Kai.

'Nothing.'

'Dr. Nakadate,' says Kai now. 'I am sorry if we have disturbed your work. Please continue with the autopsy.'

Dr. Nakadate picks up a scalpel from the tray. *Metal on metal.* Dr. Nakadate inserts the scalpel into her chest cavity. *Metal through skin.* Dr. Nakadate cuts a Y-shaped line down through the centre of her body, from the front of each shoulder down beneath each breast, around her navel to her pubic bone. *Metal through flesh to bone . . .*

She crosses her arms. She grasps her own shoulders . . .

The skin, the muscles and the soft tissues of her chest wall are now peeled back and away, the chest flap pulled upward towards her face, the ribcage and the lower neck left exposed –

She turns and gazes across at me . . .

Her body is open. Her blood flowing –

'I am here because of you . . .'

Black/white light. In/out knife –

'Here because of you . . .'

Hack away. Cut away. Piece by piece –

To weigh. Measure for measure –

Here where there is pain . . .

Dr. Nakadate removes her stomach and an assistant opens it up at one of the smaller dissecting tables, inspecting its contents as another assistant slices her liver and the smell of gastric acid –

That stench of gastric acid fills the room –

Her ribcage is opened up now –

Here where there is pain . . .

Her heart taken out –

Here.

Finally, the rubber body block is placed beneath her head. Now Dr. Nakadate opens her scalp –

I close my eyes again –

Black/white light. *The scalp of my wife.* In/out knife. *The scalp of my daughter.* Hack away/cut away. *My son . . .*

I open my eyes –

Here . . .

Her head is slumped back while her eyes stare upward, fixed in one last cold gaze at the cracked ceiling of the autopsy room, her spinal cord cut and her brain removed –

Measure for measure. . .

Piece by piece . . .

To record . . .

Inspector Kai has closed his notebook. He has put away his pencil, taken out a cigarette. The detective has finished his work –

Her suffering recorded. Her misery noted . . .

Dr. Nakadate is washing his gloves in a metal bowl. The water red, his gown black. The doctor has finished his work –

The doctor's assistants beginning to stitch –

Her suffering. Her misery . . .

I watch them work. I watch her –

Her breaking . . .

'Preliminary conclusions, doctor?' asks Inspector Kai –

'I would estimate the time of death as being somewhere between ten and eleven days ago,' says the doctor. 'And the cause of death as asphyxia due to ligature strangulation.'

'Thank you very much, doctor,' says Inspector Kai. 'I look forward to reading your full report.'

'You're welcome.'

Inspector Kai turns to me. 'I'm going back to Atago now.'

'What about the second body?' I ask him. 'You're not going to stay for the autopsy. There might be . . .'

'That's your case,' says Kai. 'It's mostly bones anyway. There will be nothing to see.'

I turn back to the autopsy table. *Back to her.* The stitching complete, her body is being lifted onto the gurney. The grey sheet is placed back over her body once more. The glass doors are opened and she is wheeled out of the autopsy room back to the mortuary –

The marble table washed down with a bucket of water –

I swallow bile. I swallow bile. I swallow . . .

Her blood running away in rivers.

*

I sit in the corridor between the autopsy room and the mortuary. I itch and I scratch. *Gari-gari.* I wait for Dr. Nakadate to drink his tea and smoke his cigarette. I itch and I scratch. *Gari-gari.* I wait for the orderlies to finish cleaning up the autopsy room. I itch and I scratch. *Gari-gari.* I wait for them to bring in the second body. I itch and I scratch. *Gari-gari.* I wait for the second autopsy to begin –

Itching and scratching. Itching and scratching –

My autopsy, my body. My body, my autopsy . . .

The bomb tape still upon the glass.

*

The second body is on a blanket on a stretcher on a gurney. The second body is mostly bones and clothes. Two orderlies take two corners of the blanket each to lift the bones and clothes off the stretcher and the gurney and place them on the autopsy table. The blanket is then removed from under the clothes and bones.

Dr. Nakadate has put back on the same stained surgical gown and the same rubber gloves and again begins the gross external examination with the measurements and the estimates, one assistant at the chalkboard on the wall, another one writing in the hospital notebook; the facts and the figures and the educated guesses; first in German and Latin, then in our native tongue –

The mumbled evocations. The muttered incantations . . .

'The body is that of a young female, a young female once again aged approximately eighteen years . . .'

The same age, the same sex . . .

The clothes are now carefully removed from the bones –

Knives and scissors through buttons and threads –

First the yellow and dark-blue striped pinafore dress, next the white half-sleeved chemise, then the white canvas shoes with their red rubber soles, and finally the dyed-pink socks –

There are no undergarments on her –

The same sex, the same place . . .

I say, 'Underwear was found near the scene.'

'Have it sent here,' says one of the assistants. 'It may still be possible to compare its age to the age of these clothes and also to search for matching threads or fibres.'

I lick the tip of my pencil –

I make a note and then I ask, 'What about time of death?'

Dr. Nakadate shakes his head. 'With the heat and humidity this summer, with the insects and vermin that found her first, it's difficult to be precise but I'd estimate about three to four weeks . . .'

I lick the tip of my pencil again. I make another note –

Three, four weeks; twentieth to the twenty-seventh of July . . .

Dr. Nakadate places his gloved fingers around the neck bones and the jawbone. Dr. Nakadate looks up at me. Dr. Nakadate sticks out his lower lip, nods to himself and then says, 'The hyoid bone at the base of the tongue is fractured, as are the thyroid and cricoid cartilages, all of which were seen on Body Number One . . .'

The same place, the same crime . . .

'This girl was strangled?'

'More likely throttled.'

'The same person?'

Dr. Nakadate nods. 'And we've both seen this before, detective. Remember?'

Back out into the light. I curse. I curse. I curse. *I don't want to remember. I don't want to remember.* The heat on the street. I sweat. I sweat. I sweat. *Keep it simple, keep it simple; two bodies, one murderer; one case, Kai's case.* The streetcar never comes or the streetcar is full. I itch. I itch. I itch. *I don't want to remember. I don't want to remember.* The trains always late, the trains always full. I scratch. I scratch. I scratch. *Fuck Nakadate, hide the link, and bury the connection.* Back down through Moto-Akasaka and along the side of the river. I run. I run. I run. *I don't want to remember. I don't want to remember.* Through the doors of Headquarters. I pant. I pant. I pant. *Hear nothing, see nothing, say nothing.* Up the stairs to the First Investigative Division and the door to the chief's office. I knock. I knock. I knock. *Remember nothing. Remember nothing. Nothing . . .*

I step into the chief's office. I apologize. I bow –

No Adachi. No Kanehara. No Kai. Just me . . .

'Please sit down,' he says. 'You look hot . . .'

I bow and I apologize again. I sit down –

He hands me some tea. 'Drink . . .'

I take the tea. I thank him –

'It's always hot in this city,' says Chief Kita. 'I hate it, this city heat. I have bought a little land, you know? Near Atami. I've started to cultivate it. Look . . .'

Chief Kita holds out his hands across his desk. There are calluses on these hands –

'These are real calluses,' he says. 'From the land. Because the land is important. The land keeps us alive. The land keeps us close to the people . . .'

Chief Kita has lost both his sons; one dead in China, one missing in Siberia . . .

I nod. I agree with him. I put down the tea –

'How was Nakadate?' asks the chief –

'Dr. Nakadate thinks that both bodies found in Shiba Park were probably murdered by the same person.'

'Does he really?' says Chief Kita. 'Now do you think that makes things easier or more difficult for us?'

'I would hope it makes things easier,' I say. 'There surely needs to be only one investigation now . . .'

I stop speaking. It's too late –

I curse! I curse! I curse!

The chief looks across his desk at me. He tuts. He smiles –

I curse myself! I curse myself! I curse myself!

'I just don't think there's any need for two . . .'

The chief has one finger raised now –

I curse myself! I curse myself!

'I am sorry,' I say. 'I don't mean . . .'

The chief sighs. The chief shakes his head. The chief asks, 'Why don't you want this case, inspector?'

'It's not that I don't want it,' I tell him. 'It's just that I –'

'You want to transfer? To transfer to Room #6?'

'Yes,' I say and then, 'But it's not just that . . .'

'You know Kanehara and Adachi think I am too soft with you? They think I indulge you when I should reprimand you?'

I bow my head. I apologize –

'And I know they are right,' he says. 'But I knew your father and your father was a good friend to me and so I have obligations to his memory and thus to his son . . .'

I apologize again –

'And in times such as these,' he continues, 'I believe honouring one's obligations is more important than anything else, that by honouring our obligations we will be able to survive these times and rebuild our country . . .'

I glance up at the scroll on the wall behind his desk, that blood-flecked scroll on which is written, *'It is time to reveal the true essence of the nation.'*

'Now is not the time to forget our obligations,' he says. 'They are who we are.'

'I am very sorry,' I tell him. 'I have made unreasonable demands on you . . .'

'Your eyes are red,' says the chief. 'Be careful how you go.'

*

The day is still unbearably hot and I need a drink. I need a meal and I need a cigarette. I take a different route back to Shiba Park through one of the many makeshift markets where street vendors have set up their stalls and stands with their straw mats and reed screens. They squat in what shade there is and shout out their wares, their faces red and their tempers short, fans in their hands and towels on their heads, the men might be women and the women might be men –

But there is drink here. Food and cigarettes –

Here among the shrieks of the vendors and the clatter of their plates, as open-mouthed customers stagger from stall to stall staring with bloodshot eyes at the goods and the food, clutching their crumpled old notes and misshapen bellies –

Drink and food and cigarettes –

I watch a vendor slap putrid sardines on a corrugated grill. I smell the oil on the metal and I listen as the hungry come running with their notes and their bellies –

I can't eat this food.

I turn away. I keep walking. I come to a woman who is selling rice-balls, each one wrapped in a thin piece of seaweed –

'Three yen,' says the woman. 'Polished rice . . .'

But there are ten or twenty flies on each rice-ball, the seaweed torn and the rice old. I turn away from the stall and stare up and down the marketplace, looking and listening out for drink or cigarettes –

I watch the man on the next stand but one. I watch him sell candies and sweets from a kerosene drum. I watch him reach inside that metal drum and also bring out packs of American cigarettes –

I walk over to the stand. 'How much for just one pack?'

'Don't know what you're talking about,' says the man –

The man wears an undershirt, shorts and army boots –

'Please?' I ask him. 'How much for just a pack . . .?'

The man stares at me and says, 'One hundred yen.'

'How about two packs for one hundred yen?'

The man laughs. 'Get lost, you bum . . .'

I look around. I take out my police notebook. I hold it in front of me so that he can see it but no one else. I say, 'Four packs.'

'Say what?' says the man. 'You're joking . . .'

I shake my head. I say again, 'Four packs.'

The man sighs. The man reaches down inside the kerosene drum. The man brings out four packs of Lucky Strike –

'There you are, officer,' he says.

I take the cigarettes. I turn –

'Stop! Put that back now you thieving little bastard . . .'

I turn back. The woman at the rice-ball stall has a young boy by his wrist. The boy has a rice-ball in his hand –

I have seen this boy somewhere before . . .

The young boy is caked black in rags and filth which the heat and his sweat have stuck one to the other, the dirt to the cloth, the cloth to his skin, his face and hands covered in blisters and boils which weep fresh pus in the market sun –

I have seen this boy before . . .

'Let go,' the woman shouts –

But the boy will not let go and he leans in towards her and bites down into her hand and the woman jumps back in pain as she pushes the young boy away –

Back into me –

Banzai!

Biting into the rice-ball as he falls, swallowing it whole as he goes, the boy sends me sprawling back into a stall and onto the ground but before I can hold him, before I can stand, the boy is up and away, into the crowd which now stands and stares down at me –

Among them the man in the undershirt, the shorts and the army boots who shakes his head and says, 'The thieving bastard.'

*

My trousers are coated in dust. My back aches from the fall. It is 4 p.m. now. I find some of my team sat on the slopes of Shiba Park; Hattori, Takeda, Sanada and Shimoda slumped in the shade with their hats in their hands, swatting at flies and mosquitoes. They struggle to their feet as they see me approach, bowing and apologizing, making their excuses and their reports. I give them cigarettes. I don't care. I'm not listening. I'm looking for the others. For Detective Fujita –

Hattori, Takeda, Sanada and Shimoda scratch their skulls and suck in air, they shake their heads and say, 'Detective Fujita was here before. He was definitely here before. But now he's not . . .'

'How about Nishi? Kimura? Ishida?' I ask them –

Hattori, Takeda, Sanada and Shimoda peer into the sun and shield their eyes, they point up the hill and say, 'Detectives Nishi and Kimura went up there with the woodcutter . . .'

'And where's Ishida?' I ask them –

Now Hattori, Takeda, Sanada and Shimoda have a think before they say, 'With Detective Fujita.'

I turn to go, to walk away, but turn instead to face Adachi –

'Hard at work as usual,' says Chief Inspector Adachi –

I bow. I apologize. I make my excuses. My report –

But Adachi doesn't care. He's not listening. Adachi is not looking for the others. He's looking for Detective Fujita –

No one is who they say they are . . .

I scratch my skull and suck in air. I shake my head and I say, 'Detective Fujita has gone back to Atago police station, sir.'

*

Back at Atago, one hour later, and Chief Inspector Adachi is staring at me. *No Fujita.* The First Team, the Second Team and all the uniforms from the other stations are gathered in the First Team's room at Atago. Adachi is staring at me. *No Fujita.* I am stood up at the front of the room beside Adachi, Kanehara and Kai, the four of us facing the First Team, the Second Team and the uniforms. But Adachi's eyes are turned to the side and fixed on me –

No Fujita. No Fujita. No Fujita. No Fujita . . .

'Attention!' shouts the sergeant –

'Bow!' he shouts. 'At ease!'

Everyone stands at ease now or sits down except Inspector Kai and me. Kai has a piece of paper in his hand; Kai reads out the findings from Dr. Nakadate's preliminary autopsy report on the first body; the physical description of the victim and her estimated age, the time of her death and the cause of her death. But I am not listening. I am looking for the face of Detective Fujita in the faces at the back and sides of this room –

'Inspector Minami!' says Adachi again. 'If you wouldn't mind giving us your report . . .'

I bow. I apologize. I begin to read aloud the findings of the preliminary autopsy report on the second body; the physical description of the victim and her estimated age, the time of her death and the cause of her death. But I am not listening to my own words. I am still looking for the face of Fujita in the faces at the back and sides of this room, still looking for Fujita when I see Ishida –

'Attention!' shouts the sergeant again –

Ishida here, his face to the floor . . .

'Bow!' the sergeant shouts –

His back bent . . .
'Dismissed!'
He runs . . .
I run.

*

Down the Atago stairs, through the uniforms, to the doors, but I am too late. *Too late. Too late. Too late.* The hand on my arm. *I jump. I jump. I jump.* I spin round but it's not Ishida. Not Fujita –

The desk sergeant asks, 'Did you speak to Detective Fujita?'

'No,' I tell him. 'Where is Detective Fujita?'

'Hayashi of the *Minpo* paper . . .'

'What about him?' I ask –

'He was here . . .'

'When?'

'This afternoon,' says the sergeant. 'Hayashi was looking for you, but you were up at Keiō, so he asked to see Detective Fujita . . .'

'And was Detective Fujita here?'

'Yes,' says the desk sergeant. 'He was waiting to see you too, kept asking me what time you were due back from Keiō . . .'

'And so when did you last see Detective Fujita?'

'I haven't seen him since he met Hayashi . . .'

'When?' I ask him. 'When was that?'

'It must have been about 3 p.m. . . .'

'Where? Where did they meet?'

'They were here first,' says the sergeant. 'In reception, but then they stepped outside and . . .'

'And what?' I ask –

'And I haven't seen Detective Fujita since he stepped outside with Mr. Hayashi.'

*

Past the pots and the pans, the kettles and the cans. Down the alleys and the lanes, the shadows and the arches. Up the stairs and through the doors. I kneel down on his tatami mats. I bow. I say, 'I'm sorry.'

Senju Akira selects a new toothpick. Senju slips it between his

84

teeth and chews. He spins his new electric fan my way and says, 'You always smell of corpses, always stink of death, detective.'

I say again, 'I'm sorry. I'm very, very sorry . . .'

'They tell me you've got yourself another dead body,' says Senju. 'They tell me you're all camped out at Atago police station.'

I say, 'Yes. Two young women were found in Shiba Park.'

'Were these two young women prostitutes?' he asks.

I say, 'Maybe not. We haven't identified them yet.'

'It's no wonder you smell like shit then, is it?' he laughs. 'They work you hard, don't they? How many hours a day is it?'

I tell him, 'Twenty-four on a murder investigation.'

'Twenty-four hours?' he laughs again. 'That's nearly as many as I work, detective! But at least I work for me and at least I get well paid and at least my kids get to eat and my mistresses get to wear silk stockings and I don't smell of fucking corpses . . .'

Now Senju Akira stops laughing. Now Senju spits out his toothpick. Now he says, 'So tell me, officer, how many detectives have they got working on these two dead girls?'

I tell him, 'About twenty detectives.'

'Twenty? For two dead whores?'

I start to say, 'I don't know . . .'

'So tell me this, detective, how many men then have you got out there looking for the killer of my boss? For the real killer? For the man who paid Nodera to pull the trigger? How many, detective?'

I bow. I apologize. I tell him, 'It's not my decision . . .'

'So what use are you to me? What use, detective?'

I bow again. I start to say again, 'I'm sorry . . .'

'Shut up!' shouts Senju and he gets to his feet and he says, 'Let's take a walk, just you and me, detective.'

I stand up. I follow him. Down his stairs. To his two goons –

In their pale suits, their patterned shirts and their shades . . .

The two goons and us stepping out into the market –

His market; the Shimbashi New Life Market . . .

Each stall-keeper bowing and thanking Senju as he ambles past them, past the fresh sardines and second-hand suits, past the coffee and the silk, each stall offering him free this and free that, bowing and thanking him as he acknowledges them all with an imperial nod or a military salute, these people on their knees, bowing and thanking him, on their worn-out knees at his leather-shod feet –

Emperor Senju, Banzai! Emperor Senju, Banzai! Banzai!

Then he turns to me and asks, 'You got a name for me?'

'I'm sorry. I'm very sorry,' I say. I bow my head –

'So why do you come around here, detective?'

'I'm sorry,' I say again. 'I'm very sorry . . .'

'Stop apologizing,' says Senju. 'And start looking around you, looking where you are. This is a market, officer, where people come to buy and sell. This is the future –

'This is the New Japan!'

'Yes,' I agree. 'Yes.'

'*Yes?*' laughs Senju. 'But you've got nothing to sell and no money to buy, detective.'

'I'm sorry,' I say again. 'I'm very sorry.'

'You're the past, Detective Inspector Minami,' he laughs again. 'With your stench of death and your one hundred yen a month, your shrieking kids and your starving mistress . . .'

I bow my head.

Now Senju stops at a *kakigōri* stall. Senju asks for two strawberry flavoured cups. The stall-owner bows. The owner hands them to Senju. He thanks Senju again and again –

Senju hands one of the cups to me –

I bow. I apologize. I thank him –

I curse him. I curse him . . .

'What is it you really want?' he asks me. 'More money, is that what you need, detective?'

I shake my head. I apologize again. Then finally I tell him, 'Please, I really need some Calmotin.'

'Calmotin?' laughs Senju. 'Why would you want to sleep? I wouldn't want your dreams . . .'

'Please,' I beg him again. 'I really need some Calmotin.'

Senju stops laughing. 'And I really need some names.'

Fujita. Hayashi. Fujita. Hayashi. Fujita. Hayashi . . .

'You give me a name and I'll give you your Calmotin.'

'But how much can you get me?' I ask him. 'I really need as much as you can give me. Please . . .'

'Don't worry,' laughs Senju again. 'You give me a name and you need never wake again.'

'Thank you,' I say, over and over. 'Thank you. Thank you.'

'*Red apple to my lips, blue sky silently watching . . .*'

'But don't dare come back here without a name.'
Hayashi. Fujita. Hayashi. Fujita. Hayashi . . .
'Thank you,' I say again. 'Thank you.'
'Or I promise you, you won't wake again.'

*

From Shimbashi to Atago. Up the stairs to the office –
No Fujita. No Fujita. No Fujita . . .
But Ishida is here; Ishida with his head down on his desk –
I shake him. I pull his hair. I whisper, 'Where's Detective
Fujita? Quickly! Come on! Where is he? Tell me! Quickly!'
Ishida shakes his head. Ishida starts to apologize –
I shake him again. I slap him. I hiss, 'Tell me!'
Ishida apologizes and apologizes –
Bodies stir. Bodies wake . . .
I push him away –
I run again.

*

From Atago back through Shimbashi. From Shimbashi through Ginza.
Through Ginza to Hatchōbori. *The city getting darker and darker,
the lights fewer and fewer.* Through Hatchōbori and across the
Kameshima River. Across the Kameshima River to Shinkawa.
Through Shinkawa and across the Eitaibashi Bridge. *The city getting
flatter and flatter, the buildings getting fewer and fewer.* Across the
Eitaibashi Bridge into Monzen-nakachō. Monzen-nakachō up to
Fukagawa, the dark burnt field where Fukagawa once stood –
Air raid! Air raid! Here comes an air raid!
The endless burnt field where now stands but a lone chimney
here, a lone chimney there; the bathhouses and the factories but
rubble and dust. *Red! Red! Incendiary bomb!* The hull of a hospital,
the shell of a school, the rest is all ash and weeds. *Run! Run! Get a
mattress and sand!* An endless field of ash and weeds –
Air raid! Air raid! Here comes an air raid!
This is where Fujita's house once stood –
Black! Black! Here come the bombs!
His house gone. His family gone –

87

Cover your ears! Close your eyes!

Fujita has nothing left to lose –

I stand before the ruins of his home, before the scorched stone steps and the charred tree stump, panting and sweating, itching and itching, and now I begin to weep as a gust of wind raises the thick, brown dust that covers the lot where his house once stood and bangs the loose sheets of iron on the neighbouring shacks, drowning out the sound of my sobs, of my scream –

Get off your knees!

4

August 18, 1946

Tokyo, 89°, cloudy

I have walked all night through fields of ash to find him here; Detective Fujita sitting in the early morning shade on the steps of the Atago police station with his face to the sun, his eyes closed, a new Panama hat in one hand and a freshly lit cigarette in the other –

I stand over him. I block out the light. I say, 'Good morning.'

'Good morning,' he replies but he does not open his eyes –

I tell him, 'Let's go for a walk, please. We need to talk.'

'Talk about what?' he asks me, his eyes still closed –

'Hayashi Jo,' I say. 'Matsuda Giichi. Senju Akira.'

Now Detective Fujita opens his eyes. He gets to his feet. He wipes away the dust from his trousers. Now he says, 'Lead on.'

My eyes ache. My head aches. My belly aches . . .

In the old grove across the road, among the cedars and the bamboo, we stand in the shadows and the sunlight, black and white patterns across our clothes and across our faces –

'They missed you yesterday,' I say. 'Adachi and Kanehara. They were both asking where you were . . .'

Fujita bows ever so slightly and says, 'I'm sorry. It couldn't be helped. I had to meet someone . . .'

'I hear you met Hayashi from the *Minpo* . . .'

Fujita laughs. '*Minpo, Minshū, Akahata* . . .'

'What did Hayashi want?' I ask him.

'Blackmail. Extortion. Money.'

'He tried to blackmail you?'

'Not only me. You too.'

'Me?' I ask. 'Why?'

'He knows things.'

'Things about you and Nodera Tomiji?' I ask him. 'Things about you and the murder of Matsuda Giichi?'

'All lies,' hisses Fujita. 'All lies.'

'Is that what you told Hayashi?'

'I didn't tell Hayashi anything,' says Fujita. 'I just wanted him gone and now he's gone and he won't be coming back.'

My stomach aches. My head aches. 'Really?'

'I paid him to go. To not come back.'

'How much did you pay him?'

'Forget it,' smiles Fujita.

'No,' I say. 'How much?'

'Forget it!' he snaps –

I nod. I bow to him. I thank him. Then I ask him, 'But do you know where Hayashi is now?'

'He's running,' says Fujita. 'Running from Tokyo. Running from this life. His turn to change his name. To change his job. He'll not be back, I promise you.'

I tell him, 'Senju Akira wants a name from me.'

'Whose name does he want?' asks Fujita.

'The name that set up Nodera Tomiji.'

'Or what?'

'Or he'll make things difficult for me.'

'So give him Hayashi's name,' laughs Detective Fujita. 'Hayashi doesn't need it any more.'

'But how do you know he won't come back?'

'I just know,' he laughs again. 'Trust me.'

'But how do you know . . .?'

Detective Fujita steps closer. Fujita whispers, 'I told him I'd kill him if I ever saw him again.'

*

I have vomited in the toilets of Atago police station. *Black bile*. Now I stand over the sink. I spit. I wipe my mouth. I turn on a tap. I wash my face. I look up into the mirror. I stare into the mirror –

No one is who they say they are . . .

I stand up in front of the First Team, the Second Team and all the uniforms from the Atago, Meguro and Mita police stations as Chief Inspector Kanehara reviews the progress of the investigation to date; the searches of the two crime scenes in Shiba Park have been completed; the statements of the witnesses have been taken; the autopsies have been conducted; the initial stages of the investigation have been successfully completed bar the identification of the bodies, which is scheduled for later this morning; then the second stage of the investigation will begin –

I swallow . . .

'All reports must be completed and submitted to Headquarters this morning,' Adachi is now telling the First Team, the Second Team and the uniforms from the Atago, Meguro and Mita police stations. 'Following the completion of the identification process, there will be a second meeting later today at 4 p.m.'

'Attention!' shouts one of the sergeants –

'Bow!' the sergeant shouts –

'Dismissed!'

I run back to the toilets. I vomit again. *Brown bile.* I walk over to the sink. I spit. I wipe my mouth. I turn on a tap. I wash my face. I look up into the mirror. I stare into the mirror –

No one is who they say they are . . .

In the upstairs corridor I wait for Nishi and Kimura. I take them to one side. I ask them, 'Have you written up your reports?'

They both nod. They both say, 'Yes, we have.'

'Then I want you to go to Toshima Ward,' I tell them. 'I want you to go to the ward office. I want you to ask again about this Takahashi of Zōshigaya, Toshima . . .'

Kimura nods again but Nishi says, 'The First Team have already been up there.'

'I know that,' I tell him. 'And I know they couldn't find him or any mention of him, but his name on a statement of employment in his bag in that park is the only name we have found so far and, remember, our body is only bones and those bones need a name or they'll always be bones . . .'

Nishi nods. Kimura nods. They both bow. They both turn to leave. I wait until they've gone and then I run. I run back to the toilets to vomit a third time. *Yellow bile.* I turn on the tap. I wash my face. I look up into the mirror. I stare into the mirror –

No one is who they say they are . . .

Ishida is wiping down the chairs and the tables, sweeping up the floor and the doorway, straightening our banner. Ishida looks up. He sees me. He flinches. Then he stands to attention –

'At ease,' I say as he bows and apologizes –

I ask, 'Have you written up your report?'

He nods. He says, 'Yes, I have, sir.'

'Then I want you to do something for me,' I tell him. 'I want you to go to the offices of the *Minpo* newspaper . . .'

Ishida nods. Ishida bows again –

'I want you to ask to see a Hayashi Jo . . .'

Ishida takes out his notebook –

'Tell Hayashi to come see me . . .'

Ishida licks his pencil tip –

'Now if he's not there, I want you to find out who he has seen recently, where he has gone and when he'll be back.'

Ishida nods. Ishida says, 'I understand, sir.'

'I'm depending on you, Ishida.'

Ishida nods. He bows. He turns to leave. Now I run again. Back to the toilets of Atago police station. I vomit again. *Grey bile.* Four times I have vomited in the toilets of Atago Police Station. *Black bile, brown bile, yellow bile and grey.* Four times I have looked into the mirror. Four times I have stared into that mirror –

I don't want to remember. But in the half-light . . .

Four times I have screamed into the glass –

In the half-light, I can't forget. I can't forget . . .

I have screamed into my own face –

No one is who they say they are!

*

Inspectors Kanehara, Adachi and Kai have already left for Metro Headquarters, left in a car without me. *Ton-ton.* But I am glad. *Ton-ton.* I don't care. *Ton-ton.* I want to walk. *Ton-ton.* In the shit. *Ton-ton.* In the dust. *Ton-ton.* In the dirt. *Ton-ton.* There is a typhoon approaching Japan. *Ton-ton.* But it won't hit Tokyo. *Ton-ton.* Not this time. *Ton-ton.* Not this one. *Ton-ton.* But the air is still heavy with its approach. *Ton-ton.* The people wilting in the streets. *Ton-ton.* The stalls at the sides of the road quiet. *Ton-ton.* Men sat on their butts slowly shelling nuts to sell, slowly stripping down old wirelesses for parts. *Ton-ton.* Nut by nut, part by part, as slowly as they can. *Ton-ton.* Frightened to finish, frightened of having no more nuts to shell, of having no more wirelesses to strip, of having nothing more to do –

Ton-ton. Ton-ton. Ton-ton. Ton-ton. Ton-ton. Ton-ton . . .

Nothing more to do but think, think about food –

Ton-ton. Ton-ton. Ton-ton. Ton-ton. Ton-ton . . .
My stomach aches. My head aches –
Ton-ton. Ton-ton. Ton-ton. Ton-ton . . .
My feet ache. My eyes ache –
Ton-ton. Ton-ton. Ton-ton . . .
I curse! I curse! I curse!
Ton-ton. Ton-ton . . .
I curse myself –
Ton-ton.

*

I knock on the door to Chief Kita's office. I open it. I bow deeply. I apologize profusely. I take my seat at the table; the same people, the same place, the same time and the same two conversations every day but today I am late so I have missed all their talk of the Tokyo trials and the rumours of purges. Now the talk around the table has turned again to SCAP, to their so-called reforms, all of which are based on the recommendations of former New York Police Commissioner Lewis J. Valentine, and to the SCAP puppet Tanikawa, the chief of the Police Affairs Bureau at the Home Ministry –

'He's helping them purge good hard-working officers,' Kanehara is saying, 'And replacing them with policewomen, turning female clerks into police officers, giving them the authority to arrest suspects or to take them back to the stations . . .'

'Tanikawa is a fool,' agrees Adachi. 'A fool and a stooge.'

'He might be a fool and a stooge,' says Kanehara, 'But he's not finished yet; have you seen the kind of reforms they want to include in the proposed new Police Bill? Not only policewomen with powers of arrest and detention, but an emphasis on the recruitment of college graduates above all other recruits . . .'

'All communists,' says Kai –

'Exactly,' continues Kanehara, 'And then let's not forget the centrepiece of the Bill; the prevention of unreasonable or unjustifiable detention in police cells or jails. You know what this will mean? That for every single suspect you pick up, there will have to be either some proof of guilt or some actual charge. There will be no more picking people up and holding them until you find the evidence or gain a confession. There will have to be either evidence

93

or a charge before you can touch them. If not, then you'll be the one charged – with violating the suspect's human rights!'

'Human rights!' everyone laughs.

'Like all this talk of new uniforms,' says Kai. 'All these calls for less militaristic ones, of blue instead of khaki, of sleeve stripes instead of shoulder boards. All this talk of new uniforms when we barely have enough men left . . .'

'We've asked and asked and asked them for new uniforms,' says Kanehara. 'New uniforms and new boots or, if not new uniforms or new boots, then new material to patch up our old uniforms or new soles for our old boots, anything that stops our men looking like tramps and being despised by the public as tramps . . .'

'And they've promised and promised us,' says Adachi –

'Yes,' says Kanehara. 'But that's all they've done . . .'

The same people, the same place, the same time and the same two conversations every day, meeting after meeting until there is another knock on the door and another interruption –

'Excuse me,' says another uniform –

'What is it?' barks the chief –

'The mothers are ready, sir.'

*

The autopsies have been performed, the search of the area has been completed, and five of the mothers have been told to come back to Headquarters. Five mothers who read the morning paper or heard the news from neighbours two days ago. Five mothers who have taken out their last good kimonos again. Five mothers who have called upon their other daughters or their sisters for a third time. Five mothers who have once again begged the streetcar or train fare up to Sakuradamon. Five mothers still looking for their daughters –

Five mothers praying we have not found them.

A uniformed officer opens the door to the reception room for Inspector Kai and me. Kai and I apologize to these five mothers for keeping them waiting, these five mothers in their last good kimonos, their other daughters or their sisters at their sides –

Praying and praying and praying . . .

These five mothers whose daughters' ages and descriptions, their heights and their weights, the scars their daughters bore or the teeth their daughters lost, the clothes they were wearing and the shoes on their feet, the bags they were carrying –

On the days they were last seen . . .

These features and descriptions that help us eliminate or match the missing to the dead, these features and descriptions that have brought these mothers back here –

Their hands in their laps . . .

These five mothers who stare up at us now as Kai asks, 'Which one of you is Mrs. Midorikawa of Meguro Ward?'

Blinking and nodding, Mrs. Midorikawa gets to her feet with the help of her two other daughters. Blinking and nodding, Inspector Kai and I lead them into a smaller room next to the reception room. Blinking and nodding, Mrs. Midorikawa sits between her two older daughters. Blinking and nodding, Mrs. Midorikawa is twisting a piece of cloth in her hands. Blinking and nodding, Mrs. Midorikawa is staring at another piece of cloth on the table. Blinking and nodding, the tears already running down her cheeks. Blinking and nodding –

The red haramaki *with the five darned holes . . .*

'It was her father's. Ryuko darned it herself,' she tells us. 'Five times. Replaced the buttons.'

Blinking and nodding as Inspector Kai picks up the *haramaki*, folding it in two and then wrapping it back up inside the brown paper, the crumpled brown paper –

'Ryuko darned it herself,' she repeats, blinking and nodding. 'Ryuko darned it herself.'

I excuse myself. I step outside. I go back into the reception room next door. The four other mothers look up at me. The four other mothers stare up at me –

Mouths open . . .

I tell the four mothers that a car will take them up to the Keiō University Hospital.

*

Mrs. Midorikawa and her two older daughters do not speak in the car to the Keiō University Hospital. They do not speak in the corridors crowded with the dying and the dead, the waiting and the grieving –

She is here. She is here. She is here. She is here . . .

They do not speak as we wait for the elevator, as we watch

the elevator doors open, as we step inside and watch the doors close –

She is here. She is here. She is here . . .

They do not speak as we ride the dark elevator down, as we watch the elevator doors open again, as the light returns –

She is here. She is here . . .

They do not speak as they walk along the corridor to the mortuary, as they put on the slippers, as they step through the doors into the half-light of the mortuary –

She is here, here . . .

They bow but do not speak when they are introduced to Dr. Nakadate, as the orderlies remove a stretcher from the refrigerator –

Here is Ryuko . . .

They do not speak as they stare at the raised grey sheet on the stretcher, as Dr. Nakadate reaches under the grey sheet, as he takes out a hand from under the sheet, as he holds up a left hand and points out a scar on the left thumb, they do not speak but they weep –

They do not speak but they weep and they weep –

'I am here because of you . . .'

They weep and they weep but they still do not speak as Dr. Nakadate slowly pulls back the grey sheet, as he shows them the bleached face of a young girl, seventeen years old –

'I am Midorikawa Ryuko of Meguro . . .'

They weep and they weep but they still do not speak until Mrs. Midorikawa finally looks up from the bleached face of her daughter, from the ruined corpse of her child and cries out, 'Kodaira!'

*

Inspector Kai and I stand in the corridor between the autopsy room and the mortuary and wait for Mrs. Midorikawa and her two older daughters to finish their discussions with the Keiō staff about the funeral arrangements for her youngest daughter. Inspector Kai is smoking a cigarette. Inspector Kai is smiling. Inspector Kai is looking at his notebook, a name written three times –

Kodaira. Kodaira. Kodaira . . .

'This time tomorrow,' laughs Inspector Kai. 'This case will be closed and I'll be drunk . . .'

Dr. Nakadate's assistant comes down the narrow corridor. He bows. He apologizes for interrupting our conversation. He hands me

96

a piece of paper torn from a newspaper and says, 'This was found folded in the pocket of the skirt of the pinafore dress on your body.'

I open out the piece of newspaper. It is an advertisement – *Salon Matsu in Kanda now hiring new staff* . . .

It is a clue, at last. It is a start, at last –

'You never know,' laughs Kai. 'Maybe this time tomorrow, we'll both be drunk . . .'

I bow and I thank Dr. Nakadate's assistant as Mrs. Midorikawa and her two daughters step out of the mortuary room –

The arrangements have been made.

Now Inspector Kai puts out his cigarette. Inspector Kai stops smiling. Inspector Kai takes Mrs. Midorikawa and her daughters back to Metropolitan Police Headquarters.

Now it is my turn –

I open the glass doors. I step inside the autopsy room. I walk over to one of the sinks. I take off my jacket. I roll up the sleeves of my shirt. I wash my hands. I dry my hands. I do up my shirt cuffs. I put my jacket back on. I walk over to one of the autopsy tables, octagonal, marble and German in design. I take out my pocket knife, blunt, rusted and Japanese. I cut the string of the three brown paper parcels waiting for me here on the table. I unwrap the brown paper of the first parcel. I take out the yellow and dark-blue striped pinafore dress, the white half-sleeved chemise, and the dyed-pink socks. I lay these clothes out on one of the other autopsy tables. I unwrap the brown paper of the second parcel. I take out the two white canvas shoes with the red rubber soles. I place these shoes on the same autopsy table. I unwrap the third brown paper parcel. I take out the ladies' undergarments we found near the bodies in Shiba, these undergarments that did not belong to Midorikawa Ryuko. I lay these garments out on one of the smaller separate dissecting tables –

Now I step back out into the corridor –

The four other mothers with their other daughters or their sisters or neighbours are waiting. Four other mothers who have lost daughters aged fifteen to twenty years old. Four mothers who lost their daughters over three weeks ago. Mothers who are wringing their hands and praying they do not find their daughters here at the end of this corridor, beyond these glass doors –

Praying and praying . . .

I ask Mrs. Tamba of Ōmori Ward to please step into the

autopsy room. Mrs. Tamba and her two sisters follow me inside –

Mrs. Tamba and her sisters stare at the yellow and dark-blue striped pinafore dress, the white half-sleeved chemise, the dyed-pink socks and the white canvas shoes with red rubber soles lain out on the autopsy table and they shake their heads. I ask them to look at the undergarments on the other table. They stare again and then they shake their heads again. I thank them and they leave –

I lick the tip of my pencil. I make a note –

Mrs. Nakahara of Yodobashi Ward and her other daughter stare at the yellow and dark-blue striped pinafore dress, the white half-sleeved chemise, the dyed-pink socks and the white canvas shoes with red rubber soles. They dab their eyes but shake their heads. I ask them to look at the undergarments on the other table. They shake their heads again. I thank them and they leave –

I turn the page. I make another note –

Mrs. Hidari of Ebara Ward and her sister stare at the yellow and dark-blue striped pinafore dress, the white half-sleeved chemise, the dyed-pink socks and the white canvas shoes with red rubber soles and finally, after five minutes, they shake their heads. I ask them to look at the undergarments. They look at each other and then shake their heads. I thank them and they leave –

I lick the tip of my pencil –

Mrs. Mitani of Jōtō Ward has no daughter or sister or neighbour with her today. Mrs. Mitani stands alone before the autopsy table and stares at the yellow and dark-blue striped pinafore dress, the white half-sleeved chemise, the dyed-pink socks and the white canvas shoes with red rubber soles. Mrs. Mitani shakes her head. I ask her to look at the undergarments. Mrs. Mitani shakes her head again. I thank her but she does not move. Mrs. Mitani continues to stare at the undergarments lain out on the dissecting table. I thank her again. She still does not move but asks, 'What happens now?'

'We will continue to try to identify these clothes so . . .'

'Not about that,' she says. 'About *my* daughter . . .'

'I'm sure the Jōtō police are trying to find her . . .'

'How can they?' she asks me. 'Have you been to Jōtō Ward? There's nothing left there. The police have nothing. No buildings. No telephones. No bicycles. How can they find her?'

'I'm sorry,' I say. 'I'm really sorry . . .'

'She was all I had,' she says. 'I have nothing now. No family.

No house. No job. No money. Nothing . . .'

'I'm sorry,' I say again. 'But I promise I will make sure that the description of your daughter is sent to every police station in Tokyo and I hope we will find her . . .'

Now Mrs. Mitani of Jōtō Ward looks up from the ladies undergarments and the dissecting table. Now Mrs. Mitani wipes her eyes. Mrs. Mitani bows and thanks me –

Now Mrs. Mitani leaves –

I make my final note –

I need a cigarette . . .

I walk back down the basement corridor past the walls of sinks and drains, the written warnings of cuts and punctures, the orderlies washing and rinsing their hands and their forearms and I push the elevator button and I watch the doors open and I am about to step inside the elevator when Dr. Nakadate catches my arm and asks, 'Did you find that file, inspector? The Miyazaki file . . .'

*

I don't want to remember. In the half-light, I can't forget . . .

The cars have gone back to HQ. The streetcar full again –

Kai has a name. Kai has a suspect. Kai will get an address . . .

I walk back to Sakuradamon, through Moto-Akasaka –

Kai will make an arrest. Kai will get a confession . . .

By the river, behind the parliament building –

Kai can close the case. Both our cases . . .

Past the imperial moat to HQ –

Both our cases closed . . .

Miyazaki Mitsuko forgotten again.

*

I knock on the door of the interview room. I open it. I bow. I take a seat next to the stenographer at the side. Inspector Kai does not look up. Mrs. Midorikawa does not look up; Mrs. Midorikawa sat next to one of her older daughters, twisting and wringing that same piece of cloth in her lap as Inspector Kai confirms again, again and again, the things she has told him during their initial two interviews –

'So you last saw your daughter on the sixth?'

99

'Yes,' whispers Mrs. Midorikawa. 'Ryuko left the house at about nine on the morning of the sixth of August.'

'And this is the house in Meguro Ward?'

'Yes,' she says. 'But it's not our house, it's the Yamamotos' house. We've been staying with them since our house was pulled down for fire defences at the end of last March.'

'And Ryuko was living there too?'

'Yes,' she says again. 'Always.'

Now Inspector Kai asks, 'And so can you tell me again what was she wearing when she left the house in Meguro on the sixth?'

'A white summer dress and white canvas shoes.'

'And did she have any money with her?'

'She would have had about ten yen,' says Mrs. Midorikawa. 'Just for the streetcar or the train fare.'

Inspector Kai turns the page of his notebook. 'And she told you she was going for a job interview?'

'Yes,' agrees Mrs. Midorikawa. 'Ryuko didn't really like the job she had as a waitress in Ginza.'

'And this was as a waitress at a café in the fourth chōme?'

'Yes,' she agrees again. 'But there were not many tips.'

'And the interview for this new job was in Shibaura?'

'Yes,' she says again. 'With the Occupation Army.'

'And this job interview had all come about through this man called Kodaira?' asks Inspector Kai. 'Kodaira Yoshio?'

Mrs. Midorikawa pauses here. Mrs. Midorikawa swallows. Now Mrs. Midorikawa says, 'Through that man, yes.'

'Please tell me again then, in as much detail as you can, how your daughter Ryuko came to meet this man called Kodaira?'

Mrs. Midorikawa sighs. Mrs. Midorikawa shakes her head. Mrs. Midorikawa says, 'By chance at Shinagawa station.'

'How was it by chance that Ryuko met this man Kodaira?' asks Inspector Kai. 'And what was the date they met?'

Mrs. Midorikawa looks at her other daughter. Mrs. Midorikawa asks her, 'You said the tenth of July?'

'Yes,' says her other daughter. 'There was an accident at Shinagawa and all the trains were delayed.'

Inspector Kai looks down at his notebook and then asks, 'And this was when Kodaira approached and spoke to Ryuko?'

'Yes,' says the other daughter again. 'Ryuko told me that he just came up to her on the platform and started talking to her.'

Inspector Kai asks, 'Do you know what they talked about?'

'Yes,' she says. 'They talked about work and about food.'

'Ryuko told him she wanted to find a new job,' adds Mrs. Midorikawa now. 'And Kodaira said he had connections with the Occupation Army and that he could help her find a job with them.'

'How exactly did he say he would be able to help Ryuko?'

Mrs. Midorikawa shakes her head. 'I don't know.'

'Through his connections,' says the other daughter. 'That's what Ryuko told me that he said; through his *connections* . . .'

'Did she say what kind of connections?' asks Kai.

'He was wearing the Shinchū Gun armband.'

Kai nods. 'So when did they next meet?'

'Not until earlier this month,' says Mrs. Midorikawa. 'Ryuko fell ill with intestinal problems and so she didn't see Kodaira again until he suddenly turned up at the house asking after her . . .'

'So Kodaira knew where Ryuko lived then?'

'Yes,' says Mrs. Midorikawa. 'She must have given him her address that day in July at Shinagawa . . .'

'And so when exactly did Kodaira make this visit?' asks Kai. 'This visit to the house in Meguro?'

Mrs. Midorikawa says, 'The day before she went missing.'

'The fifth of August,' confirms her other daughter.

'And did you both meet Kodaira?' asks Kai –

'Yes,' they both reply at the same time.

'So then tell me,' says Inspector Kai. 'What is he like?'

They are both silent for a moment until Mrs. Midorikawa first sighs and then says, 'He seemed like a gentleman. He brought us a small gift. He said he was concerned about Ryuko's health. He told us he was working as a cook with the Occupation Army. He thought he could help Ryuko find work at the same barracks.'

'Can you remember which barracks these were?' asks Kai.

'Number 589,' says the other daughter. 'In Shinagawa.'

Kai looks up from his notes. 'And you believed him?'

'Of course I believed him,' spits Mrs. Midorikawa, suddenly. 'Do you really think I would have let my daughter go off to meet him, if I didn't believe him? If I didn't trust him?'

Inspector Kai looks back down at his notebook. Inspector Kai shakes his head and now says, 'I am very sorry. I . . .'

'There are six of us in our family,' she says. 'And no man.'

Inspector Kai bows his head and says again, 'I am sorry.'

'He promised her a good job,' she says. 'Free food.'

Inspector Kai just nods and stares at his notebook.

'He was wearing the Shinchū Gun armband.'

I cough now. I edge forward on my seat. I bow and then ask, 'And so Ryuko went to meet him on the sixth of August?'

'Yes,' says Mrs. Midorikawa. 'They had arranged to meet at ten o'clock at the east gate of Shinagawa station.'

'Ten o'clock in the morning?' I ask –

'Of course,' she says. 'Of course.'

'And so when Ryuko didn't come home, what did you do?'

'I waited until the next morning,' says Mrs. Midorikawa. 'And then, first thing, I went straight to see Kodaira.'

'You went to see him at his home?' I ask. 'Where is it?'

'In Hanezawamachi,' she replies. 'In Shibuya Ward.'

'And what did he say when you went to see him?'

'He lied to me,' spits Mrs. Midorikawa. 'He said Ryuko had never turned up to meet him at Shinagawa station.'

'Let me just check this,' I say. 'When you went to see Kodaira in Shibuya it was the seventh of August?'

'Yes,' says Mrs. Midorikawa.

'And you went to see him because Ryuko hadn't come home the night before?'

'Yes.'

'But Kodaira told you Ryuko had not shown up to meet him at Shinagawa station at ten o'clock on the morning before?'

'Yes,' says Mrs. Midorikawa. 'He lied to me.'

'They all lie,' says her other daughter.

Now I take out an envelope from my jacket pocket. I open the envelope. I take out the piece of newspaper found in the pocket of the skirt of the pinafore dress on *my* body. Now I place the newspaper advertisement on the table before Mrs. Midorikawa –

I ask, 'Does this mean anything to you?'

Mrs. Midorikawa looks down at the newspaper advertisement. Mrs. Midorikawa pushes it away. Mrs. Midorikawa looks up at me. Mrs. Midorikawa says, 'My daughter was not a whore.'

*

Inspector Kai and Room #1 have been busy. Room #1 have an address for Kodaira Yoshio. Inspector Kai and Room #1 have sent two men to the address in Hanezawamachi, Shibuya Ward. Room #1 have stationed two pairs of detectives near the address –

No escape. No escape. No escape. No escape . . .

'It is Kodaira's sister's house,' Inspector Kai is telling us. 'His younger sister's house. He lives there with his wife and son . . .'

Chief Kita knows Kai wants to bring Kodaira in now –

No escape. No escape. No escape. No escape . . .

The chief asks, 'What about his place of work?'

'It is Laundry Barracks #589,' says Inspector Kai. 'Just as he told the mother, but he's not a cook. He's been working in the laundry since March this year. In Shinagawa, on the ocean side . . .'

Now Adachi glances up from his notes. Adachi looks at me –

'And we've both seen this before, detective. Remember?'

The chief asks, 'What shifts does he work at the laundry?'

'He's been working on nights this month,' replies Kai.

Adachi still looking at me. Adachi still watching my face –

'Did you find that file, inspector? The Miyazaki file . . .'

The chief asks, 'Do we have his family's address?'

'Nikkō, Tochigi Prefecture,' says Inspector Kai –

No escape. No escape. No escape. No escape . . .

The chief says, 'Arrest him tomorrow at noon.'

No escape. In the half-light, no escape at all.

*

I take a different route back to Atago, through Hibiya Park and out onto Hibiya-dōri. The branches of the trees hang low in the hot and overcast light, the leaves on the branches covered in dirt and dust. There were statues in this park before the war turned against us, when there were heroes to celebrate and metal to spare. There were fountains too, when there were hours to play and water to spare. Restaurants and tea-houses, flower exhibitions and symphony concerts, tennis courts and a baseball ground, before they converted it into vegetable gardens and anti-aircraft batteries –

Ton-ton. Ton-ton. Ton-ton . . .

I queue for a streetcar at Uchisaiwai-chō, just down the road from the Imperial Hotel; the Imperial Hotel where there are still heroes to celebrate and metal to spare, hours to play and water to spare. The old woman queuing next to me is bent double with the weight of the box tied to her back. The old woman telling the queue the story of a small boy in Hongō who waited and waited for his chocolate ration to come and was so excited when the chocolate finally came that he could not take his eyes off the chocolate, that he did not look up from the chocolate, that he did not see the streetcar coming. The queue for our streetcar says nothing. The queue just stands and waits, watching for a streetcar that never comes, listening to the hammering that never ceases –

Ton-ton. Ton-ton . . .

*

I am back in the toilets of Atago police station. I have vomited again. *Black bile again.* I stand over the sink. I spit. I wipe my mouth. I turn on the tap. I wash my face. Now I look up into that mirror again –

I don't want to remember. I don't want to remember . . .

Ishida is waiting for me beside our banner –

'Did you find Hayashi Jo?' I ask him –

'No,' says Ishida. 'He's resigned.'

'When did Hayashi resign?'

'Late yesterday evening.'

'Where is he now?'

'No one knows.'

'Good work,' I tell him. 'Dismissed.'

I wait until Ishida has stepped into our borrowed office and then I run back to the toilets. I vomit again. *Brown bile.* I walk over to the sink. I spit again. I wipe my mouth. I turn on the tap. I wash my face again. Now I stare into that mirror –

I don't want to remember . . .

No Hayashi. No Fujita –

You can tell which are the men from Room #1 and which are the men from Room #2 by the looks on their faces. *No Fujita.* The anticipation on the faces of Room #1, the resignation on the faces of Room #2. *No Fujita.* Room #1 have a name for their suspect. *No Fujita.* Room #2 still have no name for their victim. *No Fujita.* Detectives Hattori, Takeda, Sanada and Shimoda are sat at the very back of the room. *No Fujita.* Detectives Nishi, Kimura and Ishida sat at the front. *No Fujita.* None of the men from the Second Team are smiling in anticipation of an arrest as they listen to Inspector Kai –

'But the mother and sisters had already identified her *haramaki* by its five darned holes and given us details of the whitlow scar on her left thumb, so she was then formally identified by her mother as Midorikawa Ryuko, aged seventeen of Meguro Ward . . .'

Inspector Kai updating Room #1 and Room #2 about the identification of the body, about the life of the victim, about the name of the suspect and the plan for his arrest at noon tomorrow. The uniforms from Atago, Meguro and Mita have not been invited this evening. This meeting is just for detectives; detectives only –

'And our two teams of detectives in Shibuya have just reported that the suspect left for his shift as usual at 5:30 p.m. tonight and then arrived at the laundry before 6 p.m. . . .'

I am stood next to Inspector Kai at the front of the room beside Inspectors Kanehara and Adachi –

I am cursing Inspector Kai . . .

'Naturally the detectives from Room #2 will also be able to question the suspect Kodaira about the second body found at Shiba Park and to which we hope he will also provide an identity and a confession and thus spare the blushes of Room #2 again . . .'

There is laughter from one half of the room –

There is resentment from the other half –

'I'm just joking,' laughs Kai. 'We're all comrades now.'

There is more laughter and more jeering, fists on desktops and boots on floorboards, backs slapped and hair ruffled –

In anticipation, in excitement –

'Attention!' shouts Kai –

Their fists by their sides, their boots together now . . .

'Bow!' he shouts –

Backs straight and hair flat . . .

'Dismissed!'

They file out . . .

And I run out of the meeting room and down the stairs to vomit in the toilets. I vomit in the toilets of Atago police station a third time. *Yellow bile.* I spit. I turn on the tap again. I wash my face. I look up into that mirror again. I stare into that mirror –

I can't forget. In the half-light, I can't forget . . .

Adachi is waiting for me outside the toilets –

'We've both seen this before, detective . . .'

Adachi grabs my arm. 'Where's Fujita?'

'Did you find that file, inspector?'

'I sent him to the Salon Matsu in Kanda,' I lie but I don't ask him why; why Adachi wants Fujita. I don't ask him why because I turn back into the toilets. Back to vomit. *Grey bile.* Back to the sink. Back to the tap. Back to the mirror –

In the half-light . . .

Adachi is gone but Nishi and Kimura are waiting for me in the corridor. They are hot and they are dirty. They know I have forgotten about them. They are tired and they are angry –

'There are no records of a Takahashi of Zōshigaya,' says Nishi. 'Because there are no records of anyone because all their records were lost when their ward office burnt down . . .'

'But did you go to the address in Zōshigaya?'

Kimura nods and Nishi says, 'Yes.'

I ask them both, 'And . . .?'

'It's cinders,' says Nishi.

I ask, 'Have either of you seen Detective Fujita today?'

Kimura shakes his head and Nishi says, 'No.'

'Right then,' I say and I take out the envelope from my pocket and hand them the piece of newspaper. 'Find out which paper this advertisement is from and the date it was run. Then, last thing tonight, before they pull this man in tomorrow, you two are coming with me to Kanda to help me wake up the ladies of the Salon Matsu.'

Kimura nods. Nishi nods. They both bow. They both turn to leave. I wait until they've gone and then I run back to the toilets of Atago police station to vomit in the toilets –

But this time I do not vomit –

Nothing comes up.

*

Everything is falling into place. Back to Shimbashi to give Senju the name. *Everything is turning out fine.* Back to Shimbashi to get some Calmotin. *Falling into place.* Back through the pots and the pans, through the knives and the spoons. *Turning out fine.* Back through the suits and the sardines, the tinned fruit and old army boots –

'Red apple to my lips, blue sky silently watching . . .'

But tonight there are many more pale-suited goons out here, many more patterned shirts and American sunglasses in the alleys and the lanes, in the shadows and the arches –

Trains screaming overhead . . .

Eight goons tonight at the foot of the stairs that lead up to his office, their legs apart and their hands in jackets, with twitches in their cheeks and pinpricks for pupils –

In the half-light . . .

His office door is closed, his office lights out tonight –

I straighten my jacket. I ask them, 'Is the boss in?'

'And who the *fuck* are you?' asks one of them –

I tell him, 'Inspector Minami of Metro HQ.'

This goon tells that goon to go up the stairs and so that goon goes up the stairs and taps on the door to the office and then that goon comes back down the stairs and whispers in the ear of this goon and so now this goon says, 'You're to wait, Minami of Metro HQ.'

No dice tonight. No calls of odd, even and play . . .

Now the door to the office opens. A foreigner, an American, a Victor, comes down the stairs. At the foot of the stairs, this man turns to me and says, 'Good evening, inspector . . .'

'Good evening, sir,' I reply.

The foreigner, this American, this Victor, he winks at me now and Senju's goons all laugh along –

'Up you go now, Minami of Metro HQ,' says one of the goons as the Victor disappears –

And up I go now –

Senju Akira is sat cross-legged in the dark with only the street lights illuminating the sweat on his skull and the sheen on his skin; Senju Akira naked except for a traditional loincloth –

'You better have a name for me,' whispers Senju Akira. 'Or you won't be leaving here again tonight . . .'

I curse him and I curse myself . . .

I kneel before him. I say, 'Hayashi Jo of the *Minpo* paper.'

Senju says nothing. *His eyes on me.* Senju says nothing –

My face to the floor, I say, 'He was seen with Nodera.'

His eyes on me. Nothing. *His eyes on me.* Nothing –

'They were drinking together in the New Oasis.'

His eyes on me. Nothing. *His eyes on me . . .*

'The night before the hit,' I tell him –

In the dark. Senju shifts his weight. In the dark. Senju hisses, 'Get out, detective! Go now! Quickly before I change my mind . . .'

I slide back on my knees towards the door, the stairs –

'Red apple to my lips, blue sky silently watching . . .'

In the dark, Senju is getting to his feet. In the dark, Senju is rising, saying, 'You want your drugs, you be here tomorrow night.'

*

I open the door to the borrowed office at Atago. *Fujita still not here.* They are all asleep now. *Fujita gone again.* I put my head down on my desk. *But Fujita will be back.* I still can't sleep. *Fujita is safe now.* Tomorrow I will sleep. *Tomorrow Fujita will return. Tomorrow . . .*

Everything will fall into place. Everything will turn out fine –

Tomorrow Kai and the First Team will make their arrest –

Tomorrow the killer will confess to both crimes –

Tomorrow everything will fall into place –

Everything will turn out fine –

Everything will end –

'Boss . . . Boss . . .'

I open my eyes –

'The advertisement is from the *Asahi* newspaper,' says Nishi. 'It ran on the nineteenth of July . . .'

'Thank you,' I tell him –

Nishi smiles. Nishi asks, 'So is it time to go and wake up the ladies of the Salon Matsu yet?'

*

The streets are dark and silent now, the heat heavy still, as we walk up Hibiya-dōri and show our passes again and again as we walk in front of the illuminated Dai-Ichi Assurance Building, Emperor MacArthur's Headquarters opposite the darkened Imperial Palace of the old Emperor, as we walk on up past the Imperial Theatre and the Meiji Seimei building, then the Yūsen building and the Kaijō building, to Marunouchi and Ōtemachi –

The old Mitsubishi Town . . .

Here most of the modern steel and concrete buildings are still standing, just the odd ones gutted here and there; here where the

Victors rule from their offices and their barracks; here in the new heart of Occupied Tokyo –

Same as the old heart . . .

Now Kimura, Nishi and I cut under the tracks of Tokyo station to Kanda –

Here, less than a mile from the Emperors old and new, few of the wooden buildings are still standing. There were train yards here once. Family businesses. Bicycle shops. Homes. Now there are only burnt-out ruins and makeshift shelters, rare clusters of old timber houses that were spared and sudden alleys of one-storey offices that have sprung up among the fields of weeds and mountains of ashes, the braziers and lanterns, the guitars and girls, the songs and shouts –

'Asobu . . .? Asobu . . .? Asobu . . .? Asobu . . .?'

From the alleyways and the doorways with their permed hair and painted faces, they coo and they call, luring and then leading their catches back to the shabby little buildings where their foreign names and Japanese prices are written on placards or posters –

Off-limits. Off-limits. Off-limits. Off-limits . . .

The Salon Matsu is just another shabby little building stained with dirt among all the other shabby little buildings stained with dirt, an unlit pink neon sign the only new thing here. I slide open the cracked glass door. There is a young Korean man sat in the *genkan*, before a split *noren* curtain. The Korean has a pageboy haircut and spectacles, loud-coloured trousers and a grey undershirt –

He sees us. He stands up. He starts to speak –

'Shut up!' I tell him. 'Police raid!'

I tell Kimura to wait with the Korean in the *genkan* and then I lead Nishi through the split curtain into the kitchen-cum-waiting room where three Japanese women are sat with their blouses wide open and their skirts up round their thighs, fanning themselves –

They look up at us. They sigh. They roll their eyes –

'What do you want this time?' asks the oldest –

I tell her, 'We're from Tokyo Metro HQ.'

'So what?' she says. 'We've paid.'

I offer her a cigarette. She takes it. I light it for her. I ask her, 'Are you the *mama* here then?'

'So what if I am?' she asks, and then she winks and says, 'You after a free ride?'

I take out the envelope. I take out the clipping from the *Asahi*. I show her the advertisement. I ask her, 'Are you still hiring?'

'Why?' she laughs. 'You're too ugly even for here.'

The other girls laugh. I hand out more cigarettes –

I ask her, 'Do you do the interviews yourself?'

'Why?' she asks again. 'So what if I do?'

'Come on, play the game,' I tell her. 'Answer the questions and then we can all go home.'

She snorts. She says, '*Home*? Where's my *home*? This is my *home*, officer. You like it?'

'Listen,' I tell her. 'The body of a young girl was found up in Shiba Park, up behind Zōjōji. It had been there a while and it is impossible to identify . . .'

Now they are listening to me, smoking my cigarettes, sweating like pigs and fanning their thighs; the pictures in their heads, the pictures behind their eyes –

The Dead . . .

'This advertisement was in one of her pockets, so we are here to see if you can identify her, help us put a name to her body . . .'

'So how did she die?' asks one of the girls –

The picture in her head, behind her eyes . . .

'Raped and then throttled,' I say –

The pictures of the Dead . . .

There is silence here now, behind the split curtain in this kitchen-cum-waiting room, silence but for the giggles and the groans from upstairs rooms, the panting and the pounding –

Ton-ton-ton-ton-ton-ton-ton-ton-ton-ton . . .

'Who says she came here first?' asks the *mama*. 'Poor thing might have been on her way here when . . .'

'That's what I've come to find out, to talk to you about . . .'

'But you haven't given us a description,' she says. 'How would I know if she was here or not?'

I ask her again, 'So do you do the interviews yourself?'

'Not just me,' she says. 'Me and Mr. Kim do them.'

'Is that him outside?' I ask her. 'Mr. Kim?'

'He's a Kim,' she laughs. 'But not him.'

'Where's the real Mr. Kim then?'

'He'll be here tomorrow.'

'Where is he now?'

'Recruiting.'

'Where?'

'Where? Where? Where?' she laughs and rolls her eyes. She puts out her cigarette. She picks up a mirror. She primps her perm –

I think about her all the time. I think about her all the time . . .

'Ninety per cent of all the girls that come through our door have come from the International Palace,' she says. 'Now that doesn't mean your dead girl did, but it doesn't mean she didn't . . .'

I turn to Detective Nishi. I tell him, 'Please describe the body and the clothing of the victim for this lady.'

But Detective Nishi is miles away, lost between the breasts and thighs of these girls. Now Nishi blushes, reaches for his notebook and stammers, 'The victim was approximately seventeen or eighteen years old with shoulder-length permed hair, wearing a yellow and dark-blue striped pinafore dress, a white half-sleeved chemise, dyed-pink socks and white canvas shoes with red rubber soles . . .'

'We're all corpses then,' laughs the *mama*. 'All ghosts . . .'

'It could be anyone,' says another one of the girls –

Made of tears. Made of tears. Made of tears . . .

'She's all of us,' says the *mama*. 'Every woman in Japan.'

5

August 19, 1946

Tokyo, 87°, moonless & cloudy

The three of us leave the Salon Matsu, leave Kanda and walk back towards Headquarters. I itch and I scratch. *Gari-gari*. This time we walk back along the other side of the tracks, the Nihonbashi side, on the opposite side to the old Imperial Palace and the new. I itch and I scratch. *Gari-gari*. This side we don't have to show our notebooks –

There are no Victors here. No white stars. No lights at all –

From Sotobori to the Yaesu entrance of Tokyo station –

Five trucks in a row. Five trucks full of Formosans –

But not all Formosans, some are Japanese . . .

Kimura looks at Nishi. Nishi looks at me –

No radio. No telephone. No car . . .

'Boss?' shouts Nishi. 'What are you doing, Boss? Boss?'

I am walking towards the five trucks. I am taking out my police notebook. I am holding up my ID. I am approaching the passenger door of the first truck. I'm reaching up and opening the door of the truck and shouting, 'I want you out of these trucks now!'

But now I'm looking up at a submachine gun –

Skin to the metal, metal to the skin . . .

Fingers on the trigger of the gun –

Bullet through my skin . . .

I am waiting to die –

Praying . . .

But the bullet never comes; not yesterday, not today and not tomorrow; not over there and not back here –

I can't die. I can't die . . .

It's not a bullet to the gut that sends me sprawling back across the ground, it's a boot to the gut as the trucks speed away down Sotobori-dōri towards Shimbashi –

Towards Senju Akira –

I'm already dead.

By the time I have got back to my feet, by the time Kimura, Nishi and I have started to run, by the time we have reached Headquarters, by the time we have repeated and reported our story four or five times, by the time we have been given a telephone that works, by the time we have requested reinforcements, by the time the reinforcements have been raised, by the time the reinforcements have been deployed, by the time we all get down to the Shimbashi Market –

It's too late . . .

The Formosan trucks have been and gone –

The shots have been fired –

The blood spilled –

The battle over –

For now –

'*Kuso* Formosan shits,' Senju's men, the former Matsuda men, all cursing. '*Kuso* American shits. *Kuso* police shits. *Kuso* Formosan shits. *Kuso* American shits. *Kuso* police shits. *Kuso* . . .'

'*Kuso* . . . *Kuso* . . . *Kuso* . . . *Kuso* . . .'

Two dead. Eight injured –

But not Senju Akira –

Never Senju –

Senju with a short sword in one hand and a pistol in the other, his sleeveless white undershirt and the top of his *haramaki* spotted with fresh blood –

'Lucky I was elsewhere on business,' says Senju. 'A stray bullet here, a stray bullet there and then where would we be?'

Senju takes off his American sunglasses now –

Senju stood before his men, before his troops; the Shōgun of Shimbashi beneath the night sky, outside his emergency field headquarters; the emperor of all he surveys –

'Where would you be, detective?'

I shrug my shoulders but I do not reply to him. I say nothing –

Nishi, Kimura and half of Atago are here with me tonight –

I am here as a policeman tonight. I am not here to beg . . .

'More to the point,' continues Senju. 'Where *were* the police? Nowhere, that's where. These Koreans, Formosans and Chinese, they try to walk all over us and where are you? Nowhere . . .

'And what do you do? Nothing . . .' he sighs –

I curse him. I curse him. I curse him . . .

'Nothing but beg . . .'

The stall-holders of the New Life Market, all risen from their sleep, roused from their dreams, are lining up to give Senju their support and their supplies for the coming war, bowing as they offer him their best sake, meat and polished white rice –

I am here as a policeman . . .

'Because if I've got money, if I've got cigarettes, if I've got alcohol or some special food in, then I can always find a policeman, I can always count on meeting one or tripping over one grovelling around on his hands and his knees, begging for sleeping pills . . .'

And I curse myself . . .

'The Formosans are hardly walking all over you,' I tell him. 'They just want stalls in your New Life Market, just like they had stalls in your old Black Market, but you won't give them any . . .'

But Senju is not listening. Senju is just speaking –

'They act like the Victors but they won nothing! Beat no one! They didn't fight and they didn't win. They just got lucky! Lucky to be allowed over here and lucky to still be here . . .'

'There weren't only Formosans in those trucks,' I tell him. 'There were Japanese too; I know because I saw them myself.'

'When you were taking their money to keep away?'

'No one wants another war,' I tell him. 'Not now.'

'*Another* war?' spits Senju. 'It's the *same* war . . .'

I shake my head. 'GHQ will close you down.'

'See?' he laughs. 'It's always the same war!'

'Then the Formosans will have won it.'

'The Formosans win?' laughs Senju again. 'Never, and I'll tell you why, detective. Thousands of people depend on this market. If I let the Formosans or the Yankees close me down or drive me out then this market will die and if this market dies then so will the thousands of people who depend on it and depend on me . . .'

'If they close you down,' I say. 'You've lost.'

'Never! Never! Never!' shouts Senju. 'I have never lost. I have never been defeated and I never will be. Not by the *kuso* Formosans! Not by the *kuso* Koreans! Not by the *kuso* Chinese! Not by the *kuso* Yankees and not by the *kuso* police and the likes of you!

'I've never lost! Never been defeated! And I never will be!'

'So what are you going do?' I ask him –

'You kill one of mine,' says Senju –

'I'll kill ten of yours, I swear!'

I look up at the night sky above us all. There are no stars out tonight. I shake my head again. I bow to him. I start to walk away –

'See you later, detective,' he shouts. 'Don't forget . . .'

Nishi and Kimura following behind me –

'Because I never forget,' he says –

'I never forget a debt; not to the living and not to the dead.'

*

Men talk about the dead in their sleep. Men remember the dead in their sleep. Their fathers, their mothers, their wives and their lovers. Their family and friends, their colleagues and comrades. There are over one million urns containing the ashes of the war dead still unclaimed by their bereaved families. These urns contain the ashes from all ranks of the military and naval war dead. The First and Second Demobilization Bureaus who are responsible for the issuance of death notices and for the care of the dead say that many of the ashes have been transferred to their institution in a haphazard fashion and they are increasingly unable to verify whether all the ashes and remains of the war dead in their care actually belong to those of military personnel. The Bureaus are also encountering numerous difficulties in returning the ashes of the dead to their relatives who have often moved from their former addresses or had them destroyed. Moreover, the absence of claimants is usually as a result of death –

Their stomachs empty, their dreams lost . . .

Up until this June, the Demobilization Bureaus also received a grant of fifteen yen for taking care of each individual urn. However, since June, these institutions have been deprived of this grant. Lack of these finances has made it impossible for the institutions to order the construction of new boxes for depositing the ashes. Presently, new boxes are still being made out of lumber in stock but the day will soon come when the ashes of the war dead will have to be returned to their relatives in ordinary plain brown wrapping paper –

They are hungry, they are starving . . .

Men talk about the dead in their sleep. Men remember the dead in their sleep; their fathers, their mothers, their wives and their lovers; their family and friends, their colleagues and comrades. Men talk about ghosts and demons in their sleep –

Their masters gone . . .

I have sat in this borrowed chair with my head on this borrowed desk through the rest of the night. I have closed my eyes but I have not slept. I open my eyes but I do not wake. I read their reports. I read old newspapers. Now the dawn is coming up but it still feels old. Dead. Like the last light at the beginning of a long night. Lost and dead. Not a new morning. No new mornings here. I sit up in my borrowed chair. I look around. No Fujita. I close my eyes again –

Tonight I will sleep. Tonight I will sleep. Tonight I will . . .

I open them. I look up at the uniform standing over at me –

The uniformed officer has a telegram in his hand.

*

Four officers from Takanawa are unbuttoning their uniforms. *The mosquitoes circle.* The four officers strip down to their underwear. *The mosquitoes attack.* The four officers jump into the Shiba Canal. *The water stinks.* The four officers swim over to the wooden door floating in the canal. *The water black.* The four officers guide the door towards the side of the canal where we are all stood. *In the sun.* The chief nods. *In the heat.* The four officers turn over the door. *I curse.* The body of a drowned man, naked and bound to the door –

Hayashi Jo naked and bound to the back of the door . . .

Bound with his hands and feet nailed to the door –

His hands and feet then nailed to the door . . .

The door then thrown into the canal –

Hayashi face down in the water . . .

His mouth and lungs full –

He drowns as he floats . . .

Bound and nailed –

I kneel before him. I say, 'Hayashi Jo of the Minpo paper.'

*

Was it Senju or Fujita? Nobody knows his name. Everybody knows his name. *Fujita or Senju?* Nobody cares. Everybody cares. *Senju or Fujita?* The day is night. The night is day. *Fujita or Senju?* Black is white. White is black. *Senju or Fujita?* The men are the women. The

116

women are the men. *Fujita or Senju?* The brave are the frightened. The frightened are the brave. *Senju or Fujita?* The strong are the weak. The weak are the strong. *Fujita or Senju?* The good are the bad. The bad are the good. *Senju or Fujita?* Communists should be set free. Communists should be locked up. *Fujita or Senju?* Strikes are legal. Strikes are illegal. *Senju or Fujita?* Democracy is good. Democracy is bad. *Fujita or Senju?* The aggressor is the victim. The victim is the aggressor. *Senju or Fujita?* The winners are the losers. The losers are the winners. *Fujita or Senju?* Japan lost the war. Japan won the war. *Senju or Fujita?* The living are the dead. The dead are the living. *Fujita or Senju?* I am alive. I am dead –

Senju or Fujita? Fujita or Senju?

I am one of the lucky ones.

*

Two dead and eight injured down at Shimbashi; the body in the Shiba Canal; it has been a bad night and a bad morning. And the Victors want answers; the Victors have summoned the chief to the Public Safety Division. Now the chief wants answers; now the chief has summoned us all back to Metropolitan Police Headquarters –

The heads of all sections. The heads of all rooms . . .

'There will be no gang wars,' says the chief. 'I'll ask for the closure of all the markets. I'll ask for Eighth Army reinforcements from GHQ. But there will be no gang wars in Tokyo . . .

'They think they can do what they want,' the chief continues. 'But they don't appreciate the help we give them. They don't appreciate the protection we give them. They don't appreciate the trouble we spare them. And all I ask for is peace.'

'But it's not our local gangs who started this,' says Kanehara. 'It's the Formosans and the mainland Chinese muscling in . . .'

'And the Koreans,' adds Inspector Adachi –

'And the Americans are protecting them,' says Kanehara. 'They let these *immigrant* people do what they want while they punish the ordinary *tekiya* who are just trying to run their stalls . . .'

'And we can't step in,' says Adachi. 'Because if the police are seen to step in on the side of the Japanese against the Formosans or the Koreans then we risk being purged for mistreating *immigrants* and reverting to our old Japanese ways, ignoring human rights and abandoning democratic freedoms but, if not us, if not the police, then who is there left but the gangs themselves to protect the human rights and democratic principles, the lives and livelihoods of the *tekiya*?'

'Divide and conquer,' says Kanehara. 'Divide and rule.'

'And I know all that and I will tell them that,' says the chief. 'But you tell your men in the gangs that they'll have to choose . . .'

He is fighting for his rights, fighting for his freedoms . . .

'Either open war,' says the chief. 'Or open markets.'

*

They will find Hayashi's name. They will visit Hayashi's address. They will talk to Hayashi's family. They will visit Hayashi's office. They will talk to Hayashi's colleagues. They will find Hayashi's stories. They will read Hayashi's stories. They will talk to Hayashi's contacts. They will find Hayashi's notes. They will read Hayashi's notes. They will talk to Hayashi's snitches and they will tell them –

They will tell them my name and they will come for me –

Just like we have come today for Kodaira Yoshio –

Nothing moves on the streets of Shibuya. It is almost noon on the hottest day of the year. Nothing moves outside the house in Hanezawamachi. Ninety-one degrees in the shade now. Room #2 are here as back-up for Room #1. Pairs of men on every corner. Down every alleyway. In every doorway. Inspector Kai is in command. Inspector Kai has his whistle in his hand. Inspector Kai looks at his watch again. *Chiku-taku.* Inspector Kai puts his whistle to his lips –

Through the front door. Up the steps. Into the second floor room where Kodaira Yoshio is sleeping naked beneath a mosquito net, his wife covering her breasts, reaching for their child –

Kodaira Yoshio dragged out from under the net by his feet onto the mats and back down the stairs –

Kodaira pulling on his trousers. Kodaira pulling on his shirt. Kodaira buttoning up his trousers. Buttoning up his shirt as he goes, putting on his army boots –

In the back of the car. *Another middle-aged man.* Kodaira rubs the top of his skull. Kodaira scratches his balls. In the back of the car. *Face gaunt.* Kodaira blinks. Kodaira rubs his eyes. In the back of the car. *Hair thinning.* Kodaira grins. Kodaira laughs. In the back of the car. *Kodaira looks like Kai, Kodaira looks like Kanehara and he looks like me . . .*

Like me . . .

There are press all over the road and the steps outside the Atago police station. *Kodaira accepts a cigarette.* The car turns back onto Sakurada-dōri and then right onto Meguro-dōri. *Kodaira chats about the weather.* The car turns right again onto Yamate-dōri and then follows the Meguro River along to the Meguro police station –

Kodaira speaks with maturity. He speaks with authority –

This is where Kodaira Yoshio will be interrogated –

Kodaira is grinning now. Kodaira laughing –

This is where Kodaira will confess.

But the Meguro police are angry. The Meguro police have been used for legwork since the two bodies were found in Shiba Park. Now the Meguro police are being kicked out of their own offices. In the dark and out of the loop, the Meguro police sulk and sweat –

Two men from Room #1 take Kodaira up the stairs –

They give him tea. They give him a cigarette –

Then they leave him to drink and to smoke –

They leave him to wait and to think.

Chief Inspector Kanehara, Inspector Kai, and the rest of Room #1 take over another office down the corridor, clearing desks and emptying drawers, moving files and stealing pencils –

The Meguro police just watching and cursing, left sulking and sweating, in the dark and out of the loop –

I take an empty chair at the back by the window as Kanehara and Kai outline the strategy for the interview, the questions they will ask and the questions they won't –

Then Adachi is back, back with a telegram in his hand and a smile on his lips, 'This just got here from Nikkō. He's killed before.'

'And we've both seen this before, detective. Remember . . . ?'

Kai is on his feet now. Kai saying, 'Come on! Let's go!'

'Did you find that file, inspector? The Miyazaki file . . .'

'Slowly, slowly,' smiles Kanehara. 'Step by step.'

*

I follow Adachi, Kanehara and Kai. Down the corridor. Into the interrogation room. No one invites me. No one refuses me. I sit by the door. I say nothing. The room is bright. Bare but for a table and six chairs. Adachi, Kanehara and Kai sit across the table from Kodaira, the stenographer to one side with a pen and some paper –

Kodaira Yoshio with his hands on the table, smiling –

Inspector Kai asks him, 'When were you born?'

'In the thirty-eighth year of the reign of the Emperor Meiji,' says Kodaira. 'In the first month, on the twenty-eighth day.'

That is the twenty-eighth of January, 1905 . . .

Kai asks, 'And where were you born?'

'Tochigi Prefecture,' says Kodaira.

'Where in Tochigi Prefecture?'

'Kami Tsuga-gun, Nikkō-chō, Ōaza-Hosō.'

'Are you the eldest son of your family?'

'No,' he says. 'I'm the sixth son.'

'Is your father still alive?'

'No.'

'How did your father die?'

'Brain haemorrhage.'

'And when did he die?'

'Ten years ago.'

Kai nods. Kai asks, 'What kind of work did your father do?'

'Well, he used to have land, a farm and an inn,' says Kodaira. 'But he drank heavily, bought women and gambled and lost it all.'

'So he was a bankrupt?' asks Kai. 'Unemployed?'

'No,' says Kodaira. 'He always worked. His last job was working as an oil-feeder at an iron-railings factory . . .'

Kai asks, 'What about your eldest brother?'

'He's dead too,' says Kodaira.

'When did he die?'

'This year.'

'And what was his job?'

'Nothing steady,' laughs Kodaira. 'He used to work in the copper-smelting factory in Nikkō. Then he left that and came to Tokyo but I don't know what he did here. I never saw him in Tokyo.'

Kai asks, 'So who is the head of your family now?'

'It'll be my other elder brother, I suppose,' shrugs Kodaira. 'But I never see them. I never really go back there now.'

'But you still have family in Nikkō-chō?'

Kodaira nods. Kodaira says, 'Yes.'

'Let's talk a little bit about you,' says Inspector Kai now.

'You were born in Nikkō-chō? Is that where you went to school?'

'I graduated from school in Nikkō,' says Kodaira. 'Yes.'

'And then what did you do?' asks Kai. 'After school?'

'I left home and I moved down here to Tokyo.'

'And so when was that? How old were you?'

'I was about fourteen years old, I think.'

'So that would be when?' calculates Inspector Kai. 'About the seventh year of Taishō. Does that sound about right?'

'It sounds right,' agrees Kodaira. 'But I can't remember exactly. I know I was about fourteen though.'

'And so where did you work?'

'At a steel works in Ikebukuro,' he says. 'The Toyo Metals Corporation. But I didn't work there for very long . . .'

'Why was that?' asks Kai. 'Were you fired?'

'No,' he laughs. 'I'd found a better job.'

'Which was what? Where?'

'The Kameya Grocery.'

'The one in Ginza?'

'Yes.'

'That's a very famous store,' says Inspector Kai. 'And so how long did you work there?'

'Just two years.'

'Why?'

'I just got bored of working at the Grocery,' says Kodaira. 'The hours were too long, the pay was too poor and the work itself was just fetching and carrying, lifting boxes and so on . . .'

Kai asks, 'And so what did you do then?'

'I went back to Nikkō.'

'Back home?'

'Yes.'

'And so what year is this now?' calculates Kai again. 'When you left Tokyo? Three years later? Tenth year of Taishō?'

'Round about then,' agrees Kodaira. 'Yes.'

'And did you have a job back home?'

'Yes,' he says again. 'I worked for the Furukawa Company.'

'This is the big copper-smelting works, yes?'

'Where my brother had worked, yes.'

'How long did you work there?'

'I've worked there twice now,' says Kodaira. 'The first time I worked there until I enlisted.'

'When was that?'

'That was the sixth month of the twelfth year of Taishō.'

'1923 then,' says Kai. 'Before the Great Earthquake.'

'Yes,' laughs Kodaira. 'I had a lucky escape.'

'Were you in the army or the navy?'

'I volunteered for the navy,' he says. 'And I enlisted in the Marine Corps at Yokosuka.'

'As what?'

'First I was trained as an engineer on the *Yakumo* training ship, then I was stationed on the warships *Yamashiro, Kongō* and *Manshu* and I was also on the *I-Gō* submarine.'

'You were always an engineer?'

'No, no, no,' he says. 'Later I was an actual fighting marine. I was a member of the Ryojun Defence Force and then with the Rikusen Tai marines stationed in Shandong.'

'And so you saw combat then?'

'Of course,' he laughs.

'So you must have fought during the Jinan Incident?'

'Of course,' he says again. 'During the Jinan Incident itself I was part of the initial assault on the Northern Railway Depot and then I was part of the defence of the Nissei Bōseki Company . . .'

'And so you must have made a number of kills?'

'Naturally,' he smiles. 'In Jinan I bayoneted six Chinese soldiers to death and then there were others . . .'

'How long did you serve?'

'I served my six years and then I was discharged as a petty officer, first class, and I received the White Paulownia medal of the Order of the Rising Sun.'

Inspector Kai says, 'Congratulations.'

Kodaira bows his head.

Inspector Kai hands Kodaira a cigarette and then we all stand up and leave him to smoke –

In peace . . .

In the corridor outside the interrogation room, Adachi stares at the wall; Kanehara reads the telegram from Nikkō; Kai smokes –

Then Chief Inspector Adachi turns to me and smiles and asks, 'You served in China too, didn't you, inspector?'

'Yes,' I tell him. 'I was in the army.'

'And how old are you now?'

'I'm forty-one years old.'

'The same age then.'

*

The light is already beginning to fade now. The shadows falling from the wall to the floor. Kodaira has finished his cigarette. Kodaira is looking at his fingernails. I sit back down by the door again. I say nothing again. Adachi, Kanehara and Kai sit back opposite Kodaira –

Inspector Kanehara leans forward in his chair and asks him, 'So when you were discharged, you went back to Nikkō again?'

'Yes,' he says. 'I went back to work for Furukawa.'

'And how was civilian life after the navy?'

'It was good for a time . . .'

'And why was that?'

'I got a wife.'

Kanehara asks, 'And so this was your first wife?'

'Yes. My first.'

'Not your present wife?'

'No,' says Kodaira.

'So how did you meet your first wife?'

'The manager of the factory introduced her to me,' he says. 'She was his sister's child, his niece.'

'How old were you both?'

'She was twenty-one and I was maybe twenty-eight.'

'And so what happened?'

'We lived together for about six months,' he says. 'But then she went back to her parents.'

'Why was that?'

'She went to help them plant rice but she never came back.'

'Why not?'

'Because her family wanted me to divorce her.'

'Because?'

'Because I'd had an affair with another woman and this woman had become pregnant.'

'So you must have been happy then to divorce your wife?'

There is something now, something in his eyes . . .

'No,' he says. 'I was humiliated.'

123

In his eyes something flashes, in his eyes . . .
'And so what did you do?'
Torchlight in the dark . . .
'You already know.'
Death . . .

Inspector Kanehara looks down at the piece of paper on the table before him. Kanehara nods and then says, 'But please tell us again. In your own words. Tell us what happened . . .'

'I went back to their house.'

'Whose house was this?'

'Her family's house.'

'When was this?'

'Midnight on the first day of the seventh month of the seventh year of the reign of the Emperor Shōwa . . .'

July 1, 1932 . . .

'And . . .'

'I left my own house at nine o'clock in the morning. I went over to the house of my wife's family. I checked the house out carefully in the daylight and then I waited until nightfall.'

'And . . .'

'I broke into their house at midnight.'

'And . . .'

'I went from room to room.'

'And . . .'

'I hit them as they slept.'

'With?'

'An iron bar.'

'You still remember the iron bar?' asks Inspector Kanehara. 'Can you describe this iron bar for me?'

'Of course, I can remember it,' says Kodaira. 'The iron bar was about eighty centimetres long, five centimetres in diameter and it weighed about four kilograms.'

'How many of her family did you hit?'

'I think it was either six or seven.'

'How many did you kill?'

'Just her father.'

Inspector Kanehara nods. 'And so you were sentenced to fifteen years by the Tokyo High Court in February 1933 . . .'

'Fifteen years,' agrees Kodaira. 'But later it was reduced.'

'So how long were you in prison then?'

'About six and a half years.'

'In Kosuge? In Tokyo?'

'Yes.'

'So you were released under the Imperial Amnesty of 1940?'

'Yes,' says Kodaira. 'By the mercy of the Emperor.'

'And so what did you do upon your release?'

'I went to the hot springs in Kusatsu.'

'How long did you stay there?'

'About half a year.'

'Did you work?'

'Not really,' he says. 'I was recuperating from prison.'

'And then you came back to work in Tokyo?'

'I worked as a boiler-man, yes.'

'For which companies?'

'Four or five,' he says. 'But I can't remember the names of them all. This was before I went to Saipan.'

'How did you get that job?'

'I was recruited.'

'Despite your criminal record.'

Kodaira Yoshio shrugs. Kodaira smiles. He says, 'They never asked me and I never mentioned it.'

'And so what kind of work did you do in Saipan?'

'I worked in construction, building a runway.'

'And how long did you work in Saipan?'

'I was lucky again,' he says. 'I left in the April of 1942.'

'And so you came back to work in Tokyo again?'

'I worked for Nihon Steel in Kamata, yes.'

'And for how long was that?'

'About half a year.'

'And then?'

'I think it was then I worked for Suzuki Seihyo in Ōmori,' says Kodaira. 'Maintenance work on the refrigerators.'

'And for how long was that job?'

'Again about half a year.'

'And then what?'

Now Kodaira pauses for a moment but then shrugs and says, 'I was assigned to the Naval Clothing Department near Shinagawa.'

'We've both seen this before, detective. Remember?'

'Who assigned you to work in Naval Clothing?'

'*Did you find that file, inspector . . . ?*'

'I was assigned to the Naval Supplies Department by the local Labour Mobilization Office in Gotanda . . .'

'And they assigned you as . . . ?'

'As a boiler technician.'

'And when was this?'

'August, 1944.'

'And then?'

Kodaira shrugs again, then says, 'I got married. I had a kid.'

'This is with your present wife then?' asks Kanehara.

'Yes.'

'How did you meet your new wife?'

'Through a friend.'

'And when did you get married?'

'Last February.'

'And you were still working for the Naval Supplies?'

'I was then,' he says. 'Until June last year.'

'What happened in June last year?'

'Nothing,' he says. 'I just quit.'

'Why?'

'I had evacuated my wife and baby to her family home in Toyama and I was renting a house in Wakagi-chō in Shibuya . . .'

'This is the same house that you're in now?'

'No,' he says. 'The old place we were renting burnt down in the May air raids, so that was when I decided to quit my job at the Naval Supplies and go live with my wife and kid in Toyama.'

'And could you find any work in Toyama?'

'We were staying with my wife's older brother and he helped me get a job as a security guard.'

'Where was that?'

'At Fuji Seikō-zai in Higashi Toyama.'

'So when did you come back here?'

'About a week after the surrender.'

'And what did you do?'

'Well, I'd borrowed some money from a broker,' he says. 'To set myself up selling Toyama Medicine Boxes door to door.'

'And so how long did that job last?'

'Not very long,' he laughs. 'Just until I paid back the money

126

to the broker. In November last year . . .'

'And so when did you start working at the Shinchū Gun laundry, for the Occupation Army?'

'Well, my wife and my kid came back to Tokyo in December last year,' he says. 'So then I must have started at the Shinchū Gun laundry in March this year.'

'Thank you very much,' says Chief Inspector Kanehara. 'You've been very helpful. Very cooperative. Now we're going to give you a little rest and some tea and then we're going to come back in here and we're going to ask you some more questions.'

Kodaira Yoshio smiles. Kodaira nods his head.

'But these questions won't be about your life,' says Kanehara. These questions won't be about your family. These questions won't be about your work. These questions will be different questions –

'Do you know what these different questions will be about?'

Kodaira has stopped smiling. Kodaira is shaking his head –

Kanehara is smiling now. 'But I think you do know . . .'

Kodaira shaking his head again. Again and again –

'These questions will be about Midorikawa . . .'

Again and again. He shakes his head –

'Midorikawa Ryuko . . .?'

Again and again –

Now Kanehara says, 'Take off your shirt and your trousers and we'll be back soon.'

In the corridor outside the interrogation room, Adachi stares at the wall again; Kanehara reads back over the notes; Kai smokes –

Now Chief Inspector Adachi turns to me again and asks, 'Does the Naval Clothing Department in Shinagawa ring any bells?'

'Not for me,' I say. 'Why, does it ring any bells for you?'

'No,' he says. 'But I'm deaf to all bells these days.'

*

It is dark now. The table has gone. The chairs have gone. The stenographer too. The cigarettes are all smoked. The tea all drunk. The room all shadows. Ten policemen file into the room. Ten policemen with bamboo sticks. Ten policemen opposite Kodaira Yoshio. Kodaira Yoshio stood in his underwear. Kodaira Yoshio with his head bowed. Kodaira Yoshio with his tears on the floor –

Chief Inspector Adachi steps towards him –

Adachi says, 'In your own words . . .'

'I met Midorikawa Ryuko in Shinagawa station about two months ago. There had been a train accident that day and so the platform was crowded with people waiting. I saw Midorikawa Ryuko walking along the platform. I had some bread with me from the Shinchū Gun. As she walked past, I offered her half of the bread and she took it and ate it there and then. I felt sorry for her and so I gave her the other half and she stayed near me . . .'

Inspector Adachi says, 'So it was Midorikawa who followed you. You didn't follow her . . .'

'We got on the train for Meguro together and while we were on the train I put my hand up her skirt and stroked her cunt. Ryuko didn't object and when we got off the train she copied down my address from my pass. She then visited my house three times . . .'

Adachi says, 'So she obviously liked your hand up her skirt. She must have liked you playing with her cunt . . .'

'I met Ryuko again on the sixth of August at ten o'clock at the east entrance of Shinagawa station. I'd told her I could help her find a job with the Shinchū Gun but that she would first need to take a written test at the barracks; that to enter the barracks we would have to get a letter of permission; that to get the letter we would have to go to the American Club in Marunouchi. This was all a lie. But I told her to follow me and I took her up the hill in Shiba . . .'

'But once again it was Midorikawa who followed you, yeah? You didn't drag her up there, did you?'

'We found a quiet spot and we sat down together, side by side, and we began to eat our *bentō* lunches, side by side. But all the time we were eating, I couldn't stop staring at her tits, smelling her woman's smell and all the time we were eating, I really wanted to have her, to have her there and then, but she said she didn't want to do it then, said she didn't want to do it there. I was angry and I was frustrated now and so I slapped her face and then I stripped her underwear and I had her then and had her there, even though I knew it was wrong. I just lost control . . .'

'But you'd been down there before, you'd had your fingers up her skirt and in her cunt . . .'

'Then after I'd finished, she just wouldn't stop crying and crying so I strangled her.'

'She'd never been upset before, had she? She'd still come to meet you, hadn't she?'

'I strangled her with her own *haramaki*.'

'You'd not planned it that way . . .'

'Then I stripped the body and . . .'

'You were afraid . . .'

'I ran away.'

*

In the corridor outside the interrogation room, Chief Inspector Kanehara and Inspector Kai congratulate Chief Inspector Adachi. *Case closed.* Chief Inspector Kanehara and Inspector Kai tell Chief Inspector Adachi what a great job he did. *Case closed.* In the corridor outside the interrogation room, Chief Inspector Adachi congratulates Chief Inspector Kanehara and Inspector Kai. *Case closed.* Chief Inspector Adachi tells Chief Inspector Kanehara and Inspector Kai what a great job they did. *Case closed. Case closed. Case closed . . .*

They will eat good food tonight, their glasses raised –

They will sing old songs, their songs of victory –

'You saw how it was done,' Kai tells me. 'Good luck.'

*

They have switched on the light. They have brought back the table. They have given Kodaira Yoshio back his chair. They have given Kodaira Yoshio back his clothes. They have given Kodaira Yoshio tea to drink. They have given Kodaira Yoshio cigarettes to smoke –

Kodaira smiling. Kodaira grinning. Kodaira laughing . . .

I ask him, 'Is there anything else you want to tell me?'

'Like what?' he asks. 'Like about Midorikawa?'

'That's not the first time you've killed, is it?'

'You know that,' he says. 'I told you.'

'Then please tell me again . . .'

'Why?' he laughs.

'Tell me!'

He shrugs his shoulders. He says, 'I killed my father-in-law.'

'And?'

He says, 'And I've just told you I killed Midorikawa.'

'And?'

He smiles now. 'And I killed six Chinese soldiers.'

'And?'

He shakes his head. He asks me, 'And what?'

'And how many more have you killed?'

He asks, 'Killed where? In China?'

'Just tell me about the others . . .'

Kodaira asks, 'Were you a soldier, detective? Did you fight?'

'I'm not talking about China,' I say. 'What about here?'

But he asks me again, 'Did you fight, detective?'

'Yes,' I tell him. 'In the army. In China.'

He says, 'Then you saw what I saw. You did what I did.'

Half-thoughts form. In the half-light. Half-things move . . .

'I'm not talking about China,' I tell him. 'There was another body found in Shiba Park. There was another murdered girl.'

Ton-ton. Ton-ton. Ton-ton. Ton-ton. Ton-ton . . .

Kodaira shrugs his shoulders again. He shakes his head –

'Another dead girl aged seventeen or eighteen . . .'

Ton-ton. Ton-ton. Ton-ton. Ton-ton . . .

Kodaira shakes his head. He bows his head –

'In a yellow and dark-blue striped pinafore dress,' I tell him. 'A white half-sleeved chemise, dyed-pink socks and white canvas shoes with red rubber soles . . .'

Ton-ton. Ton-ton. Ton-ton . . .

Kodaira shrugs his shoulders. Kodaira shakes his head. Kodaira bows his head. Kodaira says, 'It wasn't me, detective . . .'

Ton-ton. Ton-ton . . .

I get up to go –

Ton-ton . . .

'I'm very sorry,' says Kodaira. 'But it wasn't me, soldier.'

*

I stay away from Headquarters. *They will have found his name.* They will be having their parties to celebrate. *They will have talked to his family.* They will be eating good food. *They will have found his office.* They will be raising their glasses. *They will have talked to his colleagues.* They will be taking off their ties. *They will have found his stories.* They will be tying their ties round their foreheads. *They will*

130

have talked to his contacts. They will be singing their songs. *They will have found his notes.* Their songs of endeavour. *They will have talked to his snitches.* Their songs of courage. *They will have found my name.* Their songs of battle. *They will be coming for me . . .*

Case closed. Case closed. Case closed . . .

Be singing their songs of victory –

Chiku-taku. Chiku-taku . . .

The night is heavy; the heat is dark; the Shimbashi New Life Market deserted except for a few stall-holders here and there, standing in small groups, watching the reed screens being torn down, drinking *mechiru-arukōru* and reading the signs while they still can:

Closed for the time being. Efforts being made to reopen . . .

No pots. No pans. No sardines or second-hand suits –

No tinned fruit or soldiers' boots –

No Victors on the stairs tonight –

No red apple to my lips . . .

'The boss has been waiting for you,' says the goon in the new suit as two other goons in two other new suits take an arm each and march me past the empty mats and broken stalls, down the alleys and the lanes, through the shadows and the arches to the old wooden stairs and the wide-open door at the top of those stairs –

I wipe my face. Then I wipe my neck –

Now I walk up the stairs –

Into the light –

Senju Akira is sat cross-legged before the long low polished table, bare-chested with his trousers unbuttoned at the waist and a clean white *haramaki* belt around his belly –

Senju calmer than before –

Before the storm . . .

'I attended a very interesting meeting today,' he tells me –

There are ten police revolvers laid out on the long table . . .

'All of the gang bosses and all of the police chiefs . . .'

There is ammunition for them. There are short swords . . .

'I impressed upon them all that the traditional friendship between the bosses and the followers should remain untouched, but I agreed that the system itself should be completely altered otherwise it will not survive in this age of democracy . . .'

He picks up a gun. He picks up a cloth. He begins to clean . . .

'I advocated that all of the gangs should abandon the practice

131

of living upon protection money and other such outdated and parasitic practices . . .'

Bit by bit, piece by piece, he wipes, he polishes, he oils . . .

'I advocated that the markets be drastically democratized and reorganized into modern business corporations with even their own labour unions . . .'

He sorts through the ammunition, he sifts . . .

'I told the gang bosses and the police chiefs that the old Shimbashi Black Market has already been transformed into the Shimbashi New Life Market and that the old Matsuda gang has now been reorganized into the Kantō Matsuda Group, a modern commercial organization under my presidency . . .'

He chooses. He loads . . .

'That all our members have doffed their traditional clothes for sack coats like all other white-collar workers. That unemployment insurance is being introduced . . .'

One bullet, two bullets, three bullets, four . . .

'Relief money for workers who are sick . . .'

Four bullets, five bullets, six more . . .

'And help for the families of the dead . . .'

He closes the chamber of the gun . . .

'I told them that we were here to work with the police, shoulder to shoulder, brother to brother, Japanese to Japanese. I told them we were here to help the police . . .'

Now he cocks the gun . . .

'But I also told them that we would never lie down, that we would never back down in the face of threats and intimidation from the Formosans and Koreans . . .'

Bang. Bang. Bang . . .

'Never. Ever . . .'

Bang. Bang . . .

Now Senju aims the gun in my face. Now Senju asks me, 'What do you think of that then, detective?'

Bang . . .

'Hayashi Jo is dead,' I tell him. 'They pulled him out of the Shiba Canal early this morning.'

Bound and nailed . . .

Senju lowers the revolver. He smiles. 'That's lucky for you.'

'How's it lucky for me?' I ask. 'There'll be an inquiry.'

'But it's lucky you gave me the name of a dead man.'

'He wasn't a dead man when I gave you his name.'

'So you say now,' laughs Senju. 'So you say.'

'But if I knew he was dead, why would I give you his name?'

Senju raises the revolver again. Senju says, 'Because dead men don't say very much, do they, Detective Inspector Minami?'

I curse him. I curse myself. And I curse my dependence . . .

I bow before him. I apologize to him. I tell him, 'Hayashi was nailed to a door. I thought you might have killed him.'

'So you came down here to arrest me, did you, detective?'

I bow to him again. I apologize to him again. I shake my head and tell him, 'No. I came down here for the Calmotin.'

Senju reaches under the table. Senju brings out a small box –

'And here you are,' he says. 'Sweet dreams, detective.'

I apologize again. I thank him. I take the box.

Senju Akira throws some banknotes across the table at me. Now Senju says, 'But I still need a name, detective. Understand?'

I nod. I bow again. I apologize again. I thank him again –

'A name from the living, not the dead . . .'

I start to shuffle backwards across the mats but then I ask, 'What are you going to do about the market? About the Formosans?'

'They tell me they've not finished with me,' laughs Senju.

'And what did you tell them?' I ask. 'What did you say?'

Senju raises the gun again. 'I just told them the truth –

'I told them I've not even begun yet . . .'

*

We have not found her name. I stay away from Atago police station. I stay away from Room #2. *We have not talked to her family.* My men will not be eating good food. My men will not be raising their glasses. *We have not connected her to Kodaira.* They will not be taking off their ties. They will not be singing their songs of victory. *We have not got a confession.* They will be asleep at their borrowed desks. Their stomachs will still be empty, their dreams still lost –

Our case not closed. Our case never closed . . .

I push my way off the train. I itch and I scratch. *Gari-gari.* I go through the ticket gate at Mitaka. I wipe my face. I wipe my neck. I follow the telegraph poles down the road to my usual restaurant, half-way between the station and my house –

But in the half-light, I can't forget . . .

'There have been more men looking for you,' says the master. 'They've been in here almost every night . . .'

No one is who they say they are . . .

I shrug my shoulders. I take off my hat. I order *yakitori* and a whisky. I put the glass to my lips. I knock it back –

No one is who they seem to be . . .

'In here every night asking questions . . .'

It burns. I cough. I order another –

'About your wife and children . . .'

I leave it. I leave the bar –

I walk and then I run –

I run up the road –

The house is dark. The house is silent. I wipe my face and I wipe my neck. I take out my key and I open the door. *The rotting mats.* The house smells of boiled radish. *The shredded doors.* The house smells of DDT. *The fallen walls.* The house smells of pain –

The pain I have brought them. The pain I have left them . . .

I place the money and the food in the *genkan* –

The money and the food; the blood money . . .

I step back outside. I close the door again –

The blood money and the blood food . . .

I turn away. I walk away –

The tears in my eyes . . .

I hear the door open –

Tears of blood . . .

I start to run, to run away, away again.

*

I think about her all the time. Her head slightly to the right. *In a white half-sleeved chemise.* I think about her all the time. Her right arm outstretched. *In a yellow and dark-blue striped pinafore dress.* I think about her all the time. Her left arm at her side. *In her pink socks.* I think about her all the time. Her legs parted, raised and bent at the knee. *Her white canvas shoes with red rubber soles.* I think about her all the time. My come drying on her stomach and on her ribs –

'I look like bones,' says Yuki, in the half-light –

In the half-light. I open the box of Calmotin –
I swallow some pills. In the half-light –
The dead are the living, the living are . . .
In the half-light. I close my eyes –
'Does this umbrella become me . . .?'
'I can't remember the umbrella,' I tell her. 'But I remember your hair, your freshly dressed chignon tied up in threads.'
'And you followed me,' she smiles. 'You followed me.'
Another flash of lightning. Another clap of thunder . . .
'You were afraid,' I say. 'You reached for my hand.'
'Worried you were lost. Worried you would lose me.'
She turns down the alleyway, crosses the little bridge over the ditch and waits for me before the reed awnings of her row-house . . .
'You returned my umbrella then beat the rain from my coat.'
'Your Western clothes were really very wet,' she laughs –
The thunder is in retreat now but the rain falls harder still, bouncing off the buildings and our bodies in a shower of stones . . .
'You were worried about my clothes, so you invited me in.'
'I was only being polite,' she says. 'What else could I do?'
She leads me into a back room screened off by a lattice of unpolished wood and a curtain of long ribbons and little bells . . .
'You wiped your bare feet while I untied my foreign shoes.'
'But you wouldn't take your coat off,' she laughs again –
And sits me down at the long charcoal brazier as she then begins to make tea, her left knee drawn up to her left breast . . .
'Was that well-water?' I ask her again. 'Or tap-water?'
'You were more worried about typhoid than syphilis,' she says. 'Is that why you never drink the tea in my house . . .?'
Now she wipes oil from her forehead with a piece of clear paper and then goes off through the curtains to the wash basin . . .
'You would have been twenty-three or twenty-four,' I say. 'And the skin on your face had been spoilt and dulled by cosmetics.'
'But my lips were red,' she says. 'And my eyes were clear.'
I can still see her through the ribbons, beyond the bells, bowing to wash her face, her kimono pulled back over her shoulders, her shoulders and breasts even whiter than her face . . .
'You were always alone,' I say. 'Weren't you afraid?'
In the half-light, she does not answer me. In the half-light –
Her face to the wall. To the paper. To the stains –

In the half-light, Yuki sleeps. In the half-light –
'Black! Black! Here come the bombs!'
I cover my ears. I close my eyes –
'Cover your ears! Close your eyes!'
In the half-light, she is startled and wakes, clutching her hair.
Now she sees a length of her hair has wound itself around my neck –
'My hair only grows when we sleep together,' she smiles –
I swallow some more pills. I close my eyes again –
'But I don't want to sleep,' she whispers into my mouth.
'Why do we have to sleep? Why should lovers ever have to sleep?'
'A love that never sleeps would send us mad.'
'We never slept before,' she says. 'When sleep was selfish.
When sleep was for the demons. When sleep was for the dead . . .'

II

The Bridge of Tears

procession, the coffin decorated with the images of snakes, the chief mourner in a hat of coarse hemp as the women howl with the yellow wind through the electric wires. The soil blows, the sun pales as I lie among the corpses. **Sixty Calmotin, sixty-one.** Chinese officers stuff their mouths with melon under the huge Sun in the Blue Sky flag atop the peeling red-lacquered gate. *We watch them from behind our sandbags.* Their soldiers in their grey uniforms throng the streets, overturning stalls and stealing goods. *We watch them from behind our barbed wire.* They chew food as they saunter around the city. *We watch them in our khaki uniforms.* They spit skin and bones into the faces of the local Chinese. *We watch them with our machine guns.* They love plunder, they love violence. *A shot rings out.* They knock over altars, they yank open drawers. *Another shot.* Beggars and coolies run towards the shots. *The Chinks are robbing the Japanese.* Women with bound feet and children with plaits flee. *The Japs are raping the Chinese.* Two grey armoured vehicles speed up the street. *The Chinks are murdering the Japanese.* Nationalist cavalrymen gallop south through the city. *The Japs are murdering the Chinese.* Bullets fly from the second-floor windows of Western buildings. *Artillery sounds.* Barefoot Japanese men run down the streets, their shirts unbuttoned. *Cannons fire.* Prostitutes pour out of the Yung-hsien-li district. *Windows shatter.* A woman in red satin falls to the ground. *My son said he would cut his own throat!* Houses are burnt. *Mine too!* Refugees cower in halls. *A true Japanese man!* Men lose their wives. *Run!* Mothers lose their children. *Hide!* A wire birdcage lies trampled in the street. *No!* This is how it starts, among the corpses. **Seventy Calmotin, seventy-one.** The disarmed soldiers in their grey uniforms groan and cry like animals, their hands tied behind their backs in the barbed-wire stockade. Hundreds of them, sat on the ground before the fixed bayonets of just five of our unit as our artillery thunders on until dawn. Then there is only smoke, now only rumours. Two hundred and eighty Japanese settlers massacred, say the Japanese newspapers. Japanese women stripped naked, treated with unspeakable savagery, and then butchered. Tales of stakes thrust into vaginas, arms broken with clubs, and their eyes gouged out. Houses looted, schools burnt. The mutilated corpses of three Japanese are unearthed in a field northeast of the railway bridge, six more by the water tank. Their ears have been sliced off, their stomachs stuffed with stones. **Eighty Calmotin, eighty-one.** Now the airplanes appear, dropping black bombs on Chinese districts and the street fighting ends. *The air is thick with flies.* For two days we drink sake and wander through the city. *The stench of rotten apricots.* We count the Chinese corpses but soon give up. *Dogs wag their tails among the dead.* We take photographs but run out of film. *Beggars sleep among the bones.* We find Chinese families still hiding in their houses. *Two hundred and eighty Japanese settlers massacred, say the Japanese newspapers.* We separate the men from the women. *Japanese women stripped naked, treated with unspeakable savagery, and then butchered.* The young from the old. *Tales of stakes thrust into vaginas, arms broken with clubs, and their eyes gouged out. Masaki, Banzai! Daddy,*

6

August 20, 1946

Tokyo, 87°, cloudy

Night is day. I open my eyes. *No more pills.* Day is night. I can hear the rain falling. *Hide from sight.* Night is day. I can see the sun shining. *No more pills.* Day is night. I close my eyes. *The corpses of the dead.* Night is day. The good detective visits the crime scene one hundred times. *No more pills.* Day is night. The white morning light behind the black Shiba trees. *In the long, long grasses.* Night is day. The black trees that have seen so much. *No more pills.* Day is night. The black branches that have borne so much. *The dead leaves and weeds.* Night is day. The black leaves that have come again. *No more pills.* Day is night. To grow and to fall and to grow again. *Another country's young.* Night is day. I turn away. *No more pills.* Day is night. I walk away from the scene of the crime. *Another country's dead.* Night is day. Beneath the Black Gate. *No more pills.* Day is night. The dog still waits. *Another country.* Now night is day.

*

They are all awake now. *No Fujita.* They are all hungry still. *No Fujita.* They are all waiting for me. *No Fujita.* Hattori, Takeda, Sanada and Shimoda yawning and scratching their heads. *No Fujita.* Nishi, Kimura and Ishida with their notebooks and their pencils out –

    No Fujita. No Fujita. No Fujita. No Fujita . . .

    'By now you all know that the suspect named Kodaira Yoshio has confessed to the murder of Midorikawa Ryuko,' I tell them. 'But, unfortunately for us, Kodaira Yoshio claims to know nothing about the second body, *our* body. Now I don't believe him . . .'

    No Fujita. No Fujita. No Fujita . . .

    'But first, we need to find her name . . .'

    No Fujita. No Fujita . . .

    'Now we know she was alive enough on the nineteenth of

July to clip an advertisement from a newspaper,' I tell them. 'And we know that Dr. Nakadate estimates she was murdered sometime between the twentieth and the twenty-seventh of July . . .'

No Fujita. No Fujita. No Fujita. No Fujita . . .

'Now remember, investigation is footwork; so let's take these dates and a description of the suspect Kodaira Yoshio and go back to Shiba to ask if anyone has seen a man like this?'

No Fujita. No Fujita. No Fujita . . .

'With a girl dressed like ours?'

No Fujita. No Fujita . . .

'Between these dates?'

No Fujita.

*

I take a different route back up to Tokyo Metropolitan Police Headquarters. *Ton-ton.* The air is more humid than ever. *Ton-ton.* The hammering louder than ever. *Ton-ton.* I want to wash my face. *Ton-ton.* I want to wash my hands. *Ton-ton.* I step inside the Hibiya Public Hall. *Ton-ton.* I wish I hadn't. *Ton-ton.* It is the inaugural convention of the Congress of Industrial Unions. *Ton-ton.* The now-shabby lobby of this once-grand hall is filled with counter-intelligence agents and military policemen, foreign journalists and Japanese snitches, their paperclips in their lapels and an extra ration of cigarettes. *Ton-ton.* Young men selling *Akahata*. *Ton-ton.* Young men whistling 'The Red Flag'. *Ton-ton.* I want to wash my face. *Ton-ton.* I want to wash my hands. *Ton-ton.* I walk through the Shinchū Gun armbands and the press-corps badges. *Ton-ton.* The auditorium is dark and airless, packed with men standing and sweating, either staring or shouting at the large stage. *Ton-ton.* No cigarettes in here. *Ton-ton.* No extra rations. *Ton-ton.* The stage is decorated with banners demanding that workers fight for a forty-hour week, oppose mass dismissals and battle against the remnants and resurgence of militarism and nationalism. *Ton-ton.* In front of the banners sit a dozen men behind a long table, all of them tall, all of them lean, all of them bespectacled. *Ton-ton.* They bow deeply before the hall. *Ton-ton.* They introduce themselves. *Ton-ton.* They bow again. *Ton-ton.* They sit back down. *Ton-ton.* Then the speeches begin. *Ton-ton.* These tall, lean and bespectacled men unbuttoning their jackets and loosening their ties, clenching their fists and waving their papers –

Ton-ton. Ton-ton. Ton-ton. Ton-ton. Ton-ton. Ton-ton . . .

'There are those that say, even many here in this hall today, both Japanese and Occupier, that labour should not be militant, that labour should not fight. But I ask you today, is it not our democratic right to organize and defend our jobs? Is it not our democratic right to teach our fellow workers to tell an enemy from a friend?'

Ton-ton. Ton-ton. Ton-ton. Ton-ton. Ton-ton . . .

'The Yoshida government and the American Occupiers declare that since Japan is now suffering from the consequences of defeat, all internal differences must be forgotten, all labour disputes postponed. But when have capitalists ever welcomed disputes?'

Ton-ton. Ton-ton. Ton-ton. Ton-ton . . .

'The Yoshida government is a *zaibatsu* government. It is a government hostile to labour sponsored by an occupation hostile to labour. Things are the same now as they have always been –

'New uniforms but the same old politics!'

Ton-ton. Ton-ton. Ton-ton . . .

'The tactics of the present campaign against members of the Communist Party by the Yoshida government and the American Occupiers are the same tactics that were used by the fascists and the militarists during the war years. It shows the meaninglessness of their words, words such as freedom, such as rights, such as democracy . . .

'*The red flag, wraps the bodies of our dead . . .*'

'Labour gives capital everything. Capital gives labour nothing!

'*Before the corpses turn cold, the blood dyes the flag . . .*'

'All workers must unite! All workers must fight!'

Ton-ton. Ton-ton . . .

I find the bathroom. The toilet. The sink –

I wash my face and I wash my hands –

In the warm, rust-coloured water –

I leave the building –

Ton-ton . . .

Outside the Hibiya Hall, a former communist is stood upon a soapbox. *Ton-ton.* First the man weeps as he recalls the political folly of his youth. *Ton-ton.* Then the man rails as he denounces birth control as the Victors' way to sterilize and eradicate the Yamato race. *Ton-ton.* Now the man calls for three *banzai* cheers for the Emperor –

'*Banzai! Banzai! Banzai!*' he screams, stood upon his box

against a wall still decorated with a mural of a Japanese bomber –
'Let's Boost Plane Production for an All-out Attack!'
There are red flags in the trees of Hibiya Park –
Ton-ton. Ton-ton. Ton-ton. Ton-ton . . .
I want to wash my face again –
Ton-ton. Ton-ton. Ton-ton . . .
I want to wash my hands –
In the Year of the Dog.

*

I am late, again. Chief Inspector Adachi is standing on the steps outside Tokyo Metropolitan Police Headquarters. Inspector Adachi is looking for me. Adachi is waiting for me. He is asking me, 'So where is Detective Fujita today then, Detective Inspector Minami?'

'I just left Detective Fujita back at Atago,' I tell him. 'Detective Fujita is leading the Shiba investigation in my absence.'

Inspector Adachi asks, 'So you say you've just come from Atago, have you? And you say you've just seen Detective Fujita?'

'Yes,' I say. 'We've just finished our morning meeting.'

Adachi smiles. Adachi asks me, 'And you saw Fujita?'

'Yes,' I tell him again. 'Why are you asking me?'

Adachi smiles again. Adachi takes his time now. 'Do you remember the body we pulled out of the Shiba Canal . . .?'

'It was only yesterday,' I say. 'And I was there.'

'Well, it was the body of a journalist,' says Adachi. 'A journalist who used different names for different papers, sometimes writing for *Minpo*, sometimes for *Minshū Shimbun*, even *Akahata*.'

'Really?' I ask him. 'And so what was his name?'

'You don't know?' asks Adachi. *'Really?'*

I curse you. I curse you. I curse you . . .

'Why would I know his name?'

I curse you and I curse myself . . .

'Well, just how many journalists do you know who write for three different papers under three different names, inspector?'

I smile. I say, 'I try not to know any journalists.'

'Not one called Kato Kotaro of *Akahata*?'

I laugh. I say, 'I've never heard of him.'

'Or Suzuki Nobu of *Minshū Shimbun*?'

I shrug my shoulders. I say, 'No.'

'Or Hayashi Jo of *Minpo*?'

I swallow. I say, 'No.'

I curse myself . . .

'Well, that's very strange,' says Adachi. 'Because late last night I went to the *Minpo* offices to ask them about this Hayashi Jo, about him being found in the Shiba Canal, about him being nailed and bound to a door, about him being drowned face down and why they think that might be and do you know what the first thing they said to me was? The first thing they said to me was, not again . . .'

'Not again,' I repeat. 'What did they mean, not again?'

'That's exactly what I asked them,' laughs Adachi. 'And do you know what they told me? They told me I was the third policeman to have visited the *Minpo* offices in the last three days . . .'

I swallow again as Inspector Adachi says –

'The third one asking after Hayashi Jo . . .'

I ask, 'What do you want from me?'

Chief Inspector Adachi steps closer. Chief Inspector Adachi whispers, 'I don't want anything from you, inspector, except your gratitude that it was me who pulled this case and not anyone else. But when you do see your Detective Fujita, please send him to me . . .'

I nod then I ask, 'But why do you want to see Fujita?'

'Because Detective Fujita was the first policeman to have visited the *Minpo* offices in the last three days, that's why . . .'

I curse him. I swallow. *I curse myself.* I ask –

'And so who was the second policeman?'

Ishida. Ishida. Ishida. Ishida. Ishida . . .

'You tell me, corporal,' says Adachi. 'You tell me.'

*

I need answers; I need to find Fujita and I need to see Ishida: I want to know how Adachi got this case; I want to know who identified Hayashi's body. But today is not the day to ask the chief these questions. Today is not a day for talk; today there is no talk of fresh purges; today there is no talk of the Tokyo trials; today there is no talk of SCAP reforms; no talk of better guns; no talk of new uniforms. Because the chief has heard about last night's party; the good food; their glasses raised; the songs sung; their songs of victory –

143

'The suspect Kodaira Yoshio has confessed to the murder of Midorikawa Ryuko and I know many of you think that this means that the case is now closed,' says the chief. 'But that is not true. The statements in the confession need to be verified. The addresses of the places the suspect Kodaira claims to have lived and worked need to be checked. And we still have one unidentified body –

'Inspector Minami, if you would please . . .'

'The suspect Kodaira denies any knowledge of the second body found at Shiba. Dr. Nakadate, however, believes this crime to be the work of the same person responsible for the murder of Midorikawa Ryuko, that is to say that Dr. Nakadate believes Kodaira to have been responsible for both crimes . . .'

'And you, Inspector Minami?' asks Chief Inspector Adachi. 'Do you agree with Dr. Nakadate?'

'Yes,' I tell him. 'I believe that if we can find the evidence or, better still, if we can identify the body and then find witnesses or circumstances that can connect Kodaira to the victim or even to the time we know she was murdered then, faced with the evidence, I believe he will again confess.'

'And if not?'

'The murders and rapes of two young women would bring Kodaira the death sentence,' I say. 'And he knows it. But only one, in the circumstances in which he has confessed, probably not . . .'

'Kodaira murdered his father-in-law,' says Kai. 'Midorikawa will be his second murder conviction. Kodaira will hang this time.'

'Kodaira is an old hand at this,' I say. 'If he thinks he can still escape the rope, he has no reason to confess to anything else.'

The chief asks, 'Do you have any new leads at all on the identity of the second body, Inspector Minami?'

'A newspaper advertisement seeking staff for a Salon Matsu in Kanda was found in one of the pockets of her dress,' I tell them. 'It was clipped from the *Asahi* of the nineteenth of July and this obviously led us to visit this Salon Matsu in Kanda. Unfortunately, because we had only her clothing to describe, the staff were unable to identify her or confirm whether or not she had been to the salon. However, they suggested we go out to the International Palace . . .'

Better off dead. Better off dead. Better off dead . . .

'The International Palace?' repeats the chief. 'Out near Funabashi? Why did they suggest that you ask after her out there?'

144

'Ninety per cent of their applicants used to work there.'

'But that doesn't mean that this one did,' says Kai.

I shrug. 'And it doesn't mean that she didn't.'

'Haven't the Shinchū Gun placed it off-limits?' asks Chief Inspector Adachi. 'Won't we need clearance . . .?'

The chief nods. The chief looks at his watch. The chief says, 'Report back here in three hours, inspector.'

*

I need answers; I need to find Fujita and I need to see Ishida. *Chiku-taku*. I have to go back to Atago. *Chiku-taku*. I have to find Fujita. *Chiku-taku*. I have to see Ishida. *Chiku-taku*. I have three hours before I have to go out to the International Palace. *Chiku-taku*. But I need to find Fujita. *Chiku-taku*. I need to speak to Ishida. *Chiku-taku*. But first I have to have a drink. *Chiku-taku*. First I need a drink –

Chiku-taku. Chiku-taku. Chiku-taku. Chiku-taku . . .

The bar is in the basement of a three-storey reinforced concrete shell. *Chiku-taku*. Each room above the bar has been blown out so now only exposed steel girders dangle where once there were walls and floors. *Chiku-taku*. The bar itself was once one of the government-run People's Bars; bars that opened just once or twice a week during the war to sell cheap domestic whisky, bottles of beer and the low-grade sake known as *bakudan*; bars where people queued for hours and hours; bars that were meant to lift our morale –

Chiku-taku. Chiku-taku. Chiku-taku . . .

This bar is now back in private hands, now open twenty-four hours a day but it still sells only cheap domestic whisky, bottles of beer and *bakudan* sake and people still queue for hours to have their morale lifted. *Chiku-taku*. But this morning there are only two other customers at the counter; a middle-aged woman dressed in red, smelling of strong perfume and smoking Lucky Strikes and an old man in a shabby dark suit who keeps taking out his pocket watch and winding it up and putting it away again, then taking it out and winding it up and putting it away again, taking it out –

Chiku-taku. Chiku-taku . . .

There are ugly sores on the skin of the old man's hands. *Chiku-taku*. He has had no vitamins and now he has beriberi. *Chiku-taku*. I down my glass of clouded *bakudan*. *Chiku-taku*. I feel it explode in my throat and in my belly. *Chiku-taku*. I cough and now I ask the old man, 'Is your watch broken, sir?'

'I was on the train,' he says. 'On the day of the surrender, when a woman standing in the aisle ahead of me lost her balance and the large box tied to her back hit me right here in my chest and stopped this watch in my pocket dead . . .'

Now he shows me the watch –

It says twelve o'clock.

*

I need to find Fujita. I need to see Ishida. I need to speak to Ishida. Detectives Nishi and Kimura are back at their borrowed desks. Detectives Nishi and Kimura are writing up statements –

I ask them, 'Did you get anything at all?'

They shake their heads. They bow –

'Have you seen Detective Ishida?'

They shake their heads again –

'Right then,' I tell them. 'Nishi, I want you to come with me out to the International Palace and Kimura, I want you to find Ishida and, when you do, bring him back here and keep him here but don't let him speak to Chief Inspector Adachi until I've spoken to him first. And the same goes for Detective Fujita if he comes back at all . . .'

*

On the fifteenth of August last year, minutes after the Emperor had surrendered, the Metropolitan Police Board summoned the presidents of the seven major entertainment guilds in Tokyo. These included the heads of the restaurant, cabaret, geisha and brothel associations. The chief of the Metropolitan Police Board feared the Victors would soon be upon Japan, here to rape our wives and our daughters, our mothers and our sisters. The chief wanted a 'shock absorber' and so the chief had a proposal. The chief suggested that the heads of the restaurant, cabaret, geisha and brothel associations form one central association to cater for all the needs and amusement of the Victors. The chief promised this new association that it would not lack for funds –

The Recreation and Amusement Association was born.

Recruits were found or bought among the ruins of the cities

146

and the countryside. Dancehalls and houses of entertainment were reopened or created overnight, the biggest and most infamous of them all being the International Palace, a former munitions factory out beyond the eastern boundaries of Tokyo. Five of the workers' dormitories were converted into brothels. Some of the old management stayed on to administer the new business, some of the prettier girls stayed on to service the new customers, the Victors –

Because only the Victors are welcome at the Palace –

Only Victors allowed to make the Willow Run –

But the toll is heavy and the turnover high –

Most of the first girls were hospitalized –

Many of the rest committed suicide –

Better off dead . . .

The second set of girls were geishas and prostitutes, barmaids and waitresses, frequent adulterers and sexual deviants, girls built of stronger stuff, too strong for some because the International Palace was placed off-limits this spring –

Supposedly.

Our chief has got the clearance for Detective Nishi and me to go out to the International Palace. Our chief has even found Nishi and me a ride out there in the back of a Victors' truck. In the back with Larry, Moe and Curly, three well-fed and well-scrubbed GI Joes –

They offer us chewing gum and Nishi chews their gum. They offer us cigarettes and Nishi smokes their cigarettes. They talk about their lucky days and Nishi nods and laughs along. They talk about hitting the jackpot, about kids in candy stores, about Christmases that come early and Christmases that all come at once, and Nishi is nodding and laughing along, shouting out, 'Merry Christmas!'

He is a good Jap, a good monkey. He is a tame Jap . . .

I do not chew their gum. I do not smoke their cigarettes. I do not nod or laugh along. I do not shout, 'Merry Christmas!'

Because I am the bad Jap. Bad monkey.

The Victors' truck drives southeast, out towards Funabashi, out of the city until the ruins become fields, the burnt black earth now barren brown soil, until we can see the series of two-storey barrack buildings rising up ahead, until we can read the signs in English:

OFF-LIMITS – VD. OFF-LIMITS – VD . . .

More smaller signs, hundreds of them, dabbed in red paint the closer we come, thousands of them, on the fences, on the gates:

VD VD VD VD VD VD VD VD VD VD VD VD VD VD VD
VD VD VD VD VD VD VD VD VD VD VD VD VD VD VD VD VD
VD VD VD VD VD VD VD VD VD VD VD VD VD VD VD VD VD
VD VD VD VD VD VD VD VD VD VD VD VD VD VD VD VD ...

The Victors' truck goes through the open barbed-wire gates and sounds its horn as it pulls into a small, dusty courtyard, a crowd of men and women pouring out of the buildings to greet us –

I have been here before, seen these places before ...

Little Japanese men in white waiters' tunics without trays, tall Japanese women in Western dresses without stockings, all beaming and bowing to us, clapping and calling out to us –

These places, these buildings, these women ...

'All clean, all clean, all clean ...'

'Very clean, very clean ...'

'All cheap ...'

Now the tall women lead the driver and Larry, Moe and Curly off towards one of the dormitory buildings, the Victors' hands already up their skirts, leaving just the little men in their white waiters' tunics standing with Nishi and me in the dirt of the yard –

I am ashamed to be a policeman, ashamed to be Japanese ...

I ask to speak to the manager and the waiters disappear –

I am ashamed to be Japanese, ashamed to be me ...

The Japanese manager steps out of another of the buildings. The manager straightens his tie. The manager flattens his greasy hair. He bows. He hands me his heavy, embossed *meishi* –

The manager is another oily little man –

Just another tame collaborator ...

I tell him why we are here. I tell him about Shiba Park. I tell him about a murdered girl aged seventeen to eighteen years old. *She is better off dead.* I tell him about a yellow and dark-blue striped pinafore dress and a white half-sleeved chemise. *She is better off dead.* I tell him about a pair of dyed-pink socks and white canvas shoes with red rubber soles. *She is better off dead.* I tell him about the Salon Matsu. *She is better off dead ...*

The manager shakes his head but he wants to help us because we came here in a Victors' truck. Because he thinks we have connections to the Shinchū Gun. Because he thinks we have influence. Because he thinks we can help him to get this place reopened –

This place I have seen before. I have been before . . .

He takes us on a tour. He takes us to the infirmary –

If she was here, then she's better off dead . . .

In the infirmary. A huge, bare room lined with tatami mats. Twelve girls lie perspiring on the floor under thick comforters –

They all hide their faces from us, all but one –

I squat down. I smile. 'How old are you?'

'Nineteen years old.'

'How long have you been here?'

'Six months now.'

'And before that?'

'I was a clerk.'

'Why do you stay here?'

'I owe them money.'

'How much do you owe them?'

'Ten thousand yen.'

'Ten thousand yen? What for?'

'The clothes I've bought.'

'Bought from where?'

'The shop here.'

'What about your family? Do they know where you are?'

'I haven't any,' she says. 'They died in the air raids.'

'You do know that this place is off-limits now?'

She nods her head. She says, 'Yes.'

'Because General MacArthur has banned prostitution?'

She shakes her head. She says, 'I didn't know that.'

I nod. I squeeze her hand. I look into her eyes. I start to tell her she should leave here and go back home. But then I stop –

'We are her only home now,' says the manager.

He resumes our tour. He takes us to the clinic –

If this was where she was bound . . .

In the clinic. The girls are examined once a week. In the chairs. Every week. Each chair has a tiny curtain to conceal the faces of the girls from the doctor. Two shallow pools in which each girl must bathe every other day. Every other day, every single week –

'Very clean,' says the manager –

She's better off dead . . .

He takes us on a tour. He takes us to the dining room –

In the dining room. Here the girls are fed. In shifts –

149

'Two good meals a day,' boasts the manager.

He resumes our tour. He takes us to the ballroom –

In the ballroom. There are a hundred Japanese girls. In Occidental gowns. Nothing underneath. Beneath red paper streamers that hang in the heat from the ceiling. They dance with each other to scratched and deafening records relayed through a battery of amplifiers. Back and forth across the floor in downtrodden heels or scruffy school plimsolls. They push each other. To the distorted American jazz. In the ballroom. Back and forth –

'They are all very pretty, aren't they?' says the manager. 'But inside they are all very sad and they are all very lonely because General MacArthur won't let them make friends with GIs any more and so the GIs are homesick and lonely too . . .'

She's better off dead . . .

He takes us on a tour. He takes us to the girls' rooms –

The girls' rooms. In the two-storey barracks. Fifty cubicles to a building. Each tiny room separated by a low partition. Thin curtains or sheets for doors. Each entrance with a sign written in a child's crayon, a sign that says, *Well Come, Kimi. Well Come, Haruko . . .*

Well Come Mitsuko. Yori. Kazuko. Yoshie. Tatsue . . .

Well Come Hiroko. Yoshiko. Ryuko. Yuki . . .

Inside each small cubicle is a futon and a comforter, a little make-up mirror on the floor, the odd yellowing photograph. The air humid and heavy with the smell of antiseptic –

Better off dead. Better off dead . . .

At the top of each stairway is one long, narrow room with a painted sign beside the door which says, in English and in Katakana, *PRO Station*; this is where the Victors get their prophylactics –

The smell of antiseptic. The taste of antiseptic . . .

Beside this room are two smaller rooms without windows where the girls rest after each visit from the Victor –

Antiseptic. Antiseptic. Antiseptic . . .

The tour has finished now –

The sights all seen –

Better off dead.

Back outside the two-storey barracks, the manager leads us down one of the covered passageways between the buildings to the company store where the girls buy their cheap cosmetics and their shoddy clothes on borrowed money at expensive prices –

The store is empty. The store is dead –
My heart empty. My heart dead . . .

'Now you must meet the officers of our union here,' says the manager. 'It is a real union. It is very democratic. Very democratic. Please tell your American bosses this.'

The manager disappears inside the company store but quickly returns, bringing out with him three young women –

Two in Western suits. One in a kimono –

'These ladies are the officers of the Women's Protective League,' he tells us. 'This is the president, Kato Akiko, a former geisha. This is Hasegawa Sumiko, the vice-president and a former typist. This is Iijima Kimi, a former dancer.'

The three women smile. The three women bow.

I order the manager to leave.

'We are from the Tokyo Metropolitan Police,' I tell them. 'We are trying to identify the body of a young girl found recently in Shiba Park. We have reason to believe she may have worked here. We would be very grateful for your cooperation . . .'

The three women smile again. The three women bow again.

'Do you know the Salon Matsu?' I ask them. 'In Kanda?'

The three women shake their heads.

'Do you know anyone who has ever worked there?'

The three women shake their heads again.

'Anyone who might have left here to work there?'

'I am sorry,' says Kato, the president in her bright kimono. 'But nobody really talks about what they did before they came here or what they will do after they leave here. It is much better for us not to think or talk about the world outside of here . . .'

'But you were a geisha. She was a typist. She was a dancer.'

'Maybe we were,' she smiles. 'No one remembers.'

I don't want to remember. In the half-light . . .

'But what about new recruits?' I ask. 'Don't you interview them? Don't you ask them about their previous work?'

'There are no interviews here,' she laughs. 'Only medicals.'

The chairs and the tiny curtains. Their concealed faces and their open legs. The two shallow pools. Every other day . . .

I ask all three, 'How long have you been here, then?'

'We all came in December last year,' says Kato.

'And how much do you owe the company?'

'About five thousand yen each,' she says.

'And do you have any savings at all?'

'Of course not,' she laughs. 'We have to buy our food and pay for our own medical expenses and then there are the new clothes and the cosmetics we need for our work.'

'But how much do you earn?'

'Before we were placed off-limits, we each had fifteen customers a day,' she says. 'Each customer paid fifty yen and half of that went to the manager and half to us.'

'That's almost four hundred yen a day,' says Nishi, suddenly.

'Almost four hundred,' says Kato. 'But that was before.'

'And how many customers were coming a day?'

'Almost four thousand a day back then.'

'How many girls were there?'

'Three hundred.'

'That's one hundred thousand yen a day for the company,' exclaims Nishi. 'One hundred thousand yen a day!'

'But that was before,' repeats Kato. 'That was before we were placed off-limits to the soldiers.'

'And now?' I ask her. 'How many come now?'

'Maybe ten,' she says. 'Twenty at the most.'

I ask her, 'Why do you have a union?'

'To petition General MacArthur,' smiles Kato. 'The manager thought that if we wrote to General MacArthur as a union, asking him to let his lonely and homesick GIs come here, then the general would allow the International Palace to open again.'

I shake my head. We thank them –

They bow. We leave –

Leave. Leave . . .

I want to leave this place. *This country.* I want to flee from this place. *This heart.* I want to find the driver. *Now . . .*

I walk back inside one of the barracks –

Nishi follows me. Up the stairs –

There is a girl in the corridor. There is a naked girl in the corridor. There is a naked girl in the corridor on all fours. There is a naked girl in the corridor on all fours, no older than fourteen. There is a naked girl in the corridor on all fours, no older than fourteen, being penetrated up her backside by a Victor as she stares down the long, long corridor at Nishi and I with tears running down her cheeks, down her cheeks and into her mouth, saying, 'Oh, very good Joe. Thank you, Joe. Oh, very good Joe. Thank you, Joe. Oh, oh, Joe . . .'

She is better off dead. I am better off dead . . .

This is America. This is Japan. This is democracy. This is defeat. *I don't have a country any more.* On her knees or on her back, blood and come down her thighs. *I don't have a heart any more . . .*

Her legs apart, her cunt swollen with pricks and pus –

I don't want a heart. I don't want a heart . . .

Thank you, Emperor MacArthur –

I don't want a country . . .

Dōmo, Hirohito.

*

Nishi plays the good monkey all the way back to Tokyo as field becomes ruin and ruin becomes shack and shack becomes building and I sit and I watch him and wish I'd had the foresight and the guts to walk back, to walk back barefoot into Tokyo through field and through ruin and not to be sat back here in the Victors' jeep listening to Nishi mix up his r's and his l's while the Victors laugh and throw him cigarettes and chewing gum as childish smiles light up his grateful face and so when we get out at Headquarters and we both bow down as low as we can and thank them a thousand times and they have driven off laughing and joking, throwing their cigarettes and chewing gum, and though I know tonight they'll burn and they'll itch and they'll weep and they'll scratch it's no consolation, and so I turn and I slap Nishi hard across his face, so hard across his face that he falls over in the road and does not get back up again –

Because Nishi has no guts. No guts –

Because Nishi is gutless –

Gutless. Gutless . . .

Just like me.

*

Back inside Headquarters, I go to where we keep the undead. *'And we've both seen this before, detective. Remember?'* I go to where we keep the files of the cases we have not solved. *I don't want to remember.* To the archives and the records of our defeats and our failures. *But in the half-light, I can't forget.* I ask the man on duty for one of our records of failure. *'Did you find that file, inspector . . .?'*

'It would be the fifteenth of August,' I tell him. 'Last year.'

The officer disappears and then reappears, empty-handed –

'Not there,' he says. 'Must have already been signed out.'

'Really?' I ask him. 'Do you know who signed it out?'

The officer pulls out the tatty, old battered register –

'Your Nishi of Room #2,' laughs the officer.

'You're joking?' I ask him. 'When?'

'Only yesterday,' he says, still laughing at me.

*

Through the dirt and the dust. Through the shadows and the sweat. *Chiku-taku.* Down Sakurada-dōri to Atago I run. Through the doors and up the stairs. *Chiku-taku.* Detectives Kimura and Ishida sat in their shirtsleeves on their borrowed chairs at their borrowed desks; Kimura proud to have found Ishida; Ishida nervous and waiting –

I walk straight over. I ask them, 'Where are the others?'

'They're not back from their rounds,' says Kimura –

I am staring at Ishida. I am asking, 'And Nishi?'

'I thought he'd gone with you,' says Kimura –

I'm still staring at Ishida, asking. 'Fujita?'

They both shake their heads. Kimura says, 'Not today.'

I reach down to Ishida. I grab Ishida. I pick him up. I kick away his borrowed chair. I say, 'Where is Detective Fujita?'

'I don't know,' flaps Ishida. 'I really don't know.'

I pull his face closer to mine by his shirt. There is sweat down his face. There is sweat down mine. There are tears in his eyes and there are tears in mine. 'You've lied to me before. You've lied . . .'

'No,' squeals Ishida. 'I haven't lied to you. I haven't . . .'

'You've lied and you've lied and you've lied . . .'

'No, no, no,' cries Ishida. 'I haven't . . .'

'You've lied to protect him . . .'

'No, no, no. I haven't . . .'

'Lied to save him . . .'

'No, no, no . . .'

'Yes, you have,' I hiss and I push him away from me. Back over his borrowed chair and back onto his borrowed desk. The sweat down his face and the tears in his eyes –

'I'm sorry. I'm sorry . . .'

'Fujita's finished,' I tell him. 'And you'll be finished . . .'

'I'm sorry. I'm sorry. I'm sorry. I'm sorry . . .'

'If you don't tell me where he is . . .'

'I'm sorry. I'm sorry . . .'

'Tell me! Quick!'

'Detective Fujita will be in the Ginza tonight,' sobs Ishida. 'He'll be at the New Oasis club. After nine o'clock.'

He was seen drinking with Nodera Tomiji at the New Oasis on the night of the Matsuda Giichi hit . . .

'The New Oasis? Why there?'

But Ishida looks at the floor –

Ishida shakes his head –

'I don't know . . .'

I take out my handkerchief. I wipe my face. I wipe my neck –

I lean over Ishida. I lift up his face. I dry his eyes –

I tell him, 'You stay here with Kimura, OK?'

He buries his head again and he nods.

*

There were tea-shops and cafés here once where you could listen to a gramophone recording as you watched the latest fashions stroll past. Now I stand on the Ginza and I stare into the windows of the Victors' Post Exchange. I stand and I stare with the hungry kids and teenage girls at the Victors' brand-new clothes, at their bright white towels and their real leather shoes. I stand and I stare as the children and the girls swarm around Victors laden down with shopping bags, the children and the girls begging the Victors for gum and chocolate –

I walk away. I walk away. I walk away. I walk . . .

Past the department stores, most still empty but some now opening on the lower floors, though these floors are covered with rubble and their showcases filled only with cheap junk. Past dead buildings still nothing but concrete frames, still black from the flames, along crumbling sidewalks and the endless piles of garbage –

I turn away. I turn away. I turn away. I turn . . .

From the shoddy little mats along the old broken curbs with their harsh silk handkerchiefs and their coarse picture postcards, their busted fountain pens and their flavoured cups of ice –

I look away. I look away. I look . . .

But every single rag and every single morsel has a market value here, every single grain of rice from our one bowl a day when one cup of rice, three cigarettes and four matches are our ration, when a long-dead fish is a whole week's wage –

I cannot run away. I cannot run . . .

Now it's time. *Chiku-taku . . .*

Now day is night.

*

Day is night. Night is day. Day is night. Night is day. Day is . . .

I stand before the door. I read the sign above the door –

The New Oasis is a Korean-run shithole in the shadow of the original Oasis, down another Ginza backstreet, between another bombed-out shell and another mountain-range of garbage. The original Oasis was another gift to the Victors from the Recreation and Amusement Association, another International Palace. But the New Oasis is not for the white Victors. The New Oasis is for the yellow ones, the Koreans and the Chinese. The New Oasis is not run by the Recreation and Amusement Association. The New Oasis is not owned by Ando Akira. The New Oasis is owned by Mr. Machii –

Machii Hisayuki, a Korean-Japanese, the Bull of Ginza . . .

I am itching and I am sweating and I am scared –

The old rival of Matsuda. The new enemy of Senju . . .

If Fujita is here, then Fujita has crossed a line –

Hayashi Jo face down in the water . . .

The door is closed. I open the door. I see a flight of steps down to another closed door. I walk down the steps. The door has a spyhole. I knock on the door. I know someone is staring at me through the spyhole. The handle turning now. The door opening –

'What do you want?' says a thickset Korean in a suit –

'A drink,' I tell him. 'I'm here to meet a friend.'

'This is a members' club,' he says –

'Then I'd like to join,' I say.

'It's one hundred yen.'

I curse. I curse . . .

I take out my wallet. But not my *techō*. I open it. I have one hundred yen in notes. But that is all I have. The thickset Korean takes the notes from me. The Korean puts them in his own pocket –

He laughs, 'Welcome to the New Oasis club . . .'

The ceiling is low and the lights are dim. *If Fujita is here, then Fujita has crossed a line.* The bar is long and the staff Korean –

I see Fujita. *Fujita is here.* Fujita sees me. *Fujita has crossed the line.* I think he'll run but he smiles. *Fujita smiling.* He is smiling as he stands and walks down the length of the bar towards me –

What if he has a gun? What if he pulls it here?

Down the length of the bar, still smiling –

Hayashi Jo face down in the water . . .

Fujita bows and says, 'Good evening.'

'Hayashi Jo is dead,' I say. 'And Adachi is looking for you.'

'Adachi knows nothing,' he says. 'But he says nothing and then lets you fill in the gaps for him. Congratulations, inspector –

'He's probably followed you all the way here . . .'

'I told Adachi nothing,' I say. 'But he knows things.'

'What does Adachi know? What is there to know?'

'Adachi knows you went to the *Minpo* offices,' I tell him. 'He knows you went there to see Hayashi Jo . . .'

'And so what of it?' asks Fujita.

'So they told Adachi that he was the third cop in the last three days to visit them and that you were the first . . .'

'But that doesn't mean I killed him,' says Fujita. 'Does it?'

'But yours is the only name he's mentioned,' I tell him. 'You're the only person Adachi is looking for . . .'

'I'm not afraid of Adachi,' laughs Fujita. 'The captain has his secrets, just like everyone else. Just like you.'

I curse him and now I curse myself . . .

I ask, 'Did you kill Hayashi Jo?'

'Now that's a very strange question to be asking me,' says Detective Fujita. 'Because I hardly knew Hayashi Jo at all and it wasn't me who gave poor old Hayashi's name to Senju Akira . . .'

Day is night. Night is day. Day is night. Night is day . . .

Fujita smiles, 'I thought that was you, corporal?'

Day is night. Night is day. Day is night . . .

Fujita laughs, 'That was you, wasn't it?'

Night is day. Day is night. Day is . . .

I start to speak but the lights go out –

157

Night. Night. Night. Night . . .
There's been another power cut –
Night. Night. Night . . .
'That was you, wasn't it?' whispers Fujita again, in the dark.

*

The power is still down and it is even darker now. The lights still out and I'm even drunker now. I'm drunk on Korean liquor. The stench of the liquor sticks to the sweat on my skin. My skin itches and so I scratch. *Gari-gari.* I scratch and I scratch until my arms bleed beneath my shirt. *Gari-gari.* My shirt heavy with sweat and now blood. Blood on my hands as I walk from the Ginza back towards Atago. Back towards Atago through the debris of Yūraku-chō. The debris of Yūraku-chō piled up in mountains and in monuments. In monuments to loss, loss under every archway. Under every single archway, down every single alleyway. Down every alleyway and in every shadow. In every shadow and in every shout. Every shout of –
'*Asobu . . .? Asobu . . .? Asobu . . .? Asobu . . .?*'
I look under every single archway. Down every single alleyway. In every single shadow. Until I find the one I am looking for. The one in her yellow and dark-blue striped pinafore dress –
'*Asobu . . .? Asobu . . .? Asobu . . .? Asobu . . .?*'
In her white half-sleeved chemise and pink socks –
Her white canvas shoes with red rubber soles –
'*Asobu . . .? Asobu . . .? Asobu . . .?*'
Her hair is black. Her skin is white –
Under an archway. In a shadow –
'*Asobu . . .? Asobu . . .?*'
'*Asobu?*' she asks me in a harsh Tōhoku accent and I nod and I follow her deeper under the archway, deeper into the shadows where she asks me for the money first –
'I've no money,' I tell her –
And I curse myself again . . .
I take out my police notebook. I show her my police notebook and she curses me now and says, 'I'm with the White Bird Society.'
'So what?' I tell her as I kneel her down on all-fours–
I kneel her down on all-fours and I raise her dress –
Her yellow and dark-blue striped pinafore dress . . .

She wears no underwear. She is naked beneath –
I screw her backside as she curses and curses –
On her knees. On her knees. On her knees . . .
I turn her over and I lie her on her back –
I screw her cunt and then I come –
No country. No heart . . .
'Finished?' she asks in her harsh Tōhoku accent and I nod as she pushes me off her and stands back up and dusts herself down, rubbing at her knees and then at her palms –
Night is day. Day is night. The men are the women . . .
I stand before her now and I bow. I say, 'I'm sorry I have no money. I'm very sorry. What's your name?'
The women are the men . . .
And she tilts back her head, deep under the arch, deep in the shadows, and she laughs, 'You choose: Mitsuko? Yori? Kazuko? Yoshie? Tatsue? Hiroko? Yoshiko? Ryuko? Go on, you choose . . .'
The dead are the living. The living are the dead . . .
'Your name is Yuki,' I tell her. 'Yuki.'

*

I close my eyes, but I can't sleep. *Day is night.* I can hear the rain falling. I open my eyes, but I can't think. *Night is day.* I can see the sun shining. I close my eyes, but can't sleep. *Day is night.* The good detective visits the crime scene one hundred times. I open my eyes, but can't think. *Night is day.* The black night light behind the white Shiba trees. Close my eyes, but can't sleep. *Day is night.* The white trees that have seen so much. Open my eyes, but can't think. *Night is day.* The white branches that have borne so much. Close my eyes, can't sleep. *Day is night.* The white leaves that have come again. Open my eyes, can't think. *Night is day.* To grow and to fall and to grow again. Close eyes, can't sleep. *Day is night.* I turn away. Open eyes, can't think. *Night is day.* I walk away from the scene of the crime. Close, can't sleep. *Day is night.* Beneath the Black Gate. Open, can't think. *Night is day.* The dog still waits. Can't sleep. *Day is night.* The dog still waits. Can't think. *Night is day.* The dog still waits. Can't. *Day is night.* The dog still waits. Can't. *Night is day.* The dog still waits. Can't. *Day.* The dog still waits. Can't. *Night* . . .

7

August 21, 1946

Tokyo, 89°, slightly cloudy

There are dark grey clouds in the bleached white sky as night turns to day. I am vomiting in the toilets of Atago police station. *Black bile again.* There are newly written signs on the peeling plaster walls as I walk back upstairs. I stand over the sink. There are local government warnings about fresh outbreaks of cholera. I spit. There are instructions to refrain from drinking unboiled water, especially well-water, and to refrain from eating uncooked foods, especially raw fish. I wash my face. I look up into the mirror. I stare into the mirror –

No one is who they say they are . . .

There are seven grey faces waiting for me in the borrowed room upstairs; Hattori, Takeda, Sanada, Shimoda, and Kimura; Ishida with his worries and Nishi with his black eye. *No Fujita now . . .*

They walked round Shiba all day yesterday. *Investigation is footwork.* They asked round Shiba all day yesterday. *Investigation is footwork.* They described the suspect all day yesterday. *Investigation is footwork.* They described the victim all day yesterday –

The yellow and dark-blue striped pinafore dress . . .

I ask Hattori and Takeda what they found out –

'Nothing whatsoever,' say Takeda and Hattori.

The white half-sleeved chemise and pink socks . . .

I ask Sanada and Shimoda what they found –

'Nothing at all,' they both tell me.

The white canvas shoes . . .

I ask Kimura and Ishida –

'Nothing,' they say.

But they are looking at me now with questions in their eyes. They are looking at me with doubts in their eyes –

But I am the head of the room . . .

They are looking at me now with dissent in their eyes. They are looking at me with hate in their eyes –

I am the head. I am the boss . . .

I divide them into different sets of pairs; Takeda and Ishida, Hattori and Shimoda, Sanada and Kimura. I leave Nishi for later –

I am the boss! I am the boss!

I hand two missing persons reports to Takeda and Ishida; Ishihara Michiko and Ōzeki Hiromi, aged sixteen and seventeen years old. *I am the head of this room.* I hand two missing persons reports to Hattori and Shimoda; Konuma Yasuyo and Sugai Seiko, aged seventeen and eighteen years old. *I am the Boss of this Room.* I hand two missing persons reports to Sanada and Kimura; Tanabe Shimeko and Honma Fumiko, both eighteen years old. *I am the head!* I tell Nishi to go and wait for me in the cells downstairs –

I am the boss! I am the boss! I am the boss!

'These are all reports of missing girls aged fifteen to twenty,' I tell the rest of the room. 'And these are all reports of girls who went missing between the fifteenth and the thirty-first of July this year. And so one of these girls might be our girl . . .'

I am the boss! I am the boss!

'So I want them found!'

I am the boss!

I run back to the toilets. I vomit again. *Brown bile.* I walk over to the sink. I spit. I wipe my mouth. I turn on the tap. I wash my face again. I look up into the mirror. I stare into that mirror –

No one is who they say they are . . .

Detective Nishi is waiting for me in the cells downstairs. Nishi with his black eye and darker fears. Nishi shocked now. Nishi surprised now. Nishi up against the cell wall. My face in his face. But Nishi knows what I want. Nishi *must* know what I want –

But he starts to apologize about yesterday. He starts to say, 'I'm sorry about my behaviour yesterday. In the truck . . .'

I don't want to hear his apologies or his lies –

Nishi *knows* why I'm here. He *knows* what I want. Nishi *must* know why I'm here. He *must* know what I want –

But Nishi keeps apologizing and lying –

'I'm sorry,' he says again and again. 'My behaviour yesterday, it was unacceptable, in the truck. I'm sorry . . .'

But Nishi is lying. He must be lying. Nishi *must* know what I want. He *must* know why I'm here before I say, 'I want that file.'

'What file?' asks Nishi and asks again, 'What file . . .?'

He *must* know before I ask again, 'Where is the file?'

'What file?' he asks and asks again, 'What file . . .?'

'The file you signed out!' I shout. 'That file!'

He shakes his head and says, 'I don't know.'

'The Miyazaki Mitsuko file,' I tell him –

He shakes his head again. 'I don't know.'

'You mean, you don't know where it is?'

'No, I don't know the file you mean.'

'But you remember the Miyazaki Mitsuko case?' I ask him. 'The murder on the day of the surrender? The body in an air-raid shelter near Shinagawa? You remember?'

Nishi nods his head. Nishi says, 'Now you tell me, yes.'

'So where is the file you took from Headquarters?'

Nishi shakes his head. 'I didn't take any file.'

'I saw your name in the log,' I tell him.

Nishi says, 'It wasn't me. Really.'

There are questions in his eyes . . .

'Then someone has used your name, used your seal, to sign out the Miyazaki Mitsuko case file?'

Nishi shakes his head again. Now Detective Nishi asks, 'But why would anyone do that? Why?'

Innocence in his eyes . . .

'It wasn't even our case,' he says. 'It was the Kempeitai . . .'

Ton-ton. Ton-ton. Ton-ton. Ton-ton. Ton-ton. Ton-ton . . .

'So there'll hardly be anything in the file . . .'

Ton-ton. Ton-ton. Ton-ton. Ton-ton. Ton-ton . . .

'Surely just the barest of details . . .'

Ton-ton. Ton-ton. Ton-ton. Ton-ton . . .

'The date and time of the crime . . .'

Ton-ton. Ton-ton. Ton-ton . . .

'The names of the witnesses . . .'

Ton-ton. Ton-ton . . .

'The names of the officers . . .'

Ton-ton . . .

I step back from him. I step back from the cell wall. I turn towards the cell door. I start to walk out of the cell –

'Boss?' asks Detective Nishi. 'What do you want me to do?'

I don't turn back to him. I just tell him, 'Wait upstairs . . .'

'What if Detective Fujita comes back?' asks Nishi –

'Fujita is not coming back,' I tell him and now I start to walk quicker, now I start to run, to run to the toilets upstairs –

I vomit. *Yellow bile.* I vomit again. *Grey bile.* Four times I have vomited. *Black bile. Brown bile, yellow bile and grey.* Four times I have stared into that mirror. Four times I have screamed –

No one is who they say they are!

*

In the ruins, among the rubble with a cigarette. Two little boys crouch down and watch me smoke, waiting for the dog-end. Two little boys in grey undershirts and baggy trousers, their faces and their arms as black as pitch. This ruin was once a printing shop that produced a newsletter showing daily rice prices. During the Shiba festivals, the owner would give away coloured paper to the local children and teach them how to make origami elephants and cranes. Now three little girls appear among the rubble and call to the two little boys. The little girls with their short hair and dirty faces. The two little boys ask for my dog-end and ask for my newspaper. I hand them the dog-end and I hand them the newspaper and the two little boys run over to the three girls. I watch the two little boys spread out my newspaper. I watch them crease and fold the paper into two GI hats. The three little girls stand among the rubble and call to the two little boys. In the ruins, the two little boys march up and down with their dog-ends in their mouths and their paper hats on their heads –

'*Asobu?*' call the three little girls –

'*Asobu . . .? Asobu . . .?*'

*

I knock on the door of the interview room at Meguro police station. I open it. I bow. I take a seat next to the stenographer. Chief Inspector Kanehara and Inspector Kai do not look up but the wife of Kodaira Yoshio glances up at me and then looks away again –

Mrs. Kodaira is younger than her husband, a large woman with full round breasts and a round full face. Mrs. Kodaira is wearing her best summer dress, clutching her handbag –

'I know he knew this Midorikawa,' she is saying. 'But I'm sure he did not kill her. I'm sure there is some mistake . . .'

'Your husband has already confessed to the murder,' says

Inspector Kai. 'And you've read his confession. There's no mistake.'

'But I want to see him,' she says. 'To ask him myself.'

'Later,' says Kai. 'If you answer our questions . . .'

'But in the confession it says that the murder occurred at around noon on the sixth of August,' she says. 'My husband was working at the laundry until half past two that day and then he came straight home and stayed there with us until the next morning . . .'

'How can you be so sure of that?' asks Inspector Kai.

'Because it was on that exact day that he asked me to start keeping a diary,' she says. 'To write down the times that he worked and the times he came home and the times he went back out . . .'

'And why did he ask you to do that?' says Kai.

'Because he was worried that the laundry was not paying him for all the overtime and all the night shifts,' she says. 'That's why.'

'And the first record was made on the sixth of August?'

'Yes,' she says. 'On the sixth of August and I wrote something like, *Came straight home from work at 2:30 p.m.*'

'And you still have this diary, then?' asks Kai.

'Yes,' she says again. 'Back at the house.'

Now Inspector Kanehara places a piece of paper on the table. Now Inspector Kanehara asks her, 'Do you know what this is?'

Mrs. Kodaira shakes her head and says, 'No, I don't.'

'This is your husband's time sheet from the laundry,' says Inspector Kanehara. 'This piece of paper records the actual days and shifts that your husband worked in August at the laundry . . .'

Mrs. Kodaira stares down at the piece of paper.

'And as you can see,' continues Inspector Kanehara, 'the sixth of August was actually your husband's day off that week.'

'But you see, this is why he wanted me to keep a diary,' she says. 'Because they were always making mistakes like this . . .'

'It's not a mistake,' says Kanehara. 'We've checked.'

Mrs. Kodaira clutches her handbag a little tighter –

Questions. Questions. Questions. Questions . . .

'Why would he kill?' she asks. 'Why would he?'

'You've read the confession he made,' says Kai. 'In the confession he says that he was driven by lust for Midorikawa . . .'

'She wanted my husband to get her a job,' says Mrs. Kodaira. 'And so she seduced him in order to persuade him to help her.'

'He approached her,' says Kai. 'At Shinagawa . . .'

'He gave her food,' she says. 'She was hungry.'

'He told us he put his hand up her skirt,' says Kai. 'He told us he put his fingers inside her as they rode on the train . . .'

'Exactly!' shouts his wife. 'She wanted him . . .'

'He raped her,' says Kai. 'He murdered her.'

'He *raped* her?' laughs Mrs. Kodaira. 'You're joking! This Midorikawa girl seduced him, just like all those others . . .'

Now I lean forward. Now I ask, 'What others?'

'The ones that hang around the barracks,' she says. 'He's told me about them, the shameful way they dress, the shameful way they speak. How they will do anything for food or cigarettes . . .'

I ask her, 'Does your husband often talk about women?'

'Of course he doesn't,' says Mrs. Kodaira. 'And I know you're trying to make out he's some kind of sex maniac, raping and killing young women, but he's just a normal Japanese man . . .'

'We haven't said anything about raping and murdering anyone else other than Miss Midorikawa,' I tell her. 'Have we?'

She shakes her head. She clutches her handbag –

Questions. Questions. Questions. Questions . . .

'But now I want you to think about last month,' I tell her. 'Can you remember which days your husband did not work in July?'

She shrugs her shoulders. 'He worked all of them . . .'

Inspector Kanehara places another piece of paper on the table. Inspector Kanehara says, 'Except the eighth and the twenty-second.'

'Can you remember what your husband did on those days?' I ask her. 'Did he stay at home with you? Did you go for supplies?'

'He often went for supplies,' she says. 'Back to Nikkō.'

Now Kanehara, Kai and I all glance up at each other –

'I never see them. I never really go back there now . . .'

'How often?' I ask her. 'Can you remember exactly when?'

But she says, 'We all need to eat, detective. Need food . . .'

'We know that,' I tell her. 'And we're not interested in whether your husband bought stuff legally or illegally. We're only interested in the dates you think he went looking for supplies . . .'

'I can't remember exactly,' she says. 'I'm sorry . . .'

'What about last month?' I ask her again. 'Your husband's work-sheet says he had the eighth and the twenty-second off.'

'Then he must have done,' she says. 'If you say so.'

'So can you remember what he did on those days?' I ask her

again. 'Did he stay home? Did he go out? What did he do?'

'How should I know?' she says. 'All the days are the same!'

'But surely not when your husband had a day off?'

'But I can't remember the eighth from the twenty-second,' she shouts. 'How can I remember one day from another . . .?'

Now Inspector Kanehara says, 'Then I'll try to help you remember. Do you read the newspaper in your house?'

She clutches her handbag. She nods her head.

'Well then,' says Kanehara. 'On the eighth of July there was the story of the baby born with two faces in Nagoya . . .'

She nods her head. She says, 'I remember . . .'

'And the twenty-second of July was the day that all the schools had to destroy their photographs of the Emperor . . .'

She nods her head again and says, 'I know . . .'

'Then can you remember anything else about those days?' asks Inspector Kanehara. 'Anything about what your husband did?'

'I was sure he went to work,' she says. 'I was sure.'

Inspector Kanehara nods. Kanehara says, 'I see.'

Now Inspector Kai sits forward again. Now Inspector Kai says, 'This is not your husband's first marriage, is it? Nor yours?'

'My first husband was killed in China,' she tells us.

'My condolences,' says Kai. 'When did he die?'

'Almost five years ago now,' she says.

'And so how long have you been married to Mr. Kodaira?'

'A year and a half,' she says. 'Not very long really.'

'And when did you become pregnant?' asks Kai –

'Almost straight away,' she says. 'Last March.'

Inspector Kai asks, 'Not before you married?'

'No!' she shouts. 'That's a dirty question!'

'Excuse me,' says Inspector Kai. 'And so when were you evacuated to stay with your family in Toyama?'

'It was last May,' says Mrs. Kodaira.

'But your husband stayed in Tokyo?'

'My husband hated it when I was evacuated back to Toyama,' she says. 'He cried at the ticket gate. Wā-wā. He cried on the platform. Wā-wā. He cried louder than a baby. Wā-wā . . .'

She dabs her eyes. She clutches her handbag –

Questions. Questions. Questions. Questions . . .

'I know he has done bad things in the past,' she says now.

166

'And I know he has changed jobs many times. But he was a good soldier and he's a good father to his child and since his child was born he has worked much harder and he even likes his present job.'

She clutches her handbag tighter and tighter –

Questions. Questions. Questions. Questions . . .

'My husband is a very friendly man,' says Mrs. Kodaira. 'My husband is also a very kind man. He will talk to anyone and he will help anyone and, in my opinion, this is actually his worst quality because that is why he's in trouble today. But my husband is not a violent man. Of course he gets angry if I serve him food he does not like or if there is not enough food for us all. But my husband never drinks alcohol and he is never violent and he never tells lies . . .'

'I believe you, Mrs. Kodaira,' says Chief Inspector Kanehara. 'And that's why I believe your husband's confession to be true . . .'

Her shoulders are shaking. Her shoulders trembling –

No answers. No answers. No answers. No answers . . .

In the cells downstairs, her husband is waiting.

*

I do not go back to Headquarters with Chief Inspector Kanehara and Inspector Kai. I take the Yamate Line from Meguro round to Shimbashi. I itch and I scratch now. *Gari-gari.* I get off the train at Shimbashi. I itch and I scratch. *Gari-gari.* The New Life Market is still cordoned off. I itch as I stand and I scratch as I stare. *Gari-gari.* Four military policemen in their white summer fatigues stand guard. I itch and I scratch. *Gari-gari.* Their blue eyes are blank and their black boots are rooted. I itch and I scratch. *Gari-gari.* Behind the sentries, inside the market building, I can see the rows of empty stalls. I itch as I turn and I scratch as I leave. *Gari-gari.* I walk down the back alleys and the shaded lanes, through the shadows and the arches to the old wooden stairs and the door at the top of those stairs –

I itch and I scratch. *Gari-gari.* I itch and I scratch –

But the door at the top of the stairs is closed –

The sign on Senju's door reads, *Gone to War.*

*

I walk into Tokyo Metropolitan Police Headquarters. I walk up the stairs to Police Arcade. I knock on the door to Chief Kita's office. I open it. I apologize. I bow. I apologize again. I take my seat at the table; Chief Kita at the head; Chief Inspectors Adachi and Kanehara to his right; Inspector Kai on his left; the same people and the same place but a different time and a different conversation today –

Today the conversation is just about Kodaira –

Inspector Kanehara, Inspector Kai and half of Room #1 spent yesterday questioning Kodaira while Nishi and I were chasing ghosts out at the International Palace and the rest of my room were walking the streets of Shiba, in the heat and in the dirt –

Investigation is footwork . . .

'There are some similarities with other cases,' says the chief. 'And so these other cases are going to need to be washed again. Now I know there is a shortage of manpower so, first of all, we are going to need to see how many of these other cases match up with the various places that the suspect Kodaira has lived and worked . . .'

'And the first case is that of Abe Yoshiko . . .'

Shinagawa. Shinagawa. Shinagawa . . .

'You might remember that the body of a teenage girl was found by a signal operator on the thirteenth of June this year, just over two months ago now, under a burnt-out truck in the scrapyard of the Shibaura Transportation Company at 7 Hamamachi, Shiba Ward, on the ocean side of Shinagawa train station . . .'

Adachi has his eyes on me . . .

'The autopsy revealed that the girl had been raped and then strangled with her own neckerchief on or around the ninth of June. The investigation headquarters was set up at Takanawa police station and was led by former Chief Inspector Mori who, as you all know, is now unfortunately no longer with us . . .'

Arrested and imprisoned . . .

'The body was identified as that of Abe Yoshiko who was fifteen years old and attended Dai-san Kokumin Gakkō in Hirai. However, investigations revealed she was actually in a *fūten* group with three other girls who were doing business with American soldiers. The autopsy also revealed that her last meal had consisted of macaroni and sausage, suggesting that she was being given food by American soldiers. There was also a persistent rumour that Abe had been sleeping with a uniformed officer from the Mita police station. As you may know, this officer was identified, questioned and then dismissed because of improper conduct . . .'

Dismissed and disgraced . . .

'However, because of the connection with the Shinchū Gun, because of the possible involvement of American soldiers, former Chief Inspector Mori felt unable to pursue the case and so it was recorded as unsolved and the banner rolled back up –

'The investigation officially closed.

'However, on reading through Kodaira's statements and cross-referencing them with unsolved crimes of a similar nature to the murder of Midorikawa and by further cross-referencing these unsolved crimes with the dates and places Kodaira is known to have lived and worked, Chief Inspector Kanehara now believes the suspect should be questioned about the murder of Abe Yoshiko in June.'

Inspector Kanehara thanks the chief. Then Kanehara says, 'Kodaira has already denied any knowledge of the murder of Abe Yoshiko. However, earlier this morning, Kodaira's wife inadvertently told us that Kodaira *had* mentioned the groups of young women who hang around the barracks and the laundry where he works. It is my hope that we will be able to find a witness who can place Kodaira in the company of Abe on or around the ninth of June this year and then Kodaira will have little choice but to confess again –

'So our first step will be to trace the other remaining members of Abe's *fūten* group. Fortunately, former Chief Inspector Mori interviewed them during the course of the initial investigation and their names and addresses were verified and recorded in the case files. If Abe was familiar with Kodaira then it is also likely one or more of these girls will also have been familiar . . .'

'And also,' adds the chief, 'there is a slight chance that one of these girls might be able to assist in the identification of the second body we found at Shiba . . .'

'Or even be that body,' laughs Chief Inspector Adachi –

His eyes on me, all their eyes on me now . . .

I clear my throat. I bow. I say, 'As you are all aware, as yet we have been unable to identify the body and so I very much appreciate and am very grateful for any assistance . . .'

The chief nods. The chief says, 'You will then personally go to the most likely addresses we have on file for these girls . . .'

They are punishing me, but punishing me for what?

'You will personally go to these addresses,' repeats the chief. 'It is important that you do not delegate this responsibility –'

Have there been complaints about me . . .?

'If any of the girls are found at any of these addresses, then I want you to accompany them to Shibuya police station –'

Why not Atago? Why not my room?

'There you will hand over any girls you find to Chief Inspector Kanehara. After Chief Inspector Kanehara has questioned these girls about Abe Yoshiko and the suspect Kodaira Yoshio, then you and the other men from Room #2 will be able to interview them about the second body found at Shiba Park –'

They are punishing me . . .

The chief stops talking. The chief looks up. The chief says, 'We appreciate your hard work in this, detective inspector –'

But for what?

The chief now turns to Inspector Kai. The chief says, 'Inspector Kai and the First Room will take a description of the victim Abe Yoshiko to the suspect Kodaira Yoshio's family, to his friends, to his neighbours and to his workmates –'

Questions. Questions. Questions . . .

Finally, the chief says, 'Chief Inspector Adachi and his team will continue to work on the case of the journalist Hayashi –

Answers. Answers and . . .

'Dismissed!'

Warnings!

*

I take a different route back to Atago. *They are punishing me.* The restaurant is a shack slapped together from pieces of corrugated metal. *They are warning me.* They have no white rice, but they have white bread. *They are punishing me.* They have custard cakes, but they have no white rice. *They are warning me.* I order a cup of coffee from the woman behind the counter and I squeeze onto an improvised stool. *They are punishing me.* The young man beside me is still wearing his uniform, his kitbag propped beneath the counter. *They are warning me.* He has short-cropped hair and smells of DDT. *They are punishing me.* There are no badges on his uniform and there is no light in his eyes. *They are warning me.* The woman behind the counter places a doughnut in front of him. 'You just got back, dear?'

The young man stares at the doughnut and nods his head.

170

'Got a wife waiting for you?' she asks. 'Your mother?'

The young man looks up from the plate now and says, 'They think I died honourably in battle three years ago. They received a citation from the Mayor of Tokyo which said Private Noma would forever be remembered and may his soul rest in peace. They were given a small white casket in which the ashes of my body had been brought back to Japan. They deposited the casket in our local temple. They placed a framed picture of me in my uniform on the family *butsudan*. They lit incense for me, offered white rice and sake . . .'

I don't want to remember. I don't want to remember . . .

'They wouldn't look at my face. They said Noma is dead . . .'

But here in the half-light, I can't forget . . .

'They wouldn't look at my feet . . .'

They are punishing us all . . .

'They said I'm a ghost . . .'

Warning us all . . .

No one is who they seem.

*

I stand over the sink again. *Black bile again*. I spit again. *Brown bile again*. I wipe my mouth again. *Yellow bile again*. I turn on the tap again. *Grey bile again*. I wash my face again. *Black bile, brown bile, yellow bile and grey*. I do not look into the mirror –

Cover the mirrors! Cover the mirrors!

I go upstairs into the borrowed office. Detectives Takeda and Ishida are still out looking for Ishihara Michiko and Ōzeki Hiromi. Detectives Hattori and Shimoda are still out looking for Konuma Yasuyo and Sugai Seiko. Detectives Sanada and Kimura still out looking for Tanabe Shimeko and Honma Fumiko. But Detective Nishi is sat at his borrowed desk in our borrowed office where I left him, where I left him to sit and wait for me. They are keeping me close. *Tight*. But I am keeping him closer –

'Wake up,' I say. 'Time to go . . .'

Down the Shibuya backstreets and down the Shibuya alleyways, to knock on the doors of the addresses we have taken from the Abe file, to be given another address and then another because this city is one huge sea of displaced persons, moving from here to there and back again to here, looking for a relative, looking for a home, looking for a job, looking for a meal, a familiar face on an un-bombed street in an un-burnt neighbourhood, selling this and selling that to buy a little of this and a little of that, from room to room, house to house, neighbourhood to neighbourhood, place to place, one minute here and one minute gone, gone and then back again, back and then gone again, tiny, tiny fish in a rough, rough sea –

It is late in the afternoon before we finally find one of Abe Yoshiko's friends, one of her *fūten* group, down another Shibuya backstreet, up another Shibuya alleyway, our shirts stuck to our backs and our trousers stuck to our legs –

Five in the afternoon and the girl is still asleep, says the landlady. The girl never rises before dusk. But she always pays her rent. Even brings home extra rations. Not that she should be telling two handsome detectives from the Tokyo Metropolitan Police Department. But yes, she is in her room and yes, the landlady agrees to go up and wake her –

Now the landlady mops her neck with a towel and gets up from her knees to go up the steep wooden stairs, along the narrow wooden corridor to the room of seventeen-year-old Masaoka Hisae –

Masaoka Hisae who follows her landlady back along the narrow wooden corridor, back down the steep wooden stairs to light a cigarette and tighten the belt of her *yukata* and narrow her eyes and scowl and then sigh and ask us, 'What do you want this time?'

*

The Shibuya police station is tense. The Shibuya police station is armed to its teeth. Nishi and I should have taken Masaoka to either the Meguro or the Atago police station. But the chief told us to take anybody we find into the Shibuya police station. The Shibuya station is tense. The Shibuya station is armed to its teeth. The Shibuya station raided the headquarters of Kakyō Sōkai, the association of Chinese merchants. The Shibuya station took away Kō Gyoku-Ju, the vice-president of the Kakyō Sōkai. The Shibuya station tense. The Shibuya Station armed to its teeth. The Shibuya station is holding Kō Gyoku-Ju in a cell downstairs. The Shibuya station doesn't want anyone to know. Shibuya station tense. Shibuya armed to its teeth. But everyone knows what will happen next –

Because they are coming. They are coming . . .

172

Nishi and I commandeer an upstairs room to use to interview Masaoka Hisae. Then Nishi and I send a message to Chief Inspector Kanehara at Metro Headquarters. Now Nishi and I leave Masaoka in a downstairs cell to wait until Inspector Kanehara arrives from Headquarters. Until it's time to begin the interview –

They are coming. They are coming . . .

Masaoka in the downstairs cell opposite Kō Gyoku-Ju and his bloodied face and his blackened eyes –

They are coming.

*

The night is coming down now. Chief Inspector Kanehara here now. The sweat running in rivers down Masaoka Hisae's face and neck. The fan in her hand never stops. The scowl on her face never leaves –

Never leaves until Kanehara shows her a photograph –

Masaoka stares at the photograph. Masaoka nods her head and says, 'Yoshiko and I visited his room in the barracks . . .'

'He has a room in the barracks, does he?'

'Yes,' she says. 'Just a futon and . . .'

'So you went there for sex?'

'He promised us *zanpan*,' she says. 'Bread and sausages from Shinchū kitchens. Leftovers and scraps . . .'

'Did you screw him?'

'Yes,' she says.

'Did Abe?'

'No,' she says. 'At least not while we were there together. She refused him . . .'

'And when was this?'

'May or June . . .'

'Where?'

'The Shinchū Gun barracks down at the old Naval Business and Accounting School in Shinagawa. That was where he worked and that was where he had his room . . .'

'Did you stay there?'

'Yes.'

'Both of you?'

'Three of us.'

'Who was the third girl?'

'Tominaga . . .'

'And did she fuck him?'

'Maybe,' laughs Masaoka. 'He could *fuck* all night could that one, said he was making up for all the screws he had lost . . .'

'But he wasn't Shinchū Gun, was he?'

'He had bread. He had meat.'

We have no rice. No food . . .

'You fuck for bread?'

We all beg for food . . .

'He was kind to us.'

We all beg . . .

'Kind to you?'

Beg . . .

'Yes.'

'So, after Abe was murdered, you never thought it could have been this man who killed your friend on the ninth of June?'

'No, but now you've told me all these things and now you've shown me his photograph, maybe . . .'

'But you didn't mention him to Chief Inspector Mori at the time of the murder, did you?'

'No one mentioned him to me and I didn't think he could have been her killer . . .'

'Did he tell you he'd already been convicted of the murder of his father-in-law?'

'He never said,' she smiles. 'Or I would have mentioned it.'

'He's also confessed to the rape and murder of a girl.'

'Well then, maybe he murdered Yoshiko . . .'

'But he definitely knew Abe Yoshiko?'

'He definitely knew her, yes.'

'He had asked her for sex?'

'He asked her for sex.'

'And she refused?'

'That night, yes.'

'Thank you,' says Chief Inspector Kanehara. 'You have been very helpful, Miss Masaoka.'

Masaoka Hisae narrows her eyes now and scowls at him and asks, 'Can I go home then?'

'In a little while,' I tell her. 'But I have a few more questions to ask you first . . .'

Masaoka Hisae folds her arms back in front of her and says, 'Go on then, please.'

'I want you to tell me a little bit more about your group.'

Masaoka Hisae laughs. 'My group? My *fūten* group?'

There are boots on the stairs now, boots coming . . .

'Yes,' I say. 'Their names and their ages . . .'

Boots coming down the corridor . . .

Now the door flies open without a knock, a uniformed policeman falling into the interview room, panting, 'All hell's broken loose, sir! The Formosans, the Chinese and the Koreans have all joined forces and they have attacked the markets at Shimbashi and at Ōji and they have stoned the Atago and Ōji police stations and they have injured Police Chief Hashioka of the Ōji police station . . .'

The Chinks are murdering the Japanese . . .

'There are thousands of them and they have come up from Osaka and Kobe and they have got Chinese sailors from a Chinese battleship anchored in Yokohama and they are armed with machine guns and they are firing at the police and the Japanese . . .'

The Chinks are murdering the Japanese . . .

'Now they are all heading this way, heading here to the Shibuya station to bust out Kō Gyoku-Ju . . .'

*

Kanehara, Nishi and I run downstairs and outside. *They are coming.* The night is here. *They are coming.* It is 9 p.m. and the battle lines have been drawn. *They are coming.* Two hundred policemen standing guard outside the Shibuya police station. *They are coming.* Inspector Adachi here, a short sword in one hand, a drawn pistol in the other. *They are coming.* Five trucks full of Formosans approach –

Nerves. Nerves. Nerves. Nerves. Nerves. Nerves . . .

'They are here! They are here! They are here!'

Nerves. Nerves. Nerves. Nerves. Nerves . . .

Police stop the first truck. *Nerves.* The driver tells the officers they are heading for the Kakyō Sōkai headquarters. *Nerves.* The officers make their report to the Shibuya chief. *Nerves.* The Shibuya chief tells them to let the trucks pass through. *Nerves.* The first truck is allowed through the checkpoint. *Nerves.* Then the second. *Nerves.* Then the third. *Nerves.* Then the fourth. *Nerves.* Finally the fifth –

Nerves. Nerves. Nerves. Nerves . . .

The fifth truck with its tailgate down. *Nerves*. The fifth truck with a machine gun mounted in the back. *Nerves*. The machine gun mounted in the back that now opens fire, that cuts through the night, that sends policemen running, hitting two policemen, cutting them down, other officers scrambling for their own revolvers, firing back –

Bang! Bang! Bang! Bang! Bang! Bang! Bang! Bang! Bang . . .

Now I see Senju's men and Tokyo policemen side by side –

Bang! Bang! Bang! Bang! Bang! Bang! Bang! Bang! Bang . . .

Formosans firing back from the trucks. Formosans falling from the backs of the trucks, bleeding. Formosans lying in the street –

Bang! Bang! Bang! Bang! Bang! Bang! Bang! Bang! Bang . . .

One, two, three, four, five, six Formosans lying in the street –

Bang! Bang! Bang! Bang! Bang! Bang! Bang! Bang! Bang . . .

Through the windscreen of a Formosan truck, the driver hit –

Bang! Bang! Bang! Bang! Bang! Bang! Bang! Bang! Bang . . .

The truck up on the sidewalk. The truck fast into a wall –

Bang! Bang! Bang! Bang! Bang! Bang! Bang! Bang . . .

Formosans spilling out of the back of the truck –

Bang! Bang! Bang! Bang! Bang! Bang! Bang . . .

They have iron clubs. They have pickaxes –

Bang! Bang! Bang! Bang! Bang! Bang . . .

We have revolvers. We have bullets –

Bang! Bang! Bang! Bang! Bang . . .

I see Senju Akira with his pistol –

Bang! Bang! Bang! Bang . . .

One, two, three, four –

Bang! Bang! Bang . . .

Dead Formosans –

Bang! Bang . . .

Five, six –

Bang!

*

There is blood in the entrance to the Shibuya police station. There is blood on the floor of reception. There is blood down the corridor. There is blood on the stairs. There is blood on the walls. There is blood in the cells downstairs. The cells all full. The cells all silent –

There are men with buckets. Men with mops –
The Victors will be here at any moment –
Men with cloths and men with bleach –
Men with pistols and men with gags –
The Victors will demand answers –
'They're here! They're here!'

We can hear the engines of the Victors' jeeps. We can hear their trucks. We can hear them pull up outside the Shibuya police station. We can hear their doors slam. We can hear the Victors' boots. Now we can see the Victors' faces –

Here they come again . . .

Through the station doors, the Victors and their Nisei translators, waving their arms and shouting their orders –

'What's happened here?' they ask the Shibuya police chief –

'There was an attack by a group of Formosans,' he says –

'Where are these Formosans now?' they ask him –

'They have fled in their trucks,' he tells them –

'Did you make any arrests?' they ask him –

'Not yet,' the Shibuya chief tells them –

'You have no suspects in custody?'

'Unfortunately not,' he says –

The Victors look around at the entrance to the Shibuya police station. The sparkling clean entrance to the Shibuya station. The Victors look around at the reception. The sparkling clean reception. The Victors look down the corridor. The sparkling clean corridor. But the Victors don't look down the stairs. The stairs that were covered in blood. The Victors don't look at the walls. The walls that were covered in blood. The Victors don't ask to see the cells downstairs. The cells that are full of men with gags in their mouths, full of other men with pistols in their hands, bloody gags and bloody pistols –

The Victors don't see these men with bloody pistols –

These men with bloody gags in their mouths –

See nothing. Hear nothing. Say nothing . . .

The Victors go back out through the station doors. The Victors get back in their trucks. They get back in their jeeps –

The Victors start their engines. The Victors leave –

'They're gone!'

And now so are we, back down the stairs that were covered in blood, back past the walls that were covered in blood, back to the cells that are still all full, that are still all silent –

No one can save them now . . .

They have stripped the Formosans of their pistols. *No one can save them now.* They have stripped the Formosans of their knives. *No one can save them now.* They have stripped the Formosans of their staves. *No one can save them now.* They have stripped the Formosans of their clubs. *No one can save them now.* They have stripped the Formosans of their pickaxes. *No one can save them now.* They have stripped the Formosans of their money. *No one can save them now.* They have stripped the Formosans of their clothes. *No one can save them now.* Now they will strip these Formosans of one last thing –

Every man in Shibuya police station down in the cells –

The rumours of dead Japanese policemen . . .

Policemen with guns. Policemen with swords –

I don't know why I came down here . . .

The cells have been opened –

I don't want to watch . . .

The beatings begun –

I don't want to see . . .

Chief Inspector Adachi with his short sword drawn; his lips are moving but no words are forming, tears rolling down his cheeks –

Adachi brings the blade of his short sword up close to his face. He stares into the blade, bewitched as the blade catches the light –

His eyes, red spots on white . . .

'Revenge! Revenge!'

Blood on the blade . . .

'Captain!'

There is fresh blood on the walls and there is fresh blood on the floors, on their knuckles and on their boots, on their shirt cuffs and on their pant legs, tonight the fresh blood is Formosan blood –

The blood on our hands and the blood on our lips . . .

There are lost teeth and bits of their bones –

We are the Losers. We are the Defeated . . .

There are screams and then silence.

They will drive their bodies out of the city, out beyond Kokubunji, beyond Tachikawa. They will turn their bodies into ash out among the trees of the Musashino plain. Then they will drive back into the city with the morning light. They will hose down the backs of their trucks. They will set fire to their arrest sheets. They will destroy the custody records. Then they will rewrite history –

Their history. Your history. My history. Our history . . .

They will tell lie upon lie, lie after lie, until they believe lie upon lie, lie after lie, until they believe there were no custody records. There were no arrest sheets. There were no beatings in the cells. There were no murders in the cells. There were no bloody bodies in the backs of their trucks. There are no ashes and bones out among the Musashino trees. They will tell lie upon lie, lie after lie after lie –

The caretaker and the boiler-man pick up their spades . . .

Until everyone believes these lies upon lies –

Pick up their spades and begin to heap the dirt . . .

These lies that everyone tells themselves –

Heap the dirt back into the hole . . .

Until everyone believes this history –

Back into the hole, over the man . . .

This history we teach ourselves –

Over the man, faster and faster . . .

Until I too believe these lies –

Faster and faster, as they . . .

Until I believe this history –

As they bury his cries . . .

My lies. My history.

*

Masaoka has heard the screams. Masaoka has heard the silence. Now Masaoka is ready to talk. Now Masaoka is ready to tell us whatever we want to hear. Now she will say whatever we want her to say –

But I am screaming now. *Inside.* I am shaking. *Outside –*

'There were four of us,' she is saying. 'Yoshiko, Tominaga Noriko, Shishikura Michiko and me. But after what happened to Yoshiko, then we all went our own separate ways . . .'

I am shaking. I am repeating, 'Aged approximately eighteen years old, wearing a yellow and dark-blue striped pinafore dress, a white half-sleeved chemise, dyed-pink socks and a pair of white canvas shoes with red rubber soles . . .'

Red rubber soles . . .

I am asking, 'Does this sound like Tominaga or Shishikura?'

'It could be Tominaga Noriko,' says Masaoka. 'It might be

Tominaga. It could be her. Then again, it could be anyone. But . . .'

I stare at Masaoka Hisae and I ask her, 'But what?'

'But I heard that Tominaga is missing,' she says.

I sit forward. I repeat, 'Tominaga is missing?'

'Since sometime in June,' she says. 'But . . .'

I am still staring at Masaoka. 'But what . . .?'

'But you hope it's her and I hope it isn't.'

'You're wrong,' I tell her, but Masaoka Hisae is looking past me now, looking over my shoulder to the door –

Chief Inspector Adachi standing in the doorway. Inspector Adachi asking me, 'What does she know?'

'Not much,' I tell him, still looking at Masaoka Hisae –

Shadow and sweat running in rivers down her face . . .

'Take this woman home then,' Chief Inspector Adachi tells Detective Nishi and then he says to me, 'Let's walk . . .'

*

Down another backstreet, up another alleyway, under another lantern, at another counter, Adachi orders the drinks, 'Whatever you have that won't send us insane or leave us blind or dead in the morning!'

Send us insane. Leave us blind. Dead in the morning . . .

The master puts two glasses of clear liquid on the counter –

'Cheers,' says Adachi as he raises his glass to mine –

And then adds, 'But you look terrible, inspector . . .'

'I feel terrible,' I tell him. 'Worse than terrible.'

'Because of tonight? The Formosans?'

'No, but it didn't help much . . .'

'It's the way things are,' says Adachi. 'The way things are.'

'Well then, I suppose I just don't like the way things are.'

'And you think I do?' asks Adachi. 'You think I do?'

'No,' I say. 'But you're surviving and I'm not.'

'You're still here,' he says. 'You've not run.'

'Where would I go? What would I do?'

'There's always the next life . . .'

Another life. Another name . . .

'No thanks,' I tell him. 'Twice is too many times for me. Much too many times . . .'

Adachi drains his glass. Adachi offers me a Lucky Strike.

Now Adachi asks, 'Have you seen Detective Fujita yet?'

I take his cig. I take his light. I tell him, 'Yes.'

He orders two more drinks. He asks, 'And?'

I finish my first drink. I say, 'He's gone.'

He raises his second glass. 'Gone?'

I say, 'And he's not coming back.'

'How do you know that?'

'He told me.'

'And do you always believe everything people tell you, Inspector Minami?'

'Not always, Chief Inspector Adachi. But this time I believed what he said, yes.'

'People say all kinds of things, especially these days.'

'Not Fujita,' I tell him. 'He's not coming back.'

Adachi puts out his cigarette. Adachi takes another drink. Adachi asks, 'Do you think Fujita killed Hayashi Jo?'

I put out my cigarette. I say, 'I don't know. Not any more.'

'So you think he might have? You think he had reason?'

I shrug my shoulders. I say, 'Him and everybody else.'

Adachi drains his second drink. 'Even you, then?'

I turn to look at Adachi. I ask him, 'Why me?'

Adachi smiles. Adachi laughs. 'You've got blood on the cuffs of your shirt. You've got blood on the legs of your trousers . . .'

I smile now. I laugh. I say, 'And so have you . . .'

'But mine is fresh blood, corporal.'

*

I have come again to this place. *Black bile again.* I have walked out of the light and into the shadow. *Brown bile again.* Into the temple grounds. *Yellow bile again.* But there is nothing here. *Grey bile again.* Nothing but the ruin of the old Black Gate. *Black bile.* Beneath the dark eaves of the Black Gate, I close my eyes. *Brown bile.* Under the Black Gate, I can hear a stray dog panting. *Yellow bile.* His house is lost, his master gone. *Grey bile.* In the ruin of the Black Gate, in the Year of the Dog, I stare at its feet. *Black bile, brown bile, yellow bile and grey.* I vomit and I vomit and I vomit and I vomit –

Cover the mirrors! Cover the mirrors!

This dog has no feet.

*

In the half-light, Yuki stands up. In the half-light, she picks up an unlined summer kimono draped over the rack by the mirror. In the half-light, Yuki changes into the summer kimono, a pattern printed low upon its skirt. In the half-light, she knots the red and purple striped undersash. In the half-light, Yuki sits back down beside me. In the half-light, she takes a cigarette from the package on the dresser. In the half-light, Yuki lights it. In the half-light, she hands it to me –

'It was like a fairy tale,' she smiles. 'The way we met . . .'

'Yes,' I laugh. 'A chance meeting in a sudden shower.'

'A love story from the older traditions,' she says, but Yuki is not smiling now, she is not laughing, she is crying now –

'There is tobacco smoke in my eyes,' she lies –

'Air raid! Air raid! Here comes an air raid!'

Now she lies back down next to me and she stares up into my eyes. Now she touches her finger to my nose and says, 'Don't sleep.'

But there is no more sleep because there is no Calmotin –

But I want to sleep, though I won't. I want to forget today, though I won't. I want to forget yesterday. The day before. This week. Last week. This month. Last month. This year. Last year. Every single year I have ever lived, but I won't forget because I can't forget. But here, here at least, here I can sometimes forget. For an odd hour –

In her arms. *I can forget.* Between her thighs. *I can forget . . .*

The many things I have left behind. The things I have lost –

I have failed you. I have failed you. I have failed you . . .

The many things I have seen. The things I have done –

Hour after hour. Day after day. Week after week . . .

The blood on the walls. The blood on the floor –

Month after month and year after year . . .

The blood on the cuffs of my shirt –

But in the half-light, I can't forget . . .

On the legs of my trousers –

I am sorry. I am sorry . . .

Here, in the half-light –

I have failed you all . . .

In the half-light.

8

August 22, 1946

Tokyo, 90°, very fine

Ton-ton. Ton-ton. Ton-ton. Ton-ton. Ton-ton. Ton-ton . . .

It is dawn now and the first trains have already been and gone. I itch and I scratch. *Gari-gari.* I wipe my face and I wipe my neck. There is no shadow here. No respite from the heat. I am standing at the end of my own street, watching the gate to my own house –

Ton-ton. Ton-ton. Ton-ton. Ton-ton. Ton-ton . . .

I walk down the street to my own house. I itch and I scratch. *Gari-gari.* I open the gate to my own house. I wipe my face and I wipe my neck again. I go up the path to my own house. I itch and I scratch. *Gari-gari.* I open the door to my house. I wipe my face and I wipe my neck. I stand in the *genkan* of my own house –

Ton-ton. Ton-ton. Ton-ton. Ton-ton . . .

The house is silent. *The mats are rotting.* The house still sleeping. *The doors in shreds.* I place the envelope of money and the bundle of food on the floor of the reception room. *The walls are falling in.* The house smells of my children –

Ton-ton. Ton-ton. Ton-ton . . .

I turn their shoes to face the door –

Ton-ton. Ton-ton . . .

I turn away and I walk away, itching and scratching, *gari-gari*, wiping my face and wiping my neck, as I start to run, to run away.

*

Tominaga Noriko's last known address was in Ōimachi, near to where Abe Yoshiko's body was found. Near to where Kodaira Yoshio works. *Kodaira country.* Near to where Miyazaki Mitsuko was murdered. Near to where Yuki lives. *My country . . .*

Tominaga Noriko's landlady invites me into her house and then up the stairs to Tominaga Noriko's rented little room at the end of the second-floor passage, next to a bathroom –

'I dust,' she says. 'But, other than that, it's just as she left it.'

'Why is that?' I ask her. 'Why don't you rent it out again?'

'The same reason I reported her missing, I suppose.'

'Why?' I ask her again. 'Just another tenant . . .?'

The landlady goes over to the small window and opens it. She shakes her head. 'But Noriko wasn't just another tenant, you see . . .

'She'd lost both her parents and her younger sister in the March air raids, her elder brother still missing in China . . .

'I have no one either now, you see. My husband is long dead and my sons are both dead too, one killed in the south early on and one killed in the north. My eldest was married but he had no children, his wife already remarried. I don't begrudge or blame her, these are the times we live in, but I have no one now but this house which was spared and the people who live here . . .

'Noriko had been here just over six months, a very pretty girl, a very polite and very friendly girl. Because of all your inquiries after the murder of her friend, I know now the kind of life Noriko led, but I never ever would have guessed . . .

'Noriko was so very quick to share whatever extra food or clothing she managed to get hold of, no matter what she had done for it, no matter what it had cost her . . .'

'*Asobu* . . .? *Asobu* . . .?'

I nod. I ask, 'So when did Miss Tominaga go missing?'

'About a month after her friend was killed, I think.'

'So that would be early to mid July?'

'Yes,' agrees the landlady. 'But it was definitely before the fifteenth of July because that was the date that the rent was due on her room. And so that was when I became worried . . .'

'So when did you report her missing?'

'Not until the start of this month.'

I ask her, 'Why did you wait?'

'I thought she might have just gone off for a bit, you see. Because of what had happened to her friend, because of all your investigations into her and her friends, because of all your questions, because of all your insinuations . . .'

'So if Miss Tominaga had just gone off for a bit, where do you think she would have gone?'

Tominaga Noriko's landlady turns away now. Tominaga

184

Noriko's landlady looks out of the window and does not answer –

'You said she might have just gone off for a bit; so where?'

The landlady shakes her head. 'It's too late. She's dead.'

'You don't know that,' I say. 'Maybe she's scared.'

The landlady shakes her head again. 'It's too late.'

'Maybe she just got scared and she ran away.'

Tominaga Noriko's landlady walks over to an old wooden chest of drawers. Tominaga Noriko's landlady opens the drawers. Tominaga Noriko's landlady says, 'But Noriko would never leave all her clothes behind, never leave all her cosmetics . . .'

'But you don't know that for certain,' I tell her again. 'People's plans can change quickly these days.'

'But Noriko would never not say goodbye,' she tells me. 'She would never leave like that, you see.'

I walk over to the chest of drawers. I touch the clothes inside. I walk over to the dresser. I touch the jars of cosmetics. I take the cover off the mirror. I touch the glass –

'Does this become me . . .?'

I say, 'There was a man, wasn't there?'

Tominaga Noriko's landlady catches a sob in her throat, puts a hand to her mouth. Now Tominaga Noriko's landlady closes the drawers, covers the mirror and says, 'You should know, detective.'

'What do you mean?' I ask. 'How should I know?'

'He was one of you, wasn't he?' she whispers –

'She was seeing a policeman?'

'For all the good it did her.'

Now I take out my notebook but I do not open it. I ask her, 'Did you ever see Miss Tominaga wear a yellow and dark-blue striped pinafore dress over a white half-sleeved chemise . . .'

The woman is crying. The woman nodding now –

'Dyed-pink socks and white canvas shoes . . .'

Nodding now and crying and crying –

'With red rubber soles . . .'

'Yes! Yes! Yes! Yes!' she is crying as she opens the drawers again, pulling out the clothes and sending them into the air as she frantically searches for a yellow and dark-blue striped pinafore dress, a white half-sleeved chemise and a pair of dyed-pink socks –

But these clothes are not here and neither am I –

Our body has a name. Our case closed . . .

I am running back down the stairs now –

Case closed! Case closed! Case . . .

Out of the house and straight into the face of a uniformed policeman asking, 'Are you Inspector Minami?'

'What is it?' I ask him. 'What is it?'

'Excuse me, sir,' he says. 'There is a meeting of all divisions, sections, and rooms at Metropolitan Headquarters . . .'

'How did you know you'd find me here?'

'Chief Inspector Adachi told me I'd find you here, sir.'

*

The chiefs of all the divisions are here. The heads of all the sections. The heads of every room. The chiefs of every single police station.

The Victors have also sent their observers and their spies; their Nisei translators; their collaborators in their turncoats; race traitors, these banana boys, with their yellow skins and white hearts –

'Asobu . . .? Asobu . . .? Asobu . . .? Asobu . . .?'

Down at the very front of the room, Fujimoto Yoshio, the chief of the Metropolitan Police Defence Bureau, stands up and begins his speech about the events of last night –

'Gentlemen, as you know, though such cases have occurred before in Osaka and in Kobe, this is the first case of Formosans openly attacking a police station in Tokyo . . .

'Details remain sketchy for now; however, it is reported that approximately five hundred Formosans, possibly aided by a further five hundred Chinese and Korean allies, all of whom are angry at their perceived exclusion from the New Life Market in Shimbashi, boarded at least five trucks at the Yaesu entrance of Tokyo station at about 7 p.m. last night. They then drove to the site of this Shimbashi New Life Market, where they rode about in a repetition of previous incidents at the market, hoping to confront members of the former Matsuda group. However, as the market is temporarily closed, there were no members of the Matsuda group present on this occasion and no confrontation occurred there. There are reports, however, that a few machine-gun bursts were heard . . .

'But finding no Matsuda group members at the Shimbashi New Life Market, the Formosans then headed in their trucks for the Shibuya precinct station and, on arriving there at approximately

9 p.m., they were met by over two hundred policemen who had been assigned to guard the station . . .

'Police initially stopped the trucks but then allowed them to pass when the Formosans insisted they were there only to peacefully visit the Kakyō Sōkai headquarters at the request of representatives of the Chinese Mission to Tokyo. However, as the trucks passed through the police lines, occupants of at least one truck opened fire on the police, aiming at the chief of the Shibuya police and seriously wounding two officers . . .'

Bang! Bang! . . .

'The officers were left with little alternative but to defend themselves and respond with revolvers. A fifteen-minute gun battle then ensued, wounding a further four officers, two seriously, and killing six Formosans and wounding a score more. The battle was waged with at least two machine guns, set up by the Formosans in their trucks, as well as with pistols, knives, staves, clubs, pickaxes and other weapons. One Formosan truck also ran up onto a sidewalk, injuring many of the passengers but allowing us to arrest twenty-seven of the Formosan occupants. Revolvers, iron clubs, wooden clubs and bottles of gasoline were also found inside the truck . . .'

These lies that everyone tells themselves . . .

'Unfortunately, the vast majority of the Formosans involved in this incident escaped during the course of the gun battle and the ensuing melee. These Formosan suspects remain at large . . .'

Until everyone believes this history . . .

'Furthermore, earlier yesterday evening the Ōji police station was also surrounded and attacked by a group of twenty to thirty Koreans, resulting in the hospitalization of Police Chief Hashioka of Ōji police station and the death of one Korean man . . .

'It is believed that the incident began at around 5 p.m. last night and grew out of a dispute between Japanese and Korean stall-operators in front of Ōji train station in which approximately forty or fifty people were involved in a fist fight . . .

'Police were called to restore order and to arrest the perpetrators, detaining them at the Ōji police station. It was at this point that the group of twenty to thirty Koreans surrounded the police station and began to stone the building. Police Chief Hashioka of Ōji police station went outside to remonstrate with the crowd and was himself then surrounded and stoned. Police Chief Hashioka was left with no alternative but to discharge his pistol in self-defence. His shots unfortunately pierced the lower abdomen of one of the Koreans, fatally wounding him . . .'

Bang! Bang! . . .

'However, the firing of the shot undoubtedly brought the dispute under control and order was restored. Police Chief Hashioka was then taken to the Imperial University Hospital where, we have been told, he will take about ten days to recover from his injuries.

'Finally, during the course of last night, there were also five separate reports of fights between rival Korean gangs, resulting in many injuries and much damage to property. The headquarters of the Youth League for the Promotion of Korean Independence at Denenchōfu in Ōmori Ward was attacked at around 5 a.m. by approximately three hundred Koreans in a number of trucks and vehicles, breaking windows, tables and chairs . . .

'As a result of information received, a comprehensive round-up of suspects in the Komatsugawa, Sunamachi and Kameido districts has been ordered . . .'

Bang! Bang! . . .

'But enough is enough!' shouts Chief Fujimoto now –

'The restoration and maintenance of order must be our priority as both policemen and as Japanese!

'The Tokyo Metropolitan Police will detail extra guards at all police stations with instructions to fire back in the event of a renewal or repetition of last night's attack . . .'

Bang! Bang! . . .

'To fire back not for the purpose of wounding or killing but for the arrest of the attackers and for restoring order because the restoration and the maintenance of order must be our priority . . .

'Extra guards have also been assigned to the Shimbashi Market and other markets believed to be potential targets . . .

'Today we will also urge the operators of all markets to tighten their own security and to cooperate fully with police in order to restore and maintain order in Tokyo . . .'

Bang! Bang! . . .

'But we will continue to urge them to accommodate legitimate businesses run by Chinese, Formosan and Korean operators inside their markets. We will also continue to offer ourselves as arbitrators and mediators in the case of any disputes . . .

'But enough is enough!' shouts Chief Fujimoto again –
'Restore order! Maintain order! Dismissed!'

*

Things never change. There are wars and there are restorations.
Things never change. There are wars and there are victories. *Things
never change.* There are wars and there are defeats. *Things never
change.* There are occupations and there are elections. *Things never
change.* Because there is always a second meeting. *Things never
change.* There is always a second meeting to discuss the first –

Never change. Never change. Never change . . .

For everyone to discuss the best ways in which to ignore the
conclusions of the first meeting; for everyone to pretend that the first
meeting never actually took place; to promise to keep things exactly
the way they were before the first meeting –

Never change. Never change . . .

'What a mess, what a mess, what a mess,' our chief is saying
over and over, again and again. 'The Victors will be talking about the
corruption of the police and the failure of justice again, warning of
the growth of racketeering and the power of the underground,
moaning about the mistreatment of minorities and the rebirth of
nationalism. The Victors will be wanting more reviews and more
reforms, watching us like hawks . . .'

Never change . . .

'But the Victors must let the markets reopen,' says Adachi.
'This whole situation is a direct result of SCAP's campaign against
the markets. I know they want to stop the hoarding and the pilfering
of goods meant for rations, to keep these goods out of the markets so
they are free to be distributed as rations at the official prices . . .

'But the markets and the vendors are only fulfilling a demand.
By closing the markets and then failing to meet that demand, the
Victors are only creating further hunger and frustration . . .

'And then, by forcing the markets to change, by limiting the
number of stalls, insisting on licences, then the Victors are again only
creating frustration among the excluded minorities . . .'

'Chief Inspector Adachi is exactly right,' agrees Kanehara. 'A
colleague from Chiba was telling me about this large catch of
sardines that was brought ashore. The regular rationing organization

was not properly equipped to handle such a catch. There was not enough ice to keep the fish from spoiling. There were not enough trucks available to bring the catch into Tokyo. Furthermore, the official price for the catch was so low that it couldn't cover the cost of the boats, the fishermen, the storage or the transportation . . .'

'So what happened to it all?' asks Inspector Kai.

'Well, this is my very point,' says Chief Inspector Kanehara. 'What would have happened last month, back when the markets were allowed to open, is that news of such a big catch would have caused a hoard of small stall-holders to descend on Chiba. They would have bought up the entire catch directly from the fishermen for cash. The stall-holders would then have brought the fish on their own backs into Tokyo in a couple of hours and would have had those sardines on their stalls within the day. Yes, the price would be higher than the official price but there would have been so much and from so many competing vendors that the price could not go too high . . .'

'What happened this time?' asks Kai again.

'A very small proportion of the catch was sold at a very high price to one of the gangs,' says Kanehara.

'And the rest of it?' asks Kai.

'It was all allowed to rot,' says Chief Inspector Kanehara. 'And what could be salvaged was then turned into fertilizer.'

Things never change. Things never change . . .

There is silence around the table now –

Never change. Never change . . .

There is silence until Chief Kita says, 'Chief Fujimoto wants us to keep out of the Shibuya and Shimbashi areas. Unfortunately, because of the Abe and Midorikawa cases, and because of the suspect Kodaira, we cannot keep out of the Shibuya area but we can refrain from using the Shibuya police station. Also, because of the proximity to Shiba Park, there is no way for us to avoid using the Atago police station. However, before you or any of your teams enter either Shibuya or the Shimbashi Market area, I want you to first request permission from Headquarters –

Things never change . . .

'I don't want any of my men caught in the crossfire!'

*

I go to the bathroom down the corridor. *I do not vomit*. I go into a cubicle. *I do not vomit*. I lock the door. *I do not vomit*. I stare into the bowl. *I do not vomit*. I stare at the stains. *I do not vomit*. I smell the ammonia. *I do not vomit*. The insects and the heat. *I do not vomit*. I wait for fifteen minutes inside the cubicle. *I do not vomit*. Now I unlock the cubicle door. *I do not vomit*. I rinse my face in the sink. *I do not vomit*. I do not look up into that mirror. *I do not vomit* . . .

I go back down the corridor. I knock on the door to the chief's office. I open the door. I step inside. I apologize. I bow –

'I am sorry to disturb you again,' I tell the chief. 'But I would be very grateful if you could spare me a moment . . .'

But today the chief does not offer me a seat or any tea. Today the chief does not even look up. He just asks, 'What is it now . . .?'

'I didn't have a chance to update you on our progress . . .'

Now the chief looks up. 'You've made some progress?'

'I feel we have a strong lead which I'd like to pursue.'

'Go on then, detective, what is this strong lead . . .'

'Well, as you know, we managed to locate Masaoka Hisae, who was one of Abe Yoshiko's friends. Well, Masaoka told me that the description of the second body found at Shiba Park resembled that of another of her friends, Tominaga Noriko . . .'

'Along with hundreds of other girls . . .'

'But this Tominaga girl is missing . . .'

'And who reported her missing?'

'Her landlady,' I tell the chief. 'And the dates fit because, although the landlady didn't report Tominaga missing until the first of this month, she said Tominaga actually went missing between the ninth and fifteenth of last month . . .'

'That's it?' asks the chief.

'Far from it,' I tell him. 'The landlady also confirmed that Tominaga Noriko wore clothes exactly like those that were found on the body at Shiba. A search of the missing girl's room and possessions revealed that these clothes are also missing . . .'

Now the chief is interested. 'Go on, detective . . .'

'Masaoka has confirmed that Kodaira knew Abe Yoshiko. Masaoka also confirmed that Kodaira knew Tominaga Noriko . . .'

'But that doesn't make her the dead body in Shiba Park.'

'Faced with this evidence, Kodaira will confess . . .'

'Faced with what evidence exactly, detective?' asks the chief.

'A missing girl had the same dress as a murdered girl? A missing girl was an acquaintance of another murdered girl?'

'But the dates are exactly right . . .'

'Have the landlady view the body then,' says the chief.

'But there is no body,' I tell him. 'It's just bones'

'You have her clothes, don't you, detective?'

I nod. I say, 'They're still up at Keiō.'

'Well, if she can positively identify them, through a repair or through a tear or anything, then that will be the evidence, won't it?'

'Thank you,' I say. 'And there was one other thing . . .'

'Quickly then,' says the chief. 'What is it?'

'I'd like to know the name of the uniformed officer who was dismissed during the initial Abe investigation?'

'Why do you want to know that?'

'He might know where the rest of Abe's friends have gone or he might even be able to assist in any possible identification . . .'

'No,' says the chief. 'Now is not the time.'

'I understand that,' I tell the chief. 'Then would it be possible for me to speak with former Chief Inspector Mori . . .'

'You know where Mori is?' laughs the chief –

The Matsuzawa Hospital for the Insane . . .

'Yes, but I thought he might still . . .'

I don't want to remember . . .

'And I thought you would have seen enough of that place . . .'

The blood-flecked scroll on the wall behind his desk . . .

'Inspector Mori might know what happened . . .'

But in the half-light, I can't forget . . .

'What happened is in the file. What he knew is in the file. There are no shortcuts, detective. Not any more,' says the chief –

The best friend my father ever had . . .

'Now go back to your men –

'Go back to your men,' he shouts. 'And lead your men!'

*

I do not take a different route back to Atago today. I take the same route I took two days ago. I take the same route past the bar in the basement of the three-storey reinforced concrete shell –

I don't want to remember. I don't want to . . .

I walk down the stairs but the door is closed today. I turn the handle and the door opens. I step inside the bar but the room is pitch-black. I look around the place but everything is rubble and ruin. I turn round and I go back up the stairs. I stand at the top of the stairs in the harsh white daylight, finding my bearings –

But everything looks the same . . .

The concrete shell, the blown-out rooms, the exposed girders. The young man still in his uniform who asks, 'You lost something?'

'There was a bar here,' I tell him. 'What happened to it?'

'Can't you guess?' laughs the man. 'A bomb fell on it.'

'No, no, no,' I say. 'I was only here two days ago . . .'

'You've got the wrong place then,' he says. 'This was one of those People's Bars. More than a hundred people were trapped and burned alive in there when the building took a direct hit . . .'

'But I was here two days ago,' I tell him again.

'Well, you were drinking with ghosts then.'

I stand in the harsh white daylight –

In the harsh white daylight –

'Is your watch broken, sir?'

The daylight which looks like raindrops. The raindrops good upon my face. My face to the sky. The sky blue not grey, high not low across the city. The city standing tall and shining bright in a neon night. A neon night reflected on my face. My face wet with the raindrops. The raindrops nothing but my tears. My tears in the daylight. The city fallen and drab, the sky grey and low –

'You were drinking with ghosts then . . .'

Fallen and drab, grey and low –

Now he shows me the watch . . .

In that harsh white daylight –

It still says twelve o'clock.

*

I am late, yet again. *I am looking in a mirror.* Detective Nishi is standing on the steps outside Atago police station. *I am looking in a mirror.* Detective Nishi is looking for me. *I am looking in a mirror.* Detective Nishi is waiting for me. *I am looking in a mirror.* Detective Nishi wants a word. *I am looking in a mirror.* Detective Nishi looks like shit. *I am looking in a mirror.* Detective Nishi looks like he hasn't slept. *I am looking in a mirror*. Detective Nishi telling me, 'Kodaira Yoshio has a mistress. Near Meguro . . .'

'How do you know that?'

'Masaoka told me.'

'Told you when?'

'Last night,' he says. 'When I took her back to her room.'

'Why didn't she mention it before? At the station?'

'She didn't think it was of any importance.'

I look at him. I ask, 'Did you fuck her?'

He looks away. He shakes his head –

'You're a bad liar, Nishi-kun.'

He starts to speak. He stops.

'Did you pay her for it?'

'I bought her a meal,' says Nishi. 'I bought her some drinks. I gave her a pack of cigarettes.'

'And now that's all your money gone until the end of the month,' I say. 'All your food and all your cigarettes . . .'

Nishi looks away again. Nishi nods.

I take out one hundred yen from my trouser pocket. I stuff it into his shirt pocket. I say, 'And you got a screw and a break in the case. Well done, detective . . .'

'Thank you,' he says. 'Are you going to tell Chief Inspector Kanehara and Detective Inspector Kai about this mistress?'

'No,' I tell him. 'We'll go and bring her in ourselves.'

'Thank you, sir,' says Nishi and then he adds, 'There was one other thing; about the Miyazaki Mitsuko file –'

'What about it?' I snap. 'What?'

'I think I know who took it –'

'Who?' I ask. 'Who . . .?'

'I was thinking about that day,' he says. 'The day of the case, the day of the surrender last year. Only Detective Fujita and –'

'You think Detective Fujita took the file?'

'Well, I didn't even go to the scene of the crime,' he says. 'And so I had no idea there was even a Metro file on the case. But Detective Fujita was there. Detective Fujita would have known . . .'

'So you think Fujita signed the file out using your name?'

Nishi nods. 'Who else could it have been?'

'Detective Fujita's face is well known,' I tell him. 'The duty officer wouldn't record your name instead . . .'

'Unless he had an incentive,' says Nishi. 'Or unless Fujita used a stooge to sign for it using my name.'

'A stooge?' I ask. 'Like who?'

'Detective Ishida, maybe.'

'Have you spoken to Ishida about the Miyazaki file yet?'

Nishi shakes his head. 'I wanted to speak to you first.'

'Good man,' I tell him. 'Now leave it to me.'

But Nishi won't leave it to me. Now Nishi says, 'Yet I still don't understand why Detective Fujita would want that file –'

'I'll find out,' I say. 'So you forget the file now.'

'But you do believe it wasn't me who took it?'

I nod. I say, 'Only because you're such a bad liar, detective.'

*

Back up the stairs. *Lead your men. Lead your men.* Back to the borrowed second-floor room. *I must see Ishida.* Back to the questions and the doubts in their eyes. *Lead your men. Lead your men.* Back to the dissent and the hate. *I must find that file.* But there's no drop in temperature here. *Lead your men. Lead your men.* No change in circumstances. *No Ishida. No file.* This room is still an oven, their breakfast still *zōsui; zōsui* still their only meal. *Lead your men. Lead your men.* Unwashed and unshaven, they have not seen their wives or their children, their lovers or their bastards, in well over a week –

Lead your men! Lead your men! Lead your men . . .

Sanada, Hattori, Takeda, Shimoda, Nishi and Kimura; I count my men again and then ask them, 'Where is Detective Ishida?'

They shrug their shoulders. They shake their heads –

I say to Takeda, 'I thought he was with you.'

'He was yesterday,' says Takeda.

'He was with you all day?'

'Yesterday, he was . . .'

'What about today?'

Detective Takeda shakes his head. Takeda looks at the others. Takeda says, 'Not today.'

The other detectives shake their heads again. The others agree, 'Not seen him today.'

Now Hattori says, 'Maybe he's looking for Detective Fujita.'

'What do you mean by that remark, detective?' I ask him –

Hattori shrugs his shoulders. Hattori says, 'Nothing.'

'Forget about Ishida,' I tell them all. 'But, if you do see him, you tell him to remain here until he has spoken to me. And you tell him, if he leaves again, then he leaves for good . . .'

The detectives nod their heads.

'Anyway, I have some much better news for you now,' I say. 'I have a possible name for our body; Tominaga Noriko –

'Tominaga was a friend of Abe Yoshiko who, as you know, we believe may also have been murdered by the suspect Kodaira. Tominaga has been missing since the second week of July and she was known to wear clothing the same as that found on our body . . .'

But there is no applause. There are still only doubts –

Lead your men! Lead your men! Lead your men . . .

Now I divide them into pairs again. *Lead your men.* I send Detectives Takeda and Kimura back to Tominaga Noriko's landlady in Ōimachi. *Lead your men.* I send them back to find out every last detail she knows about her former tenant's life. *Lead your men.* I send them back to arrange for her to come to the Keiō University Hospital tomorrow in order to view the clothes found on the body –

Lead your men! Lead your men . . .

I send Detectives Sanada and Shimoda back to Masaoka Hisae in Shibuya. *Lead your men.* I send them back to find out every last detail she knows about her friend's life –

Lead your men . . .

I leave Hattori in the borrowed second-floor room to wait for Ishida. *Lead your men.* Then I tell Detective Nishi to come with me.

'Excuse me, sir,' says Detective Hattori. 'But what about Ishihara Michiko and Ōzeki Hiromi? What about Tanabe Shimeko and Honma Fumiko? What about Konuma Yasuyo and Sugai Seiko?'

Lead your men! Lead your men! Lead your men . . .

'Of course,' I say. 'What did you find out?'

Lead your men! Lead your men . . .

'Nothing,' spits Hattori –

Lead your men . . . !

'Thank you, detective,' I say. 'Thank you very much.'

*

Masaoka Hisae gave Detective Nishi the name of Kodaira's mistress as one Okayama Hisayo and her address as being somewhere near Meguro, near the police station where Kodaira is now being held. Detective Nishi worked quickly and found a current address for an Okayama Hisayo, listed as living in an apartment building half-way between Meguro and Gotanda, so we walk down to Hamamatsu-chō station, take the Yamate loop train, getting off at Gotanda station –

Another shabby neighbourhood, another shabby building . . .

Kodaira Yoshio's mistress lives in an apartment building on a bluff overlooking the Meguro River. There are Western-style houses near here but they have all been requisitioned by the Victors and are now tightly guarded. Okayama Hisayo's apartment building is on the very edge of the bluff, level with the elevated line of the National Railway, level with the noise of the trains. And, while we are climbing the stairs to her apartment, it finally dawns on me that this building is one of the addresses we have listed for Kodaira Yoshio, that he and his wife used to live in this very building –

Another shabby apartment . . .

Nishi and I knock on the door of Okayama Hisayo's apartment, opening it and apologizing for disturbing her, for calling on her unannounced, introducing ourselves –

Another shabby room . . .

Okayama Hisayo is a plain, pale-skinned woman in her forties. She kneels down in the entrance to her apartment. She bows. She welcomes us. She apologizes for the poor state of her apartment. She invites us in. She has been expecting us, waiting for us –

She does not ask why we are here.

Nishi and I sit at her stained, low table in her hot, overcast room. We refuse her offer of tea. We apologize again for disturbing her, for calling on her unannounced –

But she is insisting on giving us tea, apologizing for having no snacks, leaving us alone in her room while she ducks behind a curtain to bring us some tea –

I turn away to look out of her window but the view is partially obstructed by a thick growth of trees near the edge of the cliff, though I can still see the Togoshi-Ebara heights rising beyond the Meguro River, still see the barrack houses going up, the light industry returning, but all else is burnt and ruined; the old feudal villas, their gardens now overgrown parks, their ponds diseased pools –

'It was originally a place for mistresses, up here,' says

Okayama Hisayo, placing two glasses of cold tea on the low table. 'The founder of the Shibaura Company was actually the man who first bought this land to build an apartment for his mistress. It used to be quite a fashionable address but the building has changed hands so many times now it has become quite run down . . .'

'It must still have some luck left though,' I say. 'To have escaped all the bombs and the fires.'

'Because it's up on a hill,' she says. 'And because of the railway and the river . . .'

'Do you see much of the other tenants?' I ask. 'Do you know your neighbours?'

'Not really,' she says. 'They used to be quite fussy in their choice of tenants. But the war changed all that. It turned back the clock. It's all hostesses and mistresses again now, balladeers and gangsters who sublet the rooms for hourly uses . . .'

'This building is also used as a hotel, then?' Nishi asks her. 'For prostitutes and their clients?'

'Every evening,' she says. 'Different women, different men.'

'And so do you know where they solicit their clients?'

'They work the cheap cafés near Gotanda station.'

'Each night?' Nishi asks. 'Different men?'

'The sound of laughter,' she says. 'And then of tears.'

I ask her, 'And so what do you do, Mrs. Okayama?'

'I work the cheap cafés near Gotanda station.'

Another plain woman, another shabby room, another shabby apartment, another shabby building, another shabby neighbourhood.

'Is that how you first met Kodaira Yoshio?'

Mrs. Okayama shakes her head and says, 'I am a widow now, but my husband was a bus driver. I met him when I worked as a bus girl. Mr. Kodaira's wife worked as a bus girl too. That's how I became friendly with his wife and it was her I knew first. Then, when the apartment downstairs fell vacant, I suggested Mrs. Kodaira and her husband move in. She then became pregnant and went back to her family home in Toyama to have the child. Because of the wartime situation, Mrs. Kodaira and the new baby stayed on in Toyama . . .'

'And so, when his wife was evacuated to Toyama, that was when you first became intimate with Kodaira?' asks Nishi.

'Mr. Kodaira had to stay on in Tokyo,' says the widow. 'And so his wife asked my daughter and me to take good care of him. But actually it was Mr. Kodaira who took care of us as he always had some extra food, he always had sweets and tobacco . . .'

'And what did he ask in exchange?' asks Nishi. 'For his extra food, his sweets and his tobacco . . .?'

'His wife had been pregnant,' she says. 'And then she was evacuated. He was alone and I . . .'

'Did Kodaira ever mention anyone called Tominaga Noriko?' I ask the Widow Okayama. 'Did he ever mention an Abe Yoshiko?'

'I know I wasn't the only one,' she says. 'I know there were even others in this very building. Others who were not widows, like me. Others whose husbands were soldiers . . .'

'But did you ever hear Kodaira talk about or ever see him with a girl aged approximately seventeen to eighteen years old; a girl you might have seen wearing a yellow and dark-blue striped pinafore dress over a white half-sleeved chemise?'

I think about her all the time . . .

'My daughter Kazuko had a dress just like that,' she says.

'Where is your daughter?' I ask. 'Does she live here?'

Mrs. Okayama shakes her head. 'I sent her away.'

'Where did you send her? When was this?'

'May last year,' she says. 'To Tochigi.'

The place where Kodaira is from . . .

'Did your daughter know Kodaira?' asks Detective Nishi. 'Did your daughter ever meet Kodaira?'

Mrs. Okayama nods. 'Why do you think I sent her away?'

'You sent her away because of Kodaira?' asks Nishi. 'Why?'

'Because I knew he liked my daughter, not me. But she wouldn't sleep with him and I would. He would screw me while she slept beside us; screw me while he stared at her . . .'

'How often did he come here?' asks Detective Nishi. 'How often did you let Kodaira sleep with you?'

'Mr. Kodaira had an appetite,' says the Widow Okayama. 'Mr. Kodaira was always hungry . . .'

'And was Kodaira violent with it?' I ask the widow. 'With his appetite, with his hunger?'

She haunts me . . .

Mrs. Okayama shakes her head. 'As long as you lay still.'

'He never forced you to have sex with him?' I ask her.

'We had to be quiet so we did not wake my daughter.'

'Did Kodaira ever put his hands around your neck?'

'I said it was like pretending to be dead . . .'

'Did he ever try to strangle you?'

'He said, we already are.'

We're already dead . . .

And then she says, suddenly from out of the silence, she says, 'I think death follows him, it must follow him wherever he goes . . .'

Death follows us, as we follow death . . .

'What do you mean?' I ask her –

'After I had sent my daughter away to Tochigi Prefecture, to live with my own mother, her grandmother, Mr. Kodaira kept asking and asking about her, saying we should go and visit her, saying we should see how she was, how we could go there to get *kaidashi*, to stock up on supplies. You don't know him, but Mr. Kodaira is a relentless man and he is a persuasive man and so last June, this would have been about a month after my daughter left, Mr. Kodaira and I went to Tochigi to visit my mother and my daughter . . .'

Death is everywhere. Death is everywhere . . .

But Nishi can't wait. Nishi can't let her finish. Nishi asks, 'You said death follows Kodaira; what do you mean?'

'Well, I only accompanied Mr. Kodaira to Tochigi that once,' she says. 'But I heard from my mother and my daughter that he has been back there on a number of other occasions . . .'

Nishi still can't wait, can't let her finish. Nishi asks her again, 'But your mother and daughter are still alive?'

'Of course they are,' says Mrs. Okayama. 'But my daughter told me someone had been murdered . . .'

Nishi asks, 'Murdered where?'

'In Kanuma,' she says. 'Near to the house where my mother and daughter are living . . .'

*

Detective Nishi and I take Mrs. Okayama to the Meguro police station. We take her upstairs. We sit her in a chair at a table in an interview room. We give her a glass of cold tea. We offer her a cigarette. Then we ask her to tell us again all the things she has told us before. We ask her about her late husband. We ask her about her mother. We ask her about her daughter. We ask her about the house in Kanuma. We ask her for the dates. We ask her for the places –

Personal things. Private things . . .

We ask about her lover. We ask about their sex –

Dirty things . . .

We bow. We thank her. We send her back home. We do not tell her that her former lover is sitting in the very next interview room, smoking our cigarettes and telling us jokes –

Dirty jokes.

*

Kodaira Yoshio is sat at the interview table, enjoying a cigarette and a joke with Chief Inspector Kanehara and Inspector Kai, a dirty joke from a dirty mouth. But Kodaira still notices when Adachi and I take our seats at the back of the room, he still notices the stenographer take a seat, through the smiles and the smoke Kodaira sees it all –

'Come on, Mr. Kodaira,' Kanehara laughs. 'Tell us.'

Kodaira shrugs. Kodaira smiles. 'Tell you what?'

'The youngest piece of pussy you've ever had?'

Kodaira shrugs again. Kodaira's smile widens –

'A man like you, you've had so much cunt . . .'

Kodaira laughing now, shakes his head –

'Don't be modest, we're all friends . . .'

Kodaira stops laughing and sighs –

'You're right,' he says. 'It's true I've had a lot of pussy and all kinds of pussy at that; Japanese, Chinese, Korean, Filipino, Russian, French, Australian, American . . .'

'You've had American pussy?' exclaims Inspector Kai. 'When did you have some of that?'

'When I was in the Imperial Japanese Navy,' laughs Kodaira. 'A whore in every port.'

'Go on then, tell us,' says Kai. 'What's white pussy like?'

'It's big and fucking hairy,' laughs Kodaira. 'Very big.'

'So you prefer a tight pussy?' asks Kai. 'Very tight?'

'What true Japanese man doesn't?' laughs Kodaira. 'You like a big huge bucket of a cunt to slop that tiny little cock of yours around in, do you Inspector Kai? Do you . . .?'

And we all laugh along with him. We all laugh along with our mouths wet and our cocks hard . . .

'I prefer to put it in a new pot,' he winks. 'A clean pot.'

'So the tighter the pussy, the better?' asks Kanehara –

Kodaira raises an imaginary glass and nods his head.

'And so the younger the pussy, the better then?'

'I like the taste of cherry on my cock,' laughs Kodaira again. 'What true Japanese man doesn't like to admire the first buds upon the cherry tree and then watch the blossoms fall . . .?'

'That's very poetically put,' says Kanehara. 'Very poetic.'

Kodaira asks, 'And who here doesn't agree with me?'

And we all nod along with him. We all nod along . . .

'So what is the earliest bud you've ever admired?'

Kodaira looks up at Kanehara and winks at him –

'Come on,' says Kanehara. 'You're teasing . . .'

'I don't really like them too young,' admits Kodaira. 'You see I'm a man who also likes a bit of chest, a bit of tit to suckle and to chew on, if you gentlemen understand what I mean?'

And we all nod along with him again . . .

'So, generally, sixteen years old or so would be my limit . . .'

'And there's nothing wrong with that,' says Kai –

But Kodaira doesn't answer him. Kodaira stares at Kai and then around the room; Kodaira has stopped laughing now. Kodaira has stopped smiling now. Now Kodaira whispers, 'But a man could have any age he wanted in China. Any age at all . . .'

'And did you take any age you wanted?' I ask him –

And Kodaira turns to look at me. And Kodaira recognizes me. And Kodaira laughs and tells me, 'You were there, detective. I'm sure you saw what I saw. I'm sure you did what I did . . .'

No one laughing along, no one nodding now . . .

Adachi is on his feet. Adachi says, 'Enough of this shit –'

Kodaira turns away from me. Kodaira looks at Adachi –

'You knew a fifteen-year-old girl called Abe Yoshiko. Abe Yoshiko hung around the barracks where you work. Abe Yoshiko and three of her friends were selling their cunts to the Shinchū Gun for leftovers and scraps. You fucked Abe Yoshiko and gave her scraps. On or around the ninth of June this year, you raped her, you strangled her and then you hid her body under a burnt-out truck in the scrapyard of the Shiba Transportation Company, didn't you . . .?'

Kodaira shaking his head, Kodaira whispering to himself –

'We have witnesses,' says Adachi. 'We have statements.'

Kodaira nodding his head now, Kodaira muttering –

'Be the man you are,' shouts Adachi. 'And confess!'

Kodaira is still. Now Kodaira says, 'Then I did it.'

'Did what?' asks Adachi. 'Tell us every detail.'

'I killed Abe,' he says. 'But I didn't rape her.'

'Really?' asks Adachi. 'Tell us why not?'

Kodaira laughs, 'She was too young.'

*

'Excellent work, Inspector Minami,' says Adachi. 'Excellent work.'

'If there's something you want,' I tell him. 'Just ask me.'

'You know what I want,' he whispers. 'I told you last night; I want to talk to Fujita; to talk to him about the murder of Hayashi Jo.'

'I told you,' I say. 'Fujita's gone and I don't know where.'

'Really?' he says. 'I thought a good night's sleep might have cleared your head, might have helped you remember who your real friends are; might have helped you to see things more clearly, see things my way, the clever way, the right way, the only way . . .'

'I didn't sleep at all last night and I don't know where he is.'

'That's a great shame,' he says. 'A very great shame.'

'It might well be a great shame but it's also the truth.'

'No, it's a great shame because it means you're going to have to go down to the Shimbashi Market and ask your new friend Senju Akira if he knows where his old friend Fujita might have gone . . .'

I curse him and I curse him and I curse him . . .

'If you want to know, then you go and ask Senju.'

'But Senju Akira's not my friend, he's yours.'

I curse him and now I curse myself . . .

'But why would Senju know anything?'

'You're right,' smiles Adachi. 'Senju might know nothing, but he'll know a lot more after he's finished reading the letter . . .'

I curse and I curse and I curse and I curse . . .

'What letter?' I ask. 'What are you talking about?'

'The letter about Fujita,' he smiles. 'About you.'

I curse and I curse and I curse . . .

I stare at him. I ask him again, 'What letter?'

'Can't you guess, Inspector Minami?' laughs Adachi now. 'The letter Hayashi Jo left in the drawer of his desk; the letter about

Detective Fujita and Nodera Tomiji and their plot to kill Matsuda Giichi; the letter that states Hayashi told you about this plot . . .'

'I'm a dead man then,' I say. 'It's a death sentence.'

'Who says you don't always get what you want?'

'Senju will kill me,' I say. 'I can't go to him.'

'Yes, you can,' he says. 'You'll be fine.'

'He'll kill me and you know it.'

Adachi takes an envelope from his jacket pocket. Adachi holds it up and laughs, 'Only if he was to actually read the letter . . .'

I want to kill *him*, here and now, in the upstairs corridor of the Meguro police station, stab *him*, again and again –

Blood on the blade . . .

Adachi pats my face. 'Remember who your real friends are, corporal. And remember, I want Fujita!'

*

I should not have come back in here. *I need a drink.* I should not have sat down at this table. *I need a cigarette.* I should have gone straight to Senju. *I need some pills.* I should have gone back to Atago. *I need to see Ishida.* I should have gone to see my family. *I need that file.* I should have gone back to Yuki. *I need some sleep.* Anywhere but back in here, here sat at this table, here before Kodaira Yoshio –

Kodaira Yoshio leans across the table and smiles at me again and says, 'Like I say, never heard of a Tominaga Noriko, soldier.'

'But you knew Abe and you knew her friend Masaoka?'

'Yes, I knew Masaoka and yes, I knew Abe Yoshiko.'

'Tominaga Noriko was one of their group . . .'

He laughs. 'There was no group, soldier.'

'But they were all *fūten* together . . .'

Kodaira Yoshio sighs and stretches his arms high above his head and then he says, 'It was just the two of them, soldier . . .'

'There were four of them,' I say. 'A gang of them.'

'Only time I ever saw groups of *fūten* was in China,' he says. 'But you'd know as much about them as I do, soldier . . .'

I should not have come. I should not have sat at this table –

I don't want to remember. I don't want to remember . . .

'Back in Jinan,' he laughs. 'I once saw a man who looked a lot like you. But he was Kempei and his name wasn't Minami.'

I itch and I itch. *Kodaira country*. I scratch and I scratch. *Kodaira country*. I walk and I walk. *Kodaira country*. I sweat and I sweat. From Meguro towards Shimbashi. *Kodaira country*. The route takes me close to the Takanawa police station. *Kodaira country*. Near to Shinagawa. *Kodaira country*. This is where the initial investigation into the murder of Abe Yoshiko was based. *Kodaira country*. The next police station, the one before Atago, is the Mita police station –

Kodaira country. Kodaira country. Kodaira country . . .

I change my direction. I change my course –

Kodaira country. Kodaira country . . .

I go up the steps and through the doors of the Mita police station. I show my TMPD identification at the front desk. I ask to see the duty sergeant; an old man and a suspicious man, suspicious of Headquarters and suspicious of me –

My country now, not his . . .

I tell him who I am, why I'm here and what I want –

'You're from Headquarters,' he says. 'So I've no choice but to give you his name. But I tell you this, though I no longer know his address, I wouldn't give it to you even if I did because you lot ruined his life once and no doubt you'd do it again . . .'

'Then just tell me his name,' I say. 'And I'm gone.'

The sergeant looks away as he spits, 'Murota . . .'

I turn away now, itching and scratching, *gari-gari*, as I walk back through the doors, back down the steps and back outside –

I itch and I scratch. *Gari-gari*. I itch and I scratch –

It is dark now. It is late now. But I am near.

I itch and I scratch. *Gari-gari*. My arms and my legs. *I turn their shoes to face the door*. I itch and I scratch. *Gari-gari*. My back and my front. *I turn their shoes to face the door*. I itch and I scratch. *Gari-gari*. My scalp and my groin. *I turn their shoes to face the door*. I itch and I scratch. *Gari-gari*. My nails blood, my hands blood –

Death is everywhere. Death is everywhere . . .

I take the scissors from her dresser. *I see black lice*. I take the cover off her mirror. *I see brown lice*. I begin to cut. *I see yellow lice*.

I cut the longer hairs on my head. *I see grey lice.* I cut the longer hairs on my body. *I see white lice.* Then I take the razor from her dresser. *I see black lice.* I open up the blade. *I see brown lice.* I dip the blade in the bowl of water by her bed. *I see yellow lice.* I have no soap but still I shave. *I see grey lice.* I shave off my hair. *I see white lice.* The hair on my head. *I see black lice.* The hair on my body. *I see brown lice.* Hair by hair. *I see yellow lice.* Every last strand. *I see grey lice.* In my scalp. *I see white lice.* In my groin. *I see black lice.* The skin beneath is red. *I see brown lice.* The skin beneath is raw –

I see yellow lice, I see grey lice, I see white lice . . .

The razor in my hand, the blade dull now –

Death is everywhere. Death is everywhere . . .

Black lice. Black lice. Black lice –

Death follows us as we follow death . . .

Yuki is awake. Her eyes open –

But we're already dead . . .

9

August 23, 1946

Tokyo, 87°, slightly cloudy

I turn their shoes to face the door. No Calmotin. No alcohol. No sleep. No dreams. No air. No breeze. I am out of luck. Everything is falling apart. *I turn their shoes to face the door.* No Calmotin. No alcohol. No sleep. No dreams. No air. No breeze. I am out of luck. Everything falling apart. *I turn their shoes to face the door, three times I turn their shoes to face the door.* No Calmotin. No alcohol. No sleep. No dreams. No air. No breeze. No luck. Everything falling apart again, over and over and over, again and again and again –

She is beside me now, beside me now, beside me now . . .

I cannot keep my eyes open but, when I close my eyes, I cannot sleep. I cannot sleep. I cannot sleep. I cannot sleep because I cannot stop thinking about her. I think about her all the time –

She is beside me now. She is beside me now . . .

I think about her all the time –

She is lying beside me now . . .

Her head slightly to the right. *In a yellow and dark-blue striped pinafore dress.* Her right arm outstretched. *In a white half-sleeved chemise.* Her left arm at her side. *In dyed-pink socks.* Her legs parted, raised and bent at the knee. *In white canvas shoes with red rubber soles.* My come drying on her stomach and on her ribs. *In white canvas shoes with red rubber soles.* She brings her left hand up to her stomach. *In dyed-pink socks.* She dips her fingers in my come. *In a white half-sleeved chemise.* She puts her fingers to her lips. *In a yellow and dark-blue striped pinafore dress.* She licks my come from her fingers. *In that yellow and dark-blue striped pinafore dress . . .*

She is beside me now, beside me now, beside me now –

I don't want to remember. I don't want to remember . . .

I smash my fist into her three-panelled vanity mirror –

But here, in the half-light, I can't forget . . .

I shout into her mirror, again and again –

207

No one is who they say they are . . .
'Who are you? Who are you?'

*

Through the doors of the borrowed police station. *Ishida*. I have a shaved head. *Ishida*. Up the stairs of the borrowed police station. *Ishida*. I have a bandaged hand. *Ishida*. To the borrowed second-floor room where Hattori, Takeda, Sanada, Shimoda, Nishi and Kimura have him; Ishida with a black eye, a bloody mouth and handcuffed wrists. *Ishida*. Ishida looking at the floor, staring at his boots –

'What's going on? What have you done to him?'

'You told us to keep him here,' says Hattori.

'I didn't tell you to beat and handcuff him.'

'We had no choice, did we?' says Hattori.

'What do you mean, you had no choice?'

'He was going to run,' says Takeda.

'Just like Fujita,' says Hattori –

Fujita. Fujita. Fujita . . .

I wipe my face. I wipe my neck. I walk over to Ishida. I raise his face from the floor. I ask him, 'Where have you been, detective?'

Ishida sucks the air in between his teeth but does not answer –

'We think he went to see Detective Fujita,' says Takeda –

'We reckon he knows where Fujita is,' agrees Sanada –

'And knows why Fujita has gone,' hisses Hattori –

'But he won't tell us anything,' says Shimoda –

'So I say we should turn him over to Chief Inspector Adachi,' says Hattori now. 'He'd soon make him talk . . .'

'Why turn him over to Chief Inspector Adachi?' I ask him. 'What would Chief Inspector Adachi want with Ishida?'

'The Chief Inspector was here looking for him,' says Hattori. 'Looking for Ishida, asking about Detective Fujita –'

I curse him and I curse him and I curse him . . .

'When was Chief Inspector Adachi here?'

'Yesterday evening,' says Hattori. 'When you weren't.'

I curse him and I curse myself . . .

They are mumbling now. They are muttering now –

I am the head of the room! I am the boss . . .

'Enough!' I shout. 'I want your reports now!'

They stop mumbling. They stop muttering –

Eyes full of dissent and eyes full of hate . . .

And they make their reports about Tominaga Noriko's landlady. And they make their reports about Masaoka Hisae –

'But there was one other thing,' says Detective Sanada. 'Masaoka told us that Kodaira Yoshio always had gifts on him . . .'

'You mean like food,' I ask him. 'Like *kaidashi*?'

'As well as food,' says Detective Sanada. 'Proper gifts for ladies like jewellery, watches, umbrellas, you know . . .?'

'Thank you, detective,' I say. 'Now I want you all back out on the streets today, back round Shiba and back round the park, back with the descriptions of Tominaga Noriko and Kodaira Yoshio . . .'

Investigation is footwork. Investigation is footwork . . .

'What about Ishida here?' asks Detective Hattori.

'Leave him to me,' I say. 'You just get to work.'

But Hattori doesn't move. 'What about Fujita?'

'Get to work, detective!' I shout –

But, for just one moment, Hattori still doesn't move. None of them move; Hattori, Takeda, Sanada, Shimoda, Nishi or Kimura; their eyes full of questions and doubts, full of dissent and hate –

Lead your men! Lead your men! Lead your men!

Now Hattori moves and then they all move –

I am the boss! I am the boss! I am the boss!

'Detective Nishi, you wait here,' I say –

Detective Nishi nods. Nishi waits –

'Detective Takeda! Detective Kimura!' I shout after them. 'What time will Tominaga's landlady be at Keiō Hospital?'

'I said I'd take her,' says Takeda. 'An hour ago.'

I am the boss! I am the boss! I am the boss!

'What are you standing around here for then?' I shout at him. 'You two go and pick her up and meet me up at Keiō with her . . .'

They are mumbling as they leave, muttering again.

Lead your men! Lead your men! Lead your men!

I turn to Detective Nishi. I take Detective Nishi off to one side. I ask him, 'Did you hear back from the Kanuma police?'

Detective Nishi nods. Detective Nishi takes a piece of paper from his jacket. Detective Nishi hands it to me –

'Good work, detective,' I tell him.

Nishi bows. Nishi thanks me –

I am the boss! I am the boss!
Nishi says it was nothing –
I am the boss! The boss!

I shake my head and I thank him. Now I write down a name on a piece of paper for him and tell him, 'Get me an address for this man and then meet me at Keiō with it as soon as you can . . .'

Nishi nods again. Nishi bows. Now Nishi leaves –

He leaves me alone with Detective Ishida.

*

My skin is red. *Ishida on his knees.* My skin is raw. *Where is the file?* My hand aches. *What file?* My body sweats. *The Miyazaki Mitsuko file.* The city stinks of shit. *I don't know what you're talking about.* Of shit and dirt and dust. *The Miyazaki Mitsuko file.* The dirt and the dust that coats my clothes and coats my skin. *I've never heard of it.* That scars my nostrils and burns my throat. *Liar! Liar! Liar!* With every passing jeep and with every passing truck. *No, no, no.* I take out my handkerchief. *The file Fujita asked you to sign out.* I take off my hat. *No, no, no.* I wipe my face. *The file you signed out under Nishi's name.* I wipe my neck. *I didn't.* I stare up at the bleached-white sky. *The file you were to give to Fujita.* The clouds of typhus. *No, no, no.* The clouds of dust. *The Miyazaki Mitsuko file.* The clouds of dirt. *I don't know what file you mean.* The clouds of shit. *The Miyazaki Mitsuko file!* My skin is red. *I don't know what you're talking about.* My skin is raw. *Tell me where it is!* My hand aches. *I don't know, I don't know, I don't know.* My body sweats. *I'm sorry, then.* The city stinks of shit. *But I really don't know.* The city stinks of defeat. *Because you're on your own now.* This city on its knees –

And I curse him. I curse Fujita. I curse Adachi. I curse Hattori. I curse Takeda. I curse Sanada. I curse Shimoda. I curse Nishi. I curse Kimura. I curse Kai. I curse Kanehara. I curse Kita. I curse them all but most of all, I curse myself, I curse myself, I curse myself –

'Get off your knees!' I shout. 'Get off your knees!'

*

The air is still thick with screams and sobs. *I hate hospitals.* I try not to breathe in. *I don't want to remember.* The gurneys still lined up against the walls. *I hate hospitals.* I try not to stare. *I don't want to*

210

remember. Through the waiting rooms, down the long corridors to the service elevator. *I hate hospitals.* I watch the elevator doors close. *I don't want to remember.* I ride the dark elevator down. *I hate hospitals.* I watch the elevator doors open. *I don't want to remember.* I watch them open again onto the light. *In the half-light.* I watch them open onto Dr. Nakadate; blood on his gown, blood on his mask, and blood on his gloves. *I can't forget.* Nakadate waiting for me. 'You've not spoken to Chief Kita, have you? About Miyazaki Mitsuko?'

'I'm sorry,' I tell him. 'But the file is missing . . .'

'So what? You could still go to Chief Kita.'

'Please give me a few more days . . .'

'A few more days? Why?'

Just a few more days . . .

'Please doctor, I need to find the file. I need to read it . . .'

'Why?' asks Nakadate. 'We all know what it must say.'

'But I wasn't even the senior officer,' I say. 'I need to find the file. I need to read it. And I need to speak to him . . .'

'And you think he'd do the same for you?'

'I really don't know any more.'

'A few more days,' says Nakadate now. 'But then I'll go to Chief Kita myself, Inspector . . .'

'Thank you.'

'And you really need to get that hand dressed too . . .'

'Thank you,' I say again. 'I know I do.'

'Then what are you waiting for?'

Not you. Not you. Not you . . .

I bow to the doctor. I thank the doctor. I turn and I walk away. Down the basement corridor. Past the walls of sinks and drains. Past the warnings and the signs. Past Detective Takeda and Detective Kimura now sat waiting in the corridor with Tominaga Noriko's landlady. Down to the glass doors. Into the autopsy room –

The clothing has already been laid out on one of the autopsy tables, the two white canvas shoes with their red rubber soles placed at its foot, and the ladies' undergarments found near the scene placed again on one of the smaller separate dissecting tables –

I wipe my face. I wipe my neck. I step back out into the corridor. I ask Tominaga Noriko's landlady to please step into the autopsy room. Tominaga Noriko's landlady follows me back inside. Now the landlady glances up at the autopsy table –

She is here. She is here. She is here . . .
The landlady collapses into tears –
She is here. She is here . . .
The landlady nods –
She is here . . .
'Yes,' whispers Tominaga Noriko's landlady and I turn, then I walk and now I run back down the corridor, past the walls of sinks and drains, past the warnings and the signs, into the elevator and into the dark, into the dark then back out into the light, out into the light –
Nishi waiting for me. Nishi with an address.

*

My skin is not red. *Nishi can't wait to ask.* My skin is not raw. *What happened?* My hand does not ache. *She identified the clothes.* My body does not sweat. *The yellow and dark-blue striped pinafore dress?* The city smells of flowers. *Yes.* Of flowers and blossom and perfume. *The white half-sleeved chemise?* The blossom and the perfume that coats my clothes and coats my skin. *Yes.* That tickles my nostrils and that caresses my throat. *The dyed-pink socks?* With every disappearing jeep and with every disappearing truck. *Yes.* I take out my handkerchief. *The white canvas shoes with red rubber soles?* I take off my hat. *Yes, yes, yes.* I wipe my face. *She identified all the clothing as belonging to Tominaga Noriko?* I wipe my neck. *Yes.* I stare up at the hint of blue in the sky. *Really?* The breeze in the air. *Yes.* The perfume on the breeze. *Then our body has a name?* The blossoms on the breeze. *Yes.* The flowers on the breeze. *Our body is Tominaga Noriko?* My skin is not red. *Yes.* My skin is not raw. *And her killer is Kodaira Yoshio?* My hand does not ache. *Yes.* My body does not sweat. *And you think he will confess?* The city smells of flowers. *Yes.* The city smells of garlands. *And then the case is closed?* The city smells of victory. *Yes.* My victory! My victory! My victory!

Not his victory. Not Fujita's victory. Not Adachi's victory. Not Kai's victory. Not Kanehara's victory. Not Kita's victory –
'This is my victory!' I shout. 'Mine! Mine! Mine!'

*

Murota Hideki is originally from Yamanashi Prefecture. But after he was fired from the police for his inappropriate behaviour, after he was left without a job, Murota Hideki did not go back to his family's home in Yamanashi. Murota Hideki stayed on in Tokyo. And so Murota Hideki still lives in an old wooden row house in Kitazawa, not far from the Shimo-Kitazawa station, the same old wooden row house that Detective Nishi found listed as his address in his personal records, the same old wooden row house before us now –

The knock, the bow and the introductions . . .

Murota Hideki comes to his doorway in his underwear. Murota Hideki is red faced. Murota Hideki looks at my identification. Murota Hideki is sweating heavily. Murota Hideki wipes his thick neck with a grey towel. Murota Hideki looks up into my eyes –

Eyes he has met somewhere before . . .

Murota Hideki stinks of alcohol. Murota Hideki knows he has no choice. Murota Hideki listens to what I have to say. Then Murota Hideki looks at Nishi and then back at me and now he says, 'I know I've no choice, but only one of you is coming inside.'

The spit and then the curse . . .

Murota Hideki turns back inside his house. Murota Hideki pads back across his old worn tatami. Murota Hideki sits back down at his low wooden table to wait for me –

In another shabby room . . .

For me to close the door on Nishi. To follow him inside his house. To pad across his tatami. To sit down at his table. To watch him pour himself another drink from the tall glass jug on the table –

Murota Hideki stirs the pale white mixture with a chopstick. Murota Hideki raises his glass. Murota Hideki takes a long drink. Now Murota Hideki asks, 'Come on, what do you want this time?'

'I want to talk to you about Abe Yoshiko,' I tell him –

'Not again,' he groans. 'What more is there to say?'

'Only you know that,' I say. 'Is there any more?'

'I fucked her just the once but I did not kill her,' he says. 'That's all I know. I fucked her but I did not kill her . . .'

'I know,' I tell him. 'We caught her killer.'

Now Murota Hideki looks up. 'Really?'

'You heard about the two bodies we found in Shiba Park last week? Well, one of the bodies was identified as a seventeen-year-old girl named Midorikawa Ryuko. Her family told us she was going to meet a man called Kodaira Yoshio on the day she went missing –

'We pulled this Kodaira in and now he's coughed . . .

'The Midorikawa girl had been raped and strangled and so now we're looking into any similar unsolved cases . . .'

'Abe Yoshiko,' says Murota Hideki –

'I fucked her but I did not kill her . . .'

'It's the first case we've reopened,' I tell him. 'And we've already been back through the statements, back to the witnesses and one of Abe's friends, a girl called Masaoka Hisae, she recognized this Kodaira and told us Abe knew him . . .'

'How did she know him?'

In another shabby room . . .

'The suspect Kodaira works in the laundry of a Shinchū Gun barracks in Shinagawa. As you know, Abe was part of a *fūten* group and they did their business with Americans at the same barracks. But not only Yankees; Kodaira would take them to a room he had there where they'd fuck him for food.'

'As you know . . .'

'And this Kodaira has confessed to killing Abe?' asks Murota.

'Yes,' I nod. 'When he was presented with this girl Masaoka's statement, Kodaira confessed to killing Abe Yoshiko . . .'

'What exactly did he say?' asks Murota. 'I want to know everything he said. I want to hear Kodaira's confession.'

'Everything he said . . . everything he said . . .'

'Why?' I ask him. 'What difference does it make to you?'

'What difference does it make to me?' he laughs. 'I only lost my job because of her, because of him, because he murdered her.'

'Because of him . . . because of her . . .'

I put up my hand to stop him. I nod. I take out my notebook. I flick through the pages of coarse paper. The pencil marks. And I say, 'It's not verbatim, but Kodaira confessed that on the ninth of June this year, he met Abe Yoshiko who had been coming to the barracks regularly for *zanpan*. That day, Kodaira felt a strong sexual urge and so he told Abe that if she came with him, he knew where he could get her some bread. Kodaira says he then took her to the scrapyard of the Shiba Transport Company, about two hundred metres from the barracks. Kodaira gave her some bread and then asked her to have sex with him. Abe refused and tried to run away. Kodaira caught her and throttled her. Kodaira then strangled her with her own neckerchief and fled. So far he has denied raping Abe and denied hiding the body under the burnt-out truck where it was found . . .'

'*I fucked her but I did not kill her . . . I fucked her . . .*'

Murota Hideki nods. Murota Hideki thanks me. Murota Hideki drains his glass. Murota Hideki pours himself another drink. Murota Hideki begins to stir it and stir it and stir it and stir it –

'*I fucked her . . . I fucked her . . . I fucked her . . .*'

'There were other girls in the *fūten* group,' I tell him.

Murota Hideki continues to stir his pale drink –

'One of them was called Tominaga Noriko . . .'

Murota Hideki stops stirring his drink –

'We have reason to believe that she might well be the second unidentified body we found in Shiba Park on the same day that the body of Midorikawa Ryuko was discovered . . .'

Murota Hideki begins to stir his drink again. 'And what reason is that, then, detective?'

'The second body found at Shiba was approximately the same age and height as Tominaga. The autopsy of the second body found at Shiba puts the time of death as sometime between the twentieth and the twenty-seventh of July. Tominaga went missing sometime between the ninth and the fifteenth of July. The second body was clothed in a yellow and dark-blue striped pinafore dress, a white half-sleeved chemise, dyed-pink socks and white canvas shoes with red rubber soles. Earlier this morning, Tominaga Noriko's former landlady identified these clothes as having belonged to Tominaga –

I think about her all the time, I think about her all the time . . .

'Tominaga Noriko knew Abe Yoshiko; Abe Yoshiko was murdered by Kodaira Yoshio; Kodaira Yoshio also murdered Midorikawa Ryuko; according to the autopsy reports on both bodies, Midorikawa Ryuko and the second body found at Shiba Park were both murdered by the same man; that man is Kodaira Yoshio –'

'*Never heard of a Tominaga Noriko, soldier . . .*'

'I believe the second body is that of Tominaga Noriko and that Kodaira Yoshio was her killer . . .'

Murota Hideki drains his glass. Murota Hideki claps his hands. 'So what do you need me for, then?'

'You knew Abe Yoshiko,' I tell him. 'So you might also have known Tominaga Noriko and might then be able to assist us . . .'

Murota Hideki shakes his head. Murota Hideki says, 'No.'

'No, you didn't know her or no, you won't assist us?'

Murota Hideki pours himself another drink. 'Both.'

'You knew Masaoka, another of Abe's friends?'

Murota Hideki shakes his head again. 'No.'

'You've admitted you were fucking Abe,' I tell him. 'All I'm asking is if you knew any of the other girls in the same group . . .'

'He wasn't fucking Abe Yoshiko,' says a woman's voice from out of the shadows, from out of the shadows behind the shabby curtain, behind the shabby curtain that partitions this shabby room –

Another shabby curtain in another shabby room . . .

Murota Hideki is on his feet. 'Shut up! Idiot! Shut up! Idiot!'

'He was fucking me,' says the woman, who now steps from out of the shadows and through the shabby curtain, from out of the shadows dressed in a yellow and dark-blue striped pinafore dress –

In another shabby yellow and dark-blue striped pinafore . . .

Murota Hideki grabbing hold of her bare thin white arms. Murota Hideki pushing her back through the curtain. Murota Hideki shouting, 'No! No! Shut up! You don't know what you're doing!'

Back through the curtain. Back into the shadows –

He is pleading with her now. He is begging her –

'Please shut up! Please, please shut up . . .'

Behind the curtain, in the shadows . . .

'But I won't pretend to be dead,' she says. 'I'm not a ghost.'

Murota whispering, 'But they'll come for you again . . .'

I stand up. I walk over to the curtain. 'Listen to me . . .'

I can hear Murota groaning, cursing and sobbing –

'I won't say anything to anyone,' I tell them –

Now Murota Hideki pushes the woman out of the shadows, through the curtains and says, 'Here you are, then, detective. Here –'

He pushes her chin and her face up, up towards the light –

Her chin and her face squeezed between his fingers –

'This is Tominaga Noriko,' hisses Murota Hideki. 'Are you satisfied now, detective? Are you happy now? Are you . . .?'

I shake my head. I say nothing. I wait for him –

For him to let go of her face and her chin –

For him to sit down. To pull her down –

To pour himself another drink –

For her to look up at me –

Tominaga Noriko . . .

'It was never Abe Yoshiko,' whispers Murota Hideki now. 'It

was always her, always Noriko, but it was always a secret and it always would have been had my luck not run out. But then again, my luck had already begun to run out before I even met Noriko . . .'

'*It was always a secret . . . It was always a secret . . .*'

'I suppose it's funny, really, in a way, I survived the whole of the war and then, on the very morning of the surrender, the very last day of the whole of the war, my luck finally ran out . . .'

'*My luck finally ran out . . . finally ran out . . .*'

'Towards the end of the war, that very month in fact, I had been transferred to the Shinagawa police station and so that was where I was working when, early that morning of the fifteenth of August last year, some boiler-man comes in saying he's discovered the naked body of a woman in an air-raid shelter . . .'

Miyazaki Mitsuko. Miyazaki Mitsuko . . .

'And so that was my first piece of bad luck, being at Shinagawa that morning when this man comes in, because now I and an Officer Uchida are sent up there to get the details and to wait for your mob to arrive from Headquarters . . .'

I have seen this man before . . .

'But it turns out the air-raid shelter is on naval property and so the case belongs to the Kempeitai. It's not your business. Not our business. The Kempeitai take the case . . .'

Eyes I have met before . . .

'Me and Officer Uchida were sent back down to Shinagawa police station to request an ambulance and that was that. Finished. Never heard anything more about it and never expected to. Case closed, as far as I was concerned . . .'

Now Murota Hideki points at Tominaga Noriko and says, 'Then I met her this last winter, on my beat. She's got no one and she's got nothing. I feel sorry for her and yes, I fancy her. I find her a place in Ōimachi. I give her money and I give her food –

'I take care of her and yes, I sleep with her . . .'

Murota Hideki looks over at Tominaga Noriko now and says, 'We both had nothing and now we have something.'

She haunts me here. She haunts me now . . .

Now Murota Hideki shakes his head. Murota Hideki sighs, 'But then two months ago, when this friend of hers, this Abe Yoshiko, was murdered, and in a similar manner and in a similar place to that body in Shinagawa last year, that was when I made my first mistake

217

and that was when my luck finally ran out for good . . .'

'My luck finally ran out for good . . . finally . . .'

'I tried to be a policeman. I tried to help. I was at the Mita police station by then but I went across to Takanawa, where the Abe team was based, and I asked to see the officer in charge . . .'

'Who is unfortunately no longer with us . . .'

'I met this officer, man called Chief Inspector Mori, and I told him about the body in the air-raid shelter at Shinagawa. Chief Inspector Mori thanked me and, again, I thought that was that. I'd done what I could. I'd tried to help. Finished. And I never expected to hear anything more about it. Case closed again for me . . .'

Case closed . . . case closed . . . case closed . . .

'But then, the very next day, this Chief Inspector Mori is down at the Mita police station, to question *me* . . .'

I don't want to remember . . .

'Can I remember any further details? Can I remember who was working with me at Shinagawa on that day? Can I remember the two detectives who were sent out from Headquarters? Can I remember the names of the officers from the Kempeitai? The witnesses? And so on and so on and so on . . .'

But in the half-light . . .

'All I can tell him though is what I told him the day before, same as I just told you, but that's when I should have known, that's when I should have guessed . . .'

I can't forget . . .

'Because no sooner is Mori gone than some other Metro detective is down at Mita to see me, hauling me back up to HQ, telling me I've been a bad cop, that he's heard all about me, screwing *pan-pan* girls on my beat, like I'm the only cop in the city who's ever had a whore on his beat, like he hasn't got better things to do than chase after me, but he's relentless, this detective, he never gives up, asking me to confess to this, to confess to that, asking me for the name of my girl, for Noriko's name, and now I get the picture –

'He is here to punish me. He is here to warn me –

'And I don't know why I ever thought it would work, or why I ever thought it was a good idea, but there's no way I'm ever going to give him Noriko's name, so I tell him I was seeing Abe, that I fucked her but I never killed her, and guess what . . .?

'He bought it, believed it was Abe –

'And so they fired me –

'For conduct unbecoming a police officer, but I didn't care because they didn't know about Noriko and that meant she was safe. Safe. Ten days later, I read that this Chief Inspector Mori has been purged by the SCAP and gone insane. Mad. Then I knew I'd made the right decision, knew I'd made the right choice . . .'

The Matsuzawa Hospital for the Insane . . .

'Until today. Until you turned up . . .'

'My luck finally ran out . . .'

'I knew we should have run, we should have gone as far away as we could from here . . .,' and now Murota Hideki's words trail off, trail off back into the shadows, back into the shadows behind the shabby curtain, behind the shabby curtain that partitions this shabby room, the shadows from the light and the light from the shadows –

The voices from the echoes and the truth from the lies . . .

This shabby curtain, this shabby country –

'Are you satisfied now, detective?' asks Murota Hideki. 'Are you happy now? Have you heard and seen enough now? Heard enough about me and seen enough of her, have you now, officer?'

'No,' I tell him. 'I want the name of the detective.'

'Why do you want that?' he laughs. 'What for?'

'Tell me his name,' I say. 'And then I'm gone.'

Murota spits, 'Said his name was Adachi . . .'

'Are you satisfied now, detective?'

'For what that's worth,' laughs Murota now. 'Because no one is ever who they say they are . . .'

Here in the half-light . . .

'Not these days . . .'

I have nothing more to ask them. *My skin is red.* Nothing more to say to them. *My skin is raw.* I pick up my hat. *My hand aches.* I get up from their low table in their shabby room. *My body sweats.* In this shabby house, in this shabby city, in this shabby country –

In this place of defeat. In this place of capitulation . . .

'You be careful out there, detective,' Murota Hideki tells me. 'And you remember my face and remember what happened to me. And remember the name of Chief Inspector Mori and you remember what happened to him. You remember us both now, detective . . .'

This place of surrender. This place of occupation . . .

'I'll remember you,' I say. I turn to Tominaga –

In this place of ghosts, this place of ghosts . . .
I turn to Tominaga Noriko and I say, 'Thank you, miss.'
And she thanks me back and then she bows her head –
In her yellow and dark-blue striped pinafore dress . . .
'And you remember this as well then,' says Murota Hideki.
'If you ever tell anyone about her, you ever tell anyone where she is,
that she's here with me, then I will find you and I will kill you . . .'
In this place of death. In this place of silence . . .
I turn back to Murota. I bow to him –
In this place of no resistance.

*

My skin is red. *Nishi can't wait.* My skin is raw. *Nishi wants to know
what happened.* My hand aches. *I say nothing.* My body sweats.
What did Murota say? The city stinks of shit. *I say nothing.* Of shit
and dirt and dust. *Did he know Tominaga Noriko?* The dirt and the
dust that coats my clothes and coats my skin. *I say nothing.* That
scratches my nostrils and burns my throat. *Did he remember her?*
With every passing jeep and with every passing truck. *Nothing,
nothing, nothing.* I take out my handkerchief. *It isn't her, is it?* I take
off my hat. *No.* I wipe my face. *The body in the park?* I wipe my
neck. *I'm sorry.* I stare up at the bleached-white sky. *It isn't
Tominaga Noriko, is it?* The clouds of typhus. *I'm sorry.* The clouds
of dust. *The case isn't closed, is it?* The clouds of dirt. *I'm sorry.* The
clouds of shit. *This isn't victory, is it?* My skin is red. *I'm sorry, I'm
sorry, I'm sorry.* My skin is raw. *This is defeat again.* My hand aches.
Yes. My body sweats. *We haven't won.* The city stinks of shit. *No.*
The city stinks of defeat. *We have lost again.* This city on its knees.
Yes. Nishi on his knees. *We always lose. Always, always lose . . .*
      'No! No! No!' I shout. 'Get off your knees!'

*

I walk up the stairs to Police Arcade. *To the smells and the stains.*
Chief Inspector Adachi is standing in the corridor. *There is no escape.*
Chief Inspector Adachi is looking for me. *We should turn him over to
Chief Inspector Adachi.* Chief Inspector Adachi is waiting for me.
The Chief Inspector was here looking for him. Chief Inspector
Adachi walks me to the end of the corridor. *Looking for Ishida,*

asking about Detective Fujita. Chief Inspector Adachi pulls me into the bathroom. *Said his name was Adachi.* Chief Inspector Adachi pushes me into a cubicle. *No escape from the smells and the stains . . .*

Chief Inspector Adachi puts me up against the wall –

The smells of ammonia and the stains of shit . . .

Chief Inspector Adachi stares into my face and then he says, 'You haven't been to see Senju yet, have you, detective?'

The smells of amnesia, the stains of blood . . .

'You've been following me, sir?'

The stains on his hands . . .

'I'm not the only one.'

The stains on mine . . .

'Then you'll know I've been busy,' I tell him. 'Busy searching for the Miyazaki Mitsuko file, chief inspector, sir.'

Now he takes his hands off me. Now he steps back. Now he asks, 'And which Miyazaki Mitsuko file would that be?'

'The Tokyo MPD file on the murder of Miyazaki Mitsuko. The file that was signed out just four days ago –'

'Signed out by whom?' asks Adachi –

'Detective Nishi,' I say. 'But he denies it and I believe him.'

'So who do you *believe* signed it out, detective?'

'I think Fujita got Ishida to sign it out under Nishi's name.'

'Why?' asks Adachi, but Adachi already knows –

'Insurance,' I say. 'Extortion. Blackmail . . .'

'Blackmail?' he asks, but he knows –

'You.'

'And what about *you*, corporal? Mine won't be the only name in that file, will it?'

'I don't know,' I tell him. 'I haven't read it, have I?'

'*But I wasn't even the senior officer,*' I say. '*I need to find the file. I need to read it. And I need to speak to him . . .*'

'Then go to Senju and go soon,' hisses Adachi. 'Ask him where Fujita is. If Senju says he doesn't know, you tell him about Fujita and Nodera Tomiji. You tell him about the plot.'

'*And you think he'd do the same for you?*'

'But then Senju will rip Tokyo apart looking for Fujita,' I say. 'He'll find him and he'll kill him before we . . .'

'*I really don't know any more.*'

'Exactly,' smiles Adachi.

Adachi and Kanehara are sat on his right, Kai and I on his left, the chief telling us, 'As you all know, we had a quick success yesterday in attaining Kodaira Yoshio's confession to the murder of Abe Yoshiko. And I think we should all thank Chief Inspector Kanehara for his legwork and Chief Inspector Adachi for his interrogation . . .'

Inspector Kai and I nodding our heads –

'As we said, there are similarities with other cases and, after this early success with the Abe case, I feel there is every reason to go ahead and wash these other cases, manpower permitting. And so Inspector Kai, I believe you have the next one . . .'

Inspector Kai stands up now. Kai nods. 'Shinokawa Tatsue; seventeen years old; raped and strangled . . .

'Her body was found on the sixteenth of January this year in the basement of the annex of the former Toyoko Department Store at 20 Namiki-chō, Shibuya Ward, next to Shibuya station This basement formerly housed the employee canteen of the Toyoko Department Store but, since it was badly damaged during the air raids, it is now used only for storage . . .

'On the sixteenth of January this year, a guard checking the storage area in the basement, removed some shelves and found the body of Shinokawa . . .

'The body was in a state of some decay and the autopsy, which was conducted by Dr. Nakadate at the Keiō University Hospital, concluded that Shinokawa had probably died between the last week of October and the first week of November last year. However, the autopsy also revealed that Shinokawa Tatsue had most probably been raped before being strangled to death . . .'

'Probably?' asks Chief Inspector Adachi. 'Why probably?'

Kai says, 'Presumably because of the state of the body.'

'Where was the investigation headquarters?'

Kai says, 'The Shibuya precinct station.'

'And who was in charge?'

Kai says, 'Mori.'

'Chief Inspector Mori,' says Chief Kita. 'Former Chief Inspector Mori was in charge.'

Kai blushes now. Kai bows. 'Former Chief Inspector Mori.'

'But that's strange, don't you think?' asks Adachi. 'I've read the entirety of the Abe Yoshiko case file, every single scrap of paperwork, and former Chief Inspector Mori never once mentions the Shinokawa case in his notes on the Abe case, never once . . .'

Inspector Kai shakes his head. Kai says, 'No.'

'And yet, both victims were of a similar age,' continues Adachi. 'Both had been raped and strangled. Both were his cases . . .'

'But let us not forget the particular and peculiar circumstances of our times, Chief Inspector Adachi,' interrupts Chief Kita. 'Former Chief Inspector Mori was a very competent and a very diligent police officer but, and as you are well aware, there has been a marked rise in crimes and lawlessness in Tokyo over the past year and, equally, there has been a marked fall in the number of police officers and the resources and equipment available to us –

'Now Chief Inspector Mori and I discussed this particular case at length and we both felt that, because of the state of the body, because of the shortage of manpower, the shortage of resources, our efforts were better directed towards other cases . . .

'And so, ultimately, it was my decision to roll the banner back up again and close this case.'

Chief Inspector Adachi has his head bowed. Inspector Adachi does not look up. Adachi says, 'I am sorry. Please excuse my rudeness and my presumption. I am sorry. It was not my intention to cast aspersions or make insinuations about the competence of Chief Inspector Mori. We all worked with him and we all learned from him. We all valued him and we all miss him . . .'

'Thank you, chief inspector,' says Chief Kita. 'Inspector Kai, is there anything else you would like to add about the case?'

Inspector Kai closes his mouth. Kai nods. He says, 'Her umbrella and twenty yen in cash were also reported missing.'

'*Kodaira Yoshio always had gifts on him . . . Proper gifts for ladies like jewellery, watches, umbrellas, you know . . . ?*'

'Thank you, inspector,' says the chief. 'Right, as you all know, at the time of Shinokawa's murder, Kodaira was living in Wakagi-chō in Shibuya Ward. And, as Chief Inspector Adachi stated, the age of the victim and the cause of death are the same as both those of Midorikawa Ryuko and Abe Yoshiko. So I want Inspector Kai and his Room to reopen this case, to reinterview the original witnesses from the original investigation as well as Kodaira's wife and his immediate family living here in Tokyo . . .

'Unfortunately, we will also have to make use of the Shibuya police station again as Inspector Kai will need officers from the Shibuya precinct to question local residents about Kodaira and Shinokawa. Hopefully a lead or a witness will quickly turn up that will again prompt Kodaira Yoshio to make another confession . . .'

More legwork. More questions. More reports . . .

'Finally,' says the chief. 'Inspector Minami . . .'

There are things to say. Things not to say . . .

I wipe my neck. I stand up. I tell them about Kodaira Yoshio's mistress, Okayama Hisayo. I tell them about the rumours of a murder in Kanuma in Tochigi Prefecture –

There are things to say . . .

'Baba Hiroko, aged nineteen, found raped and strangled with her own scarf on the third of January this year, in Nishi Katamura, Tochigi. This fell in the jurisdiction of the Kanuma police, Tochigi. As you all know, Kodaira is originally from Nikkō in Tochigi Prefecture. His mistress, the widow Okayama Hisayo, has told us that Kodaira accompanied her on a visit to her mother's house which is located one mountain away from Kanuma station. Okayama also told us that Kodaira has been back to the area on numerous occasions ostensibly for *kaidashi* and supplies and so on . . .

'I think there is a strong possibility, given the age of the victim, the cause and circumstances of her death, the proximity to Kodaira Yoshio's known haunts and the timeframe, that Kodaira should be questioned about this murder . . .'

There's no applause here either . . .

I do not tell them about Tominaga Noriko's landlady and the clothing. I do not tell them about visiting Murota Hideki. I do not tell them about seeing Tominaga Noriko –

Things not to say . . .

But Adachi is waiting for me. Adachi is always waiting –

'But are you any nearer identifying the second Shiba body? What about this missing friend of Abe Yoshiko? What about the statement by her landlady? You said there was a possibility that the body might be this missing girl? This friend of Abe?'

But I told you nothing. I told you nothing . . .

'I am very sorry,' I tell him now. 'But we no longer believe that to be the case, Chief Inspector Adachi, sir.'

'Is that right?' asks Adachi. 'And yet only yesterday you

seemed so very, very sure . . .'

'And I'm very, very sorry,' I tell him again. 'And we are equally disappointed, sir.'

'So are you now saying this friend of Abe is alive?' he asks. 'You've actually found her? Eliminated her?'

Tell him nothing . . .

'No, sir,' I lie. 'I just mean that her landlady failed to identify the clothing as hers . . .'

Nothing . . .

'So she is still missing, then? This friend of Abe Yoshiko?'

I nod. I say, 'She may be missing, but she's not our body.'

But Adachi doesn't give up. Adachi never gives up . . .

'And what about all the other girls?' he asks me –

I shake my head. I ask, 'What other girls?'

'All the other girls aged fifteen to twenty years old reported missing in the past two months. These other girls that you have had your own men combing the streets of Tokyo for . . .'

I curse him. I curse him. I curse him . . .

'The enquiries are still ongoing, sir.'

I curse him and I curse myself . . .

'So are you then any nearer actually identifying the body?'

I meet his eyes now. I stare back at him. I say, 'No.'

No, no, no, no, no, no, no, no, no, no, no . . .

'That's enough,' says Chief Kita –

No, no, no, no, no, no, no, no, no . . .

Now the chief stands up –

It's finished. It's over . . .

And we all stand up and all bow and now all start to leave –

'Chief Inspector Adachi,' says the chief. 'Please wait.'

Chief Inspector Adachi bows and sits back down.

'And Inspector Minami, please wait outside.'

I bow my head. Then I step outside.

*

Thirty minutes later Chief Inspector Adachi steps out of Chief Kita's office into the corridor. Chief Inspector Adachi stands in front of me and says, 'The chief would like to see you now, Inspector Minami.'

I nod and I thank him. But I sit and I wait until he is gone –

Now I open the door. I step back inside the chief's office –

The blood-flecked scroll on the wall behind his desk –

'It is time to reveal the true essence of the nation . . .'

'Please sit down,' he says. 'You look tired . . .'

I bow. I apologize. I thank him. I sit down –

Then he asks, 'What happened at Keiō?'

'The landlady believes that the clothes found on the body in Shiba Park are not the same as those worn by Tominaga Noriko.'

'So you said,' says the chief. 'And so?'

I shake my head. 'And that's it.'

'But you were convinced that this missing girl could be the body at Shiba Park,' says the chief. 'You know the landlady could be mistaken about the clothes. You must have found out more?'

I shake my head again. I say, 'I'm sorry. No.'

'You've nothing else to say, then?'

I say again, 'I'm sorry. No.'

Things not to say . . .

'So why were you down at Mita police station last night?'

I have no answer. I say nothing. There is nothing to say.

'You went there to try to find the name of the officer who was dismissed over Abe, didn't you, detective? Didn't you?'

I bow my head now. I say, 'I am sorry, sir.'

'You went there even after I told you now was not the time, didn't you, detective? You still went there, directly disobeying me.'

My head still bowed, I say again, 'I'm sorry, sir.'

'Did they tell you his name?' asks the chief.

'Yes,' I say. 'They told me his name.'

'Did they tell you his address?'

'No, they did not.'

'But you still found it out, didn't you?' asks the chief. 'You still went to see Murota, didn't you?'

'No.'

'Why not?'

'I . . .'

'Did you ever stop to think why I said now was not the time to be asking about Murota? Did you, detective?' the chief asks me –

My head still low, I apologize. I apologize and I apologize –

'Did you ever stop to think I might have had a reason?'

I apologize and I apologize and again, I apologize –

226

'Did you ever think of anyone but yourself in this?'

I apologize and I apologize again, over and over –

'Do you ever think of anyone but yourself . . .?'

I say, 'I am sorry. I am sorry. I am sorry . . .'

The chief leans forward now. The chief whispers, 'You are being watched. You are being followed. Everywhere you go –

'Did you know that? Did you even suspect that?'

My head still bowed, I say, 'I had no idea . . .'

'The Public Safety Division has been sniffing around again, seeking to draw up fresh lists of the guilty. There are rumours of a second Purge Directive, this time against lower ranking officers . . .

'They are trying to match histories to names . . .

'And yours is one of the names . . .'

I curse him and I curse myself . . .

I want to know what he knows. *I curse him!* I want to know what he has heard. *I curse myself!* I want to know how he knows what he knows. *I curse him!* I want to know who told him what he knows. *I curse myself!* But I don't ask anything or say anything –

I just curse him and I curse myself . . .

Because there's nothing to say –

No point. No point. No point –

Chiku-taku. Chiku-taku . . .

No point. No point –

Chiku-taku . . .

I am out of time –

'I don't know if these are just shots in the dark,' the chief is saying now. 'Or if they have some actual information, some witnesses or statements but, either way, it is best you get lost . . .'

'Best I get lost?' I repeat. 'What do you mean?'

'I want you to go up to Tochigi,' he says.

'Tochigi Prefecture? When?'

'Tomorrow,' he says –

Now the chief picks up a file and passes it across his desk. 'Yesterday we actually had a call from the Utsunomiya Chihō Kensatsu-chō, the Utsunomiya District Public Prosecutor's Office, about two unsolved murders in their jurisdiction that they wanted to pass on to the Kodaira investigation team. One of the murders was your Baba Hiroko and the other was a Numao Shizue, aged sixteen, who was found stabbed on the thirtieth of December last year, in the

227

jurisdiction of the Nikkō police. Baba Hiroko, as you know, was found strangled with her own scarf on the third of January in Nishi Katamura, in the jurisdiction of the Kanuma Police . . .

'But Baba Hiroko was actually living here in Kyōbashi Ward so, before you go up to Tochigi tomorrow, I think it would be a good idea to first speak to her family in Tokyo . . .'

I say, 'I want to take Nishi . . .'

'No,' says the chief.

'Am I to go alone?'

'Chief Inspector Adachi has recommended young Ishida . . .'

'Excuse me,' I say. 'I don't think he's a suitable officer –'

'This is not a debate,' says the chief. 'This is an order.'

I bow my head again. I apologize again, and again –

And then I ask, 'How long should I stay away?'

'Only for a couple of days,' says the chief –

Now I ask, 'And then what happens?'

The chief clears his throat. The chief stands behind his desk. Now the chief says, 'Inspector Minami, as of midnight tonight, I am forced to relieve you of your command of Room #2 . . .'

I am on my knees. I am on my knees . . .

'There have been complaints about you . . .'

I am on my knees in his office . . .

'Complaints from your own men . . .'

On my knees, on his floor . . .

'Complaints about your lack of leadership,' says the chief. 'Your lack of organization. Complaints about your inability to command. Your inability to delegate. Complaints about the continued absence of Detective Fujita and about your own absences . . .'

On his floor. In his office. On my knees . . .

'But you tell me to lead my men and then you send me away and you demote me. Who will lead my men now . . .? Who will take charge of this case . . .? Please give me a second chance . . .'

Begging him, pleading with him . . .

'In the continued absence of Detective Fujita, I'm promoting Detective Hattori under the supervision of Chief Inspector Adachi.'

'And what happens to me when I get back . . .?'

Pleading for a second chance . . .

'Until this situation is clarified, you will be assigned to a local police station upon your return from Tochigi . . .'

'And so what about my transfer . . .?'
Begging for a second chance . . .
'There will be no transfer . . .'
No second chance.

*

There is no route back to Atago today. *In the half-light.* I walk down the stairs into the bar. *They are following me.* There are only two other customers at the counter; the same middle-aged woman, now dressed in brown, smelling of local perfume and smoking Golden Bat cigarettes; the same old man in his dark suit, taking out his pocket watch and winding it up and putting it away again, then taking it out and winding it up and putting it away again, then –
Chiku-taku. Chiku-taku. Chiku-taku . . .
The woman opens her purse. The woman places chocolates on the bar. The woman says, 'Please help yourself . . .'
But they taste bitter. They taste of ash –
The *bakudan* explodes in my belly –
The man shows me the watch –
It still says twelve o'clock –
But in the half-light –
His watch has no hands and we both have no feet.

*

Through the doors of the borrowed police station. I have a shaved head. Up the stairs of the borrowed police station. I have a bandaged hand. To the borrowed second-floor room. I have a pair of bloody knees. Hattori, Takeda, Sanada, Shimoda, Nishi, Kimura and Ishida. I have a broken heart. They are all here and they already know –
I am not the head of the room. I am not their boss . . .
Now they all look away. They all hide their eyes –
Their eyes full of questions. Eyes full of doubts . . .
Eyes full of whispers, rumours and complaints . . .
I have nothing to say to any one of them –
I hate them. I hate them. I hate them all . . .
I walk over to Takeda's borrowed desk and I bow and I thank him for all his hard work and for all his help. I walk over to Sanada's

borrowed desk and I bow and I thank him for all his hard work and for all his help. I walk over to Shimoda's desk and I bow and I thank him for all his hard work, for all his help –

I hate them all. I hate them all . . .

I stand before Nishi's desk and I bow and I thank him for all his hard work and for all his help and I wish him luck. I turn to Kimura and I bow and I thank him for all his hard work and for all his help and I wish him luck. Then I bow and I thank Ishida for all his hard work and I wish him luck –

I will see him again . . .

I walk over to Detective Hattori's desk and I bow low and I congratulate him on his promotion and I wish him luck in his promotion and with the investigation and I thank him for all his hard work and all his help –

I hate him . . .

Finally, I stand before them all and I bow deeply and I apologize to them for my lack of leadership, my lack of organization, my inability to command, my inability to delegate and my absences –

'I am sorry,' I say. 'And I hope to earn your forgiveness.'

*

It is night now. *They are following me.* It is hot still. *They are following me.* I have places to visit, people to see before we leave for Tochigi tomorrow afternoon. *They are following me.* The sound of a balladeer and his guitar trails me up the hill as I walk away from Shibuya station. *They are following me.* I don't recognize the words of the song, I don't recognize the music. *They are following me.* I stop at the mouth of the dark alley. *They are following me.* I glance back down the hill. *They are following me.* I sit down on a broken wall. *They are following me.* I take off my hat and I fan myself –

They are following me. They are still following me . . .

I put on my hat and I stand back up. I walk down the alley and I knock on the door. I slide it open and I make my apologies –

'But I have some good news,' I tell her –

Tominaga Noriko's landlady looks up from another shabby low table in another shabby little room in another shabby little house in another shabby neighbourhood –

'Noriko's not dead.'

There are questions and doubts in her red eyes now, questions and doubts among the tears, the tears she has wept since she glanced up at the clothing lain out on that autopsy table –

'The clothes were not hers,' I tell her –

Hope among the questions now, hope among the doubts, hope that cries, 'Really? So Noriko is still alive?'

'Yes,' I say. 'I saw her today.'

Hope that asks, 'Is she coming back, then? Back here?'

'I don't know,' I tell her. 'But I don't think so . . .'

No more questions, no more doubts and no more hope now, only rage and only grief that shouts and screams out –

'Then she's still dead to me, detective!'

*

The Shimbashi New Life Market is back in business. But among the kettles and the pans, the crockery and the utensils, among the clothes and the shoes, the cooking oil and the soy sauce, among the fruit and the vegetables, the sardines and the second-hand suits, the coffee and the silk, in their patterned shirts and their American sunglasses, Senju's men are still licking their wounds, still counting their dead –

Sharpening old blades and swearing new oaths –

Exchanging sake cups with any old soldier –

'Let's all sing the Apple Song . . .'

These are desperate times . . .

But defiant times –

'Let them come in their hundreds,' Senju Akira is telling me. 'Let them come in their thousands. For I am assembling the largest organization of patriotic Japanese men this country has seen since the end of the war. Then let the Chinese, the Koreans and the Formosans try to take away what has been left us, the little that has been left us by the many that sacrificed themselves before us –

'For I tell you this, in the centuries to come, generations of Japanese, generations who will be living only because of our stand, these generations will hear tales of the things we did to protect our fellow countrymen and save the Japanese nation and they will shed tears for us under the cherry blossoms and raise their glasses under the full moon and pray for our souls at Yasukuni, honouring us as the true keepers of the Japanese spirit . . .'

I have no time for this –

Chiku-taku . . .

I bow lower on the tatami. I say, 'I am very sorry to trouble you at a time like this . . .'

'I am always happy to see an old friend,' says Senju now. 'And I was worried about you, detective. I'd begun to think you might be avoiding me. I'd even begun to think that maybe we weren't really friends, that maybe you only came to see me when you wanted something from me, when you wanted money or wanted drugs . . .'

'I do need money,' I tell him. 'And I do need Calmotin.'

'That's very honest of you, detective,' says Senju. 'And also very refreshing in such duplicitous and deceitful times as these –

'I admire your honesty, Inspector Minami . . .'

I bow. I thank him. I start to speak but –

'But did you just come with a shopping list, detective?'

I bow again. I apologize again. I tell him, 'It isn't easy for me. There's an investigation into the murder of Hayashi . . .'

'You sound surprised?' laughs Senju. 'It's your job, isn't it?'

'But it's not my case,' I tell him. 'And there's a problem . . .'

'A problem for who?' asks Senju. 'For you or for me?'

'For both of us,' I tell him. 'Fujita is missing . . .'

'And why is this a problem for either of us?'

'Do you know where he is?' I ask him.

'No,' says Senju. 'But I'll ask you again, why would a missing Detective Fujita be my problem?'

'He's wanted for questioning about the death of Hayashi Jo,' I say, and then I pause, I swallow, and now I say, 'He's wanted for questioning because Hayashi Jo left behind a letter, a last testament, in which he claims to have information putting Fujita in the New Oasis with Nodera Tomiji on the night of the hit on Matsuda . . .'

Senju has stopped listening. Senju is stood up now –

Senju showering me with money and with pills –

'This is not a problem,' Senju is shouting –

'This is going to be a pleasure!'

*

It will be hours before I lie again here upon the old tatami mats of her dim and lamp-lit room. It will be hours before I stare again at her

232

peeling screens with their ivy-leaf designs. Hours before I watch her draw again her figures with their fox-faces upon these screens –

I cannot stay tonight. I cannot take the Calmotin –

I do not want to close my eyes tonight –

For I have one last place still to go.

'I wish it would rain,' she says –

'I cannot stay tonight,' I tell her. 'I won't be here tomorrow. But, as soon as I return to Tokyo, I'll come straight here . . .'

Now Yuki puts down her pencils and reaches for a piece of tissue paper. Now she covers both her eyebrows with the paper and stares at me in the panels of her mirror –

'Does this become me?'

I leave her money –

I leave her pills.

10

August 24, 1946

Tokyo, 90°, fine

The Matsuzawa Hospital for the Insane is on the border between the Setagaya and Suginami wards, half-way between my own house in Mitaka and the house of Murota Hideki in Kitazawa. *I thought you would have seen enough of that place.* I know the Matsuzawa Hospital for the Insane well, but I'm not sure why I'm here today –

I thought you would have seen enough of that place . . .

The Matsuzawa Hospital was built during the reign of the Emperor Meiji and survived the fires and the famines of the last two years to still be standing in the reign of the Emperor MacArthur –

I hate hospitals. I hate all hospitals . . .

But its buildings are in disrepair and its grounds untended now, the gates long taken for the war effort and the trees cut down for winter fuel. Inside the reception, the paint on the walls has faded and the linoleum on the floor is worn, the staff anaesthetized –

But I hate this hospital the most . . .

'Former Police Inspector Mori,' I say again –

But the receptionist still shakes her head –

'Please check for me,' I ask her. 'It is very important and he was only admitted last month. Mori Ichiro . . .'

The gaunt receptionist in the stained uniform does not speak but turns away and disappears now, disappears into the grubby office behind the grimy counter. I wait and I wait –

Chiku-taku. Chiku-taku. Chiku . . .

The same sounds of screams and sobs as at Keiō Hospital, the same smells of DDT and disinfectant –

I hate this place. I hate . . .

'Here it is,' says the receptionist now with a file in her hand. 'Mori Ichiro was admitted on the thirtieth of June this year.'

'And is Mr. Mori still here?' I ask her –

The receptionist nods. 'Yes, he is.'

'I'd like to see him then, please.'

The receptionist shakes her head now. The receptionist says, 'But you know I can't just let you –'

'Then please tell me the name of Mr. Mori's doctor,' I say. 'And tell me where I can find him.'

The receptionist looks down at the file and says, 'Dr. Nomura. His office is on the second . . .'

'I know,' I tell her and I start to walk away, to walk away and then to run, to run down the corridor and up the stairs, up the stairs and along another corridor, along another corridor to bang on the door, to bang on the door to the office of Dr. Nomura, to bang on the door and then open it, open it and bow and say, 'Excuse me . . .'

Dr. Nomura looks up from the papers on his desk –

'Inspector?' he says. 'It's been a while . . .'

'And I am sorry to call on you unannounced,' I say again. 'But I am here on police business this time . . .'

'Please sit down, then,' says the doctor now. 'And can I offer you a drink of cold tea, detective . . . ?'

I wipe my face and I wipe my neck. I glance at my watch and I shake my head. I say, 'Thank you but I haven't much time, doctor.'

The doctor nods. 'What is it I can do for you, detective?'

'You have a patient I would like to see,' I tell the doctor. 'A former chief inspector of police called Mori. Mori Ichiro . . .'

The doctor nods again. The doctor says, 'I know.'

'Well, I'd very much like to see him,' I tell the doctor again. 'It is important I speak with him about an investigation.'

Now the doctor shakes his head. Now the doctor says, 'I very much doubt that that will be possible, inspector . . .'

'Why not?' I ask him. 'It's important.'

'I understand that,' says the doctor. 'But, unfortunately, Mr. Mori has not responded to any of our treatments or our regimens –

'And so, for the moment, Mr. Mori does not speak . . .'

'I would still like to see him,' I tell the doctor.

The doctor shakes his head. The doctor says, 'As you know better than most, detective, recovery from the kind of sudden mental collapse which former Chief Inspector Mori suffered on learning he was to be purged, such a sudden mental collapse takes a very, very long time to recover from, if at all, and any further shocks to the brain can cause irreparable damage to the patient . . .'

I bow. I nod. I say, 'I know that.'

The blood-flecked scroll . . .

'In the case of your father, for example,' continues the doctor. 'One sudden moment of lucidity, a moment of clarity, proved fatal.'

I don't want to remember. I don't want to remember . . .

I nod again. I say again, 'May I see him but not speak?'

The blood-flecked scroll on the wall . . .

'Yes,' says the doctor. 'Though I'm not sure why . . .'

In the half-light, I can't forget . . .

'He was a policeman,' I tell him. 'Like my father . . .'

The blood-flecked scroll on the wall behind his desk . . .

'Like my father,' I say again now. 'And like me . . .'

I can't forget. I can't forget . . .

Dr. Nomura nods. Dr Nomura says, 'Follow me –'

And so I follow Dr. Nomura out of his office, out of his office and down another long corridor, another long corridor through locked metal doors, through locked metal doors into the secure wards, into the secure wards and down more corridors, down more corridors to the secure rooms, the secure rooms and more locked metal doors –

Now Dr. Nomura stops before one locked metal door –

One locked metal door with a bolted metal hatch –

'Here we are,' says Nomura. 'But just look . . .'

Nomura slides back the bolts on the hatch. Nomura lowers the metal hatch. Now Nomura steps back and says, 'There you are . . .'

I step towards the door. I look through the hatchway –

I stare through the hatchway at the man inside –

The man inside, cross-legged on his cot –

I have seen this man before . . .

This man in a shapeless gown of yellow and dark-blue striped Chinese silk, with his close-shaven head and his unblinking eyes –

Eyes I have met before . . .

'Have you seen enough now?' asks Nomura –

I step away from the hatch now and I nod –

'I have seen enough,' I say. 'Thank you, doctor.'

Nomura closes the hatch. Nomura bolts it –

No one is who they say they are . . .

But I have seen this man before –

No one is who they seem . . .

This man is not former Chief Inspector Mori Ichiro.

236

I have haggled and I have bartered. *Just to eat.* I have threatened and I have bullied. *Just to work.* But I itch and I scratch again. *Gari-gari.* My hand aches and my body stinks. *Of defeat.* I wipe my face and I wipe my neck. *And I curse.* I have come to the end of my own street. *Ton-ton.* I walk down the street to my own house. *Ton-ton.* I open the gate to my own house. *Ton-ton.* I go up the path to my own house –

Ton-ton. Ton-ton. Ton-ton. Ton-ton. Ton-ton . . .

There is a bonfire of bedding in my garden –

There is fire and there is smoke here.

I open the door to my own house –

I have come to say goodbye –

Their shoes face the door . . .

This time I cannot turn away. This time I cannot run away –

The rotting mats, the shredded doors, the fallen walls . . .

From the smell of the children. The smell of the pain.

I stand in the *genkan.* I call out, 'I'm home . . .'

My wife comes out of the kitchen, her face is stained with soot, her hands brushing dust from her worn *monpe* trousers –

'Welcome home,' she says –

Home. Home. Home . . .

I take off my boots. I ask her, 'Where are the children?'

'Masaki! Sonoko!' my wife calls. 'Father is home!'

Father. Father . . .

My children do not run to greet me. My children do not smile when they see me. They stand before me now but do not speak –

Their heads shaved. Their eyebrows shaved –

'Are you well?' I ask each of them –

Heads bowed, they both nod –

I lift their faces to mine, lift their little faces to the light, and Masaki looks up at me now and smiles, but Sonoko still can't look up, she still cannot smile, her eyelids swollen and her features distorted –

I force open her eyelids with my fingers –

Her eyes inflamed and festering –

The eyes of a dead fish –

Pinkeye.

I turn to my wife. 'When did you last take her to the doctor?'

'But I think her eyes are getting a little better,' says my wife.

'Two days ago, they were so swollen and so inflamed that she could not see anything at all. So I took her to the doctor then and . . .'

'Maybe it's a bacterial infection, not pinkeye?'

'That's what I said to the doctor.'

'And what did he say?'

'It's just pinkeye.'

'Just pinkeye!' I shout. 'Just look at her. She still can't see. She could be permanently blinded! She could be blinded forever!'

'I know,' says my wife. 'But the doctor said be patient.'

'Doctors make mistakes,' I say. 'They usually do.'

'But what should I do?' asks my wife. 'Tell . . .'

I ask, 'Which doctor did you take her to?'

'To our usual doctor,' replies my wife.

I look at my watch. 'I'll take her . . .'

'Take her where?' asks my wife –

'To a different doctor I know.'

'What about the money . . .'

'Forget the money!'

*

Through the doors of the Atago police station. Up the stairs of the Atago police station. My shirt is stuck to my back. My trousers wet behind my knees. I walk along the corridor. I walk past the banner, two metres tall and fifty centimetres wide in bright-red stitching:

Special Investigation Headquarters.

I should have collected all my belongings and made these arrangements yesterday. I would then have saved myself this –

This sudden silence. This sudden blindness –

There have been complaints about you . . .

But at least Hattori is not here this morning; probably up at Headquarters for the morning meeting with Kai, Kanehara, Adachi and the chief. But I'm not going to ask Takeda, Sanada, Shimoda, Nishi, Kimura or Ishida, I'm not going to ask them –

I hate them. I hate them all . . .

Ishida looks up. Now Ishida asks, 'Are you here for me?'

Ishida has his orders . . .

'It's a bit early yet,' I tell him. 'And I've some things to do before we leave for Tochigi, so I'll meet you at the ticket gate of the

Asakusa Tōbu station at three o'clock this afternoon . . .'

Chiku-taku. Chiku-taku. Chiku-taku . . .

Ishida nods. Ishida says, 'I've been told to buy the tickets . . .'

'Well, I hope they've given you the money, then.'

Ishida nods again. 'I've enough for three days.'

'I won't be needing a return ticket,' I laugh –

But no one else laughs. No one even smiles . . .

Ishida just asks, 'How much rice should I bring with me?'

'Rice?' I ask him. 'Surely we'll be bringing rice back?'

'I heard we'll not find an inn unless we take rice.'

'Do you have any rice, detective?' I ask him –

Ishida whispers, 'I have a little at home . . .'

'Then bring enough for both of us,' I say and I turn to go –

'Why should he take any rice for you?' asks Kimura –

I turn back round. I ask him, 'What did you say?'

'I said, why should he bring any rice for you,' repeats Detective Kimura. 'You're not his boss any more, are you?'

'Maybe not now,' I tell him. 'And maybe not in this room. But on that train and in Tochigi, I'll still be the senior officer . . .'

'Senior officer? Really?' snorts Detective Kimura now. 'Well, I'd save my rice if I were you, Detective Ishida . . .'

I walk over to Detective Kimura and I pick up one of the telephones on the desk, one of the telephones that cannot ring, and I smash it into the side of Kimura's face and then, as he cries out and reaches up to hold his face, I punch him in his gut and I bend his left hand back until he howls out in pain and begs me to stop as I slap him and slap him and slap him, again and again and again across his face and then I push him back onto his desk and I watch him roll onto the floor and now I lean over him and I tell him, 'And I'd learn some manners and I'd learn some respect if I were you, Detective Kimura.'

Now I walk over to Detective Sanada and I say, 'You said something very interesting yesterday, Detective Sanada. You said Masaoka Hisae told you that Kodaira always had gifts on him . . .'

Detective Sanada sweating. Detective Sanada nodding –

'You said he had ladies' gifts; jewellery, watches and . . .'

Detective Sanada nodding and saying, 'Umbrellas.'

'That was good work,' I tell him. 'Because after you said that, when I was up at Headquarters, I heard that we are going to wash another unsolved case as a possible Kodaira Yoshio job –'

I am not their head. I am not their boss . . .

'Shinokawa Tatsue, seventeen years old, found raped and strangled in the basement of the Toyoko Department Store in Shibuya on the sixteenth of January this year. However, the autopsy estimated she'd been dead since late October or early November last year –

'And guess what?' I ask. 'Her umbrella had been stolen.'

Again, there is no applause. But I don't want any . . .

'So if any of you want to impress your new boss,' I tell them. 'I suggest you go back to Masaoka, back to the Widow Okayama and back to all the other people who knew Kodaira, his family and his workmates, and you try to trace all these gifts he kept giving away –

'Because somewhere out there in Shibuya or Shinagawa, in Toyama or Tochigi, are the belongings of our own Shiba body –

'Excuse me,' I tell them. '*Your* Shiba body . . .'

No applause. Just silence. Just blindness . . .

I walk over to my desk now, my former borrowed desk, and I open the drawer ready to tip out the entire contents into my old army knapsack. But the drawer of my desk is empty –

My desk has already been cleared –

I curse and I curse and I curse . . .

'Inspector Hattori took all your things up to Headquarters,' says Ishida. 'He didn't think you'd be coming back here again.'

I hate him. I hate him. I hate them . . .

I say nothing. There is nothing to say. I leave –

I hate them. I hate them . . .

Down the corridor. Down the stairs –

I hate them all . . .

Detective Nishi is standing on the steps outside Atago police station. *I am looking in a mirror.* Detective Nishi must have ducked out of the room while I was beating the shit out of Detective Kimura, while I was lecturing the hell out of the rest of them. *I am looking in a mirror.* Detective Nishi is waiting for me. *I am looking in a mirror.* Detective Nishi wants another word, a last and final word. *I am looking in a mirror.* But Detective Nishi still looks like shit. *I am looking in a mirror.* Nishi still looks like he hasn't slept. *I am looking in a mirror.* Nishi telling me, 'I had nothing to do with any of it . . .'

I laugh. 'Had nothing to do with any of what, detective?'

'Your demotion,' he says. 'All their complaints.'

I ask, 'What complaints are they then, Nishi?'

'Hattori's complaints to Adachi,' he says.

I shake my head. 'I despise all of you.'

'But I'm on your side,' pleads Nishi –

On my side. On my side. My side . . .

I shake my head again. 'No you're not, and you never were.'

*

In another ruin, among another heap of rubble, with a last cigarette. Two stray dogs circle and watch me smoke, waiting for me to die. Two stray dogs in dirty coats on skinny legs, their pale tongues hanging loose from their dark mouths. *The sparrow sings, the nightingale dances.* This ruin, this rubble, was once a grand house and ornate garden owned by a family of Satsuma Samurai stock, a family that had once given the country ministers and generals, given her industrialists and financiers, from a house that once hosted banquets and balls, a garden that echoed to the songs of victory –

And the green fields are lovely in the spring . . .

Now three more stray dogs appear among the rubble and bark at the other two strays. Three more stray dogs in dirty coats on skinny legs with pale tongues and dark mouths. The five dogs form a pack, circling me. *The pomegranate flowers crimson, the willows green-leafed.* I watch the dogs circle closer and closer. I watch them sniff the ground. I watch them sniff the air. I watch them circle closer and closer. The first two dogs are the bravest, marching up and down before me, closer and closer. The three newcomers less certain. I put out my last cigarette. Now I pick up a stone –

And there is a new picture.

*

Through the doors of the Tokyo Metropolitan Police Headquarters. Up the stairs of the Tokyo Metropolitan Police Headquarters. *The sudden silence.* My shirt is still stuck to my back. My trousers still wet behind my knees. *The sudden blindness.* I walk along the corridor, the Police Arcade. I walk past the chief's room. *I shouldn't have come here.* I walk past the meeting room. I walk past Room #1. *I should have stayed away.* I come to Room #2. My former room –

No one will see me. No one will speak to me . . .

But Room #2 is empty. The Metro Arcade –

No one here. No one here . . .

I walk over to my desk, my former desk at the head of the room, and I open the drawer to tip out the contents into my knapsack. But the drawer of this desk is empty too –

This desk has also been cleared –

I curse. I curse again . . .

I go back out into the corridor to look for someone; anyone –

There's a familiar face on the stair; a familiar face from Room #1 and Inspector Kai's team. But this familiar face, he sees me first, he sees me first and he looks away, he looks away and he turns away, he turns away to walk away, to walk away the other way –

But he knows. He knows. He knows . . .

So I stop this familiar face and I bow and I apologize, and he bows back, and I bow again and I apologize again and then I ask him, 'Where is everyone? What's happened?'

'Haven't you heard?' he asks. 'They found Detective Fujita.'

I bow. I thank him. I excuse myself. I turn away –

I walk away. Back down the stairs –

Through the doors. I run –

I run, run, run away.

*

I take my daughter's red *geta* clogs in my hand. My wife puts my daughter on my back. I carry my daughter down the garden path. I carry my daughter down the street. I carry my daughter through the mulberry fields on a shortcut to another hospital, a different doctor –

The hospital has just opened. The queue already formed –

I open my police wallet. I tell them it's an emergency –

I shout. I threaten. I bully. I jump the queue –

The ophthalmologist is a woman –

'My daughter can hardly open her eyes,' I tell the doctor. 'They've been like this for almost two weeks. I am concerned it's something more serious than pinkeye, that it might be a virulent bacterial infection that could permanently damage her eyesight. I have to go away for a time and I'm worried that the situation will worsen while I am away. My wife and I are really at an utter loss . . .'

'Don't worry,' says the lady doctor. 'This will clear up in a –'

'But when?' I ask her. 'It's been nearly two weeks now . . .'

'She smells of smoke,' says the doctor. 'She's been sprayed with DDT. The smoke and DDT have aggravated her eyes . . .'

'We had no choice,' I tell her. 'We had lice . . .'

'Please don't worry,' says the doctor. 'The eyes themselves haven't actually been infected. By the time you return from your trip, I'm sure your daughter's eyes will have completely recovered . . .'

'Isn't there anything you can give her to hurry things along?'

'There's an injection,' says the doctor. 'But it's expensive.'

'I have money,' I tell her and I bow. 'Please, doctor . . .'

*

Was it Senju or Adachi? They have found Detective Fujita. *Adachi or Senju?* Do they weep for him? Or do they laugh at him? *Senju or Adachi?* Is day night? Or night day? *Adachi or Senju?* Is black white? Or white black? *Senju or Adachi?* Are the men the women? Or the women the men? *Adachi or Senju?* Are the brave the frightened? Or the frightened the brave? *Senju or Adachi?* Are the strong the weak? Or the weak the strong? *Adachi or Senju?* Are the good the bad? Or the bad the good? *Senju or Adachi?* Are strikes legal? Or are strikes illegal? *Adachi or Senju?* Is democracy good? Or democracy bad? *Senju or Adachi?* Is the aggressor the victim? Or the victim the aggressor? *Adachi or Senju?* Are the winners the losers? Or the losers the winners? *Senju or Adachi?* Did Japan lose the war? Or Japan win the war? *Adachi or Senju?* Are the living the dead? Or are the dead the living? *Senju or Adachi?* Am I alive? Or am I dead . . . ?

Was it Adachi or Senju? Senju or Adachi?

Now they have found Detective Fujita –

Adachi or Senju? Senju or Adachi?

Now they will find me –

Adachi or Senju?

But I have to take a chance; I have to take a chance that they won't catch Ishida before he leaves Atago, that Ishida will have already left Atago and be on his way back home now for his rice; have to take a chance that Ishida will then go straight to Asakusa, that either Headquarters won't know what time we're set to leave Tokyo for Tochigi, or that they won't think to send anyone to stop us –

Senju or Adachi? Adachi or Senju? Senju or Adachi . . .

243

These are the chances I take. The chances I take –
Or was it me? Was it me? Was it me?
I take as I cut and run through Tokyo –
Was it me? Was it me?
The City of the Dead –
The Shōwa Dead . . .

*

Baba Hiroko was found dead on the third of January this year in Tochigi Prefecture in the jurisdiction of the Kanuma police station. But Baba Hiroko was not from Tochigi Prefecture. Baba Hiroko was from Tokyo. Baba Hiroko lived at 1–9 Shin-Tsukuda Nishimachi, in Kyōbashi Ward with her mother and her uncle, Kobayashi Sōkichi.

I run through Kyōbashi Ward, looking for the street and keeping in the shadows of the old office buildings still standing. I find the street and I walk down it, looking for the address and dodging the sunlight in the empty spaces created by the bombsites –

The shadows and the sunlight, the black then the white . . .

I come to a battered board fence; a huge pile of rusty iron, a cabin with a glass door and a stained tin roof visible through the gaps in the wood; this place must be 1–9 Shin-Tsukuda Nishimachi –

Behind the fence, an old man in overalls stands in front of the cabin, a handkerchief around his head. I call through the fence. I tell him who I am; Inspector Minami of the Tokyo MPD. He tells me who he is; Kobayashi Sōkichi. He tells me he is Hiroko's uncle –

I tell him why I'm here and where I'm going –

I ask if I can speak with him. He nods –

I think about her all the time . . .

I step through an opening in the boarding into the scrapyard. He takes off the handkerchief and wipes his neck. He shows me inside the cabin. He points to a small stool, which is the only piece of furniture in the cabin. He sits down on an empty packing case, an old colour postcard of the Itsuku-shima Shrine still tacked to the wall –

'Me and this shack is all that's left,' says Mr. Kobayashi –

I stare up at the boarded ceiling, still black with winter soot, the blackboard by the window, and now I stare across at the *butsudan* on which a potted sakaki tree sits before three framed photographs; two are of older women, the third of a much younger woman –

'Hiroko left here early on the morning of the thirtieth of December last year. Her mother had been evacuated to the employee apartments of the Furukawa Denki copper factory in Nikkō . . .'

The same company Kodaira twice worked for . . .

'But because of the situation here in Tokyo and because of the better standard of living out in the country, her mother was still living up there. Hiroko wanted to spend New Year's Eve and New Year's Day with her and she had some gifts to give her . . .'

'Do you remember what these gifts were?'

'There was a red scarf she'd knitted herself, I do remember that. Then I think there were some bits of food and what-have-you. I mean, her mother was probably eating better than us, but Hiroko saved up her rice ration for the whole month . . .

'But Hiroko never arrived and then, four days later, her body was found in that field near that mountain in Nishi Katamura, Kami Tsuga-gun. In that lonely field . . .'

She haunts me . . .

'Hiroko had been dragged across the field, her face had been beaten, she had been throttled, she had been raped and then she had been strangled with her own scarf. The murderer had then stolen all her belongings, the two hundred yen she had had with her, as well as her coat and her scarf and all the presents she had for her mother . . .

'Hiroko's mother blamed herself. Her mother felt she shouldn't have stayed in Tochigi, that if she had retuned to Tokyo then Hiroko would never have gone up to Tochigi that day, that she'd never have met the beast that did those things to her . . .'

'Where is her mother now?' I ask. 'Not still in Tochigi . . . ?'

'Hiroko's mother died of the shame and a broken heart . . .'

'I'm sorry to hear that,' I tell him. 'I'm very sorry . . .'

'Whoever killed Hiroko, killed her mother too.'

I nod and I tell him he is right. I ask if I may pay my respects and then, for the second time today, I kneel before a *butsudan* –

But this time I do not ask for forgiveness –

This time I ask only for guidance –

The guidance for justice –

Justice & vengeance . . .

I stand back up and he thanks me for my time and he thanks me for my trouble and then he shows me back out of the cabin –

Back out into the sunlight and the scrapyard –

'My own son is still in Mulchi,' he says. 'Least, that's what they tell me. I've heard nothing. But, until I do hear otherwise, while he's chopping wood on the Amur River, I'll keep this business going so there's something for him to come back to . . .'

But now Hiroko's uncle stares across the street at the buildings going back up, and he says, 'Then again, perhaps he's already just another ghost . . .'

*

The Ginza Subway Line terminates at Asakusa station in the basement of the Matsuya Department Store. The Tōbu Line starts and finishes on the second floor of Matsuya; Ishida will be there at three o'clock. I look at my watch. *Chiku-taku.* I am early. I need to keep my distance for now. I come up for air out of the subway –

Ton-ton. Ton-ton. Ton-ton. Ton-ton. Ton-ton. Ton-ton . . .

But there is no air in Asakusa; just markets to the left, looking north, and ruins to the right, across on the other bank of the Sumida River. There is no air; the same burnt field, flat but for the black scorched concrete and the new yellow wood. No air; this place is death, always death, death before and death again now –

Ton-ton. Ton-ton. Ton-ton. Ton-ton. Ton-ton . . .

I came here the day after the Great Kantō Earthquake; that day the whole city stank, stank of rotten apricots, and the closer I walked to Asakusa and to the winds that blew across from east of the river, the stronger the stink of apricots became –

Ton-ton. Ton-ton. Ton-ton. Ton-ton . . .

The stink of rotten apricots that was the stench of the dead, the mountains of dead lain out under a burning sky among the charred ruins on both banks of the Sumida –

Ton-ton. Ton-ton. Ton-ton . . .

I stood among those corpses piled up high along the riverbanks and the body of one young boy it caught my eye, his body caked black in rags and filth, his face and hands covered in blisters and boils, I wondered where his father was, I wondered where his mother was, his brothers and his sisters, and I prayed that they were dead, better everyone was dead –

Ton-ton. Ton-ton . . .

Everyone dead –

Ton-ton . . .

Hammering then and hammering now. *Better everyone was dead.* Hammering then and hammering now. *Better everyone was dead.* Hammering then, hammering now –

Better everyone was dead . . .

Dead then, dead now –

Everyone dead . . .

Then, twenty-two years after that first fire rose up with the earth, I watched as a second fire rained down from the skies onto Asakusa and Tokyo, borne on a loud wind that swept the fire over the low half of the city, that swept half the people away in its wake –

A century of change in one night of fire . . .

Fires unfolding like fans, burning buildings, boiling rivers, bodies suffocated by smoke, scorched by flames –

I smelt them then. I smell them now –

That stench of rotten apricots . . .

Now I walk away from the Matsuya Department Store, towards the Niten Shinto Gate, onto the empty black square where the great Kannon Temple once stood, past hundreds of tiny stalls, trumpets and saxophones wailing from amplified loudspeakers –

Ton-ton. Ton-ton. Ton-ton. Ton-ton. Ton-ton . . .

I make my way through the old clothes market, I push my way through the crowds, and I come to a row of food stalls wedged together by the side of the Asakusa Pond, the air here thick with the smell of burning oil. I stop to drink among the old soldiers –

Ton-ton. Ton-ton. Ton-ton. Ton-ton . . .

I stare out at the billboard advertisements –

Ton-ton. Ton-ton. Ton-ton . . .

For the restaurants and revues –

Ton-ton. Ton-ton . . .

Movies and musicals –

Ton-ton . . .

The sun falling in black and white lines through the bamboo roof, I stare out into the face of a young boy, caked black in rags and filth, his face and hands covered in blisters and boils, he weeps pus and tears, now he raises his hand and he points his finger –

Ton-ton. Ton-ton. Ton-ton. Ton-ton . . .

Hammering then, hammering now –

Masaki, Banzai! Daddy, Banzai!
The hammering never stops –
Ton-ton. Ton-ton. Ton-ton . . .

*

I put my daughter on my back again and I carry her home through the mulberry fields, back towards our house but then, when we get to an old well, I put her down. I take out my handkerchief. I wash and soak it in the well. I wring it out. Then I put it over my daughter's eyes –

'Just until the smoke has gone,' I tell her.

I put my daughter on my back again and I carry her home, through the gate and up the path to the door and the *genkan* –

'We're home,' my daughter and I shout together.

I fetch some water and I go back out into the garden. I pour the water onto the flames and I put out the bonfire of bedding –

'The smoke irritates her eyes,' I tell my wife.

My wife bows down. My wife apologizes –

'Don't,' I tell her. 'You had no choice.'

My wife bows again. My wife thanks me again. My wife says, 'I am very sorry you had to take her to the hospital. You must be tired now. I have made you some breakfast . . .'

'Not now,' I say. 'There are some things I must tell you . . .'

'Daddy's going away again,' sings my daughter.

My wife begins to scold my daughter –

'Sonoko is right,' I tell my wife. 'But I am going away because I have been demoted. I have lost my command and I have lost my rank. I have been ordered to go to Tochigi Prefecture as part of the present investigation. However, it is only for a few days and I would hope to be back by Tuesday or Wednesday. But, when I return, I will then be transferred to a local police station and I don't know where that will be or for how long –

'I have been told that the Public Safety Division of GHQ has been asking questions about my previous record and career, about my suitability as a police officer. It is possible that my name will appear on the next Purge Directive. It is certain that this will mean dismissal. It is also possible that this might even mean a trial and imprisonment. Even execution . . .'

Now I bow low. 'I am truly sorry to have to tell you this . . .'

My wife bows deeply too, her shoulders shaking, her tears falling on the tatami, and she sobs, 'I am sorry. This is all my fault.'

'The fault is mine,' I tell her. 'Don't reproach yourself . . .'

'I am sorry,' she sobs again. 'I have been a poor wife . . .'

'Please don't cry,' I ask her. 'And please don't reproach yourself any further. You have looked after our children and you have maintained our house under difficult circumstances. We continue to face a difficult and uncertain future and so we must both be strong for our children. We must both try our very hardest . . .'

My wife nods her head. My wife bows her head.

'Did you get the money out of the post office?'

'We've queued every day, but still nothing . . .'

I take out an envelope from my jacket pocket. I tell her, 'There's some food in my backpack, some rice and some vegetables, and this money will be enough until I get back.'

My wife bows. My wife thanks me –

We are both on our knees –

Get off your knees!

I get up from my knees. I walk through to the other room where our *butsudan* alcove is. I kneel down before our *butsudan*, before the photographs of her parents and mine, her sister and my brother. I lean forward on my knees to light three sticks of incense. I tap the metal bowl three times. I kneel back down before the altar –

Now I pray to my father, my mother and my brother –

To apologize for my behaviour and for my failings –

To beg for their forgiveness and their guidance –

To ask for their help and for their protection –

I lean forward on my knees again. I place the envelope of money on the *butsudan*. I place the bag of food before the altar –

The air is heavy with the smell of incense –

The smell of smouldering bedding –

My eyes sting. My eyes smart . . .

The smell of DDT –

My own tears.

*

I am late now and the Asakusa station is crowded, dark and hot. *Every station.* Hundreds, maybe thousands of passengers in queues for tickets which take hours, even days to get, tickets for trains which take hours, even days to arrive. *Every station, every train.* The whole of Japan, the survivors, *the lucky ones,* on the move, on the move –

I look to the left and to the right. In front then behind me –

No men from Headquarters. No men in uniforms . . .

I push my way through the crowds. I push my way up the stairs to the second floor, towards the platforms and the trains –

I look to the left and to the right. Behind me then –

I see Ishida up ahead. Ishida at the ticket gate –

Does he know they found Detective Fujita?

Ishida bows. Ishida hands me my ticket –

Does he know? Does he care . . . ?

I hurry us along. We show our train tickets and our police notebooks at the gate. *Quick!* We walk briskly along the platform. We pass the long string of run-down third-class carriages for the unprivileged Losers. *Quick!* We come to the second-class hard-seat carriage, reserved for the privileged Losers like us, our carriage –

Quick! Quick! Quick! Quick! Quick!

I glance back down the platform –

No one chasing after us . . .

Ishida and I board the train –

No one here waiting . . .

The conductor has kept two seats for us opposite each other; Ishida facing back towards the third-class carriages where the passengers are packed in, sitting, standing and hanging off the steps while I am facing forward to the Victors' carriage, the two reserved carriages for *Victors Only* which, for once, are full of GIs returning to their Tochigi postings from leave in Tokyo –

The whistle blows . . .

A conductor in a shabby brown Tōbu uniform stands guard on the connecting door to the first of the Victors' carriages, a steady stream of Japanese people still trying to steal a seat through there –

Each time the conductor in his shabby suit stops them –

The locomotive starts to move. The wheels start to turn . . .

'For Americans only,' the conductor tells them –

We are pulling out of the Asakusa Tōbu Station . . .

I wait for one of them to argue back with him –

We are crossing the Sumida River now . . .

But the Japanese all retreat silently –

I am getting away, getting away . . .
The laws of victory and defeat –
I have escaped. For now . . .
The wheels that turn and turn again.

*

I itch and I scratch. *Gari-gari.* The first part of the journey, to Sugito, is not long but the train is slow and the carriage is hot. I itch and I scratch. *Gari-gari.* Ishida and I do not speak. We close our eyes –

Please let my daughter's eyes be open now . . .

But I do not sleep. I itch and I scratch. *Gari-gari.* I listen to the railway announcements and the running feet as we stop at stations, then the short, sharp whistle of the locomotive. I itch and I scratch. *Gari-gari.* From station to station, whistle to whistle –

Kita-Senju. Soka. Kasukabe . . .

Until the train finally pulls into the Tōbu Sugito station and we fight our way out of the carriage and onto the platform. I itch and I scratch. *Gari-gari.* Then we cross the bridge to the other platform to wait for the Tōbu Nikkō Line train –

To Kodaira country . . .

It is a two-hour-wait on another platform crammed from end to end with men and women, their children and their belongings. I itch and I scratch. *Gari-gari.* Many with screaming babies strapped to their backs, others with the silent bones of the dead in boxes around their necks, returnees from Manchuria, refugees in their own country. I itch and I scratch –

Gari-gari . . .

Ishida and I find a small space at one end of the platform in which to crouch down with our knapsacks to wait, to wait and to wait, to itch and to scratch, *gari-gari.* Ishida still doesn't speak and I still don't talk, so again we both close our eyes, we both close our eyes until I sense the people on the platform moving, rising and picking up their children and their belongings, their babies and their bones at the approach of a train, the sound of a whistle and the sight of steam –

Every station. Every train. Every station. Every train . . .

The people on the platform trying to board the train before it has stopped, before its passengers can get off, pushing and shoving, shouting and arguing, onto the steps, through the windows –

Every station. Every train. Every station . . .

There are no reserved seats on this train. Every man, woman and child for themselves. Ishida and I get onto the footplate at the end of one of the carriages and we push our way inside –

Every train in the land . . .

Ishida and I stand crushed in the passageway outside the toilet, the toilet itself filled with an entire family and their possessions, as the train jolts forward, this train that once carried only tourists and day-trippers to such sights as the Shinkyō Bridge and the Tōshōgū Shrine, Lake Chūzenji and the Kegon Falls, this train that now carries only the starving and the lost –

The lucky ones.

I stand wedged between Ishida and a young girl. I itch and I scratch. *Gari-gari.* I try to turn my head to see out of the window, to find some air and to watch for the stations, but all I can see are lice crawling over the scalp of the young girl in front of me, in and out of her hair they crawl, burrowing and then surfacing, surfacing and then burrowing again, in and out of her hair. I itch and I scratch. *Gari-gari.*

Maybe thirty minutes later, the train jolts over joints and begins to slow down once again. But there is no announcement –

I turn to Ishida. I ask him, 'Where are we now?'

Ishida strains to see. He says, 'Fujioka.'

In the small of Ishida's back . . .

The train shudders to a stop in the station. People push and shove again, shouting and arguing as they struggle to get on and off –

In the small of his back, something cold and metallic . . .

I move away from Ishida. I itch and I itch. I move away from the young girl and her lice. I stand by a window, finally able to breathe, to scratch myself, *gari-gari, gari-gari, gari-gari . . .*

The locomotive begins to pull out of the station. Ishida moves closer to me. Now Ishida stands beside me again –

The sun is setting. It is getting dark . . .

Detective Ishida tells me we should get off the train at Shin-Kanuma station, that we should be there in another hour or so, that he knows the way to the Kanuma police station, that he has already looked it up on a map, that they will be expecting us, that they will have reserved an inn for us for tonight –

They will be waiting for us . . .

But I have also looked at maps. I have looked at maps of my

own. I tell him we're not getting off the train at Shin-Kanuma station, that we are not going to Kanuma police station –

Not to their inn. Not tonight –

Where they'll be waiting . . .

'Ienaka,' I tell him. 'That's where we'll get off.'

*

Ienaka is about fifteen kilometres before Kanuma. Ienaka is the closest station to the house where the mother and daughter of the Widow Okayama live. Ienaka is also near to the field in which the body of Baba Hiroko was found on the third of January –

But it is night now. It is dark here . . .

Ishida and I pass through the ticket gates and walk out of the station into the deserted town. No markets here –

No one waiting for us here . . .

Nothing here but the silhouettes of dark mountains and the hints of hidden trees looming up over the town and leering down at us as I squat down to open my knapsack and take out my notebook, Ishida beginning to mumble about the lateness of the hour, about it being too late to call on the mother and daughter of the Widow Okayama, too late to visit the field in which Baba Hiroko was found, too late to find an inn for the night –

Everything too late . . .

'Here it is,' I tell him and show him the address of an inn in my notebook and its location on my map. Now I lead Ishida up the slope out of town towards the address. We find it easily –

The Beautiful Mountain Inn . . .

The detached hotel faces the road and there is still a light on in the porch, moths smashing into the glass which covers the bulb, mosquitoes biting into our foreheads and our necks as we open the door to the inn and apologize to the maid for the late and abrupt nature of our unannounced visit, offering her some of the rice Detective Ishida has brought from his home –

Dark outside, dark inside . . .

The maid scurries off with the rice and our papers and returns with an older woman who thanks us for the rice and copies down our details. The woman tells us that we are too late for an evening meal, that these days they need a day's notice to buy and prepare meals, that we are also too late to use the bath, that they heat the bath water only when they have a day's notice and then only once a day –

No bath. No late night snacks. No sake. No beer . . .

'But there will be breakfast,' she tells us.

The older woman then instructs the younger maid to show us to our room, our room which the woman assures us is the best room that they have, and so we follow the young maid down a dim and humid corridor of unlit alcoves and shuttered windows –

Now the maid unlocks and slides open a door –

Now the maid switches on the light –

And I wish she had not . . .

The screens have been shredded to strips and the tatami are crawling with bugs, the mosquitoes eating us raw as Ishida and I sit down at a low table beneath a small electric bulb to count the cockroaches, the maid putting out our futons and our bedding, apologizing for the smell and the temperature but assuring us it is better, much better, to keep the windows closed at this time of year –

'Thank you,' we say as she bows to wish us goodnight.

*

In insect silence, they gather in the *genkan* of our house to watch me leave. *This is defeat.* They watch me put on my boots. *This is defeat.* They follow me out of the door of our house. *This is defeat.* They follow me down the garden path of our house. *This is defeat.* They stand at the gate to our house. *This is defeat.* They watch me walk away from our house and they wave. *This is defeat.* They watch me walk down our street and they wave. *This is defeat.* Every time I turn around. *This is defeat.* Every time I turn around. *This is defeat . . .*

'Please remember us. Please don't forget us, Daddy . . .'

For my wife, for my daughter and for my son –

Defeat. Defeat. Defeat. Defeat . . .

For my father and for my mother –

Defeat. Defeat. Defeat . . .

For my elder brother –

Defeat. Defeat . . .

This defeat that lasts for every minute of every hour of every day of every week of every month of every year –

I am one of the survivors . . .

This is surrender. This is occupation –
One of the lucky ones . . .
This is defeat.

*

We have washed our faces and we have pissed. We have taken off our trousers and taken off our shirts. We have said goodnight and switched off the electric bulb. Now I lie awake and wait for Ishida to fall asleep. Until I hear his breathing begin to slow –

Until I hear him sleeping deeply now –

It is oven hot and pitch black . . .

I turn slowly and quietly onto my chest. I move off my futon and onto the tatami mats. I crawl with the bugs and the cockroaches across the floor, across the room towards his knapsack. Now I ease open the bag and I search around inside –

Something cold, metallic . . .

I take out the gun. It is a 1939 army-issue pistol. It is loaded. Now I raise the pistol in the dark. I aim and I point it at Ishida –

I could kill him here. I could kill him now . . .

But I lower the pistol. I put the gun back inside his knapsack. I close the bag. I crawl back across the floor, back across the tatami to my own futon and my own knapsack. Now I open the bag –

I have to sleep. I have to sleep . . .

I take out the pills that Senju gave me. Not Calmotin tonight. Senju had no Calmotin. But Senju has a hoard –

Veronal. Muronal. Numal . . .

Senju always has a stock –

I do not count.

III

The Mountain of Bones

Banzai! **Ninety Calmotin, ninety-one.** Four in the morning, the eastern sky is whitening. The road wet with dew, we march towards the hospital. The streets are deserted, the Sun in the Blue Sky flag already fallen. Lieutenant Shigefuji leads the charge inside the hospital. *The Chinks robbed the Japanese.* Nurses in white cower before us, patients still lain in their beds. *The Chinks raped the Japanese.* Muddy boots now jump upon the beds, upon the white uniforms. *The Chinks murdered the Japanese.* A child stabbed against a wall, blood gushing from his chest, crouches on the floor. *Masaki, Banzai!* A pale woman sleeping in her bed, mouth open, never to awaken. *Daddy, Banzai!* We kick the corpses of the Chinese dead as they would kick the corpses of our dead. *Banzai!* Tomorrow the main units will move out but we shall remain. *Acacia leaves fly down the streets.* To keep the peace. *In the dust and the dirt.* To maintain law and order. *On the yellow wind.* Among the corpses. **One hundred Calmotin, one hundred and one.** Kasahara and I transport the three bandits by rickshaw down the T'ai-ma-lu Road. *The old mother grows weary.* The first bandit groans. A cigarette! Give me a cigarette! Their arms are twisted behind them, their legs locked with large shackles. Beggars and coolies, Germans and Japanese swarm around the rickshaw. *Waiting for the return of her beloved child.* The second bandit cries. Give me a P'ao-t'ai-pai! No cheap shit! The crowd pour wine into the mouths of the bandits. The rickshaws enter the square in front of the station. *The young wife adorned in red.* The third bandit screams. The rickshaw pullers lower their staffs. Soldiers push back the black crowds. Kasahara and I order the three men to be dragged out of the carriages. *Keeps a lonely watch over the empty bed.* The eldest bandit begins to sing a song of war. Sons of bitches! Did I murder anyone, you sons of bitches? *These Chinks robbed Japanese settlers.* Kneel! I shout. Go ahead and do it! I'm not scared! *These Chinks raped Japanese settlers.* Turn to the west! I shout. Bring me pork dumplings! Give me pork dumplings! *These Chinks murdered Japanese settlers.* The crowd surges forward again. *That fat bastard cries like a little baby.* The smell of garlic, the metallic whispers. *Do it! Do it!* I give the order. Two soldiers are covered in steaming blood as the headless corpse pitches forward. *Hurrah! Hurrah!* My mouth full of bile. The crowd applaud. I swallow the bile. *Hurrah! Hurrah!* Three women, their feet bound in black, totter out of the crowd. *Hurrah! Hurrah!* The women carry peeled buns impaled on the ends of three long chopsticks. *Don't let her see!* My mouth full of bile again. The three women press the three buns into the wounds of the three dead bandits. *Don't let her see!* I swallow the bile. The white buns soak up the blood and turn red. *Don't let her see!* My mouth fills again. The three women eat the three blood-soaked buns. *Don't let her see!* I vomit behind a rickshaw. *Yuan-na!* A woman has fought her way through the crowds. *Yuan-na!* An older man checks her in his embrace. *Yuan-na!* He was innocent, she cries. It was the Japanese! It was the Japanese! **One hundred and ten Calmotin, one hundred and eleven.** Fields of pampas grass, mountains of pine woods. *Down with Japanese Imperialism!* Every wall of every house of every town

11

August 25, 1946

Tochigi Prefecture, 89°, very fine

Ton-ton. Ton-ton. Ton-ton. Ton-ton. Ton-ton. Ton-ton . . .
    The sound of hammering, the hammering on a door –
Ton-ton. Ton-ton. Ton-ton. Ton-ton. Ton-ton . . .
    I open my eyes. I don't recognize this ceiling –
Ton-ton. Ton-ton. Ton-ton. Ton-ton . . .
    Now I recognize this room, and this door –
Ton-ton. Ton-ton. Ton-ton . . .
    I get up. *No Ishida.* I go to the door –
Ton-ton. Ton-ton . . .
    I don't open it. 'Who is it?'
    'The Kanuma police . . .'
I curse and I curse again . . .
    I slide open the door –
    'I am Tachibana, the chief of police for Kanuma,' says the small, fat, youngish man who now bows. 'Pleased to meet you –'
His uniform too tight. His buttons polished too bright . . .
    'Detective Minami,' I tell him. 'Pleased to meet you.'
Has he spoken to Tokyo? Has he heard about Fujita?
    Tachibana says, 'I am sorry to have woken you . . .'
    'Don't apologize,' I tell him. 'It was difficult to sleep with the heat and all the insects. I should have been awake hours ago . . .'
    Tachibana says, 'We were expecting you in Kanuma but . . .'
    'My mistake again. I am sorry. I should have called you . . .'
    'Don't worry about it,' laughs Tachibana. 'The telephones are often down; you probably wouldn't have got through to us.'
He has not spoken to Tokyo, not heard about Fujita . . .
    'Have you met Detective Ishida yet?' I ask him –
    Tachibana shakes his head. 'Your colleague?'
He hasn't met Ishida, not spoken to Ishida . . .
    'Yes,' I tell him. 'He's here somewhere . . .'

'He might have gone for his breakfast . . .'

Now I ask Tachibana, 'How did you know we were here?'

'Inns are obliged to report all guests,' laughs Tachibana again. 'Even guests from the Tokyo Metropolitan Police Department.'

Welcome to the countryside! Welcome to Tochigi!

I smile now and I nod and I say, 'Of course . . .'

'I'll wait for you in the entrance, inspector.'

I bow again and I excuse myself. I turn back into the room –

The room dark. The windows and the screens still closed –

I close the door. *No Ishida.* I look at his folded-up futon –

His knapsack gone. I go over to my own bag. I open it –

I root around inside until I find the boxes and bottles –

I count all the pills. *Enough.* They are still there –

Now I lie back down. I close my eyes again –

I still itch and so I scratch. *Gari-gari . . .*

I want to forget these dreams . . .

I sit back up again and I open up my bag again. *In the half-light.* I root around again until I find my notebook, until I find my pen. *I cannot forget these dreams.* I must write them down. *In the half-light.* These dreams, these half-things. *I cannot forget.* These things I dream, these dreams I remember; all these half-things I remember –

These things that don't make sense, these things that do . . .

Now I put my notebook away and I put my pen away –

I go into the small toilet. I piss. I wash my face –

I get dressed. I itch and I scratch again –

Gari-gari. I itch. I scratch. *Gari-gari . . .*

I pick up my bag. I leave the room –

I walk down the corridor –

The corridor still dark . . .

Ishida is here now –

His knapsack . . .

Ishida sat at the low table in the entrance to the inn, talking with Chief Tachibana, nodding and smiling along to his conversation. They both stand up and bow when they see me and Detective Ishida says, 'I'm sorry, sir. I went looking for breakfast without you . . .'

I no longer know who this Detective Ishida is. This man . . .

'That's all right,' I tell him. 'I must have needed the sleep.'

Has he spoken to Tokyo? About Fujita? About his orders?

'I tried to wake you,' nods Ishida. 'But you were dead.'

This man I don't know. This man I don't recognize . . .

Now Tachibana asks me, 'Would you like some breakfast?'

'They have *miso* soup,' says Ishida. 'You should have it.'

I shake my head. 'I'm not very hungry, thank you.'

Who is this man who calls himself Ishida?

Tachibana nods. But Tachibana says, 'You've paid for the breakfast. You should eat something while we talk . . .'

'I am fine, thank you,' I tell him but this Chief Tachibana is already on his feet, walking over to the reception desk, banging on the wood and shouting for my breakfast to be brought out –

I don't look at Ishida. Ishida doesn't look at me –

No one is who they say they are . . .

Tachibana comes back over. Tachibana sits back down. Tachibana picks up his briefcase. Tachibana opens it up. Tachibana takes out two thin files. Tachibana places the two files on the table –

One marked *Baba Hiroko*, the other *Numao Shizue* –

'Excuse me for interrupting,' says the young maid, the same maid as last night, as she puts down a bowl of rice-porridge topped with a thin slice of pickle on the low table before me, then a second bowl of green leaves floating in some *miso*-flavoured water, and now places a pair of chipped chopsticks beside the two bowls of food –

I suddenly feel very hungry. I apologize to Tachibana and Ishida. I excuse myself as I begin to eat the cold porridge and the pickle, to wash them down with the tepid brown soup and leaves –

I am a stray dog, his house lost and his master gone . . .

I swallow. I say, 'Tell us about Numao . . .'

'She was a local Nikkō girl,' he says, opening the file out on the table. 'On the evening of the second of December last year, she told her family she was going to visit her friend's house. She never arrived there and she never returned home. Just over one month later, on the third of January this year, her body was found –

'Numao Shizue had been stabbed to death.'

I put down the chipped chopsticks. I wipe my mouth and I say, 'I thought Numao was found on the thirtieth of December?'

'Sorry, sorry,' says Tachibana. 'Yes, you're right, of course.'

I ask, 'Was there any evidence at all that she'd been raped?'

'None,' says Tachibana. 'She was found fully clothed.'

I lean forward. I push the file away. 'It's not Kodaira.'

Tachibana bows his head. Tachibana nods his head –

261

I tell him, 'Kodaira Yoshio only murders for sex.'

'There are some other cases,' he tells me –

I ask, 'Do you have the files with you?'

'No, they are back at Kanuma.'

Back at the police station . . .

'All right,' I tell him. 'Thank you. We'll take a look at them later but, for now, we have two requests to make of you . . .'

'Please,' he says. 'We are here to help you . . .'

'We'd like to visit a girl named Okayama whose mother is an acquaintance of Kodaira Yoshio. We'd like to talk to her and anybody else who may have met Kodaira up here. Then we'd like to examine the site where the body of Baba Hiroko was found . . .'

'Of course,' says Chief Tachibana, getting to his feet now. 'These places are not far and I have a small truck we can use. I'll bring it round to the front while you settle up with the inn.'

I nod my head. I say, 'Thank you for your help.'

Tachibana gathers up the files from the table and puts them back in his briefcase. Tachibana then bows and leaves us.

I wipe my mouth again. I wipe my neck.

'He seems very helpful,' says Ishida.

'Because he's afraid,' I tell him –

'Afraid of what . . .'

'Does he need a reason?' I ask him. 'This is Japan. This is the twenty-first year of Shōwa. The Year of the Dog –

'Everybody is afraid, detective . . .'

Now Ishida suddenly asks, 'What happened to your hair?'

I rub my scalp. I say, 'I shaved it a few days ago . . .'

'But it's growing back grey,' says Ishida.

I touch it again. I shrug my shoulders –

'I almost didn't recognize you.'

*

The truck is ancient and small and there is an old policeman in the driving seat in a frayed and soiled cap. Tachibana gestures for me to sit up in the front on the small seat to the left of the driver while he and Ishida climb into the back where there is some corrugated iron and what look to be carpenter's tools. The driver starts the truck –

Now I hold on tight as off we set. No windscreen or hood, the daylight is blinding, my eyes squinting as the sunlight illuminates the Tochigi countryside; this Land of the Living. This Land of Plenty –

There are mountains. There are trees. There are fields –
There are leaves and there are flowers here –
There are rivers and there are streams –
There are greens and blues here –
In the Land of the Living –
There are colours.

*

The truck labours up the side of one small mountain and down its other side and then up another until it pulls up outside a detached house that faces out onto the road and we all climb out. There is a dog asleep in the shade of the wall but it is still tethered to a pole –

It is not a stray, its house not lost, its master here . . .

Black and large, better fed than most of the people of Tokyo, I watch its belly rise and fall, its eyes closed, tongue hanging out –

'That lazy dog is a guard dog,' laughs Chief Tachibana.

'Do you get much burglary round here?' asks Ishida.

'There are always the Scavengers,' nods Tachibana. 'And before that were the Chinks, always escaping from the factories . . .'

'He'd have been a hunting dog, then,' says the driver.

Tachibana looks at the dog and laughs again. Then the chief excuses himself as he goes into the house ahead of us –

The old driver lights a cigarette and tells us, 'A lot of them old hunting dogs are running wild now, in packs . . .'

Tachibana returns with the mother of the Widow Okayama, who bows and welcomes us as Tachibana introduces us and explains to the old woman why we have come as Ishida and I apologize for the early hour and abruptness of our visit, calling on her unannounced.

The mother of the Widow Okayama bows again and invites us into her house. The mother is very old and her granddaughter is not here today. But the mother is not alone. An old man is sat in the empty fireplace. The mother of the Widow Okayama rents this house from this man. This man named Koito. This man Koito doesn't usually much like the police and he doesn't usually much like city folk. The mother of the Widow Okayama doesn't really remember anyone called Kodaira Yoshio but this man Koito remembers him –

'I liked Mr. Kodaira because he was born round here, born up in Nikkō. He came here a number of times hunting for supplies –

'He was a friendly fellow was Kodaira, very friendly. He always had money to buy with or things to exchange, did Kodaira. I introduced him to a number of other people round here, folk I knew would be willing to trade with a local fellow like him . . .'

I ask him for their names and their addresses –

'I know it's not strictly legal,' he says, looking at Tachibana. 'But everybody does it. If they didn't they'd starve . . .'

I ask him again for names and addresses –

'Not all as lucky as the likes of you . . .'

I hate the countryside. I hate it . . .

I crack my knuckles and I ask him for their names again, their addresses. I ask him one last time and now Koito sighs and begins to list the names, the names of local farmers and their families, every local farmer, every family he can think of, he can remember –

Kashiwagi, Kiyohara, Fujisaki, Yoshimura . . .

'How many times did Kodaira come up here?' I ask him but this man Koito shrugs his shoulders and says he can't be sure, he didn't keep a record, did he? Then I turn to the old grandmother –

The grandmother asks again, 'Who is this Kodaira?'

Dr. Nakadate estimated that the second body in Shiba Park had been killed sometime between the twentieth and the twenty-seventh of July, and the advertisement found in the pocket of her dress was dated the nineteenth of July, so I want to know if Kodaira Yoshio came here again after the nineteenth of last month, if he was here and what he brought, what he brought and exchanged . . .

I turn back to Koito. I ask, 'When was his last visit?'

But Koito just shrugs his shoulders again and says he can't be sure, that he doesn't keep records, does he? But now I crack my knuckles again and I lean forward and I hiss, 'Then think!'

'Her granddaughter would know better than me,' he says. 'There may have been times when he was here and I was not, for all I know, and it was her he came to see anyway . . .'

And the grandmother asks again, 'Who is this man?'

I need to speak to the granddaughter but they don't know where she is or what she's doing though they swear she will be back tonight, that she will be here if we come back tomorrow . . .

'We'll be back then,' I promise them.

The Kashiwagi family lives further up the same mountain. *He walks behind me.* There is only so far the truck can go so then we walk, Tachibana showing me the way, Ishida walking behind –

He walks behind me. He walks behind me . . .

Up the mountain and through the heat –

No one is who they say they are . . .

Through the insects and their teeth –

No one is who they seem . . .

The Kashiwagi family makes fuel for the hand-warmers that are used in the winter. Last winter was the worst winter on record. The Kashiwagi family made a lot of fuel for hand-warmers last winter. The Kashiwagi family also made a lot of money last winter. And a lot of visitors called upon the Kashiwagi family last winter –

Kodaira called upon the Kashiwagi family last winter –

Baba Hiroko was murdered last winter.

Baba Hiroko was found dead on the third of January this year. Baba Hiroko was last been seen alive on the thirtieth of December –

Kodaira was here last winter. Kodaira was here . . .

The Kashiwagi family is a nervous, sullen family. The Kashiwagi family just sits and stares and offers us no tea or water –

'Do you remember exactly when Kodaira came here . . .?'

But the Kashiwagi family does not remember exactly –

'You remember if it was before or after New Year . . .?'

The Kashiwagi family does not want to remember –

'But you remember what he traded . . .?'

The Kashiwagi family claims not to remember what Kodaira Yoshio traded for their hand-warmer fuel. But the Kashiwagi family is lying because country-folk never forget anything –

I hate the countryside. These country-folk . . .

Because country-folk remember everything; every last piece of fuel and every last grain of rice; every single coin and every single note they have ever received; every single item accepted in a trade –

I hate them. I hate them all . . .

That is why their unmarried daughter is fiddling with her wristwatch. That is why she has been fiddling with it since we sat down. That is why I reach across their hearth to grab her wrist –

Why I hold this watch on her wrist up to her face –

'Is this what friendly Mr. Kodaira gave you?'

Chiku-taku. Chiku-taku . . .

This watch I now tear from her wrist. This watch I turn over in my hand to the light. This watch with an inscription on its back –

An inscription that states, *Miyazaki Mitsuko* . . .

This watch that was not Kodaira's to trade –

That screams, *Miyazaki Mitsuko* . . .

This watch. This watch . . .

Not theirs to keep –

This watch . . .

That I stuff into my knapsack as I get to my feet to leave –

Tachibana asking, 'But who is Miyazaki Mitsuko?'

*

The daylight blinding, my eyes squinting, in this Land of the Living, in this Land of Plenty, before their mountains, before their trees, before their fields, their leaves and their flowers, their rivers and their streams, their greens and their blues, in this Land of the Living –

Before *his* mountains, *his* trees, *his* fields –

I say, 'Miyazaki Mitsuko was a nineteen-year-old girl from Nagasaki whose naked body was found on the fifteenth of August last year in an air-raid shelter of the Women's Dormitory Building of the Dai-Ichi Naval Clothing Department near Shinagawa in Tokyo.

'The autopsy revealed that she had been raped and then murdered around the end of May last year. At that time, Kodaira Yoshio was working at this Women's Dormitory.

'The autopsy on Miyazaki was performed by a Dr. Nakadate of the Keiō University Hospital. Dr. Nakadate also performed the autopsies on the body of Midorikawa Ryuko and on the unidentified body found near Midorikawa in Shiba Park. Dr. Nakadate believes that all three women were murdered by the same man; Kodaira Yoshio. As you know, Kodaira Yoshio has already confessed to the murder of Midorikawa Ryuko . . .'

Tachibana nods. 'But not to the second unidentified body from Shiba Park?'

'No.'

'And not to this Miyazaki Mitsuko . . .?'

'He's not been asked.'

'Why not?'

'Because I have not mentioned Miyazaki to either Chief Kita or Chief Inspector Kanehara, who is leading the interrogation team.'

'But why not?' asks Tachibana again.

I look at Ishida as I say, 'Two reasons; the Miyazaki case is officially closed and, secondly, the case file is missing.'

Tachibana is shaking his head, glancing from me to Ishida and back again. 'Someone was actually charged?'

'Yes,' I tell him. 'They were.'

Tachibana asks, 'Who?'

'A Korean labourer . . .'

A Yobo . . .

'And so what happened to this Korean labourer?'

'He was shot and killed resisting arrest . . .'

'Shot by whom?' asks Tachibana.

'An officer from the Kempei.'

'Case closed, then?'

'Yes,' I tell him, still looking at Ishida; Ishida saying nothing, Ishida asking nothing. 'Until today . . .'

Chiku-taku. Chiku-taku . . .

Her watch in my hand –

Chiku-taku.

*

Beyond another pine grove, beyond more dwarf bamboo, the next house, the next family, the same as the last house, the same as the last family. The grove after that, the house after that, the family after that, the same as the last grove, the same as the last house, the last family –

I look back down the mountainside, at the mainly thatched roofs and the odd tiled one on the odd two-storey house, at the crops in the fields and the leaves on the trees and I wonder where I am, where this place is, this place of plenty, this land of the living –

No dead without name, dead without number . . .

This place of mountains. This place of rivers –

Piled up high along the riverbanks . . .

In this place of greens and blues –

No stench of rotten apricots . . .

In this place of colour where Kodaira came with his many pickings from the dead, with his trophies and his spoils, the trophies and the spoils he had brought to barter –

From the dead . . .

Every house Kodaira ever visited, every family he spoke to, every thing he traded, every single house, every single family, every single thing he showed them –

His trophies . . .

But in the next house, the next family, the house after that, the family after that, they sit in shame, sit in silence and they will not remember, will not try –

His spoils . . .

'Because so many people come,' they tell us. 'So many people, so many things, every day a different person comes, every day with different things . . .'

So many people . . .

And in the next house, the next family, the house after that, the family after that, they shake their heads when we say his name, they shake their heads when we describe his face, they shake their heads when we ask for dates, they shake their heads and tell us –

'So many people come, so many things . . .'

*

We stand beside the truck and wipe our faces and wipe our necks, the cicadas deafening and the mosquitoes ravenous, the sun high in the sky but there is a darkness here now, in the shadows from the mountains, from the trees and in the fields, darkness and shadow –

The slopes are purple, the leaves black now, the grass grey . . .

In the rivers that do not flow, the streams that stand still –

There are no currents and there are no fish, only insects . . .

Tachibana asks, 'What do you want to do now?'

Insects feasting in the still and stagnant pools . . .

I look up at the sun then back down at the shadows and I say, 'Take me to the place where you found Baba Hiroko.'

*

Up the side of another small mountain and down its other side, then up and down another until the truck stops on the narrow road where the woods at the foot of this small mountain look out over a ditch onto a patchwork of fields and ditches, more fields and more ditches, and Tachibana says, 'These are the woods. This is the place.'

Nishi Katamura, Kami Tsuga-gun, Tochigi . . .

Tachibana, Ishida, and I climb out of the truck and wipe our faces and wipe our necks and turn away from the fields and the ditches to stare up into the woods on the slope of the mountainside, up into the shadows of the black trunks of the trees –

Their branches and their leaves . . .

Tachibana points up the slope and says, 'It's that way . . .'

'But I thought Baba was found in a field?' I ask him –

'It seems that she was attacked down here,' he says. 'But then her body was dragged from the field up this way . . .'

Now I follow Tachibana as he climbs up off the narrow road and into the woods, waving away the mosquitoes and the bugs with the file in his hands, Detective Ishida following behind –

He walks behind me. He walks behind me . . .

Tachibana leads us through the trees to a slight hollow in the side of the mountain; a slight hollow surrounded by fallen logs and filled with broken branches and dead leaves –

He walks behind me, through the trees . . .

'This is the place,' says Tachibana now, handing me the file –

The cicadas are deafening, the mosquitoes hungry . . .

In this place, in this hollow, I take her case file –

Between the trees, the black trunks of the trees . . .

I open the file. I take out the photographs –

Their branches and their leaves . . .

Now I see her in this place –

Her white, naked body . . .

Her face in this place –

Her beaten face . . .

Her face –

Black . . .

In this place, in this hollow, beneath these trees, I close my eyes and I see her face; I see her say farewell to her uncle, with her gifts for her mother; I see her take the Ginza Line to Asakusa; I see her climb with the crowds up the stairs to the second floor of the Matsuya Department Store; I see her join the queue for her ticket –

How long did you stand in that queue? How long did you wait?

That cold and desperate queue of cold and desperate strangers, pushing and shoving, those desperate, defeated strangers with their desperate, hungry eyes, pushing and shoving –

Is this where you met him? Is this him behind you now . . .?

In his ancient winter suit that is far too loose beneath his frayed army coat with its Shinchū Gun armband, his hair tight against his scalp, skin tight against his skull –

Did he offer you a piece of bread? A rice-ball? Candy?

In that cold and desperate queue of cold and desperate strangers, pushing and shoving, this one smiling, friendly man, this one small, friendly act of kindness –

Did you eat it there and then? That one small gift?

Now he asks you where you are going, this smiling, friendly man and between your hurried, grateful mouthfuls, you tell him you are going to visit your mother in Nikkō. He asks you where your mother lives in Nikkō and you tell this smiling, friendly man about the Furukawa Denki apartments. Now he says he once worked for Furukawa and he tells you Nikkō is where he's from and he tells you he knows a farmer from whom you can buy some very cheap rice, some rice to surprise your mother with, some rice to take back for your uncle in Kyōbashi. And he smiles and he smiles and he smiles, this friendly man with his small acts of kindness and he even makes you laugh, this smiling, friendly man in that cold and desperate queue, among those cold and desperate strangers, this smiling, friendly man he puts an arm around you now to guide you through the crowds, the pushing and the shoving, to shepherd you onto that train, among those cold and desperate strangers, this smiling, friendly man, he helps you to find a place to stand on the train among those desperate, hungry eyes, among the ringworm and the lice, on that train with its windows of cracked plywood and bits of tin through which blow the wind and the snow as the train crosses over the Sumida River and steams up through Kita-Senju, on and on, up and up the Tōbu Line –

Does he press against you now, on that cold, cold train?

All the way up and up the Tōbu Line he smiles and he smiles and he smiles and you laugh and you laugh and you laugh as he talks and he talks and he talks, and it's like you've known him all your life, this smiling, friendly man, like he's your uncle, this smiling, friendly man, or even the father you lost so young, for you feel so safe in his smile, this one smiling, friendly face on this cold, cold train, among these strangers, these desperate, defeated strangers who stare at you with their hungry eyes and their dried lips, their sunken cheeks and their frayed collars on this cold, cold train that takes forever –

Is his smile too close? Are his hands too free . . .?

But now the train is pulling into Kanazaki and he's telling you this is where you should both get off, that this is the quickest way to the farmer he knows, the farmer with the very cheap rice he'll sell you, the rice for your mother, the rice for your uncle, and now you're not so sure because you do not know this place, this land, and it's getting darker and darker and darker but you've eaten his bread, taken his rice-balls and sucked on his candy, and now he takes you by your arm and leads you through these cold and desperate strangers, through the pushing and through the shoving, and off that cold, cold train and onto that cold, cold platform and now the train is gone and the platform is gone and you're walking through the ticket gates and now the station is gone and soon the town is gone because you are walking and walking and walking away, minute after minute, hour after hour, and now the day is gone and the road is narrow, walking and walking and walking, and the mountains are dark and the fields are lonely and still he smiles and he smiles and he smiles, this smiling, friendly man, but his teeth are pointed now, his eyes hungry now –

Is this when his grip tightens? His words harden . . .?

His lips wet and his tongue long, this man is not smiling now, this man is not friendly now, this man with his pointed teeth and his hungry eyes, his wet lips and his long tongue whispering what he wants from you now, in those woods or in that ditch, telling you exactly what he wants from you now and you're turning away from this man, turning away from him now, on this narrow road, beside these lonely fields, beneath that dark mountain, below those black woods, but he's pulling you back and he's slapping your face, punching your face and kicking your legs, and you're asking him to stop and you're begging him to stop and you're pleading with him to stop, but he's pulling you off that narrow road and away from those lonely fields, up this dark mountain, into these black woods, putting a hand around your neck and another between your legs and you know what he wants and you know what he wants and you know what he wants and you're trying to tell him to take it and you're begging him to take it and you're pleading with him to take it, to take it and then leave you alone, please leave you, please leave you alone but he's squeezing your throat, he's squeezing your throat, he's squeezing your throat, snot in your nose and piss down your legs and shit from your backside, as he squeezes your throat tighter and tighter, the mountain darker and darker, the woods blacker and blacker –

As black as your hair that will never turn grey . . .

Now you open your eyes and you know you are still living, lying on your back on broken branches and dead leaves in a hollow in these woods, you have survived, you are one of the lucky ones, freezing and bleeding on these branches and these leaves, but you have survived, you are lucky and now you raise yourself up from the branches and the leaves, but this is when you know you have not survived, you are not one of the lucky ones, when you see him sat on the trunk of a fallen tree, staring at you and smoking a cigarette, this once smiling, friendly man who now finishes his cigarette and gets up off the trunk of this fallen tree, walking towards you over broken branches and dead leaves as he unbuttons his trousers again –

You try to speak but you cannot speak, you cannot scream . . .

Because this once smiling, friendly man has your scarf in his hands and he is pulling it tighter and tighter as the mountain turns darker and darker, the woods blacker and blacker again –

Freezing and bleeding and choking here . . .

Here on these broken branches and these dead leaves, here in this hollow, in these woods, on this mountainside –

As he fucks you again and again . . .

Beside those lonely fields –

Again and again . . .

Kodaira fucks the dead.

*

I hate the countryside. He walks behind me. *I hate the countryside.* Back down the slope. *I hate the countryside.* Back to the truck. *I hate the countryside.* Ishida walks behind me. *I hate the countryside.* Ishida says nothing. *I hate the countryside.* I say nothing. *I hate the countryside.* Tachibana says nothing. *I hate the countryside . . .*

I hate the countryside. I hate the country-folk –

By these ditches. In this terrible place . . .

There is nothing else to say.

Down the side of another mountain and into a valley, we follow the signs for Kanuma, a river to our right and a railway line to our left –

Lines of people making their way back towards the station . . .

'Local people call it the Scavenging Line these days,' shouts Chief Tachibana from the back of the truck. 'Because the only people who ever use the trains on that line now are city people from Tokyo, up here to scavenge after our rice and our sweet potatoes . . .'

Lines of people with their supplies on their backs . . .

'They've turned them into freight trains,' agrees the driver. 'No panes of glass in the windows, old boards for doors . . .'

Lines of people with their backs bent double . . .

'Difficult to tell what's human and what's luggage . . .'

Lines of people under the setting sun . . .

'The early morning trains are the worst, packed . . .'

Lines of people all reduced to this . . .

'Infested as well, with fleas and with lice . . .'

Lines of people, beaten to this . . .

And on and on they drone, on and on about city-folk; how it was city-folk who had brought all these problems onto Japan, how it was all the fault of city-folk, but now city-folk demand and expect the country-folk to help them and look after them when it was city-folk who had brought this mess on Japan, the city-folk who got us into this mess, and on and on they drone, on and on about city-folk –

I hate the countryside and I hate the country-folk . . .

But I'm not listening to them. I am looking out for Kanuma police station. They are looking out for us too. The Kanuma police –

They are waiting for us. They are waiting for me . . .

They are watching for us. They are listening out for the sound of Tachibana's battered old mountain truck coming through the town towards their quaint old rural police station –

We are here. I am here . . .

The driver pulls up right outside the pristine police station, right outside the eight pristine police officers who have lined up in the sinking sun to greet us, to bow, to salute and welcome us to Kanuma police station. Detective Ishida and I bow back and salute and thank them and then we follow Chief Tachibana up the clean little steps and into his police station where two officers behind the front desk bow and salute and welcome us again to their station –

'I have a telegram from Tokyo for a Detective Ishida,' announces one of the two men. Ishida quickly steps forward –

I curse! I curse! I curse! I curse! I curse! I curse!

Ishida takes the telegram from the officer behind the desk. Ishida steps to one side to open and read the telegram –

My heart is pounding. My heart is pounding . . .

But Tachibana is taking me down the side of the front desk, leaving Ishida to his telegram, and leading me along a corridor to his office, telling me the local history of Kanuma –

I curse him! I curse him! I curse him!

Police Chief Tachibana sitting me down and promising me tea, searching for the other files, the other dead women he feels might have been murdered by Kodaira Yoshio –

Other women, other deaths . . .

There is a soft knock on the door now as Detective Ishida steps into the room, excusing himself –

Eyes blank, eyes dead . . .

'Here we are,' says Chief Tachibana, handing me two thin files across his desk. 'In the face of any initial evidence to the contrary both these deaths were originally recorded as *ikidaore*, accidental deaths due to injury or disease, mainly because of the deterioration of the corpses. But, to be honest, I've always felt that there might have been more to their deaths than simple accident or disease and now, with this Kodaira suspect you have in Tokyo . . .'

I open the top file as he speaks, *Ishikawa Yori . . .*

'Thirty years old and the wife of a tailor, Ishikawa was an evacuee living at Imaichimachi, Kami Tsuga-gun. She was last seen on the twenty-second of June last year, waiting for a train at Shin-Tochigi station and then travelling on a bus from Tochigi station to Manako station, which is near to where her body was found. We believe that Ishikawa died some time towards the end of June last year but her body was not discovered until . . .'

'The tenth of September,' I read –

'Yes, the tenth of September,' continues Chief Tachibana. 'Thank you. An old farmer had gone up into the woods at Manako-mura to pick leaves to smoke as a tobacco substitute and that's when he found the body, or the skeleton as it was by that time . . .'

'But it was never treated as murder?' asks Ishida.

'Difficult,' says Tachibana. 'Because of the state of the body and also, of course, there are many animals in these woods.'

I pick up the second file. There is no name on this second file. I hold up the second file. I ask Tachibana, 'And this one?'

'Even more difficult,' says Tachibana. 'The owner of a small mountain at Kiyosu-mura, again this is Kami Tsuga-gun, he'd gone up onto the slopes to prune away some of the branches around his cypress trees and he came upon a perfect skeleton. This was only last month and we think the body may have been there for over a year.'

I ask, 'Did you find out anything else about the body?'

'Yes,' says Tachibana. 'The autopsy was conducted in Utsunomiya and although we were unable to determine the exact cause of death we do believe it to have been the body a young woman aged approximately twenty to twenty-five years . . .'

'But again you had it listed as *ikidaore*?'

'Yes,' he says again. '*Ikidaore*.'

'Why?' I ask him. 'You find many such bodies, do you?'

Tachibana nods. Tachibana says, 'In the last three or four years, yes. Older people particularly, they come out here from Tokyo to scavenge and they get lost in the woods. They have never been out here before. In the summer, some simply collapse of exhaustion. Others, in the winter, lose their way and freeze in the night . . .'

'But these two weren't old,' says Ishida. 'You often get young women walking in your woods, dropping down dead, do you?'

'They were younger, yes,' says Tachibana. 'But we do get younger ones, but for different reasons. Only two days ago, for example, in some other woods, we found the body of a twenty-three or twenty-five-year-old woman. Dead about one month and animals had been there but we know it wasn't murder. It was suicide.'

'How do you know?' asks Ishida. 'If animals . . .'

'Well, this one had at least left us a suicide note.'

'What did it say?' I ask. 'This suicide note?'

'That she had lost all her relatives during the war. That she was completely alone. That she saw no point in living any more –

'She was from Tokyo too,' he says. 'Mitaka.'

Please let my daughter's eyes be open now.

*

Below another dark mountain, with its overhanging eaves and the shade of its hearth, this inn seems much grander than the one we stayed in last night. *This place in the shadows*. At the foot of the mountain, with its pond and its bridge in the garden round the back, this inn seems much older but is better maintained. *This place from the past*. This inn still accepts Ishida's rice but they are able to offer us a hot bath in their bathhouse and the room we are shown seems much bigger and cleaner too, with its fresh mats and its rosewood table, the tasteful alcove and the red camellia in a celadon vase. *This place from another century, this place from another country ...*

Because of the chief of the Kanuma police, because of Tachibana. He tells us he will join us for the evening meal. He promises there will be fresh food, and even some sake –

In this other country, in this other century ...

Tachibana tells us to enjoy our baths, that the water will be hot now. Then he leaves us alone, Ishida and me –

In this place, so very far from home ...

Ishida and me in this beautiful room, alone and silent –

No talk of messages from Tokyo. No talk at all ...

Until Detective Ishida says, 'Please take your bath first.'

*

The inn has been built around the garden and the room we have been given is at a right angle to the long plank walkway which separates the bathhouse from the main building. *Sara-sara*. It would also be possible to reach the bathhouse by crossing the small garden and the bridge over the pond, but I choose to walk across the planks, oak and zelkova trees to my right, the magnolia and camellia bushes in the garden on my left, listening to the sound of running water. *Sara-sara*. There is a room of toilets and basins before the door to the bathhouse. *Sara-sara*. The taps in the basins are all running and I can smell the scent of heated bathwater. *Sara-sara*. I open the door to the bathhouse and I step into the changing room. *Sara-sara*. It is dark and windowless in here, the only light coming from a small lamp in one of the corners. *Sara-sara*. The bathtub must be on the other side of the second door. *Sara-sara*. I unbutton my shirt. *Sara-sara*. I take it off. *Sara-sara*. I unbutton my trousers. *Sara-sara*. I take them off. *Sara-sara*. I am ashamed of this shirt and these trousers. *Sara-sara*.

This shirt and these trousers that my wife has tended and mended, stitched and re-stitched. *Sara-sara.* I take off my undershirt. *Sara-sara.* I take off my undershorts. *Sara-sara.* I fold and pile up these clothes. *Sara-sara.* I place them in one of the changing-room baskets. *Sara-sara.* I never want to wear these clothes again. *Sara-sara.* I pick up one of the clean white bathing cloths. *Sara-sara.* I go through the second door and I close it behind me. *Sara-sara.* The room is filled with steam. *Sara-sara.* The only windows are narrow and high in one of the walls and admit little light. *Sara-sara.* The bathtub though is big and raised. *Sara-sara.* I pick up a small wooden bucket. *Sara-sara.* I climb up the three small steps to the bath. *Sara-sara.* I fill the bucket with water from the tub. *Sara-sara.* Now I crouch down and tip the bucket of hot water over my body. *Sara-sara.* I find the soap and the brush and I begin to scrub myself clean. *Sara-sara.* Then I take another bucket of water and I rinse myself. *Sara-sara.* Now I climb the small steps for a third time. *Sara-sara.* Now I get into the bath. *Sara-sara.* I put my cloth upon the edge of the wooden tub and stretch myself out. *Sara-sara.* The water is hot. *Sara-sara.* The water is pure. *Sara-sara.* I do not itch. *Sara-sara.* I do not scratch. *Sara-sara.* I fold the bathing cloth into a small pillow. *Sara-sara.* I rest the back of my neck on the edge of the tub. *Sara-sara.* I close my eyes. *Sara-sara.* I listen to the sound of the running water. *Sara-sara* . . .

I am sleeping not waking, I am waking not sleeping –
Sara-sara. Sara-sara. Sara-sara. Sara-sara. Sara –
The sound of the running water has stopped –
I hear the door open. I feel the air change . . .
I open my eyes but there is only steam –
I think I see the figure of a woman . . .
I cannot stand. I cannot breathe –
The figure of a woman facing away from me, staring into a mirror that is not there, she is dressed in a yellow kimono with a dark-blue stripe, its skirts dripping onto the tiles of the floor, her hair tied up with silk threads which expose her pale neck . . .
The water is cold. The water is black –
The woman holds a hairbrush in one hand as she leans forward to stare at herself in the mirror, suddenly turning to face me now, dropping the hairbrush to the floor, ton, *she puts her hands to her face and covers both her eyebrows* –
'Does this become me?'

Ishida looks up startled and embarrassed when I come back from the bath. He is sat cross-legged on the floor of the room by the table. He has already changed into the same *yukata* provided by the inn that I am now wearing. He quickly stuffs something back into his knapsack and shoves it under the table. Now he picks up a towel from the mat –

'Excuse me,' he mumbles, telling me he'll take his bath now.

I listen to his feet trail off down the corridor. I wait a moment before I look out the door to make sure he has gone. Now I pull his bag out from under the table to see what he'd been so quick to hide –

And here it is, lying on the top inside his knapsack; his underwear and a needle. Detective Ishida had been hunting fleas in his underwear with a needle, piercing and spearing flea after flea on the end of the needle. But the old army pistol is still here too –

The old army pistol at the bottom of his knapsack –

I fight back the visions. I fight back the tears . . .

Here waiting for something, there waiting for someone.

*

It is dark and it is silent outside when Tachibana joins us for dinner. Tachibana has changed out of his uniform and into an evening kimono. Tachibana summons two maids who serve the food in our room on three small lacquered butterfly-legged tables, the food as good as he promised; bonito, smoked eggs, *soba*, and a bowl of fishcake in a cold soup of grated arrowroot. Ishida and I eat it up like a pair of hungry dogs. The sake is equally fine and we lap that up until Ishida begins to worry about the expense of all this food and all this drink, but Police Chief Tachibana just claps his big hands –

'It's my inn,' he laughs. 'And you're my guests . . .'

And after the dinner, after the two maids have cleared away the tables but left us with three fresh bottles of sake, Tachibana suddenly gets to his feet and begins to dance, this small, fat, youngish man whose eyes are now old and hard as he performs the violent, jerky dance of a warrior, lungeing at Ishida with an invisible sword –

This dance from the shadows, this dance from the past . . .

Then, just as suddenly, his violent, jerky dance is over and Tachibana is sat back down, his face still red and angry –

278

In the half-light, no one is who they seem . . .
Filling our cups and offering up a toast –
From the past and from the shadows . . .
'To Japan and to the Emperor . . .'

*

We have pissed and we have washed our faces. I switch off the electric bulb and now, in the dark of the room, before I say goodnight, I ask him, 'What was the message they gave you back at the station?'

Ishida is silent for a time before he says, 'What message . . .?'

'The one you got when we arrived at Kanuma police station.'

Ishida says, 'It was just from Inspector Hattori. That's all.'

'And what did *Inspector* Hattori have to tell you?' I ask –

'Nothing,' he says. 'He just wants any leads we find . . .'

'What do you mean, he wants any leads we find?'

'He wants me to telephone or telegram him . . .'

'Telephone him about what?' I ask again –

'Just if we find any new leads, that's all.'

'There was no other request or news?'

'That was all the message said.'

'Goodnight, then,' I tell him –

But now, in the dark and in the silence of this room, Detective Ishida asks me, 'Do you think we are the only guests in this inn?'

'I don't know,' I tell him. 'Why do you ask?'

'It's nothing,' he says. 'I'm just tired . . .'

'No, tell me,' I say. 'What's wrong?'

'I just don't like it here,' he says. 'I wish we'd never come.'

12

August 26, 1946

Tochigi, 87°, fine

In the night, he shrieks. In the night, he howls. In the night, he wails. In the night, the grinding of teeth. In the night, the weeping of tears –
Not sleeping, not waking. *I can hear him crying*. In his sleep. Not waking, not sleeping. *I can hear him weeping*. In my dreams. Not sleeping, not waking. *I can hear him crying*. In his sleep. Not waking, not sleeping. *I can hear him weeping*. In my dreams. Not sleeping, not waking. *I can hear him crying*. In his sleep. Not waking, not sleeping. *I can hear him weeping*. In my dreams. Not sleeping, not waking. *I can hear him crying*. In his sleep. Not waking, not sleeping. *I can hear him weeping*. In my dreams. Not sleeping, not waking –
Ton.
Before the dawn, before the light, the dull thud upon the mat –
Ton.
The only sound as it hits the floor, just beyond my pillow –
Nothing before, nothing after, the dull thud on the mat –
Ton.
I lie on the futon and I do not, dare not move –
What was that noise? What was that sound?
Ton.
Ishida is awake now. I can feel him –
He asks, 'What was that noise?'
Ton.
I turn over on the futon. I raise my head up. I look beyond my pillow. I can see it now. In front of the alcove –
It lies on the matting. It lies neck up –
Like an inverted, severed head –
The red camellia –
Ton.

*

It is dawn now and it is light. I get up from my futon but I do not wake Ishida. I take off my *yukata*. I pull on my undershorts. I put on my undershirt. I pull on my trousers. I put on my shirt. I gather up my jacket, my knapsack, my hat. I leave the room. I walk down the corridor to the reception area. There is no one here. *In this place of shadows*. The hearth deserted. *This place from the past.* I pick up my boots from the *genkan*. I squat down beneath the eaves of the inn. *In this other century.* I pull on my old army boots and I leave this inn –

    This other country, so far from home . . .

    I walk back towards the town, back towards the station; the first train must have already arrived as there are Scavengers walking past me out of town, mumbling and muttering and moaning –

    Their clothes are almost rags, half of them have no shoes . . .

    'This is a bad place to buy anything, a terrible place . . .'

    They are weighted down and they are sweating . . .

    'These farmers have us where they want us . . .'

    The weight of the bundles on their backs . . .

    'They won't take money, only goods . . .'

    Dirty towels tied around their faces . . .

    'They're getting choosier by the day . . .'

    Or old yellow caps on their heads . . .

    'Used to be just fabrics or cloth . . .'

    The weaker ones slowing down . . .

    'Now only jewellery will do . . .'

    Falling behind the others . . .

    'Kimonos or shoes . . .'

    Resting already . . .

    'It'll be much better in autumn,' they convince themselves –

    But it's not autumn yet, the tips of the branches still green –

    The persimmons on the trees still to fatten and brighten –

    To ripen, to fall and to splatter . . .

    There is an old man still dressed in his civil-defence uniform sat down at a curve in the road. His trousers tied with a rope and his jacket already soaked through with sweat, he has propped his backpack up under a nettle tree and sits rolling a cigarette from old dog-ends, staring vacantly ahead at a clump of flaming daisies –

    He looks up as my shadow falls on his face –

    I ask him if we might share a match –

    He nods and we share the light as he tells me, 'The shoddier these matches get, the more expensive their price becomes . . .'

I nod and I agree. Then I start to walk away –

But the old man asks, 'What time is it?'

I stop now and I turn back to him –

I ask, 'Is your watch broken, sir?'

Chiku-taku. Chiku-taku . . .

The man has taken out his pocket watch and is winding it up. The man shakes his head. The man shows me his watch –

The old man says, 'It keeps stopping dead . . .'

This watch. This watch. This watch . . .

His watch says twelve o'clock –

Now I show him my watch –

I say, 'It's eight o'clock.'

'I'm already late, then,' he sighs. 'Missed all the good stuff.'

I nod and I agree. I start to walk away again but again he calls after me and again I stop and I turn back to him as he asks me –

'Do you know the roads around here, do you?'

I shake my head and I apologize. 'I've not been here before.'

'I think I came here once before,' he says. 'But that was with someone from the neighbourhood and so it must have been quite a time ago now. I think it was here. The war had started, I know that. But not the air raids. I'm sure it was before the air raids . . .'

I nod again but I don't know what to say –

'I lose track of the time,' he sighs. 'Because there's no end, is there? They tell us that it's over, that we're at peace, but it doesn't feel like peace, doesn't feel like it's ended to me. What about you?'

I shake my head. I say something like, 'You're right.'

'I'm sixty-nine years old,' he tells me. 'What good am I to anyone any more? I might as well be dead and be done with it. But I remember when I could carry sixty or seventy pounds, no trouble . . .'

'But you look like you're doing all right to me,' I say –

He thanks me and asks me where I am from –

'Mitaka,' I tell him. 'What about you?'

'Kinshi-chō originally,' he says. 'But not any more, of course. I tell you, I was lucky to get away with the clothes on my back. I'm staying with my daughter-in-law in Hakozaki now. But you can't depend on anyone these days, can you? And now they say my son is dead, she'll be looking to remarry and then what will I do . . .?'

I nod and I watch him untie the towel from around his face

and wipe the sweat from his forehead and then from his neck –

Now the old man gets to his feet and he looks at me –

'Forgive me,' the old man says. 'But are you ill?'

I shake my head. I say, 'Why do you ask that?'

'I'm sorry,' he says. 'You're just very pale.'

'Don't worry,' I tell him. 'I'm fine . . .'

I pick up his bundle for him –

I hoist it onto his back –

It is a heavy load . . .

'Thank you,' he says as he walks off. 'And good luck . . .'

I raise my cigarette to wave and I watch him go –

'Don't give up,' he shouts back. 'Never!'

*

I walk up the clean little steps into Kanuma police station where the two officers behind the front desk bow, salute and welcome me back.

'I have a message from Tokyo for a Detective Ishida,' announces one of the two men behind the desk –

'Thank you,' I say as he hands me the piece of paper and I put it in my pocket and thank him again –

'Is Chief Tachibana here yet?'

'No,' he says. 'Maybe he's gone to the inn . . .'

'It's okay,' I tell him. 'I'll go for a walk . . .'

'Where will you go?' he asks me.

'To the river,' I say. 'The . . .'

'The Black River?' he asks.

'The Black River,' I nod.

I walk out of the police station. I do not run. *My pocket on fire.* I walk down the clean little steps. I do not run. *My pocket on fire.* I walk across the road. I do not run. *My pocket on fire.* I turn down another road. I do not run. *My pocket on fire.* I see the Black River –

And now I run. *My pocket on fire.* Now I run. *My pocket on fire.* Now I run. *My pocket on fire.* Down the banking –

My pocket on fire. And then I stop –

I take out the piece of paper:

'Leave Minami in Tochigi. Return to HQ. Inspector Adachi.'

Then, suddenly, a shout, 'There you are, Inspector Minami!'

I look up. Tachibana and Ishida coming down the banking –

283

Ishida; I no longer know who this Detective Ishida is . . .

'Thought you'd run back to Tokyo,' shouts Tachibana –

'I am sorry,' I say. 'I just needed to go for a walk . . .'

'Don't apologize,' says Tachibana. 'I bet you're not used to so much sake and good food these days, are you now, inspector?'

'You were very generous,' I tell him. 'Thank you.'

'It's nothing,' he says. 'We're all policemen . . .'

I look at Ishida as I nod, 'All policemen . . .'

'Where to first, then?' asks Tachibana, clapping his hands.

*

The same ancient small truck. The same old policeman in the driving seat. Tachibana gestures for me to sit up in the front while he and Ishida climb into the back again. The corrugated iron and the carpenter's tools gone today. The driver puts out his cigarette, straightens his cap and he starts up the truck as I hold on tight again –

I hate the countryside and I hate the people who live here –

This Land of the Grasping. This Land of the Greedy . . .

My eyes squinting in pain as the sunlight blinds me –

Everything black today. Everything black here . . .

The mountains black. The trees black –

No grey, no green and no purple . . .

No leaves and no flowers here –

There are no colours here . . .

Here, here, here, here –

In Kodaira country . . .

Here in Ōaza-Hosō, in Nikkō-chō, where our small truck now pulls up outside the family home of Kodaira Yoshio, the ramshackle, broken-down family home where the uncle, the aunt and the cousin of Kodaira Yoshio still live, still working for Furukawa –

The uncle, the aunt and the cousin of Kodaira Yoshio who know why we are here, who know why we will keep knocking –

Until the cousin finally opens the door to invite us in, in through their rotting door and filthy *genkan*, through their stinking, fetid kitchen and into their dark and humid hearth and home –

Home. Home. Home. Home. Home. Home. Home . . .

The aunt scuttling off on her hands and her knees down another dark corridor. The uncle cross-legged in the hearth with a pipe. The uncle is an old man. The uncle does not speak –

'He hates the police,' says his son, the cousin. 'He thinks the police have got it in for him, got it in for our family . . .'

'Shut up, idiot!' shouts the uncle as he picks up his pipe and gets to his feet. He walks off into the other half of the room, closing the screen doors behind him, still shouting, 'Idiot!'

'What do you want?' asks the cousin –

'I want to know how often your cousin Yoshio comes back here,' I tell him. 'I particularly want to know how often he came back here in the last two years, the dates he came and the things he might have brought back with him. It's important you remember . . .'

'Well, that's easy to remember,' laughs the cousin now. 'Easy because we never saw him. He never came back here . . .'

'I don't believe you,' I tell him. 'I don't believe you because I have already met six or seven other families near here who do remember that he came back, who do remember the dates and the things he brought back. So, I'll ask you again, to remember . . .'

'And I'll tell you again,' says the cousin. 'He was never here. We heard he'd been back to Tochigi, but we never saw him.'

'You never saw him?' I ask. 'He never came here?'

'Why would he come here?' asks the cousin. 'We've nothing to sell him, nothing to buy from him. Why come?'

'Because you're his family.' I say. 'That's why.'

'He never came back here,' repeats the cousin –

In the dark, humid hearth and family home –

'That's all I know, so that's all I'll say,' the cousin says now. 'If you want to hear more, just knock on any door in the village.'

*

His father was the eldest of the brothers, the neighbours tell us. He was a drinker, a gambler and a womanizer. He'd had a farm, he'd had an inn, the Hashimoto-Ya, the best in the village. But he lost them all through his gambling, his drinking and his womanizing. Even his horse. He ended his days at Furukawa Denki with the rest of them –

The father's first younger brother worked there all his life, the neighbours tell us. He was a slow worker but he was never absent. He worked only nights and he handed over all his pay to his mother. He was a stutterer and an idiot and he was the best of them –

285

The second younger brother is the uncle you met, the neighbours tell us. He was once the most dangerous man in the village; drank heavily and carried a knife. He has been in prison. He is still a short-tempered and aggressive man, but now he rarely speaks.

The eldest brother of Kodaira Yoshio is not long dead, the neighbours tell us. He worked at Furukawa with the rest of them but he was fired because he stole from the other workers and he slept on the job. He went to Tokyo but soon came back, wandering from job to job, living off odd jobs and handouts. He was another one who rarely spoke. Even made his own wife and children eat their meals outside so he could eat in peace. In April last year he was arrested for stealing potatoes but he died before the case ever came to court –

His elder sister was much the same, the neighbours tell us. She worked at Furukawa Denki too, just like the rest of them. She married a man who was working there, but it didn't last more than a year. Then she married a Korean, again for less than a year. She was often hysterical and always a liar and died in January this year –

He was a bad lad himself, the neighbours are quick to tell us. But he wasn't the worst of the family. He was poor at his schoolwork, lazy and careless, but he never drank and he never gambled. He had the Kodaira family temper but he never fought with strangers –

It was a shock, then, when he killed his father-in-law –

He has a bastard son, the neighbours whisper to us. He must be about sixteen years old. Not a nice boy, a creep to the older kids and a bully to the younger ones. This was the son he had by the woman he had his affair with. This was the affair that made his first wife's family ask him to divorce her. That was the request that caused him to attack her family and murder her father –

That got him sent to prison –

That broke his mother's heart, the neighbours tell us now. For his mother was kind and honest, a loving and long-suffering woman –

'But she lived her life in tears,' they tell us. 'In tears . . .'

*

These mountains and valleys, these forests and fields, all look the same to me. Up the side of one small mountain and down the other side, a short tunnel here, a longer tunnel there, then up and down another slope and along another narrow road until the truck stops outside another small farm set back from the road by another small ditch at the foot of another small mountain. Now, again, Tachibana climbs out of the back of the truck and goes inside the house while Ishida, the driver and I sit and sweat inside the truck until Tachibana returns with another old farmer and introduces us to Mr. Samura –

'The man who found the body,' he says. 'Ishikawa's body.'

Then the driver starts the ancient truck again and slowly, very slowly we climb up the narrow road that leads up the small mountain slope behind the farm until Mr. Samura nods and grunts and Tachibana calls out to the driver who pulls up on the mountainside –

'This is where he found her,' says Tachibana. 'This place.'

Ōaza Mizuki-chi, Manako-mura, Kami Tsuga-gun . . .

Everyone climbs out the truck. Everyone wipes their faces, wipes their necks and looks back down the mountain at the patchworks of fields and ditches, of farms and houses, and then everyone turns back round to stare up into another wood on another slope of another mountain, up into more shadows and more trees –

More black trunks, their branches and their leaves . . .

Samura points into the woods, 'It's that way . . .'

He walks behind me. He walks behind me . . .

Now Tachibana and I follow the old farmer as he clambers up off the narrow road and into the woods, pointing this way and that as he goes, mumbling things we can't catch as the trees and their trunks stand closer and thicker together, Ishida following behind –

He walks behind me, through the trees . . .

Samura comes to a stop up ahead and looks round for us, shouting, 'This is the place. This is the place. This is the place . . .'

The cicadas are deafening, the mosquitoes hungry again . . .

'Last September,' he says. 'I was looking for leaves . . .'

Between the trees, the black trunks of the trees . . .

'Leaves to dry out and to mix with tobacco . . .'

Their branches and their leaves . . .

'I trod right on her bones,' he says –

Her white, naked body . . .

'I'd smelt her too,' he says. 'As I was gathering up my leaves. But I'd thought it was an animal, same as when I first trod upon her bones, then I slipped, I fell and I saw it wasn't no animal bones . . .'

'*I look like bones . . . I look like bones . . .*'

'I knew they were human bones . . .'

287

I turn round and around, among these trees and these branches, and I ask Samura, 'Are you sure this is the exact place?'

Samura nods. 'Can't you feel her still . . .?'

Round and around, among these black trees and their trunks, asking Tachibana, 'Was this place ever examined as a crime scene?'

Tachibana lowers his eyes. Tachibana bows his head –

'Shit,' I curse, again and again, as I turn round and around, the black trunks and their branches turning round and around –

The cicadas are deafening, the mosquitoes hungry . . .

As I drop to my knees to begin to search –

Digging and digging and digging . . .

To search, again.

*

'Over here,' shouts Ishida. 'I've found something here. Look . . .'

Namu-amida-butsu. Namu-amida-butsu. Namu-amida . . .

Police Chief Tachibana and I clamber over fallen tree trunks and duck under broken branches to get to where Detective Ishida is on his knees, bent over the decaying log of another fallen tree –

Namu-amida-butsu. Namu-amida-butsu . . .

'Look at all these,' he says, standing and holding up bones, white and obviously human bones wrapped in rotting cloth –

Namu-amida-butsu . . .

'This must have been where he hid her body,' says Ishida, kneeling back down to peer under the log. 'The bones the old man found last year had probably been pulled out of here by animals . . .'

I look back through the trunks and the branches, back over towards the road where the old farmer Samura has gone to wait and smoke with the driver. I turn back to Chief Tachibana and I ask him, 'Which of Ishikawa Yori's bones have you got listed in the file?'

Tachibana opens the *Ishikawa Yori* file. He flicks through the papers until he reaches the autopsy report. Now he begins to list aloud the bones they found here last year as Ishida and I lift up the decaying log, lift it up to stare down into the damp black soil at more cold white bones, cold white bones that were lost and now found –

Ishida and I on our knees, with our hands, to dig –

To dig and to clean. To clean and collect –

Her bones once lost and now found . . .
To put them in my army knapsack –
In my bag and upon my back . . .

'We'll take these back with us to Tokyo,' I tell Tachibana. 'Where I'll give them to Dr. Nakadate at the Keiō University Hospital. But please, still try to track down the other bones that were found here and listed as belonging to Ishikawa Yori . . .'

'They'll be in Utsunomiya,' says Tachibana –

'Maybe,' I tell him. 'But it's been almost a year since they were found and, because she was listed as *ikidaore*, Utsunomiya will probably have returned her remains to her family for cremation . . .'

Tachibana bows very low. 'I am truly very, very sorry . . .'

'Don't be,' I tell him. 'We've done what we can for her.'

*

The truck goes back down the mountain and drops Old Man Samura back outside his farm. Then the truck labours up the side of another small mountain and down the other side, through one tunnel and through another, and then up another slope until it stops again outside the detached house of the mother of the Widow Okayama, the black dog still asleep in the shade of the wall, still tethered to its pole –

Not a stray, its house not lost, its master still here . . .

Police Chief Tachibana looks at the dog again but today he does not laugh. He excuses himself and goes into the house ahead of us again as the driver takes off his cap and lights another cigarette –

'Not short of tobacco round here these days,' says Ishida –

But the old driver doesn't speak. The driver just smokes.

Tachibana returns with the mother of the Widow Okayama who bows once more and welcomes us again and invites us into her home as Tachibana tells us that the old woman's granddaughter, the daughter of the Widow Okayama, is waiting for us inside –

Okayama Kazuko bows as we enter the house –

In a yellow and dark-blue striped pinafore . . .

Kazuko invites us to sit around the unlit hearth and offers us cold tea and apologizes that they have no snacks and we all thank her for her hospitality as we take our seats and we drink our drinks and we cannot help but stare at her face and her eyes –

Her worried face and her red, red eyes . . .

'I am so sorry,' she says. 'My grandmother, my mother and I, we had no idea about the kind of man Mr. Kodaira really was . . .'

She is not a country person. She was born in the city –

She heard the bombs. She saw the fires –

She hands a box to Ishida and says, 'These are all the things that Mr. Kodaira brought. These are all the things he gave me . . .'

There are tears in her eyes –

Tears down her cheeks –

'I had no idea . . .'

Ishida opens the box. Ishida takes out a large arabesque-patterned *furoshiki* cloth, a *bentō* box, another wristwatch and an elliptical-shaped ammonite brooch –

Nakamura Mitsuko . . .

I stand up. I reach across. I snatch the brooch from Ishida –

'The other body?' I am asking Tachibana. 'The unidentified body you mentioned yesterday? It must be Nakamura Mitsuko –

'How far are we from where it was found . . .?'

But before Tachibana can answer me, Ishida has picked up the wristwatch and turned it over in his hand to read the inscription on its back and now he is holding it out towards me –

Another watch. Another stolen watch . . .

I take it from him and I hold it up –

This watch. This watch . . .

Up to the light and I read –

Tominaga Noriko . . .

'I had no idea . . .'

The watch still turning in my hand. *I had no idea.* The hearth and the room turning. *I had no idea.* The house and the gate turning. *I had no idea.* Turning and turning and turning. *I had no idea . . .*

My hands in the dirt outside their house. *Day is night.* In the dirt on my hands and on my knees. *Night is day.* Turning and turning round and around. *Black is white.* Round and around in the dirt and the sun. *White is black.* Turning and turning round and around and cursing and cursing. *No truth, only lies.* Itching and scratching. *Gari-gari.* Itching and scratching. *Gari-gari.* Itching and scratching –

Gari-gari. Gari-gari. Gari-gari. Gari-gari. Gari-gari . . .

Lies upon lies upon lies upon lies upon lies upon –

Gari-gari. Gari-gari. Gari-gari. Gari-gari . . .

The mountains and mountains of lies –

Gari-gari. Gari-gari. Gari-gari . . .
These lies that make no sense –
No one who they say they are . . .
No sense, no sense at all –
No one who they seem.

*

Detective Ishida has stayed behind with the daughter and the mother of the Widow Okayama to go through the dates of each of Kodaira's visits, to list each day that he visited and each item he brought, to write down each of these dates, to catalogue each of these items –

My hands are still dirty. My knees are still bloody –

I itch. I scratch. *Gari-gari.* I scratch. I itch –

I am in the truck again, going up another mountain and down its other side, through another tunnel and up another slope, until we stop in front of another farm where Tachibana returns with yet another old man and says, 'This is the man who found the skeleton.'

Then this old man leads us on foot up another small mountain and into the cypress woods behind his farm, this small mountain and cypress woods that his family have tended for generation after generation, and where, for generation after generation, his family have come to chop and to cut and to clear away the dead wood and branches so that their cypresses might grow, their cypresses through which Tachibana and I follow him now, between trunk after trunk until the old farmer comes to a stop up ahead and turns back round –

'This is where I found it,' says the old man. 'Right here . . .'

Ōaza Fukahodo, Kiyosu-mura, Kami Tsuga-gun . . .

'A month ago,' he says. 'A perfect skeleton . . .'

'So there was no clothing here?' I ask him –

'None that I could see,' he tells me –

And again I turn and I turn, round and around again, I turn and I turn, among the trees and the branches, I turn and I turn, round and around, among these trees and their trunks, I turn and I turn –

The cicadas deafening, the mosquitoes still hungry . . .

As I drop to my knees and begin to search –

Again and again, again and again . . .

To search on my hands and –

Again and again . . .

On my knees –

Again . . .

On my hands and my knees, among these trees and these branches, searching for the only daughter of Nakamura Yoshizo –

'But what are you looking for?' asks Police Chief Tachibana. 'She was a perfect skeleton. There were no bones missing . . .'

Does he stand behind you in the queue for tickets at Shibuya?

'No bones missing,' I agree. 'But where were her clothes?'

Does he befriend you with tales of farmers and cheap rice?

Her brown *monpe* trousers and her pale yellow blouse –

Do you go to Asakusa? Then the train to Kanasaki . . .?

Her sandals, her socks and her underwear, all near –

This is the way, he says. This is the way, he says . . .

Here among these trees, among these branches –

He walks behind you. He walks behind you . . .

To the neatly chopped logs piled over there –

His hair stretched tight against his scalp . . .

Through these trees and these branches –

But it's not the way. Never the way . . .

On my hands and on my knees –

His skin tight against his skull . . .

I'm lifting up log after log –

He looms and he leers . . .

Looking for her clothes –

Kodaira, Kodaira . . .

Under log after log –

Looms and leers . . .

This one last log –

Here, here . . .

Here, buried deep in this pile of neatly chopped logs, one rotting wet pair of brown *monpe* trousers, one pale yellow blouse much better preserved through last autumn and winter to this spring and this summer, preserved and protected from the seasons and their weather by these neatly chopped logs, piled one on top of another among these well-tended cypress trees, in the midst of this small wood on the side of this small mountain, in this other world, this other country, so very, very far from home, his only daughter here –

This is where Mitsuko died on the twelfth of July, 1945 . . .

I am still on my hands and on my knees among the logs –

This is where Mitsuko was beaten unconscious . . .
On my knees and with my hands, I begin to dig –
This is where she was stripped and raped . . .
To dig and to clean. To clean and to collect –
This is where she was throttled . . .
To collect all the pieces of her clothing –
This is where she was killed . . .
To put the pieces in my knapsack –
This is where Nakamura Mitsuko died and then was raped again, again and again, raped and then robbed of her money, her wrist watch, her round silver spectacles and her brooch . . .
Her elliptical-shaped ammonite brooch . . .
To take them back to Tokyo –
The gift from a father to . . .
To take it back –
His only daughter . . .
Back home.

*

Detective Ishida climbs into the back of the truck and we all bow and thank the daughter and the mother of the Widow Okayama for their help and for their hospitality. Now we drive back down the mountain, then up and down another until we come back out into the valley, the Black River to our right again, the Scavenging Line still to our left –
More lines of people making their way back to the station . . .
But today there is no talk of city-folk. No talk of Scavengers –
Lines and lines of people with their supplies on their backs . . .
No talk of potatoes and rice. No talk of fleas and lice –
The bones of one dead girl and the clothes of another . . .
Today there is only silence in the front and back –
In an old army knapsack upon my knee . . .
They are looking out for us again, listening out for the sound of Tachibana's battered old mountain truck coming to a stop outside their quaint old police station, uniforms running out to bow and salute and to welcome us back, Detective Ishida and I bowing, saluting and thanking them again. Then we follow Chief Tachibana up the clean little steps into his station where the two officers who are stood behind the front desk bow and salute and welcome us again –

'I have another message for Detective Ishida,' says one of the men. Ishida steps forward and takes the message –

Another message. The final message . . .

Ishida asking to use their telephone –

'Leave Minami in Tochigi . . .'

Police Chief Tachibana leading me away, down the side of the front desk, along the corridor to his office where he talks about train timetables and the journey back to Tokyo and home –

Home. Home. Home. Home. Home. Home . . .

There is another soft knock on the door now as Detective Ishida steps into Police Chief Tachibana's office –

Detective Ishida; this man I don't know . . .

Tachibana asks, 'Everything all right?'

'Everything is fine now,' says Detective Ishida. 'Thank you.'

*

The entire police force of Kanuma has accompanied us down to the train station, here to wish us a safe journey and to bid us farewell. Tachibana has even held up the departure of the train for us –

Now his officers bow and then he bows –

Tachibana apologizes for the failings of himself and his men. Then he bows again, thanking us for our hard work and our help –

'And we hope to work with you again,' he says –

Detective Ishida and I salute Tachibana and bow to him and thank him for all his hard work and for all the hard work of his men, for all his assistance, for all his generosity and for all his hospitality –

Police Chief Tachibana salutes and bows one last time –

Then, finally, Ishida and I board the Tōbu train –

The Kanuma police clearing a path for us –

The doors close and the whistle blows –

No seats, so Ishida and I are stood –

The locomotive jolts as it starts –

In the small of Ishida's back . . .

Ishida and I stood pressed together again, both of us staring through a window without glass, watching Kanuma disappear –

In the small of his back, something cold and metallic . . .

I try to turn from the window, away from Kanuma –

This other world, this other country . . .

The carriage packed tight with people and their baggage, the people not meeting our eyes, afraid for their baggage –

We are the police. We are the law . . .

There is no glass in any of the windows but still there's no air in this carriage, just the stench of soiled babies –

The stench of human shit . . .

'This Tōbu Line train will stop next at Momiyama station,' begins the conductor. 'Then Niregi, Kanasaki, Ienaka, Kassemba, Shin-Tochigi, Tochigi . . .'

Suddenly Ishida says, 'I want to get off at Ienaka.'

'Leave Minami in Tochigi. Return to HQ . . .'

I ask him, 'Why do you want to do that?'

Something cold and metallic . . .

'I want to look over the Baba crime scene again,' he says. 'We found so much they had missed at the Ishikawa and Nakamura sites that I think we should look again . . .'

He walks behind me . . .

I have a bagful of bones, scraps of clothing on my back –

I curse him . . .

I nod. 'If you're sure that's what you want to do . . .'

*

The sun is setting now and soon it will be dark in Ienaka –

The shadows of the mountains lengthening . . .

Ishida and I pass through these ticket gates for a second time in three days and walk out of the station into the town –

No one is here, no one here at all . . .

The town is deserted again as I lead Ishida up the slope out of town, past the Beautiful Mountain Inn where we stayed –

He walks behind me. He walks behind me . . .

'Are you sure this is the right way?'

I do not answer him because he knows it does not matter, because he knows it could be any woods on any mountain and so up and down we go, up and down again we walk until we come to another narrow road, perhaps the same narrow road up which Kodaira Yoshio led Baba Hiroko on the thirtieth of December, last year –

'Are you sure this is the place?' he asks again –

Nishi Katamura, Kami Tsuga-gun . . .

I do not answer him because it does not matter. I put down my old army knapsack. I wipe my face and I wipe my neck –

I turn away from the fields and the ditches –

I stare up into the woods on the slope of the mountainside, up into the shadows of the black trunks of the trees –

Their branches and their leaves . . .

I point up the slope. 'It's that way . . .'

Detective Ishida follows me now as I climb up off the narrow road and into the woods, waving away the mosquitoes and bugs with my hand as Ishida walks behind me –

He walks behind me . . .

Between the trunks, beneath the branches and over the leaves, I lead him towards the slight hollow in the side of the mountain –

Between the trunks, beneath the branches and over the leaves, he follows me to this slight hollow surrounded by fallen logs –

Between the trunks, beneath the branches and over the leaves, he walks behind me to this slight hollow in the side of the mountain, this hollow filled with broken branches and dead leaves –

He walks behind me through the trees to here –

He walks behind me, through the trees . . .

'This is the place,' I tell him but I do not turn around –

The cicadas silent now, the mosquitoes sated here . . .

In this place, in this hollow, I can hear him now –

Between the trees, the black trunks of the trees . . .

I can hear him behind me. I can feel him –

Beneath the branches and their leaves . . .

I can hear him raise his army pistol –

I can feel him point it at my back –

I can hear him cock the pistol –

Cold and metallic . . .

Now I hear him shout, 'Get down on your knees, detective!'

I do not speak. I do not turn around. I get down on my knees –

On my knees, in these woods, in this hollow, in this place –

I feel the nose of the gun against the back of my skull –

In this place, in this hollow, in these woods –

I close my eyes and now I see her face –

I see her face and all their faces –

Masaki, Banzai! Daddy, Banzai!

Then I hear him pull the trigger. *Click.* I hear him pull it again.

Click. I hear him pull it again –

Click. Click.

And again –

Click –

Now I get up off my knees. *Click.* Now I turn around. *Click.*
Now I take his pistol by its nose. *Click. Click . . .*

Now I have his pistol in my hands –

Bang! Bang! Into his face –

Bang! Bang! And again –

The stench of shit.

*

In this place, in this hollow, between these trees, beneath these
branches, Ishida tries to open his eyes now as I bend down over him
to wipe away some of the blood and now he tries to speak, to thank
me, and I smile, a friendly man with my small acts of kindness, a
smiling, friendly man who puts an arm around him and smiles again
and laughs as he talks and he talks, talking about this and talking
about that, telling me that and telling me this, this about that man and
that about this man, and it's like we've known each other all our lives,
this crying, bloody man and this smiling, friendly man, like I'm his
uncle, this smiling, friendly man, or even the father he lost so very
young, but I know he does not feel so safe in this smile on my face,
this one smiling, friendly face between these trees and beneath these
branches, this desperate, defeated man who stares up at me now with
pleas for mercy and pleas for forgiveness in his black and blood-
soaked eyes in this place, in this hollow he does not know, this land,
this country getting darker and darker, hour after hour, and now the
day is gone and the mountain is gone and there is only this place, this
hollow now, between these trees, beneath these branches, but still I
smile and I smile, a smiling, friendly man between the trees, beneath
the branches, in this hollow, in this place, but now my teeth are
pointed and my eyes are hungry, my lips wet and tongue long –

Is this when my grip tightens? My words harden . . .?

My lips wet and my tongue long, I am not smiling now and I
am not friendly now, this man with my pointed teeth and my hungry
eyes, my wet lips and my long tongue whispering what I want from
him now, in this place, in this hollow, between these trees, beneath

these branches, telling him exactly what I want from him and he's turning away from me now in this place, in this hollow, between these trees, beneath these branches, but I'm pulling him back and I'm slapping his face, punching his face and kicking his legs, and he's on his hands and on his knees among the branches and the leaves, asking me to stop and begging me to stop and pleading with me to stop, to spare his life, to let him live, to let him get away but I cannot hear him asking, I cannot hear him begging, I cannot hear him pleading because I'm pulling him deeper into this place, into this hollow, this land and this country, putting a hand around his neck and another inside his chest and he knows what I want and he knows what I want and he knows what I want and he's telling me to take it, begging me to take it, pleading with me to take it, to take it and then leave him alone, please leave him, please leave him alone but I'm squeezing his throat, I'm squeezing his throat, I'm squeezing his throat, snot in his nose and piss down his legs and shit from his backside, as I squeeze his throat tighter and tighter, this place blacker and blacker –

As black as his hair that will never turn grey . . .

Now you open your eyes and you know you are still living, lying on your back on broken branches and dead leaves in this hollow, in this place, you have survived, you are one of the lucky ones, bleeding and beaten on these branches and leaves, but you have survived, you are lucky and now you raise yourself up from these branches and leaves, but this is when you know you have not survived, you are not one of the lucky ones, when you see me sat on the trunk of a fallen tree, staring at you and smoking a cigarette, a once smiling, friendly man as I finish my cigarette and get up off the trunk of this fallen tree, walking towards you beneath these branches and over these leaves, putting the bullets back into your gun –

You try to speak but you cannot speak . . .

Because a once smiling, friendly man has your gun in his hand and now I'm putting it into your mouth –

Bleeding and beaten here . . .

Here on these branches and leaves in this hollow, here in this place, I pull the trigger of your gun –

Bang!

*

In the night, he shrieks. I walk back down the mountain. *Leave Minami in Tochigi.* This mountain of lies. *Tell me who you are working for!* I hear snatches of Ishida's confession. *Not sleeping, not waking.* I do not run. *Return to HQ.* A man could live on this mountain. *Tell me!* Names and places and dates. *In the night, he howls.* I walk across the ditches and the fields. *Inspector Adachi.* A man could hide on this mountain. *Tell me who wanted me dead!* Ishida's confession and Ishida's lies. *I can hear him crying.* I do not run. *Leave Minami in Tochigi.* A man could renounce the world. *Tell me!* Ishida mumbles about Fujita. *In the night, he wails.* The whistle of a train coming down the line. *Return to HQ.* A man could forget the world. *Tell me who ordered you to kill me!* Ishida moans about Senju Akira. *In his sleep.* Now I run. *Inspector Adachi.* But I cannot forget this world. *Tell me!* Now Ishida lies and he lies about Adachi –

The bloody mouth from which the gag has been ripped . . .
Lies upon lies upon lies upon lies upon lies upon lies –
In the night, the grinding of teeth, the weeping of tears . . .
It is time to come down from this mountain of lies –
I can hear Ishida crying. I can hear him weeping . . .
To come down from this mountain of bones –
In the half-light, I can hear them all . . .
It is time to go home.

*

I struggle but manage to get on board at the couplings between two of the carriages. I struggle but manage to get from the couplings into the freight wagon. The freight wagon full of people packed like cattle –

Human cattle. Human cattle. Human cattle . . .

There is a woman attacking a rice-ball, another crunching a pickle, little kids crying and old folk snoring, itching and scratching, *gari-gari*, the reek of human piss, the stench of human shit –

Human shit. Human shit. Human shit . . .

'No luck at all,' someone is saying. 'Nothing at all . . .'
'They're all so rich now they've no need to sell . . .'
'They keep the good stuff hidden out of sight . . .'
'Or they just ask for whatever they want . . .'
'They aren't satisfied with money . . .'
'Some of the older ones want a fuck and if you put some

effort into it and promise to come back again, they'll give you a quart for a hundred and fifty yen, not bad for ten minutes' fucking . . .'

'You could sell it in Tokyo for two hundred yen . . .'

'Your rice and your cunt,' they laugh, *ha, ha* . . .

I stare out of the wagon, between the boards –

There is no hindsight. No foresight . . .

Just blindness, just darkness –

Ha, ha, ha, ha! He, he, he, he! Ho, ho, ho, ho!

13

August 27, 1946

Tokyo, 85°, fine

I itch and I scratch. *Gari-gari.* The bodies rock from side to side with the motion of the train as the dawn begins to pick them out through the holes in the boards and the gaps by the doors. I itch and I scratch. *Gari-gari.* There is an old white-haired woman sat across from me, wedged between a younger man and woman. I itch and I scratch. *Gari-gari.* The younger man and woman both trying to wake her up now, whispering, 'Wake up. We'll soon be in Asakusa. Wake up . . .'

But there is no movement or answer from the woman –

'Wake up!' hisses the other woman. 'I can't move my arm.'

The train jumps a joint now. The old woman falls forward –

The man on her left, sensing something is not quite right, lifts up her head to the light. The old woman's eyes are still closed –

There is froth round her mouth and down her chin –

'What's the matter with you?' asks the man. 'Wake up!'

The train jumps another joint. The old woman rolls over –

'She's dead,' says the woman to the man. 'She's dead . . .'

Now they both try to push the old woman's body off them, to push her away, but the woman's body won't move because it is held in its place by the weight of the bundle strapped to her back –

The weight of the bundle, the supplies on her back . . .

'Take it off,' the man is whispering to the young woman as they struggle with the body. But the young woman has had a better idea as they separate the body of the old woman from the bundle on her back, the younger woman opening the bundle and the man doesn't need telling and now he joins her picking through the ropes and the knots, each of them glancing this way and that to check that no one else is awake, the ropes and the knots now gone, that way and this to make sure no one is watching as they take the polished rice and the sweet potatoes from out of the bundle on the dead woman's back and hide it in the bundles on their own backs –

This way and that, that way and this . . .

I lower my head and I close my eyes –

I turn their shoes to face the door . . .

But not for long –

The other bodies in the freight wagon begin to stir now. I itch and I scratch. *Gari-gari.* The whispers with them. I itch and I scratch. *Gari-gari.* The rumours that the police will be waiting at Asakusa to search the passengers and their bundles for any black-market goods –

People thinking about getting off at Kita-Senju station –

People saying Kita-Senju will be just as bad –

People talking about jumping off –

I have heard enough –

I put my knapsack of bones and fragments of clothes on my back and I jump down from the freight wagon at Kita-Senju station –

But I do not go through the ticket gates at Kita-Senju. I walk up the stairs and down another flight to another platform. Then I stand on the roofless platform and I wait for the train to Ueno –

It is the twenty-seventh of August. *I think.* It is just gone 7 a.m. It is hot and humid and the sky is a dirty grey stain –

I itch and I scratch. *Gari-gari . . .*

Gari-gari. Gari-gari . . .

Gari-gari . . .

This platform for Ueno and Tokyo is not very busy but across the tracks the platforms for Saitama and Chiba are both crowded –

I itch and I scratch. *Gari-gari.* I itch and I scratch –

Gari-gari. Gari-gari. Gari-gari. Gari-gari . . .

I hear my train approaching now. I step forward towards the edge of the platform. I itch and I scratch. *Gari-gari.* The train pulls in and hundreds of people get off, pushing and shoving. I get on board, the carriage still full of hundreds of people, still pushing and shoving. I itch and I scratch. *Gari-gari.* I stand by the door as the train pulls out. I itch and I scratch. *Gari-gari.* There is silence inside the carriage. The people are nervous. The people are worried. The people afraid –

I am nervous. I am worried. I am afraid. I am scared . . .

There are always police at Ueno station, always searches of clothing and baggage. But I will not go through the ticket gates here. I will change to another platform. I will change to another train –

They will not see me. They will not stop me . . .

I will take the Yamate Line to Kanda –

They will not find me. Not catch me . . .

The Chūō Line to Shinanomachi –

I will be safe this way . . .

But there are police at Shinanomachi station. *I curse.* I am on the platform now. *I curse.* I am walking towards the ticket gate. *I curse.* They are stopping people. *I curse.* They are searching people. *I curse.* I can't show my notebook. *I curse.* I can't tell them my name. *I curse.* I am stood in the line for the gates. *I curse.* I am in the queue now. *I curse.* I hand my ticket to the station staff. I keep walking –

'You there,' commands the voice of a policeman. 'Stop!'

I curse and I curse. I stop. *I curse again.* I turn around –

There are two uniformed policemen. 'Come here!'

I curse. I curse. I curse. I curse. I curse . . .

I bow before them and I ask, 'What's wrong?'

'What have you got in your knapsack?'

I curse. I curse. I curse. I curse . . .

'Just my clothes and things . . .'

'Show us then,' they tell me.

I curse. I curse. I curse . . .

'But it's just clothes.'

'Just open it then.'

I curse. I curse . . .

'Really, just . . .'

'Open it!'

I curse and I curse but I nod. I take off my knapsack and I start to open it up but one of the officers snatches it from out of my hands. He sets it down on the floor and he starts to go through it –

I can feel the gun in the small of my back . . .

'What is all this?' he asks now, dropping the pieces of cloth and the fragments of bones onto the floor and standing back up –

Ishida's gun tucked in my belt . . .

The other man bending down to look at the cloth and the bones, now staring back up at me with horror in his eyes –

I have no choice now . . .

I take out my *keisatsu techō*, my police notebook, and I hand it to them. I tell them, 'I'm taking this evidence to the autopsy department at Keiō . . .'

No choice . . .

But the two policemen are both smiling at me now, their caps in their hands, wiping their faces and wiping their necks –

'Why didn't you just say you were one of us?'

'I didn't want to draw attention to myself.'

'Just show your *techō* next time . . .'

'I am sorry,' I say. 'My mistake.'

'We're not looking for policemen,' they laugh as I walk out of the station with the clothes and the bones in the bag on my back.

*

It is still early but the Keiō Hospital is still busy; queues through the gates, queues to the doors, queues in the corridors. I walk through the gates, through the doors and down the corridors; past the queues, past the patients and past the gurneys to the elevator. I push the button –

I hate hospitals. I hate all hospitals. All hospitals . . .

I step inside. I press another button. The doors close –

I have spent too long in hospitals . . .

I ride the elevator down in the dark –

I have spent too long here . . .

The doors open. Light returns –

In the half-light . . .

I walk past the tiled walls of sinks, of drains, the written warnings of cuts, of punctures, down the corridor to the mortuary and the autopsy room. I knock on the door to the office –

'Yes,' shouts Dr. Nakadate from inside –

I open the door. I step into his office –

The smell of death, then disinfectant . . .

Dr. Nakadate sat at his desk, his face unshaven, his eyes red –

'What happened to your hair?' he asks. 'It's gone grey.'

'I almost didn't recognize you . . .'

I say, 'I've brought you some souvenirs from Tochigi . . .'

Dr. Nakadate puts down his pen. He shakes his head –

I put the knapsack down on his desk. I open it up –

I take out the clothes. I take out the bones –

Nakadate looks at them. Then he looks up at me. 'Kodaira?'

'Yes,' I tell him. 'But I think it's going to be hard to prove, unless he confesses when faced with the evidence we have . . .'

Dr. Nakadate asks, 'Why? Where's the rest of it?'

'Utsunomiya,' I tell him. 'There are three cases but only one of them was ever treated as a crime. I have asked Utsunomiya to send any remains and any reports they can find here to you.'

'What are the names of the victims?' he asks.

'These bones here were taken from the scene where the body of a woman named Ishikawa Yori was found in September last year. The Kanuma police believe Ishikawa died in the June. Then, at a second site, I found these pieces of clothing which I believe belong to a girl called Nakamura Mitsuko, who was reported missing last July. Just last month, Kanuma police found a skeleton which I believe to be hers, though I have not seen the autopsy report. However, I am going to take these pieces of clothing to her family to try to confirm her identity. The third case is that of a young woman named Baba Hiroko who was murdered in January this year . . .'

Nakadate stops writing. Nakadate nods.

'You know about that one?' I ask. 'Then I can also tell you that we found no evidence to connect Kodaira to a fourth case, that of a Numao Shizue and which had been forwarded to us by Nikkō.'

'You've been very busy, detective,' says Dr. Nakadate now. 'Don't tell me that you're after a promotion . . .?'

'So you heard what happened to me?'

'Yes,' says Nakadate.

'Who told you?'

'Chief Kita himself,' he says.

'When did you see him?'

'When I took him the Miyazaki Mitsuko autopsy report.'

'You told me you were going to wait a few days . . .'

'I'm very sorry,' he says. 'But I had no choice.'

I have no choice. I have no choice . . .

'There's always a choice,' I hiss –

'Not this time,' says Nakadate. 'The Public Safety Division came here asking to see all reports involving the Kempeitai . . .'

'So you gave them the Miyazaki autopsy report?'

'No,' he says. 'I gave it to Chief Kita.'

'And what did Chief Kita say?'

'He already knew about it.'

'But he hadn't connected it to Kodaira?'

'I don't know,' says Nakadate.

'Did Chief Kita say what he was going to do about it?'

'He said they would question Kodaira about it.'

'What about Chief Inspector Adachi?'

'What about him?'

'Did Chief Kita say anything about Chief Inspector Adachi and the Miyazaki case?'

'No.'

'Did the Public Safety Division ask you about Adachi?'

'No.'

'So what did they ask you about then?'

'Kempeitai cases,' he tells me again.

'About me?' I ask him –

Nakadate nods –

'What . . .?'

'I'm very sorry,' he says again. 'But they have statements. They have witnesses, detective. There was nothing I could do . . .'

I had no choice. I had no choice. I had no choice . . .

In the corridor of tiled walls and written warnings, I push the button and I wait for the elevator to come. Dr. Nakadate bows. Nakadate apologizes again. He wishes me luck and then he asks –

Finally he asks, 'What will you do now?'

'I have debts to pay,' I tell him –

'You owe them nothing . . .'

'Not to the living,' I say. 'Debts to the dead.'

*

The last streetcar hit a youth and a woman jumped in front of a train so the streetcar is late and the trains have stopped and so I am stood in the queue next to a woman of about fifty in a pair of brown *monpe* work trousers similar to the rotten pair in the knapsack on my back. I itch and I scratch. *Gari-gari.* To my left is a youth of about fifteen or sixteen. There is a tear in the shoulder of the coarsely woven factory uniform he is wearing and beneath the visor of his army cap his eyes are closed and his jaw hangs open, his body swaying slowly back and forth in the morning heat, back and forth. I itch and I scratch. *Gari-gari.* Back and forth, back and forth until, just as it seems he'll fall forward flat onto his face, the youth pulls himself up –

'Is he drunk or is he sick?' asks the woman –

'Probably just tired and hungry,' I say.

The woman leans across me. She puts a hand on the youth's

shoulder. She asks him, 'Are you all right? Where are you going?'

The youth does not answer. The woman asks him again –

This time the youth says, 'I'm going to Ueno.'

'Then you're on the wrong side,' says the woman. 'You need to go and wait on the other side of the road for Ueno. Over there . . .'

The youth stares at the streetcar stop on the other side of the road. But he does not move. Under his cap, he closes his eyes –

'Over there,' says the woman again. 'Can you see?'

Now the youth's jaw hangs open again.

'You're on the wrong side,' the woman persists –

But still the youth doesn't open his eyes.

'This bus won't take you to Ueno . . .'

The youth sways back and forth again.

Now she turns to me. 'He's going the wrong way.'

I nod. I say, 'But it makes no difference.'

*

I walk down the street to the Nakamura house but keep on past it and do not stop until I reach the corner. Then I stand there and I stare back at the house, the bad news I bring in the knapsack on my back. Now I turn and I walk back down the street towards the house. I stop in front of the latticed door to the entrance. I reach up to open it but it is locked and will not move. I knock on the doorframe but no one comes. I knock again, louder this time, calling out in apology –

'Who's there?' asks Nakamura Mitsuko's father.

'Detective Minami,' I say. 'From the Metropolitan Police.'

I hear his slippers in the *genkan*. Then the door opens –

'I am sorry to disturb you,' I say. 'But I have some news . . .'

Nakamura Mitsuko's father does not ask me what kind of news I have brought them. Nakamura Mitsuko's father does not ask my anything. He just nods once and invites me into their house –

These things I have brought. These things I will leave . . .

I feel sick as I take off my boots, nauseous as I follow Mitsuko's father into the reception room at the front of the house, as I set down my army knapsack, as I sit down on the tatami across the low table from Mitsuko's father, as I open the knapsack –

The pain I have brought. The pain I will leave . . .

I take out the rotten pair of brown *monpe* trousers. I take out

307

the pale yellow blouse. Finally, I take out the elliptical-shaped
ammonite brooch. I place each of the items on the table before him –
  Nakamura Mitsuko's father reaches out his hand –
  I tell him about the skeleton in the woods . . .
  Mitsuko's father picks up the brooch –
  I tell him about the cypress trees . . .
  He brings the brooch to his chest –
  I tell him where she is now . . .
  He holds the brooch there –
  How she'll soon be home . . .
  He bows his head –
  'She was my only daughter,' he says. 'Thank you.'

*

I sit down on a pile of broken concrete. I take out a cigarette. I light it.
There is a row of barrack housing on the other side of the road. I
watch a young woman hanging out a futon from one of the second-
floor windows. I watch her beat the futon with a stick, dust coming
off. Every now and again she turns to say something to someone
inside the house. She says it with a smile or a song in her voice. But
now the woman sees me watching her and quickly pulls the futon
back inside the room and closes the window. I see her peep again at
me from inside the room, a small child in her arms, her eyes filled
with hate and fear. I want to ask her who she thinks she is to look at
me with such contempt, such fear, to ask who raised her up to look
down on me. But I look away from the window. I look down at my
boots, my soldiers' boots. There is the corpse of a pregnant collie dog
lying on its back just a metre or so from my right boot. Its stomach
has been split open by some other animal. Half-rotten but fully
formed puppies have been dragged from out of her stomach and
savaged, staining the soil and the stones a deep, dark and bloody red.
Now I stand up. In the Year of the Dog, I sweep dirt and dust over the
black dried fetuses with the side of my soldier's boot –
  Masaki, Banzai! Daddy, Banzai!

*

Ton-ton. Ton-ton. Ton-ton. Ton-ton. Ton-ton. Ton-ton. Ton-ton . . .

I walk through Kyōbashi Ward. I come to the battered board fence, the huge pile of rusty iron and the cabin with its glass door and tin roof. Behind the fence, two men in labourers' clothes, one short and one tall, are carrying the small stool and the empty packing cases out of the cabin. I go through the opening in the boarding into the scrapyard. I say who I am and ask if Kobayashi Sōkichi is around –

In the sunlight and shadows, the white and the black . . .

'Don't you know?' asks the tall one. 'He died yesterday.'

'Mr. Kobayashi is dead?' I repeat. 'How did he die?'

'He was killed about eight o'clock last night,' says the man. 'He'd gone in his truck to pick up some scrap in Ōmiya and on the way back his truck turned over on a narrow bridge. Both Kobayashi and the other man who was with him were killed . . .'

'I heard one of the Victors' trucks ran them off the road,' says the shorter man. 'That they couldn't get out of the way . . .'

'You don't know that,' says the tall man. 'It's just gossip.'

'No, it's not,' says the short one. 'This old man who lives by the bridge, he saw the whole thing and made a statement to the police and he said that there was a convoy of four or five US army trucks heading for the bridge, which is just this old wooden bridge, that it is so narrow that it's impossible for two vehicles to pass, and that the US army trucks were sounding their horns and flashing their lights but Kobayashi's truck was almost on the bridge, so he couldn't turn back but the US army trucks were coming too fast and so it looked to this old man like Kobayashi tried to pull over at the side of the bridge but that the first army truck that came across the bridge, it clipped Kobayashi and sent his truck rolling right down the banking . . .'

'And he told all this to the Ōmiya police?' I ask –

'Yes,' says the short man. 'But the police said there was nothing they could do, not when it's Shinchū Gun . . .'

I shake my head. I thank them for telling me the details of what happened. I ask if I might step inside the cabin for a moment –

They nod. 'We're just here to tidy things up.'

Now I step inside the cabin. The old colour postcard of the Itsuku-shima Shrine is still tacked to the wall. The potted sakaki tree sat on the *butsudan* before the three framed photographs; the three photographs and now one small candle burning on the shelf –

'Perhaps he's already just another ghost . . .'

Now I kneel down before the *butsudan*. I make my report –

To the three photographs and to the burning candle –

I tell them I have found justice for Hiroko –

I promise there will be vengeance.

I stand back up. I take the old colour postcard of the Itsuku-shima Shrine down from the wall. I turn it over. It's from Hiroko –

A school trip in a happier time . . .

I put the postcard in the pocket of my jacket. I walk back out of the cabin, into the sunlight and the scrapyard, the two men still talking, the taller man saying, 'You live through all that he lived through, you survive all that he survived, the war, the bombs, the fires, you survive all that just to die in a stupid traffic accident . . .'

'It doesn't make sense, does it?' says the short one –

'Except when your time comes, it comes . . .'

I thank them again and then I step back through the boarding and out into the street. I look at the buildings going up, the offices and the businesses, and I think about Kobayashi's son, still chopping wood on the Amur River, not knowing his father died in a traffic accident at eight o'clock last night, not knowing his aunt died of a broken heart, not knowing his cousin was raped and murdered, not knowing he is better off dead, he's better off dead, better off dead –

Ton-ton. Ton-ton. Ton-ton. Ton-ton. Ton-ton. Ton-ton . . .

*

I itch and I scratch. *Gari-gari.* I am hungry and I am starving. I need a drink and a cigarette. I itch and I scratch. *Gari-gari.* I walk through another makeshift market, through its stalls and its stands. I itch and I scratch. *Gari-gari.* I stop before a stall where a young woman is selling sweet potatoes. I stare at the potatoes and now at the woman –

Her sunburnt skin and her short skirt . . .

The frayed hem of her skirt hiked up, the woman sits on a crate with one leg crossed over the other –

'Are you just going to stare up my skirt, old man?' she asks. 'Or are you going to buy a potato . . .?'

I blush now and I look away.

The woman uncrosses her legs and stands up. She wipes her face and she wipes her neck. She looks at me and she laughs –

'Come on,' she says. 'They're just two yen.'

I take out the money and I hand it to her –

'Help yourself,' she laughs now.

I pick up a sweet potato and I begin to walk away. I itch and I scratch. *Gari-gari.* I glance round at the woman but she has already sat back down on her crate, one leg crossed over the other –

Her sunburnt skin and her short skirt . . .

And now I see him; I see him among the crowds, among the stalls; caked black in rags and filth, his face and his hands covered in blisters and boils, the boy is weeping pus and tears. I keep walking through the crowds, through the stalls. I glance back again. I see him again, among the crowds, among the stalls, caked black in rags and filth, covered in blisters and boils –

He walks behind me . . .

I keep walking. I am hungry and I am starving. I need a drink and a cigarette. I itch and I scratch. *Gari-gari.* I turn a corner and I turn another. I glance back over my shoulder but I cannot see him. Now I stop walking. I sit down in another ruin, among another pile of rubble. I bite into the potato –

It is cold, it is old . . .

But it still tastes hot, it still tastes fresh to me. Now a shadow falls across my face and hands and I look up. The boy is stood before me, caked black in rags and filth, covered in blisters and boils, just centimetres before me –

He points . . .

His belly distended, his bones protruding, he smells of rotten apricots. Now he raises his hand and he points his finger at me –

His yellow eyes, stained a deep, dark and bloody red . . .

I start to break the sweet potato in half, to give him one half, but the boy snatches the whole potato out of my fingers and now, with his other hand, he throws dirt and dust into my face –

Dust into my eyes as he turns and he runs –

Runs away weeping and laughing –

Tears and pus, *Ha, ha, ha, ha . . .*

Daddy, Banzai!

*

I knock on the door of the old wooden row house in Kitazawa, not far from the Shimo-Kitazawa station. There is no answer. I knock again. There is still no answer. I try the door. It is not locked. I open it.

There is silence. I step inside the *genkan*. The kitchen is deserted –

I call out, 'Excuse me, Mr. Murota? Excuse me . . .?'

But there is still no answer, still only silence –

I take off my boots. I step inside the house. I walk across the old tatami mats. I go through the shabby curtain that partitions the downstairs. Nothing but stale air and shadows –

Nothing but shadows here . . .

I go up the steep, narrow wooden stairs. There are two rooms, one at the back and one at the front of the house. The room at the front is the larger one. There is a chest of drawers stood in one corner on the dirty mats. I open the drawers. They are empty. The window in the back room has been left open. There are mosquitoes here. There is also a closet but, again, it is empty –

Nothing but shadows now . . .

I go back down the wooden stairs. Back through the shabby curtain. I stand in the kitchen. There are mosquitoes here too. The smell of old meals. Murota Hideki and the woman who called herself Tominaga Noriko are long gone –

No one who they seem . . .

I sit down at the low wooden table on the old worn tatami. I take out one of the two wristwatches from my pocket. I turn it over in my hand. I hold it up to the light. I read its inscription –

Tominaga Noriko . . .

I place the watch on the low wooden table –

I take out my notebook of rough paper –

I lick the tip of my pencil stub –

In the half-light . . .

I write, over and over –

I write my name –

Over and over –

My name.

*

The sky has turned a darker shade of grey now. *Not you.* The air is heavy with dread and heat. *Not you.* The branches and their leaves hang low. *Not you.* The street stalls have all been covered over with straw mats. *Not you.* Men and women squat among the rubble, watching the sky and fanning themselves. *Not you.* Jeeps and trucks roll past with their huge white stars on their doors, their canvas canopies rolled up. *Not you.* Men with white faces and men with black faces sat in the backs of the jeeps and the trucks. *Not you.* They have guns in their hands or guns on their knees. *It was not you.* They are smiling and they are laughing. *It was not you . . .*

It was not you we were waiting for . . .

*

They are searching for me, on the trains and at the stations, but I have found them first, back here where they least expect me, back here at the Atago police station. I stand across the road and I watch and I wait, I watch and I wait. I watch them come and I watch them go and I wait. I wait until I see Detective Nishi and now I move –

Nishi on his own coming down the road –

Ten quick steps and I'm behind him –

The pistol pressed into his ribs –

Eyes in the back of my head –

'This way,' I tell him and force him to turn around, to turn back and walk across the road, to stand him up against the trees, here among the weeds and the garbage, the black metal drums full of ashes and remains, an army-issue pistol pressed into his belly –

He looks like shit, like he still hasn't slept –

I am looking in a mirror, in a mirror . . .

'Where is everyone?' I ask him –

Nishi stares at the pistol stuck in his stomach. Nishi says, 'They're all celebrating, aren't they?'

'Celebrating what?'

'A case closed.'

'Which one?'

'Kodaira.'

'So they couldn't even wait for me to get back from Tochigi. They couldn't even wait to see the evidence I found, to read my report. They couldn't care less about all the others, could they?'

There have been others. There have been others . . .

'But they've been looking for you, you know that don't you?' he tells me now, still staring down at the pistol stuck in his stomach. 'You should go to Daimon. You should go and join the party. Talk to Chief Kita, but you should go now before it's too late . . .'

'Shut up!' I tell him. 'It's already too late.'

Nishi shakes his head. 'No, it's not.'

Liar! Liar! Liar! Liar! Liar! Liar! . . .

'Shut up!' I hiss again. 'And just answer my questions . . .'

Now Detective Nishi bows his head. Now he nods –

'What happened to Detective Fujita?' I ask him.

Nishi looks up. 'You don't know?'

I push the pistol deeper into his gut. 'Just tell me!'

'They found his body in the Shiba Canal,' says Nishi. 'Hands and feet nailed to the back of a door, drowned face down, just . . .'

'Just like Hayashi Jo,' I say for him –

Nishi nods again and says, 'Yes.'

'And whose case is it?' I ask –

'Chief Inspector Adachi's.'

I curse him. I curse him . . .

'And so who does your great inspector think killed Fujita?'

'The chief inspector thinks that Fujita was somehow involved with Nodera Tomiji in the murder of Matsuda Giichi, that Hayashi Jo tried to blackmail Fujita and so Fujita killed him to silence him, that Boss Senju then somehow found out about it and had Fujita killed.'

'This is not a problem . . . this is going to be a pleasure . . .'

'And me?' I ask him. 'What's he saying about me . . .?'

Nishi shakes his head. Nishi says, 'Nothing . . .'

I raise the pistol so it is level with Nishi's eyes, the space between his eyes, and I say, 'I don't believe you. You're lying . . .'

'But it's the truth,' pleads Nishi. 'Please . . .'

I ask, 'Then what about Ishida?'

'What about Ishida?'

'What has Adachi said about Ishida?' I ask. 'Where does Detective Ishida fit into all this?'

Nishi shakes his head again. Nishi says, 'I have no idea . . .'

'Ishida was working for Adachi all along,' I tell him –

But Nishi is still shaking his head, 'I don't know . . .'

'Adachi had him spying on me, on you, on us all.'

'I don't know what you're talking about . . .'

'Maybe now it's you, now he's gone . . .'

'Now who's gone? What's me?'

'Ishida's not coming back.'

'Where's he gone?'

'Hell,' I tell him –

Nishi staring down the barrel of the gun. Nishi sweating. Nishi telling me now, 'That's between you and Detective Ishida –

'It's nothing to do with me,' he begs. 'Please . . .'

'Is that what Adachi told you to tell me . . .?'

'He's told me nothing,' shouts Nishi –

I touch the barrel to his forehead –

'Nothing!' shouts Nishi again –

I press the barrel into him –

'Adachi is trying to help you,' cries Nishi. 'To save you!'

'Liar! Liar!' I whisper as I pull the trigger. *Click* –

'No! No!' he screams. 'It's the truth . . .'

'Adachi sent Ishida to kill me!' I tell him as I pull the trigger, again and again, as I pull it. *Click. Click* –

Nishi dropping to his knees –

Click. Click –

Nishi on his knees –

'Please, no . . .'

I lower the pistol now. I take out my notebook of rough paper from my jacket pocket. I bend down over him. I lift his face up to the light. I push the notebook into his face. I force open his mouth –

Now I stuff the notebook inside Nishi's mouth –

'That's the truth in there,' I say. 'My truth . . .'

In the half-light, the half-things . . .

'Read it and remember it!'

*

The nighthawks under the tracks are out early tonight. *Asobu? Asobu?* In their yellow and dark-blue striped pinafore dresses. *Asobu? Asobu?* They have had their radios on, their newspapers open, and have heard there is a typhoon approaching. *Asobu? Asobu?* In their white half-sleeved chemises. *Asobu? Asobu?* They know there will be no business later, only rain and only wind. *Asobu? Asobu?* In their dyed-pink socks. *Asobu? Asobu?* They know they have to earn what they can now. *Asobu? Asobu?* In their white canvas shoes with their red rubber soles. *Asobu? Asobu?* But they do not try to grab my hand –

In their yellow and dark-blue striped pinafore dresses . . .

They do not try to lure me into the shadows tonight –

'Get away!' they scream. 'Get away from here!'
They look into my eyes, then hide their own –
'We don't fuck the dead! We don't fuck ghosts!'

*

Potsu-potsu, the rain is beginning to fall now, hot fat drops on the kettles and the pans; *potsu-potsu* it falls in a terrible rhythm on the crockery and the utensils; *potsu-potsu* as the stall-holders still left outside the Shimbashi New Life Market struggle to cover the clothes and the shoes; *potsu-potsu* on the cooking oil and the soy sauce; *potsu-potsu* as the canvas and the straw mats are hauled out –

Potsu-potsu as it drowns out even the 'Apple Song' –

'If two people sing along, it's a merry song . . .'

Potsu-potsu on the patterned shirts and American sunglasses of the goons guarding the foot of the stairs to Senju Akira's office –

Potsu-potsu on the patterned shirts and American sunglasses as they frisk my body and clothes for guns and knives –

Potsu-potsu on the patterned shirts and American sunglasses as they only glance inside my old army knapsack –

Potsu-potsu as it falls on the corrugated tin roof which covers the stairs up to Senju Akira's office –

Potsu-potsu on the blue-eyed Victor coming down the stairs; *potsu-potsu* as he winks at me –

'Good evening . . .'

Potsu-potsu as I push past him up the staircase to the office; *potsu-potsu* . . .

Senju Akira sat cross-legged before his long low polished table; bare-chested again with his trousers unbuttoned at the waist, there are revolvers and short swords lain out on the table before him –

Senju Akira is preparing for war, preparing for another war –

I put down my knapsack. I bow low on the tatami mats –

'There's always a war somewhere,' he tells me –

My face to the floor, I do not answer him –

'At home or abroad,' he says. 'There's always war and always profits to be made for the bold and the brave among us!'

I raise my head. 'Always war . . .'

'The great Matsuda Giichi taught me this,' continues Senju. 'He was among the very first to see the opportunities on the continent;

first he went to Shanghai, then he went to Dairen. He made money. He invested money. In transportation. In industry. His efforts supported the Kantō army in northern Manchukō. And the Kantō army appreciated and rewarded him well. But, when he returned home in the sixteenth year of Shōwa, was he rewarded for all he had done for the Japanese army, for the Japanese Empire?'

I shake my head. I say, 'No, he wasn't . . .'

'No, he wasn't!' thunders Senju. 'This man who had built railways for the Japanese army, this man who had provided supplies for the Japanese army, that the Japanese army might expand and protect the Japanese Empire on behalf of the Emperor, what welcome did this man receive upon his return home . . .?'

I shake my head again. 'None . . .'

'Worse than none!' shouts Senju. 'No parades. No medals. No honours. They sent him to prison for assault and battery!'

I bow my head low again and I say nothing –

'But was this great man defeated?' cries Senju. 'Was this great man reduced to nothing?'

'No, he wasn't . . .'

'Of course, he wasn't!' laughs Senju. 'Matsuda Giichi organized the inmates of the prison, he protected and he helped them, no matter what their trouble, no matter what their background –

'Matsuda Giichi became their leader –

'So then, on his release, each of these men he had protected, who he had helped inside the joint, each man came to thank him and to pledge their undying loyalty to him –

'I was one of those men!'

I nod. 'I know . . .'

'In defeat . . .'

'I know . . .'

'That was how the Matsuda gang was born,' says Senju. 'From the ashes of his own personal defeat, Matsuda rose up again. Because you could not defeat a man such as Matsuda Giichi. You could not beat him down. You could not hold him down. Because Matsuda Giichi was a bold man. Matsuda Giichi was a brave man. And, most importantly of all, Matsuda Giichi was a man of vision –

'A man of vision!' shouts Senju Akira. 'A man of vision!'

I do not speak, my head still low against the mats –

Low until Senju says, 'But you are a blind man –

317

'And so you are a defeated man! Defeated!'

I still do not speak. I still wait for him –

Chiku-taku. Chiku-taku. Chiku-taku . . .

Now Senju Akira puts a bundle of money on the table. Now Senju puts a bag of pills on the table. I lean forward –

I curse myself, I curse myself . . .

I bow. I thank him –

And I curse him . . .

But now Senju moves the money and the pills just out of my reach and says, 'You kill Adachi, you get all these and also these . . .'

Ishida mumbles about Fujita. Ishida moans about Senju . . .

Now Senju holds up a file in one hand and a piece of paper in the other; the Miyazaki Mitsuko file and a demobilization paper –

'The end of one life and the start of a new one . . .'

I curse him, I curse him and I curse myself . . .

I ask him, 'But how did you get that file?'

'I've told you before,' he winks. 'Those in the know, know, and those who don't, don't, eh, corporal . . .?'

I look down at the tatami –

And I curse him . . .

'You do this one last job for me, then you run,' smiles Senju. 'You burn this file, you fill in this paper, then you live again –

'A new name in a new town with a new life –

'A new life among the living, detective –

'A third and final chance!'

I bow low. I thank him –

And I curse myself . . .

Now Senju throws some cash down onto the mat by my face. Now Senju says, 'You do the job and you get the rest. But do it soon, before you're picked up by the Public Safety Division . . .'

Ishida lies and he lies about Adachi . . .

I nod. I clutch my knapsack. I start to shuffle backwards towards the door, on my hands and on my knees –

Ha, ha, ha, ha! He, he, he, he . . .

Senju laughing at me now as he asks, 'You didn't bring me back any souvenirs from Tochigi, then? Not very thoughtful . . .'

'I am very sorry,' I tell him and I bow again –

But now Senju has said too much . . .

On my hands and on my knees –

He has said too much . . .
I get off my knees.

*

Every station, every platform, every train, every carriage. *Zā-zā, zā-zā*. The rain is coming down in sheets of sheer white water now, bouncing back off the train tracks and the umbrellas on the platform at Shimbashi. *Zā-zā, zā-zā*. Now the headlights of the Shinjuku train appear and the pushing begins, the shoving begins, the umbrellas adding to the confusion and the chaos of the bundles and baggage everyone carries. *Zā-zā, zā-zā*. I push my way forward and I shove my way on board. *Zā-zā, zā-zā*. I have food in my knapsack now. *Zā-zā, zā-zā*. I have money in my pocket now –
    But Senju has said too much . . .
    The train doesn't move and the doors don't close so there is still pushing, still shoving, one man asking another, 'Excuse me, can I put this up there next to your bag?'
    He has said too much . . .
    'There isn't room, is there?' snaps the other man, looking up at his knapsack on the rack –
    Now the doors close and the train starts. *Zā-zā, zā-zā*. I itch and I scratch. *Gari-gari*. Pushed and shoved as we crawl along the tracks through the rain. *Zā-zā, zā-zā*. I itch and I scratch. *Gari-gari*. Passengers get off at Hamamatsu-chō and Shinagawa but just as many push and shove their way inside. *Zā-zā, zā-zā*. I itch and I scratch. *Gari-gari*. But now I cannot see the passengers any more. *Zā-zā, zā-zā*. I itch and I scratch. *Gari-gari*. I cannot see their bundles and their baggage. *Zā-zā, zā-zā*. I itch and I scratch. *Gari-gari*. I cannot see this train at all. *Zā-zā, zā-zā*. Now I do not itch and I do not scratch. *Zā-zā, zā-zā*. I close my eyes –
    Zā-zā, zā-zā. Zā-zā, zā-zā . . .
    I am not here any more –
    I am sat cross-legged on a cot, a blood-flecked scroll on the wall above my bed. My head shaven and my belly bandaged.

*

I have no umbrella and I have no raincoat so, with my hat pulled down tight upon my skull and my jacket stretched over that, I run past the crooked, impotent telegraph poles down the road to my usual restaurant, half-way between Mitaka station and my own house –

The one lantern swinging in the rain and in the wind –

Ha, ha, ha, ha! He, he, he, he! Ho, ho, ho, ho!

I pull back the sheet that acts as a door on a night like this and the jokes, the smiles and the laughter stop dead. *Dead.* No more jokes. No more smiles. No more laughter. Everyone stares at me and then glances up at the master behind the counter –

I ignore them. I shake the rain from my jacket and from my hat. I sit down in a space at the counter –

I order *yakitori* and sake –

'Men were here again,' says the master. 'Asking about you.'

'Who were they?' I ask him. 'Good guys or bad?'

'What do you mean, good guys or bad?' asks the master. 'How would I know? You tell me. All I know is that they weren't friendly and they were asking after you . . .'

'I'm sorry,' I tell him. 'I don't like to see you frightened . . .'

'I'm not frightened,' says the master. 'But I don't want trouble with the Yankees and I don't want trouble with the gangs and I don't want trouble with crooked cops either . . .'

I take out some money. I put it on the counter and I tell him, 'I know I have run up debts . . .'

Debts to the dead . . .

The master picks up the money from the counter. The master puts the money back into my hand. He closes my fingers round it –

'I don't want your money and I don't want your custom either. The slate's clean but, remember, you're not welcome here any more.'

'Idiot!' I shout and storm out of his little shithole of a bar –

I walk down my own street cursing him, over and over –

'Idiot! Idiot! Idiot! Idiot! Idiot! Idiot! Idiot! Idiot!'

In the rain and in the wind, over and over again –

'Idiot! Idiot! Idiot! Idiot! Idiot! Idiot! Idiot!'

Hat on tight and jacket up over my head –

'Idiot! Idiot! Idiot! Idiot! Idiot! Idiot!'

I scratch and I scratch and I scratch –

Gari-gari. Gari-gari. Gari-gari . . .

'Idiot! Idiot! Idiot! Idiot! Idiot!'

In the rain and in the wind. *Idiot . . .*

On my hands, on my knees –
Idiot. Before the gate –
The idiot . . .

*

The gate to my house is closed. I open it. The door is locked. I open it.
The house is dark. The house is silent. I stand in the *genkan* –
The rotting mats, shredded doors and fallen walls . . .
The house still sleeping, always sleeping –
I wipe my face and I wipe my neck –
The house smells of children –
Their shoes face the door . . .
It smells of pain –
'I'm home . . .'
My wife comes out of the kitchen, her face is stained with
soot, her hands brushing dust from her worn *monpe* trousers –
She smiles and she says, 'Welcome home . . .'
Home. Home. Home. Home. Home . . .
I have brought cherries home, cherries for my children, their
stems tied in a necklace around my neck –
Home. Home. Home. Home . . .
I never want to leave again –
Home. Home. Home . . .
I close my eyes –
Home. Home . . .
Now I am –
Home.

14

August 28, 1946

Tokyo, 79°, rain

Night is day again. I open my eyes. *No sleep.* Night is day. I can hear the rain falling. *No pills.* Night is day. I can see the sun shining –

I don't want to remember. I don't want to remember . . .

I walk out of the sunlight and into the shadow. *Investigation is footwork.* I walk back up the hill to the scene of the crime. *The good detective visits the crime scene one hundred times . . .*

The scene of the crime. *Hide from sight.* The white morning light behind the black Shiba trees. *The corpses of the dead.* The black trees that have seen so much. *In the long, long grasses.* The black branches that have borne so much. *The dead leaves and weeds.* The black leaves that have come again. *Another country's young.* To grow, to fall, to grow again. *Another country's dead . . .*

I walk away from the scene of the crime. *Another country.* To stand beneath the Black Gate. *Another century . . .*

In the half-light, I can't forget . . .

The day is finally here. *Oh so bravely, off to Victory.* I leave for the front tomorrow. *Insofar as we have vowed and left our land behind.* My wife and family wake early and head for Shiba Park. *Who can die without first having shown his true mettle?* In the inner compound of Zōjōji Temple a large crowd has gathered to say goodbye. *Each time I hear the bugles of our advancing army.* They leave the compound and make their way through the crowds of school excursions to stand before the Black Gate. *I close my eyes and see wave upon wave of flags cheering us into battle.* My son has a little flag in his hand, my daughter has a little flag in hers. *The earth and its flora burn in flames.* My parents are here. *As we endlessly part the plains.* Friends from school, teammates from my high school baseball club, and colleagues with whom I graduated; each holds aloft a big banner, each banner bearing my name, each before the Black Gate. *Helmets emblazoned with the Rising Sun.* The clock strikes noon, the cries rise as my truck approaches and stops before the Black Gate. *And, stroking the mane of our horses.* I jump down from the back of the Nissan. *Who knows what tomorrow will bring – life?* I stare into the crowd, up at the banners and the flags, and I salute. *Or death in battle?* Now the departure signal sounds –

No one is who they say they are. No one . . .

Beneath the Black Gate. *Another country.* Day is night again. *Another century.* Huge scorched trees, their roots to the sky. *A different world.* Nothing but the ruin of the old Black Gate. *A different time.* Branches charred and leaves lost. *Another country.* In this place, I stand beneath the dark eaves of the gate. *A different world.* We have seen hell. *Another century.* We have known heaven. *A different time.* We have heard the last judgment. *In the half-light.* We have witnessed the fall of the gods. *I can't forget.* Night is day, day is night. *In the half-light.* Black is white, white is black –

But the good detective knows nothing is random . . .

Under the Black Gate, the stray dog waits –

The detective knows in chaos lies order . . .

His house lost and his master gone –

He knows in chaos lie answers . . .

The stray dog has no feet –

Answers, answers . . .

The dog is dead.

*

I put my daughter on my back. I take my son by the hand. In the half-light, I lead them down the garden path, down the street to stand in the queue for the post office, in the hope that the government insurance has arrived, in the hope I can cash the last of our bonds.

The queue moves slowly forward. The bench outside becomes free. I sit my daughter and my son down upon the bench next to an old man who stinks of drink. He winks at my daughter and he smiles at my son. Now he turns to me and holds out a withdrawal slip and asks, 'Will you fill this out for me . . .?'

I nod. 'For how much?'

The old man opens his post office savings book and says, 'Forty yen should do today.'

I write forty yen on the withdrawal slip. Then I copy down the number of his savings account and the address –

Now I fill in the name –

A woman's name.

I hand the withdrawal slip and the savings book back to the old man and he thanks me.

The queue moves forward again. I pick my daughter and my son up from the bench. We follow the old man inside the post office. The old man presents his withdrawal slip to one of the post office clerks as I do the same at the next window along –

Now we all sit back down to wait.

The old man winks at my daughter and smiles at my son again.

Now the clerk at the payments desk calls out the name –

'Are you Yamada Hanako?' asks the clerk.

No one is who they say they are . . .

'No,' says the old man. 'But she's my youngest daughter.'

The clerk shrugs his shoulders. He counts out the forty yen. He hands over the cash and says, 'Better if she comes in person . . .'

The old man nods, thanks the clerk and now walks past us –

The old man winks at my daughter, he smiles at my son –

'She can't come in person,' he whispers. 'She's dead.'

The clerk at the payments desk calls out my name –

The clerk hands over our cash and I thank him.

No one is who they seem to be . . .

I put my daughter on my back. I take my son by the hand. In the half-light, I lead them up the street, up the garden path, to stand them in the *genkan* of our house, to watch me as I say goodbye –

I say goodbye, as I turn their shoes to face the door –

'Please don't go, Daddy,' says my daughter –

'I have to go back to work,' I tell her –

'But not tonight,' says my son –

Now my wife comes out of the kitchen, her face is hot from cooking, her hands brushing water from her trousers –

'Let your father go to work,' she says –

I pat their heads. I say, 'Goodbye . . .'

'Please remember us,' my daughter and my son call after me. 'Please don't forget us, Daddy . . .'

Daddy, Banzai! . . .

Now I walk down the path, through the gate, up the street –

I don't want to remember. I don't want to remember . . .

I do not turn around. I cannot turn around –
But in the half-light, I can't forget . . .
I am not going back to work –
No one is who they seem . . .
Tonight I am going to her.

*

Night is day again. *There have been others.* In the ruins, in the rain. *There have been others.* The children watch me, the dogs watch me. *There have been others.* I smoke a cigarette, I read a newspaper –

SEX MANIAC CONFESSES KILLING FOUR YOUNG WOMEN

Kodaira Yoshio, 41, a sadistic sex maniac who had been under investigation by the Metropolitan Police Board for the raping and strangling to death of Ryuko, the sixteen-year-old daughter of Midorikawa Isaburo of Meguro, Tokyo, on the sixth of August, has confessed to the raping and killing of three other young women in the past one year.

On the fifteenth of July last year, the sex crazy laundry man admitted killing Kondo Kazuko, aged twenty-two years old, in Saitama Prefecture while the young woman was on a food shopping trip to the district. Luring her into a forest with promises of leading her to a good place to buy food, Kodaira violated and killed the unsuspecting young girl.

On the twenty-eighth of September of the same year, Kodaira killed Matsushita Yoshie, aged twenty years, using similar means. The girl's body was found stripped naked lying in a forest in Kiyose-mura, Kita Tama-gun, the same place where he had committed his previous crime.

In a similar manner, the maniac admitted killing Abe Yoshiko, aged sixteen years, in

Shinagawa, Tokyo, on the ninth of June this year. This girl was also raped.

In all cases, rape accompanies the killing, and in each instance, the body was hidden or buried under dead leaves about thirty to fifty metres away from the scene of the crime. Each victim was strangled to death by her own haramaki *sash.*

The only case in which the murderer knew the victim and the family well was in the instance of Midorikawa Ryuko, the last of his victims, and which was the first clue to the identity of the killer and which eventually led to the arrest of Kodaira. All the rest of his victims were total strangers to the murderer.

The Tokyo Metropolitan Police Board plan to question the sex crazed killer about four further murders; seventeen-year-old Shinokawa Tatsue who was raped and murdered in the basement of the Toyoko Department Store in Shibuya and whose umbrella was found at the home of Kodaira's wife's family in Toyama, and the murders of Baba Hiroko, Ishikawa Yori and Nakamura Mitsuko, whose bodies were all found in Tochigi Prefecture near Kodaira's family home.

I finish the newspaper. *There have been others.* I finish the cigarette. *No mention of Miyazaki Mitsuko.* The dogs wait for me. *There have been others*. The children wait for me. *No mention of the second Shiba body*. In the rain. *There have been others*. In the ruins.

*

In the half-light, I can hear the wind against the door, rattling around the roof and under the eaves of her house. But there is no rain, there is no thunder tonight, just the clatter of sandals and the calls of children in the streets outside. *I shouldn't have come here, not tonight.* Tonight I should have stayed at home with my wife and children. My wife serving up their dinner of *zōsui*, my children's bowls in their outstretched hands, asking their mother for more –

'Okawari . . . Okawari . . . Okawari . . .'

Yuki stands hands on hips, barefoot on the earthen floor of the hallway, and looks out between the ribbons –

I should not be here, not tonight . . .

'But you'll stay awhile longer?'

I nod and I thank her.

Yuki opens a cupboard. She takes out a saucer of pickled radish and a small aluminium saucepan. She sniffs at the contents of the pan and shrugs. She places it on the charcoal embers –

'And you'll eat with me, won't you?'

I nod again and I thank her again.

She lifts up the lid of the pan –

'Are you married?' she asks.

*

Night is still day here. The queues through the gates, the queues to the doors, the queues in the corridors. *I have spent too long here.* I run through the gates, through the doors and down the corridors. Past the queues, past the patients and past the gurneys to the elevator. *Hours, days and weeks.* I push the button, I step inside, and I press another button. The doors close and I ride the elevator down in the dark. *Weeks, months and years.* The doors open –

Here in the half-light, the half-things . . .

I run past the tiled walls of sinks, of drains, the written warnings of cuts, of punctures, to the mortuary –

She is here. She is here. She is here . . .

I read the names of the dead –

326

She is here. She is here . . .
I pull open the casket –
She is here . . .
No name –
Here . . .
I take out her clothes and now I take out her bones –
Half-things in the half-light, the half-things . . .
I put her clothes in my army knapsack –
Here, here in the half-light . . .
I put her bones in my bag –
Debts to the dead . . .
Down the corridor of tiled walls and written warnings, I push the button and I wait for the elevator. I glance into a mirror above a sink. I glance away. Now I glance back into the glass –
'I almost didn't recognize you . . .'
Her bones on my back, I stare into the glass –
No one is who they seem . . .
I vomit in the sink. *Black bile.* I vomit again. *Brown bile.* Four times I vomit. *Black bile, brown bile, yellow bile and grey . . .*
I stare into the mirror above the sink –
I scream, 'I know who I am!'
Now I smash the glass, breaking the mirror into one thousand pieces, one thousand pieces falling, falling to the ground –
Broken and splintered . . .
'I know who I am!'

*

I shouldn't still be here. Not tonight. I should have gone home to my wife and children. But in the half-light, I watch Yuki at dinner. There is still no rain tonight, no sound of thunder, only the wind, louder than the radio now. She finishes her second bowl of rice. She rinses her chopsticks and then her bowl. She puts the utensils back into the cupboard. She puts a hand to her mouth, stifles a belch and laughs –
'I suppose your wife is much more polite than me?'
My heart aches and my body stinks –
I itch and I scratch. *Gari-gari . . .*
Behind the six-panel screen, two pillows placed side by side, she is dressed in a yellow kimono with a dark-blue stripe; the collar is

off her shoulder, her hand upon my knee –

I think about her all the time . . .

I run my hand up her back –

She haunts me . . .

Her hairbrush in one hand, she leans forward to stare at herself in the three panels of her vanity mirror –

She turns to look at me and smiles –

She has dyed her teeth black –

She drops the brush, *ton*, and asks, 'Does this become me?'

*

The chief has reserved the same room in the same recently reopened restaurant near Daimon, the one near the kitchens of the Victors. The chief is treating the whole of the First Investigative Division to a celebratory meal. The whole of the First Investigative Division sitting sleeve against sleeve, knee against knee on the new mats –

There is no Ishida. No Fujita. No Adachi or me . . .

There is beer and there is food; *zanpan* from the Victors' dustbins, the men grateful not to eat *zōsui* again –

Raising their glasses, taking off their ties, tying them around their foreheads and singing their songs; their songs of endeavour, their songs of courage, their songs of battle –

Their songs of victory –

Case closed!

But there are only the names of three detectives on the interrogation report; Adachi, Kanehara and Kai –

Three names and one signature –

Kodaira Yoshio.

The other detectives from Room #1 and Room #2, the uniforms from Atago, Meguro and Mita, the other detectives and uniforms from Saitama and Tochigi Prefectures –

Dogs starved at their masters' feet . . .

Their names are all missing –

Beneath their tables . . .

But no one cares; everyone still talking about Kodaira Yoshio, about his confession to the murder of Kondo Kazuko, twenty-two years old, of Jūjō, Kita Ward, Tokyo, whom Kodaira had met queuing for a ticket at Ikebukuro station on the fifteenth of July last year, whom he took into the woods at Kiyose-mura, Kita Tama-gun, out in Saitama Prefecture, and throttled and raped and then robbed of sixty yen and her paulownia *geta* clogs –

Death is here . . .

Everyone still talking about Kodaira Yoshio, about his confession to the murder of Matsushita Yoshie, twenty years old, also of Kita Ward, Tokyo, whom he had met in a queue at Tokyo station on the twenty-eighth of September last year, whom he took into the same woods at Kiyose-mura and throttled and raped and then robbed of one hundred and eighty yen, her handbag, her best black suit jacket and her mother's umbrella –

Death . . .

Everyone now whispering about the rumours of purges, about Kempei in hiding, Kempei on the run. Everyone whispering about trials and hangings, Kempei taking new names and new lives, the names of the mad and the names of the dead. Everyone whispering about death and the dead, the dead and their ghosts –

Everyone now whispering about me –

Me and Ishida. Me and Fujita . . .

Me and Adachi . . .

In this room of this recently reopened restaurant near Daimon, the whole of the First Investigative Division sitting sleeve against sleeve, knee against knee on these new tatami mats –

On the mountains and mountains of lies . . .

Chief Kita and Chief Inspector Kanehara –

On those lies upon lies upon lies . . .

Inspector Kai and Inspector Hattori –

Lies upon lies upon lies . . .

Their glasses raised, their ties around their foreheads, their songs sung, they look up at me now –

All their lies on my back . . .

They look up at me like they don't know who I am, like they cannot see me standing here, standing here before them –

Her bones on my back . . .

I should not be here –

Debts to the dead . . .

Now I'm gone.

*

The wind is still blowing as the siren starts up, as the voice on her radio announces that enemy planes are at the southern tip of the Izu Peninsula, the sirens louder now, the voice more urgent as Yuki runs to the closet, sliding open the door, diving in among the bedding, heart hammering and eyes wide, listening for the rattle of the incendiary bombs or the swish of the demolition bombs –

First comes the rain, then comes the thunder . . .

'I'll be back in a moment,' I tell her –

I should not be here, not tonight . . .

I go downstairs, out into the street –

People are running, digging –

I should be home . . .

Hiding things in the dirt –

In their shelters –

Boom! Boom!

The anti-aircraft batteries have begun, the searchlights crisscrossing the sky, catching the planes as the fires start –

People with suitcases now, people on bicycles –

'Air raid! Air raid! Here comes an air raid!'

I smell smoke. I put on my air-raid hood –

'Red! Red! Incendiary bomb!'

Thousands of footsteps up on the road –

'Run! Run! Get a mattress and sand!'

The deafening sound from above –

'Air raid! Air raid! Here comes an air raid!'

I fall to the ground, to the earth –

'Black! Black! Here come the bombs!'

But there is only silence now –

'Cover your ears . . .'

I get back up. I run inside –

'Close your eyes!'

Up the stairs, into the closet, to gather Yuki up, to carry her out, into the street, the houses ablaze, the corner shop, as the wind rises and the sparks fly, I carry her across the bridge, the canal filled with people, one alley on fire, the next and the next, the crossroads blocked in all four directions with pets and babies, dogs and children, men and women, old and young, soldier and civilian, hustling and jostling, pushing and shoving, staggering and stumbling, now falling to the ground with every fresh rattle, every new swish, crushing and trampling the very young and the very old, letting go of a hand and losing a child, calling out and turning around, screaming out and turning back, hustling and jostling, pushing and shoving, staggering and stumbling, crushing and trampling –

I should not be here . .

I have to choose which way to go, which way to run; the houses on three sides are now aflame, the people all pushing one way but that way lie no fields, that way lie only buildings –

'Air raid! Air raid! Here comes an air raid!'

I jump down into the ditch by the side of the road with Yuki still in my arms and I smear our hoods and our bedding with black mud and dark water. Now I lift Yuki up again and I carry her out of the ditch, back towards the fire, back into the flames but she is struggling to break free from my arms, desperate to flee –

'Black! Black! Here come the bombs!'

'Forget the fire,' I whisper. 'Forget the bombs and trust me. Through these flames is the river, through these flames is life . .'

'Cover your ears! Close your eyes!'

Now Yuki tightens her grip, and she nods her head, as we rush back into the fires, back into the flames –

Back into the war, my war . . .

*

The chiefs, the inspectors and all their detectives will still be at the restaurant in Daimon; their glasses empty and their songs sung now, they will be flat on their backs and out for the night; only the uniforms here tonight at the Meguro police station –

The uniforms and the suspect –

Kodaira Yoshio . . .

In their interrogation room, at their table, he sits in his chair –

Kodaira smiling. Kodaira grinning. Kodaira laughing . . .

'I heard you were no longer with us, soldier . . .'

'Shut up,' I say. 'It's just you and me now . . .'

But Kodaira Yoshio leans across the table and smiles at me again and says, 'Bit like an old regimental reunion.'

'Here's another reunion for you,' I say and I pick up my army knapsack and empty the contents onto the table –

All her clothes and all her bones . . .

'Recognize these?' I shout –

Kodaira still smiling . . .

'Or these or these?' I shout again, picking up the yellow and dark-blue striped pinafore dress and the white half-sleeved chemise, then the dyed-pink socks and the white canvas shoes with their red rubber soles, now her bones –

Kodaira grinning . . .

'Well those bones could be anybody's, soldier . . .'

But now I take out the other wristwatch from my pocket. I put it down in front of him –

'And that . . .'

Kodaira picks up the wristwatch from the table. Kodaira turns it over in his hand. Kodaira reads the inscription on its back –

The inscription that says, *Miyazaki Mitsuko . . .*

That screams, *Miyazaki Mitsuko . . .*

'Could that be just anybody's wristwatch?' I ask him –

Kodaira laughing . . .

'Now you got me, soldier,' he says. 'Because I did know a Miyazaki Mitsuko, back when I was working for the Naval Clothing Department near Shinagawa. Lovely thing she was too, pure clear skin and firm fresh body she had . . .'

Licking his lips . . .

'And after I left there, I kept in touch with the old caretaker who ran the place and he did tell me that poor Mitsuko had been found naked and dead in one of the air-raid shelters . . .'

'It was you, you dirty fucking animal!'

'Hold your horses there, soldier,' he says. 'Because my old friend told me that she'd actually been killed by a *Yobo* who used to work there, that it was this *Yobo* who had desecrated her skin, violated her body; made me sick to think of such a dirty, filthy third-class person fucking a pure Japanese girl like her . . .'

'It was you, you fucking monster!'

'You're not listening to me, soldier,' says Kodaira. 'The Kempeitai caught this *Yobo*; they caught him, they tried him and they executed him there and then on the spot, that's what the old caretaker said. Made me proud to be Japanese . . .'

'It was you, wasn't it?'

'Are you deaf, soldier?' Kodaira laughs now. 'You got shellshock, have you? It was a *Yobo* . . .'

'It was you . . .'

Kodaira shakes his head. He puts the watch back down on the table and now he stretches his arms high above his head and says, 'You know, none of it makes much sense to me . . .'

I ask him nothing. I say nothing –

'Take the Kempeitai, or even me, for example; they give us a big medal over there for all the things we did, but then we come back here and all we get is a long rope . . .'

I still say nothing –

'Come on,' he laughs. 'You were over there; you saw what I saw, you did what I did . . .'

'Shut up!'

'You know, soldier, you really do look like a man I once saw over there in Jinan . . .'

'Shut up!'

'Why?' laughs Kodaira again. 'It couldn't have been you, could it, soldier? He was Kempei and he was a corporal.'

'Shut up! Shut up! Shut up!'

'And his name wasn't Minami . . .'

'Shut up! Shut up!'

'I think it was Katayama . . .'

'I know who I am,' I shout. 'I know! I know who I am!'

Now Kodaira leans across the table towards me. Now he puts his hands on mine. Now he says, 'Forget it, corporal . . .'

No one is who they say they are . . .

'But I know who I am,' I hiss. 'I know . . .'

No one is who they seem . . .

'It was a different world,' says Kodaira. 'A different time.'

*

A century of change takes place in one night of fire; neighbourhoods bombed to the ground, their people burnt to death; where there were factories and homes, where there were workers and children, now there is only dust, now there is only ash, and no one will remember those buildings, no one will remember those people –

No one will remember anything . . .

Things that happened last week already seem as though they happened years, even decades before. Things that happened only yesterday, no longer even register –

This is the war now . . .

There are severed legs and there are severed heads, a woman's trunk with its intestines spilt, a child's spectacles melted to its face, the dead in clusters, pets and babies, dogs and children, men and women, old and young, soldier and civilian, each one indistinguishable from the other –

The smell of apricots . . .

Each burnt, each dead –

This is my war now . . .

The air warm and the dawn pink. *The smell of apricots.* Black piles of bedding, black piles of possessions strewn on either side of the road. *The stench of rotten apricots.* Their black bicycles lie fallen, their black bodies huddled together. *The smell of apricots.* Black factories and black bathhouses still smouldering –

That stench of rotten apricots . . .

The all-clear signal now –

I should not be here . . .

The orders to assemble at various elementary schools, the orders to avoid certain other schools. *The smell of apricots.* I stagger and I stumble on, Yuki still in my arms. *I should not be here.* I want to leave her, I want to go home, but I cannot. *The stench of rotten apricots.* I stagger and I stumble, through the black columns of survivors, their black bedding on their backs, their black bicycles at their sides. *I should not be here.* I stagger and I stumble on until we reach the Sumida River, the river now black with bodies. *The smell of apricots.* I carry Yuki across the black bridge. *I should not be here.* I stagger and I stumble past soldiers clearing the black streets, shifting the black bodies into the backs of their trucks with hooks. *The stench of rotten apricots.* I stagger and I stumble as the black flesh tears, the black bodies fall apart. *I should not be here.* Until the air is no longer warm, the dawn no longer pink. *Just the smell of apricots . . .*

Until I can look no more, I stagger and I stumble –

I should not be here. I should not be here . . .

Until hours, maybe days later, I carry her up the stairs of a deserted block of apartments in Shinagawa –

I should not be here . . .

Until I lay her down on the pale tatami mats of a second-floor room, frayed and well worn, the chrysanthemum wallpaper limp and peeling. *Here in the half-light.* I take the bottle out of my pocket. I unscrew the cap of the bottle. I take the cotton wool out of the neck of the bottle. I begin to count the pills –

I should not be here . . .

One Calmotin, two. I count and I count. I take out a second bottle. I count out the pills. *Thirty-one Calmotin, thirty-two.* I count and I count. I take out the third bottle. *Sixty-one Calmotin, sixty-two.* I count and I count. The fourth bottle and then the fifth –

One hundred and twenty-one Calmotin . . .

I should not be here, on my knees –

This is surrender . . .

I should not be here –

This is defeat . . .

*

Potsu-potsu, the rain is still falling, the hot fat drops on the kettles and the pans; *potsu-potsu* it falls in its terrible rhythm on the crockery and the utensils; *potsu-potsu* on the clothes and the shoes; *potsu-potsu* on the cooking oil and the soy sauce –

No 'Apple Song' here tonight –

Potsu-potsu it falls on the corrugated tin roof which covers the stairs up to Senju Akira's office –

Potsu-potsu, potsu-potsu . . .

Heavier and heavier –

Zā-zā, zā-zā . . .

I clutch my knapsack. I start to shuffle backwards towards the door, on my hands and on my knees –

Ha, ha, ha, ha!

Senju laughing at me now as he asks, 'You didn't bring me back any souvenirs from Tochigi then? Not very thoughtful . . .'

'I am very sorry,' I tell him and I bow again –

But now Senju has said too much . . .

On my hands and on my knees –

He has said too much . . .

I get off my knees. *He has said too much.* I open my old army knapsack. *Get off your knees!* I take out the 1939 army-issue pistol. *He has said too much.* I raise it. *Get off your knees!* I aim and I point it at Senju Akira. *He has said too much.* Senju sat cross-legged before

335

the long low polished table. *Get off your knees!* Bare-chested, with his trousers unbuttoned at the waist. *He has said too much.* Revolvers and short swords lain out on the table before him –

Get off your knees! Get off your knees!

'It was you,' I tell him. 'You who ordered Ishida to kill me. You who ordered Ishida to steal that file because Fujita told you it would buy Adachi's silence. Because you knew Adachi would find out. You knew he would find out it was you; you who introduced Fujita to Nodera; you who set them up to kill Matsuda, your own boss, your mentor, the man you called brother; it was you . . .

'You who ordered the hit on Matsuda . . .'

Now Senju looks up at me and smiles –

Senju laughing at me again now –

He, he, he, he! Ho, ho, ho, ho . . .

'Suddenly you're a brave man, are you? With your grey hair and your stench of death, suddenly you're a hero again, are you? Suddenly, back from the dead. Go on then, corporal . . .'

The 1939 army-issue pistol pointed at him –

'Corporal what . . .? What's your name . . .?'

The 1939 army-issue pistol aimed at him –

'What is it this week, corporal . . .?'

The army-issue pistol in my hand –

'Who are you today, cor–'

I pull the trigger. *Bang!*

His forehead shatters –

I am off my knees . . .

I can hear feet coming. I pick up the file and the papers, the money and the drugs. Feet up the stairs, through the doors –

Through the doors, and I shoot again –

Bang! Bang! Bang!

The first one falls, the other turns –

I run to the door and I shoot –

Bang! Bang!

The man falls down the stairs as I follow him –

As I step over the bloodstained patterned-shirt. *Zā-zā, zā-zā.* As I stamp on the American sunglasses. *Zā-zā, zā-zā . . .*

Now I run. Now I run away again –

Zā-zā, zā-zā. Zā-zā, zā-zā . . .

Run to the station –

Zā-zā, zā-zā . . .

The rain coming down in sheets of sheer white water, bouncing back off the train tracks and the umbrellas on the platform. *Zā-zā, zā-zā.* Now the headlights of the Shinjuku train appear and the pushing begins, the shoving begins. *Zā-zā, zā-zā.* I push my way forward and I shove my way on board. *Zā-zā, zā-zā . . .*

He said too much. He will say no more . . .

Now the doors close and the train starts. *Zā-zā, zā-zā.* I itch and I scratch. *Gari-gari.* Pushed and shoved as we crawl along the tracks through the rain. *Zā-zā, zā-zā.* I itch and I scratch. *Gari-gari.* But I cannot see this train at all. *Zā-zā, zā-zā.* Now I do not itch and I do not scratch. *Zā-zā, zā-zā.* I close my eyes –

Zā-zā, zā-zā. Zā-zā, zā-zā . . .

I am not here.

*

My hat pulled down and my jacket stretched over, I run down the road to the restaurant, half-way between the station and my house –

The one lantern swinging in the rain and the wind –

Ha, ha, ha, ha! He, he, he, he! Ho, ho, ho, ho!

I pull back the sheet that acts as a door and the jokes, the smiles and the laughter stop dead. *Dead.* No jokes. No smiles. No laughter. Everyone has gone. There is no one here –

No one but the man behind the counter –

No one is who they say they are . . .

'Welcome home, corporal,' says Chief Inspector Adachi –

'This is not my home,' I tell him. 'This is not my home!'

But Adachi nods. Adachi says, 'This is all you have.'

'Stop!' I shout and scream, 'You're lying!'

'They shipped you home from China in a strait-jacket,' he says. 'And they would have locked you up in Matsuzawa with your father, if it hadn't been for me and Chief Kita.'

'I don't want to hear this!' I shout.

'I took you in as a favour to Kita and then, after the surrender, he repaid us both with these jobs –'

'Stop!' I shout again –

'With these names –'

I can't forget . . .

But I am not listening to Adachi now. Now I am ripping apart the walls of this shack. Now I am tearing off the roof –

And now in the light, here in the bright and shining light, Adachi is gone; this man is Captain Muto again –

'And I am all you have,' he says –

'They are coming for you.'

And I can hear them. *They are coming for me.* Door to door. *They are coming for me.* I can hear them. *They are coming for me.* Kita is coming, the Victors are coming. *They are coming for me . . .*

Now Captain Muto puts down a razor on the counter –

I should not be here, not tonight. I should be home . . .

Next to the razor, the bottles of Calmotin –

'Sweet dreams, Corporal Katayama.'

*

She is lying naked on the futon. *Her eyebrows shaved, her teeth black.* Her head is slightly to the right. *Her eyebrows shaved, her teeth black.* Her right arm outstretched. *Her eyebrows shaved, her teeth black.* Her left arm at her side. *Her eyebrows shaved, her teeth black.* Her legs parted, raised and bent at the knee. *Her eyebrows shaved, her teeth black.* My come drying on her stomach and on her ribs. *Her eyebrows shaved, her teeth black.* She says –

'Marry me, please marry me . . .'

Now she brings her left hand up to her stomach. She dips her fingers in my come. She puts her fingers to her lips. She licks my come from her fingers and she asks –

'Does this become me?'

Dressed in her yellow and dark-blue striped kimono, I smile, 'It more than becomes you . . .'

The pills all gone . . .

'Marry me . . .'

I pick up the razor. Nobody knows my name. Everybody knows my name. *I open up the razor.* Nobody cares. Everybody cares. *I untie the kimono.* The day is night. The night is day. *The yellow and dark-blue striped kimono.* Black is white. White is black. *It falls open.* The men are the women. The women are the men. *The razor in my right hand.* The brave are the frightened. The frightened are the brave. *I lower my right hand.* The strong are the weak. The weak are the

338

strong. *I lower the razor.* The good are the bad. The bad are the good. *The blade touches my skin.* Communists should be set free. Communists should be locked up. *I lift up my cock with my left hand.* Strikes are legal. Strikes are illegal. *The blade is cold.* Democracy is good. Democracy is bad. *My mouth is dry.* The aggressor is the victim. The victim is the aggressor. *My stomach aches.* The winners are the losers. The losers are the winners. *My heart aches.* Japan lost the war. Japan won the war. *I start to cut.* The living are the dead –

I cut and I cut and I cut and I cut and I cut . . .

Until the dead are the living. *I cut . . .*

I am one of the survivors!

Until the walls of her room are stained red with blood, the tatami mats soaked black, and now her walls are gone, her mats are gone, and I am running through the streets –

One of the lucky ones!

Down these streets that are no streets, past shops that are no shops. In this city of the dead –

The Shōwa Dead . . .

Their voices calling to me, their hands reaching out to me. *The Shōwa Dead.* The master of my usual restaurant. *The Shōwa Dead.* The friend from elementary school. *The Shōwa Dead.* The old man in the bar. *The Shōwa Dead.* My teammates from my high school baseball club. *The Shōwa Dead.* The woman at the streetcar stop. *The Shōwa Dead.* The colleagues with whom I graduated. *The Shōwa Dead.* The children, the children –

In the City of the Dead –

The Shōwa Dead . . .

They call me –

Home.

*

Running down my street, running towards my house. *In the half-light, I can't forget.* The dirt on my knees, the blood on my hands –

The sun setting in the west, rain threatening –

The sides of the road littered with corpses on mats, men and women, young and old, soldiers and civilians, their eyes blank or closed, their flesh rotting and their bones dust –

The stench of rotten apricots . . .

But there are no cars upon my street, the bridge collapsed into the river, all the restaurants destroyed and the farms abandoned –

Endless burnt fields, burnt fields of ash and weeds –

I cannot tell which of these houses is mine –

I cannot see for the tears in my eyes –

Now I remember. I remember . . .

I have been away for too long –

I remember. I remember . . .

I have failed my wife –

Now I remember . . .

My children.

But then I recognize the gate to my house, now I recognize the path to my house. I open the gate, I go up the path –

Now I open the door to my house –

Their shoes face the door . . .

I stand in the *genkan* –

'I'm home . . .'

Home . . .

My wife and my children step out of the half-light, their air-raid hoods are scorched, the bedding on their backs is black, their faces blistered and their eyes sunken, but they are alive –

I rush towards them, my arms around them –

I fall to my knees as I bring them close –

'I thought you were dead,' I cry –

'I thought I had lost you . . .'

But now they push me away, they step back into the shadows as they raise their fingers and point at me –

The rain falling on me now . . .

'We're already dead . . .'

Now there is no roof and there are no walls, only ashes, no mats and no screens, only ashes, no furniture and no clothes, only ashes, no *genkan* and no door, only ashes –

Their shoes are cinders . . .

My right hand trembles, my right arm, now my legs –

For I have no wife, I have no children, only ashes –

Masaki, Banzai! Sonoko, Banzai! . . .

I have no son and I have no daughter –

Daddy, Banzai! Banzai! . . .

I have no home. I have no family –

Daddy, Banzai!
I have no heart –
Banzai! . . .
In this House of Oblivion, I am death.

*

Through the buildings in disrepair and the grounds untended, the gates gone and the trees cut down, they are coming; past the faded paint and the worn linoleum, the stained uniforms and the grubby offices, they are coming; through the sounds of screams and sobs, the smells of DDT and disinfectant, they are coming now –

To the Matsuzawa Hospital for the Insane –

They are coming now. They are coming . . .

Down these corridors and up these stairs, up these stairs and along another long corridor of locked metal doors, they are coming now; through locked metal doors into the secure wards, into the secure wards and down more corridors, they are coming now; down more corridors to the secure rooms, they are coming now –

They are here! They are here! They are here!

Dr. Nomura before the locked metal door –

Before the bolted metal hatch –

'Here we are,' he says.

Nomura slides back the bolts on the hatch. Nomura lowers the metal hatch. Now Nomura steps back and says, 'There you are . . .'

I step towards the door. I look through the hatchway –

I stare through the hatchway back into their eyes –

Pairs of brown eyes and pairs of blue . . .

These men have looked into my eyes before –

My unblinking eyes and my shaven head –

Now I step away from the hatchway –

I sit back cross-legged on my cot –

In my shapeless gown of yellow and dark-blue striped Chinese silk, with my close-shaven head and my unblinking eyes –

The blood-flecked scroll on the wall above my cot –

'It is time to reveal the true essence of the nation.'

A colour postcard of the Itsuku-shima Shrine –

My hands folded in my bandaged lap –

I am one of the survivors . . .

'Have you seen enough?' asks Nomura –
The men step away from the hatch –
'We've seen enough,' says Chief Kita. 'Thank you, doctor.'
Dr. Nomura closes the hatch. Dr. Nomura bolts it –
The walls are white, but the cell is dark now –
In the half-light, the half-things move –
I close my eyes and I begin to count again; one hundred and twenty Calmotin, one hundred and twenty –
One of the lucky ones.

of every province through which we pass. *Datō Nippon Teikokushugi!* Trenches dug at six-metre intervals, strewn with hats, leather belts and birdcages. *This is not conquest, this is emancipation!* The unburied bones of the Chinese dead stand like sticks stuck in the soil. *The Light from the East.* Brown thighbones shine in the sunlight, vertebrae glisten. *Bright Peace.* The flies swarm, the air stinks. I lie among the corpses. **One hundred and twenty Calmotin, one hundred and twenty-one.** The Chinese couple are streaked with dirt, their faces expressionless. The interpreter spits out the match and shouts at the man. The garlic stench, the metallic words. The woman answers the question. The interpreter strikes her. The woman staggers. The interpreter nods. Kasahara and I march the couple to the outskirts of the village, the red sky reflected in the willow-lined creek. The trees are still tonight, the farmhouses abandoned. The couple stare into the waters of the creek, the clusters of wild chrysanthemums, the corpse of a horse, its saddle tangled in weeds. Kasahara draws his sword and I draw mine. The man and the woman drop to their knees. His hands clasped together, her frantic metallic pleas. The blade and then the silence again. Blood flows over their shoulders but neither head falls. The man's body tilts to the right and topples into the wild chrysanthemums. *Masaki, Banzai!* I help the woman's body into the creek, the muddy soles of her feet turned up to the sky. *Daddy, Banzai!* In the village by the riverbank, lined by willow trees, the group of young able-bodied men poses in front of a half-destroyed house. Our captain in the centre, he rests his hands on the heads of two small children. No tears for the rivers and mountains of their land, no sadness for their father and mother no longer here. *I see your little figure, waving a little flag in your little fist.* His body among the chrysanthemums, her feet turned up to the sky. *Daddy cherishes that picture forever in his mind.* By the riverbank, lined by willow trees. In a half-destroyed house, I lie among the corpses. Thousands of them, millions of them. **One hundred and thirty Calmotin, one hundred and thirty-one.** The sunlight streams in through the windows of the carriage, gaiters hang from the overhead baggage net. A child unsheathes a toy sword. *Banzai!* **One hundred and forty Calmotin, one hundred and forty-one.** In the House of Oblivion, there are no flags. *Ton-ton.* Death is a man from Tochigi. *Ton-ton.* There are no songs. Death is a man from Tokyo. *Ton-ton.* Death is a man from Japan. *Ton-ton.* There are only drums. Death is a man from Korea. *Ton-ton.* Death is a man from China. *Ton-ton.* Drums of skin, drums of hair. Death is a man from Russia. *Ton-ton.* Death is a man from Germany. *Ton-ton.* Beaten by thighbones. Death is a man from France. *Ton-ton.* Death is a man from Italy. *Ton-ton.* Beaten by children. Death is a man from Spain. *Ton-ton.* Death is a man from Great Britain. *Ton-ton.* Banging the drum, after we're gone. Death is a man from America. *Ton-ton.* There are no exits, in the House of Oblivion. *Ton-ton.* Death is a man. *Ton-ton.* Cut off your cock! *Masaki, Banzai!* Death is a man. *Ton-ton.* Tear out your heart! *Daddy, Banzai!* Death is a man. *Banzai!* **One hundred and fifty Calmotin...**

The spirits of the dead from my past crimes
Startle me,
And, while in despair, I spend days
Awaiting my death
Thinking of the kindness bestowed on me
Even to the very end,
Which causes tears to flow without limit.

Kodaira Yoshio, 1949

Author's Note

Kodaira Yoshio was executed at the Miyagi Prison in Sendai
Prefecture on the fifth of October, 1949.
He was forty-four years old.
Kodaira Yoshio had confessed to the rapes and murders of ten
women, including Miyazaki Mitsuko and the second woman found
in Shiba Park, Tokyo, in August 1946.
However, this woman has never been identified.
She was aged approximately seventeen to eighteen years and
died on or around the twenty-second of July, 1946 –
Namu-amida-butsu . . .

David Peace, Tokyo, 2006
The Year of the Dog

Glossary

Throughout the text, I have followed the Japanese convention in which the family name precedes the personal name.

Akahata	The *Red Flag*, a daily communist newspaper
Asahi Shimbun	a daily newspaper
Asobu . . .?	Shall we play?
ayu	a type of fish
bakudan	the explosion of a bomb; also the name given to low-grade alcohol that had a similar effect on the drinker
Banzai!	Hurrah!
bentō	a prepared lunch box
butsudan	a family or household Buddhist altar upon which photographs of the dead are displayed
Calmotin	a brand of sleeping pill
chiku-taku	tick-tock
-dōri	street
Formosans	people from the former Japanese colony of Formosa, now Taiwan
furoshiki	large handkerchief used for wrapping articles
fūten	group or gang of prostitutes
futon	a mattress

gari-gari	the sound of scratching
genkan	the entrance to a house, inside the front door, used for taking off, putting on and storing shoes
geta	wooden clogs
GHQ	General Headquarters (of SCAP)
gumi	group or gang
haramaki	a belly band
ikidaore	an accidental death while on an excursion
Jinan Incident	also known as the May 3rd Incident in Chinese; the battle between the Japanese army and the Southern Army of the Chinese Kuomintang Nationalist Army in May 1928, when the Japanese army entered Jinan, the capital of Shandong province in China, in order to protect Japanese citizens and businesses
Minshū Shimbun	a daily newspaper
kachō	the chief of a section
kaidashi	used to describe scavenging for food or hunting for supplies
kakigōri	a flavoured cone of shaved ice
Kantō	the region of Japan in which Tokyo is situated
Katakana	a basic written form of Japanese syllabary
Kakyō Sōkai	a post-war association of Chinese immigrant businesses
keisatsu techō	a policeman's notebook and credentials
Kempei	a Kempeitai officer
Kempeitai	the Japanese wartime military police

kuso	an expletive
mechiru-arukōru	low-grade wood alcohol
Meiji	the name given to the reign of the former Emperor Mutsuhito, 1866–1912
meishi	a business or name card
Minpo	a daily newspaper
monpe	women's pantaloons
Namu-amida-butsu	'Save us, merciful Buddha', or 'May his/her soul rest in peace'
okawari	a second-helping
pan-pan	post-war Japanese prostitutes
potsu-potsu	drip-drop, drip-drop
Public Safety Division	the branch of SCAP responsible for the reform of the Japanese police
Rikusen Tai	Japanese Naval Marine Corps
sara-sara	in this instance, the sound of running water
SCAP	Supreme Commander for the Allied Powers
SCAPIN	SCAP Instruction (i.e. directive)
Shinchū Gun	the Army of Occupation
Shōwa	the name given to the reign of the former Emperor Hirohito, 1926–1989
soba	buckwheat noodles
Taishō	the name given to the reign of the former Emperor Yoshihito, 1912–1926
tatami	rush-covered straw matting
tekiya	a stall-holder, but also a racketeer
Tōhoku	the north-eastern regions of the main Japanese island of Honshu

Tokkō	the 'Thought Police'
ton-ton	tap-tap; the sound of hammering
wā-wā	the sound of a baby crying
yakitori	grilled pieces of chicken on a stick
Yobo	in this instance, a derogative term for an old man
Yomiuri	a daily newspaper
yukata	a light summer kimono
zaibatsu	a financial clique
zanpân	a meal made from leftover scraps
zā-zā	the sound of pelting rain
zōsui	a porridge of rice and vegetables

Acknowledgements and Sources

In the thirteen lucky years I have lived in Tokyo, many, many people have helped me and, in many, many ways, contributed to this book, most of all my family: Izumi, George, Emi, Shigeko and Daisuke.

However, in the preparation and research for the actual writing of this book, I would like to pay particular thanks to the following people for their help, their knowledge and their time:

Firstly, my dear agent William Miller, along with Sawa Junzo, Hamish Macaskill, Peter Thompson, and all the staff of the English Agency Japan. Also Koyama Michio, Hayakawa Hiroshi, Chida Hiroyuki, Yoshida Tomohiro, Hamaguchi Tamako, Nagayoshi Yuki, Edward Seidensticker, Donald Richie, David Mitchell, Mark Schreiber, Michael Gardiner, Justin McCurry, Koizumi Atsuko and Matsumura Sayuri.

In London, I would like to thank Stephen Page, Lee Brackstone, Angus Cargill, Anna Pallai, Anne Owen, Trevor Horwood, and all the staff of Faber and Faber; in Yorkshire, my mother and father; in New York, Sonny Mehta, Diana Coglianese, and Leyla Aker; in Paris, François Guérif, Agnès Guery, Jeanne Guyon, Daniel Lemoine, and all the staff of Payot & Rivages, and Jean-Pierre Deloux; in Milan, Luca Formenton, Marco Tropea, Cristina Ricotti, Marco Pensante, Seba Pezzani, and all the staff of il Saggiatore, and Elio De Capitani; in Munich, Juergen Kill and Susanne Fink of Liebeskind, Markus Naegele of Heyne, and Peter Torberg.

I would also like to thank Shimoyama Susumu of my Japanese publisher Bungei Shunju for his advice and support, and finally, but most of all, my editor Nagashima Shunichiro, who gave me the confidence and help to finally begin writing this book. Shunichiro provided and translated materials which otherwise would have been beyond me and then diligently and incisively edited both the English and Japanese manuscripts. In short, any qualities this book might have, are his. The faults, as ever, are all mine.

FICTION

An Artist of the Floating World by Kazuo Ishiguro (Faber, 1986)

Childhood Years by Tanizaki Jun'ichiro, translated by Paul McCarthy (Kodansha International, 1988)

'The Camelia' by Satomi Ton, translated by Edward Seidensticker, from *Modern Japanese Stories* (Charles E. Tuttle, 1962)

The Essential Akutagawa Ryūnosuke, edited by Seiji M. Lippit (Marsilio Publishers, 1999)

The Girl I Left Behind by Endo Shusaku, translated by Mark Williams (New Directions, 1994)

A Gray Moon by Shiga Naoya, translated by Lane Dunlop (Charles E. Tuttle, 1992)

'The Hole' by Kuroshima Denji, from *A Flock of Swirling Crows & Other Proletarian Writings*, edited and translated by Zeljko Cipris (University of Hawaii Press, 2005)

'The Idiot' by Sakaguchi Ango, translated by George Saitō, from *Modern Japanese Stories* (Charles E. Tuttle, 1962)

The Journey by Osaragi Jiro, translated by Ivan Morris (Knopf, 1960)

The Legend of Gold and Other Stories by Ishikawa Jun, edited and translated by William J. Tyler (University of Hawaii Press, 1998)

'Militarized Streets' by Kuroshima Denji, from *A Flock of Swirling Crows & Other Proletarian Writings*, edited and translated by Zeljko Cipris (University of Hawaii Press, 2005)

Musashi by Yoshikawa Eiji, translated by Charles S. Terry (Kodansha International, 1981)

'Nonresistance City' by Maruo Suehiro, from *Ultra-Gash Inferno*, translated by James Havoc and Shinkado Takako (Creation Books, 2001)

Occupation by John Toland (Doubleday, 1987)

One Man's Justice by Yoshimura Akira, translated by Mark Ealey (Canongate, 2003)

Palm-of-the Hand Stories by Kawabata Yasunari, translated by Lane
   Dunlop and J. Martin Holman (North Point Press, 1988)
'A Quiet Obsession' by Kyōka Izumi, from *In Light of Shadows*,
   edited and translated by Charles Shirō Inouye (University of
   Hawaii Press, 2005)
The Saga of Dazai Osamu by Phyllis I. Lyons (Stanford University
   Press, 1985)
'Sakurajima' by Umezaki Haruo, translated by D. E. Mills, from *The
   Catch and Other War Stories*, edited by Saeki Shōichi
   (Kodansha International, 1981)
The Scavengers by Kafū Nagai, translated by Edward Seidensticker
   (Stanford University Press, 1965)
Self Portraits by Dazai Osamu, translated and introduced by Ralph F.
   McCarthy (Kodansha International, 1991)
'Shitamachi' by Hayashi Fumiko, translated by Ivan Morris, from
   Modern Japanese Stories (Charles E. Tuttle, 1962)
Soldiers Alive by Ishikawa Tatsuzō, translated by Zeljko Cipris
   (University of Hawaii Press, 2003)
'The Sound of Hammering' by Dazai Osamu, translated by James
   O'Brien, from *Crackling Mountain and Other Stories* (Charles E.
   Tuttle, 1989)
A Strange Tale from East of the River by Kafū Nagai, translated by
   Edward Seidensticker (Stanford University Press, 1965)
Tales of Moonlight and Rain by Ueda Akinari, translated by Hamada
   Kengi (Columbia University Press, 1972)
This Outcast Generation by Takeda Taijun, translated by Shibuya
   Yusaburo and Sanford Goldstein (Charles E. Tuttle, 1967)
Wheat and Soldiers by Hino Ashihei, translated by Ishimoto Shidzue
   (Farrar & Rinehart, 1939)
Where are the Victors? by Donald Richie (Charles E. Tuttle, 1956;
   republished as *This Scorching Earth*, 1986)
A Wife in Musashino by Ōoka Shōhei, translated by Dennis
   Washburn (University of Michigan, 2004)

NON-FICTION

Embracing Defeat by John Dower (W. W. Norton, 1999)
Geisha, Harlot, Strangler, Star by William Johnston (Columbia
   University Press, 2005)

Japan at War: An Oral History by Haruko Taya Cook and Theodore
F. Cook (The New Press, 1992)

Japan Diary by Mark Gayn (Charles E. Tuttle, 1981)

Japan's Longest Day by the Pacific War Research Society (Kodansha,
1968)

Keiji Ichidai: Hiratsuka Hachibei no Shōwa Jiken-shi by Sasaki
Yoshinobu (Sankei Shimbunsha; Nisshin-Hōdō Shuppanbu,
1980)

Nippon no Seishin Kantei edited by Fukushima Akira, Nakata Osamu,
Ogi Sadataka, Uchimura Yushi and Yoshimasu Shufu (Misuzu
Shobo, 1973)

The Other Nuremberg by Arnold C. Brackman (William Morrow,
1987)

Oyabun: Nippon Outlaw Retsudan, edited by Jitsuwa Jidai Henshubu
(Yosensha, 2005)

The Phoenix Cup: Some Notes on Japan in 1946 by John Morris (The
Crescent Press, 1947)

The Police in Occupation Japan by Christopher Aldous (Routledge,
1997)

Sensō to Kodomotachi (Nihon Toshokan Centre, 1994)

Shocking Crimes of Postwar Japan by Mark Schreiber (Yenbooks,
1996)

Showa by Tessa Morris-Suzuki (Methuen, 1984)

Tokyo Rising by Edward Seidensticker (Charles E. Tuttle, 1990)

Tokyo Underworld by Robert Whiting (Vintage, 1999)

Typhoon in Tokyo by Harry Emerson Wildes (Macmillan, 1954)

Valley of Darkness by Thomas R. H. Havens (University Press of
America, 1986)

War, Occupation and Creativity, edited by Marlene J. Mayo and
J. Thomas Rimer with H. Eleanor Kerkham (University of Hawaii
Press, 2001)

The Yakuza by David E. Kaplan and Alec Dubro (University of
California Press, 2003)

FILMS

Drunken Angel (Kurosawa Akira, Toho, 1948)

Gate of Flesh (Suzuki Seijun, Nikkatsu, 1964)

Senso to Heiwa (Yamamoto Satsuo and Kamei Fumio, Toho, 1947)

Story of a Prostitute (Suzuki Seijun, Nikkatsu, 1965)
Stray Dog (Kurosawa Akira, Shintoho, 1949)
Ugetsu (Mizoguchi Kenji, Daiei, 1953)
Under the Flag of the Rising Sun (Fukasaku Kinji, Toho, 1972)

SONGS

'Ringo no Uta' (the Apple Song), sung by Namiki Michiko, on
  Nippon Columbia, was the hit song of 1945–46 in Japan
'Roei no Uta' (the Bivouac Song), with lyrics by Kozeki Yuji and
  music by Yabuuchi Kiichirō, on Victor Records, was the
  winning entry in a 1937 nationwide patriotic songwriting contest
Plus the collected works of Les Rallizes Dénudés, The Stalin,
  Ningen-isu, Sigh and Church of Misery